MW00941875

Peaks and Valleys

donna coulson

Copyright © 2016 donna coulson

All rights reserved.

ISBN-10: 1534956220
ISBN-13: 978-1534956223

Front cover photograph by donna coulson:
Battle Lake from the top of Bridger Peak, Wyoming
Back cover photo by donna coulson: View near Dillon, Wyoming
Picture of donna by Hillary Wilkerson

No part of this publication may be reproduced in any form, or by
any means, electronic or mechanical, including photocopying,
recording, or any information browsing, storage, or retrieval
system, without permission in writing from the author.

To God be the Glory, great things He has done.

1

June 5, 1894
Atley farm - near Mitchell, South Dakota

The faded yellow curtains turned her shabby furniture a muted safflower hue as the morning sun's rays peeked over the roof of the barn and slid gently into her room. She stood before the mirror her grandmother had left her, gazing and smiling. *Today is my 16th birthday* she quietly whispered to the girl staring back at her. She focused on each feature. Her long brown hair fell gracefully in waves over her shoulders. Her rich, dark brown eyes were ringed by long lashes. Her small, button nose was sprinkled generously with freckles. Claire rarely had leisure to study her face in the mirror, but today she afforded herself an extra minute. She pinched her cheeks a few times to make them red, rouge was a luxury she'd heard about but could not even imagine possessing. Feeling festive and grown up, she slid her blue everyday dress, one of only two dresses she owned, over her head and settled it over her petticoat and chemise. Then she pulled on white anklets and slipped into her shoes. A frown crossed her brow as she looked at how worn and broken down they were, but she shrugged it off and smiled. She left her pinafore apron hanging on the hook beside her door and prepared to go down to the kitchen. The world seemed wonderful at that moment.

Mama was already at the stove, her back to the small stairway that led up to the attic that served as Claire's bedroom. The smell of frying ham greeted Claire as she made her way to the white shelf that held the family's dishes. Mama and Claire always had breakfast ready for Papa and Marcus when they came in from milking and chores, but now that Uncle Horace and Uncle Clancy lived with

1

them and there were seven mouths to feed instead of just five, the work for the women started earlier. Claire brought down seven plates from the shelf and turned to set the table. Mama turned around with a smile. "Happy Bir-,"

She stopped in mid-word as she turned and looked at her daughter. Claire watched as Mama's expression turned from pleasant to angry in an instant.

"What are you doing?" Her tone was fierce though very quiet.

"Good morning Mama," was all Claire could say. In a heartbeat, Mama crossed the kitchen and was standing right in front of her. An instant later, her hand flashed up and Claire felt the quick sting as Mama slapped her.

"Get upstairs and finish dressing." Mama scolded. "I'll not have you dressed like a hussy in my house. You need your hair braided and your pinafore on before you come down again. I don't have time for foolishness, the men will be in any minute."

Mama turned to the stove, leaving Claire staring at her cold back and mentally reeling at the meanness in her voice. Silently, Claire climbed the stairs. The room wasn't drenched in saffron happiness when she gained the top of the steps. Instead, it looked poor and threadbare, dusty and old. She grabbed the apron from the hook. Made of heavy white cotton, it slipped over her head and covered her, front and back. As she tied the lacings on each side, her surprise at her mother's reaction turned to indignation. *She makes me dress like a little girl! Other girls stop wearing pinafores and braiding their hair when they become teenagers, but Mama insists that I continue.* Claire fought back tears as she parted her hair and plaited it into two braids.

She stared at her face for the second time this morning. This time, she saw the small scar on her eyebrow where she'd hit the table when Papa backhanded her when she was nine, and she frowned at the small gap between her front two teeth. The mirror, too, looked different. Instead of a precious gift from a dearly remembered grandmother, now she saw the edges where the silver was flaking off the back of the glass and the chip at one edge of the ornately gilded frame.

She heard boots on the back porch and quickly finished her hair, smoothed her apron and slipped downstairs. She didn't want Mama any madder at her, and she certainly didn't want Papa to think she'd been dallying.

The table was set and when Mama saw her, she smiled softly. Claire tried to smile back and then turned to get the jam and butter for the table. Mama was usually quiet and meek, never saying much especially when the men were near. Claire knew that this was the only apology or explanation she'd get.

Marcus and Clancy arrived in the kitchen punching and pushing each other. While Clancy was their uncle, he was a year younger than Marcus and only a month older than Claire. They hadn't wiped their boots, and Claire noticed that each was leaving a trail of soiled straw and who knows what else. She took a deep breath, knowing that it would be up to her to scrub the floor after breakfast dishes were done. Uncle Horace sauntered in next. He was taller, four years older than Marcus, and had an arrogance about him that made Claire nervous.

Mama dried her hands on the edge of her apron and left the room. No doubt, she was hunting Jesse, her youngest son, to call him for breakfast. At four, Jesse was all the baby of the family should be, thought Claire, spoiled and willful. He could cry and look pitiful as needed, so any time anything went awry or Jesse did something wrong and was about to be caught, he'd make a fuss and Claire would catch the blame.

The older boys began to settle into their chairs around the large kitchen table. Marcus and Clancy were taunting each other about who could pitch the most hay in an hour. Jesse slid into his seat atop a Sears and Roebuck catalog to help him reach the table, dressed but with disheveled hair and sleepy eyes. Mama put plates of scrambled eggs and thick ham slices on the table. Claire added warm bread and sat down. Papa bowed his head and intoned a prayer, "Father, bless this food which is thy bounty to us. Amen."

The kitchen was quiet while the men ate. Claire pushed the small helping of eggs around her plate and kept her eyes down.

"Now that I have more strong help around here," Papa began as he pushed his plate away, "We can handle a few more milk cows. Milk prices are up, it seems like a good investment. I'd also like to buy twenty head of yearlings to feed on the south pastures to sell for meat."

"Have you ever met Bill Rideout? He's got a farm just south of Mitchell," Horace asked.

"Heard of him only."

"Pa and I met him a while back when we were in Mitchell for

an auction. He told Pa he was looking to sell a large lot of yearlings this spring."

Papa was quiet for a minute. Marcus and Clancy finished eating and began nudging each other under the table.

"Since you boys have so much energy," Papa looked sternly at Marcus. "I want you both to spend the day checking the fences. Take extra wire and nails with you and ride every fence. Make sure they are all tight and tied. Horace and I are going to town to get some supplies and see if we can meet up with this Mr. Rideout."

"I want to go with you," chirped Jesse. "Can I Papa?"

Mama cleared her throat quietly and looked across the table at Papa. "There are a few supplies I am running a bit short on. Would you be willing to pick up bags of flour and sugar and some coffee for the house? I can send in some eggs to trade, and I've got some egg money to pay for it."

Papa didn't look pleased, but answered that he could have Horace stop in at the mercantile. Horace shrugged. All the while, Jesse had been bouncing in his chair. Claire knew she had to speak up or she'd miss her chance.

"Papa, may I go with you to town? It has been nearly six months since I've been off the farm. Could I ride along and help?"

Papa looked over at Horace and shook his head. "I told you they couldn't leave men well enough alone, didn't I?" They both smiled at the inside joke. He turned his eyes to Claire. "I'm sure you have work to do around here. In fact, the chicken coop is pretty ragged, I'm sure your time will be better spent mucking it out and putting in a fresh bed of straw for the layers."

Then Papa turned to Jesse, acting as if he just noticed the boy's wiggling and squirming. "Well now, I'm pretty sure there's enough room for a cowboy like you. Go wash up and get your hat. We'll leave directly."

Jesse whooped and jumped up from the table. He ran from the room.

Marcus and Clancy stomped out, arguing about who would ride Whitey and who would ride Red. Papa and Horace each put their napkins on the table and slid out their chairs. As they were leaving the room Papa told Horace that he'd hitch up the wagon if Horace would slop the pigs. Mama went into the parlor. Claire could hear her at the desk, sliding open the drawer that held her egg money.

Claire stayed at the table. She felt like crying. No one even remembered it was her birthday. Not only did she not get to go into town, but now she had to do the worst chore on the place instead. She hated the chickens and the chicken house. The layers were mean, and any time Claire entered the coop, they flapped at her and squawked. Knowing Claire hated it, usually Mama herself gathered the eggs. Claire shivered a little when she remembered last spring when Marcus snuck up behind her while she was gathering eggs. He slammed closed the chicken house door and wedged it shut so Claire couldn't get out. When she yelled at him to open the door, the chickens went berserk and started flapping and pecking at her. She tried to be quiet and calm, but the longer she was trapped, the more frightened she felt until she started pounding on the door. Chickens flew at her. Thankfully, Mama heard her and opened the door.

"I'm sure he meant it in good fun," was all Mama would say when Claire told her how she had come to be trapped in the coop. Mama smoothed Claire's hair and then hugged her. "You're alright now."

Claire knew that she'd never be as important to her parents as her brothers were. While the words were never said, it was clear that the boys were cherished and she, just a girl, was not. When she was little, her father's backhand had convinced her to keep her thoughts to herself and stay out of his way as much as possible. Mama did the same.

Claire hadn't been exaggerating when she'd said that she'd not been to town for six months. Papa believed that his wife and daughter should stay on the farm, quiet and obedient. He and the boys went to town, which was about three miles away, once or twice a week. Papa didn't like getting house supplies while he was there, and usually gave Marcus the task.

The kitchen was clean, dishes washed and dried, counters and table washed. She was just finishing the mopping when Mama appeared behind her. "I'm going down to the big garden to weed. I am hoping there will be some early peas to pick."

Normally, Claire accompanied her mother to the vegetable garden plot, but they both knew that Papa would be sure to check the chicken house when he returned, and he'd be furious if it wasn't done. Fighting tears, Claire turned back around and picked up the scrub bucket. "Okay, Mama," she answered quietly.

Mama put her hand on Claire's shoulder and said quietly, "I went out and shooed all the chickens out of the coop. They are in the yard. If you keep the back gate shut until you are done, they shouldn't bother you."

"Thank you, Mama."

The warmth of Mama's hand comforted Claire. Later, while she was raking out soiled straw from the coop, Claire thought about her family. There was no doubt that Mama was as afraid of Papa as Claire was. Claire had seen him slap her mother many times. The worst had been just a month ago.

"We need help around here, Dori. Marcus is good help, but I need another hand. You and the girl are always needing cloth or flour or something, and I just can't do it all myself. My Ma and Pa have the two older brothers helping out, so Horace and Clancy aren't really needed on their place." Papa's voice was loud and angry. Mama and Papa had been in the front room talking for several minutes before his voice became loud enough for Claire to hear.

"Hiram, I beg you to reconsider. Your younger brothers have gotten themselves into trouble in town. The sheriff warned your Pa to keep control of Horace or he'd end up in trouble with the law. We have Claire and Jesse and even Marcus to think of and protect."

Papa was shouting now, "Dori, enough. I will not have you disrespect my own brothers. They are good boys and they are welcome here!"

"But-" Claire jumped at the crash that followed. There was no more noise downstairs besides Papa's boots on the wooden floor and the back door slamming. Shaking, Claire stayed where she was, at the top of the stairs to the attic, until she heard a small moan. Hoping her father was out in the barn, she quietly made her way through the kitchen and to the parlor. Mama was just sitting up. The small curio table was on its side, chess pieces scattered everywhere. When Claire caught sight of her mother's face, she gasped. Blood was dripping down her chin.

Claire quickly ran to the kitchen sink and grabbed a dish cloth. When she returned to the parlor, Mama was standing, though a bit wobbly, and gratefully accepted the towel. It took a few minutes to stop the nosebleed and assess the damage. "This tooth is a bit loose," her mother whispered, "but I think it will be alright. My nose is fine, Claire. Don't look so worried. My eye will be fine by tomorrow. I shouldn't have disagreed with your father. It is my own fault."

Claire was furious and opened her mouth to argue, but one look from her mother stopped her. "Claire, the good Lord has put us here. The Bible tells us to obey our husbands and fathers. We can't fight it, so let's just accept it."

Claire pictured her mother's bruised face as she carried itchy armfuls of clean straw into the henhouse and filled the boxes where the chickens lay their eggs. It had taken almost two weeks before the angry marks faded from bright blue, to sickly green, then finally a fading yellow. As she finished the henhouse, Claire thought about the last thing her mother had said to her that day.

"But Mama, how can we accept meanness from someone who is supposed to love us?"

"Hiram is a hard man to understand. He does love us in his own way."

Claire was quiet, watching her mother try to believe the words she had just spoken when her mother spoke again. "Claire, stay as clear as you can of Horace."

"I will, Mama," was all Claire could answer.

2
June, 1894
Atley farm - near Mitchell, South Dakota

Claire surveyed the chicken coop one last time. The Jamesway chicken waterers were filled and sitting in the shade of the coop. Mama had been pleased when she found them at the feed store last summer. *Chickens are so dumb*, Claire thought. *They can drown getting a drink of water.* The waterers were just right so that even the chicks could get a drink but not get their heads in far enough to drown. She made sure there was grain in the pans, then walked around and opened the gates. Within just a few seconds the chickens started making their way back into the coop. Claire picked a pin feather out of her hair and sighed.

Out on the road, a horse whinnied. Almost immediately, Claire could hear the squeak of wagon wheels and a clanging she couldn't identify. She walked quickly across the yard and peeked around the corner of the barn. As she watched, a caravan of three wagons moved slowly by the front gate. Pulled by two large draft horses, each wagon was dome-shaped like a sheep-herder wagon, but painted in bright reds, yellows and greens. The clanking that she heard came from assorted pots and pans hanging on the curved wall of the middle wagon. Just past the front gate, the wagons stopped. Claire didn't want to be seen, so she stayed close to the barn, but moved forward a little, staying behind a lilac bush and peeking out through the branches. The first two wagons were now beyond her view and she had no idea why they had stopped. She studied the third wagon. The driver was dark skinned, old and wrinkled. He looked a bit as if his face were a dried apple. The man looked around and Claire shrunk back farther into the lilacs. The fragrance of the blossoms was heavy and sweet. A movement at the rear of the wagon caught her attention. Two women stepped into view. They stretched and looked around. Both wore full skirts – colorful and flowing, topped with white blouses gathered at the neck. One had a shawl casually lying across her shoulders. Kerchiefs were tied around their heads, but long, curly dark hair cascaded down their backs. The shorter of the two pulled her black shawl closer around her as if she were cold, and moved forward toward the driver. The taller woman's eyes swept past the gate and towards the barn.

Claire marveled at her beauty – exotic and a little frightening. The woman was quite young, *Not much older than me*, Claire guessed. Her black eyes shined against her cocoa skin. She wore crimson on her lips and a lighter shade on her cheeks. The woman stood studying the farm, then something at the front of the caravan caught her attention and she moved out of Claire's view.

Claire quietly let out the breath she had been holding. She had only heard about gypsy caravans, but knew with certainty that this was one. Her heart raced as she realized that she was alone at the house.

Gypsies came to America from Europe. Many were horse traders or sold wares from their wagons. During a storm last winter while Claire and her mother were tearing rags to make braided rugs with, Mama told Claire a story about a caravan that had come to the family farm when she was young. While the man sharpened knives and scythe blades for Claire's grandfather, his wife offered to tell Dori's fortune. That woman, as Mama recalled, was old and hag-like with gnarled fingers and a missing tooth. Claire remembered the fear mixed with a kind of forbidden awe in her mother's memory. Mama warned Claire that gypsies also had an unsavory reputation for petty thievery.

Frightened and awestruck at the same time, Claire stayed frozen behind the bush, wondering what she would do if they came up to the house. After what seemed like hours but was only a minute or two, she heard the drivers chirrup to the horses. The wheels of the wagons protested with rusty screeching and the melodic clanging began again. She stayed hidden until she could no longer hear the caravan, then she slowly surveyed the empty road. *Gone, just as they had never been*, she thought as she made her way to the house.

The mantle clock chimed eleven as Claire stepped into the kitchen. She stopped for a minute to enjoy the sound and allow her heart rate and nerves to return to normal. The clock sat proudly on a small hutch in the parlor. The hutch and clock had both belonged to Claire's grandmother. Claire loved that it chimed once at the quarter hours and played Westminster Chimes on the hour. Smiling, Claire thought of the day Gramma Lara had taught her the words to the chiming tune, as she recalled her grandma's thin, high voice as the clock chimed.

Lord in this hour
Be thou our guide
For by thy power
No foot shall slide.

Claire took a breath and enjoyed the fact that she had seen the gypsies, her odious job was done, and that the house was quiet. She felt scratchy and dirty from the straw and the chicken feathers, so she made her way into the kitchen and pumped some water into a pitcher. She carried it up to her room, then took off her apron and dress, and unbraided her hair. She washed up, enjoying how refreshing the clean water felt, then brushed out her hair and re-braided it. She opened the window and peered out, listening for anything that might evidence the return of the gypsies or her family.

Claire studied her home. The yard was dusty, packed dirt that turned into a mucky, sucking mud bog in the rain or when the snow melted in spring. The nearby barn had once been a proud structure that could be seen on the flat plains for over a mile. Now, it sported peeling, dingy white paint while buckling and missing wooden shingles at one corner allowed rain to seep into the hayloft. Claire curled her nose at the thought of the resulting sour smelling, moldy hay.

From her window, Claire couldn't see Mama's garden, which was a hundred yards or so to the east, behind a small rise. She recalled how Papa snorted in disgust every spring when Mama asked him to till it for her so she could plant. Grudgingly, he'd take the team and plow it for her, acting as if Mama was imposing a huge favor upon him, yet he benefitted from the harvest along with the rest of the family.

The barnyard was quiet in the warm afternoon sun. Even the rooster was dozing in the shade of the coop, and Claire reveled for a moment in the solitude and stillness. She felt comfortable in her aloneness and rested with her elbows on the windowsill, feeling calm and safe. Finally, pulling herself out of her musings, she moved from the window and shook out her dress and apron, then put them back on. She left the window open since it was hot and stuffy in the attic and made her way downstairs. Looking around, she remembered that her mother had mentioned last night that she wanted to have scalloped potatoes and sausage for supper tonight. She decided that it would be a nice surprise for Mama if she had the potatoes all peeled and ready by the time she got home.

Claire walked out the kitchen door and around the corner of the house to the root cellar door. She opened the heavy door and went down the four stairs, careful in the dim light not to misstep or bang her head on the low beams. A sack of carrots had somehow toppled from the shelf it had been on, spilling its contents across the floor. It took her several minutes to pick them all up and return them to their rightful place, then she filled her apron with enough potatoes for dinner and climbed back into the daylight.

As she was rounding the corner of the house she could see dust on the road and assumed her father and Uncle Horace were returning. Hurrying now, she returned to the kitchen. She held her full apron with one hand while reaching for an enamel cookpot on a shelf above the counter. She had to stand on her tiptoes to reach it, and the weight of the potatoes in her apron made it hard to stretch that far.

"Let me get that for you."

Claire jumped and sucked in a breath, turning toward the voice. Behind her was Horace, smiling. "You about scared me to death," she said, first annoyed then embarrassed. "I didn't hear you get home."

"Your Pa and I just got here, he's still in the barn." Horace's voice was low, like he had a sore throat. Claire realized she was still holding the potatoes and turned to once more reach for the pot. Horace took three quick steps, coming up very close behind her. She could feel his body press into hers as he reached over her to get it. She tried to move, but even after he had the pan in his hand, he didn't move away. Instead, he brought it down in front of her, so that his arms now encircled her. She could feel his breath against her neck. He tightened his embrace and leaned gently into her, pushing her against the counter.

Papa's boots sounded loud on the porch. As he opened the door, Horace's hold loosened and Claire spun away from him. His eyes were hard and threatening.

Papa walked in at that moment. Horace smiled and leaned against the counter while Claire hastily pulled the pan toward her and moved out to the back porch.

She emptied her apron onto the bare wooden porch and sat down beside them. With the pot on the lower step in front of her, Claire kept her head down and began peeling the potatoes. She let the peels fall into her apron and dropped the white spuds into the pan as she finished with them. She willed herself not to cry, and concentrated on breathing and peeling. She refused to let herself think, either, at least until she knew that her heart had returned to a normal rhythm and that her urge to sob had passed.

Her peeling slowed as she replayed the scene in the kitchen. *Had Horace meant to be so close? What was he doing?* She struggled to understand why his actions made her feel so frightened and threatened. He was her uncle, surely she was misreading the situation. *That's it,* she told herself. *After seeing the gypsies you are just letting your imagination run away with you!*

She finished the last potato and looked up just as Mama turned into the gate. *She walks as though she is carrying a ton of trouble in that basket,* Claire thought.

Leaving the pot on the step, Claire gathered up the peelings in her apron and stood up. She walked out toward the pig pens, meeting her mother. Claire dumped her apron over the fence into the pen holding the piglets. They squealed and fought to get at the treasure. Mama joined her at the fence. She sat her basket down and rested one hand on the post. "Thank you, Dear Heart, for getting supper potatoes ready. I didn't expect to be gone so long, but the garden was overrun with weeds."

The screen door slammed and there was a crash. Claire turned in time to see that Papa had just stepped out on the porch and kicked over the potatoes she'd left there.

"Oh for heavens' sake," she muttered as she ran toward the house. She glanced at Papa's face as she neared. He was frustrated but not too angry. "I'm sorry Papa," she started. "I had to dump out these peelings for the piglets and I only left that there for a minute."

"Be more careful next time," was all he said as he walked by her to the barn. "I left your groceries on the counter. Get them put away and get supper on. Horace and I have chores to do."

Claire picked up the scattered potatoes and returned them to the pot. She was on her way into the kitchen when Horace came out the back door. She backed up and gave him plenty of room to pass her. He hesitated for a minute, then his eye caught his sister-in-law's approach and he continued on to the barn.

Mama looked at Claire, then at Horace's retreating back. Claire tried to make her face blank as she followed her mother into the kitchen.

They worked in silence. Just as Claire was setting the table and putting out the pickles and pickled beets, Clancy and Marcus arrived. Mama smiled. "Those two are never late for a meal," she quipped.

Supper was noisy. Marcus and Clancy reported on their day's work and the state of the fences around the farm. Papa told them that he and Horace had been able to meet with Bill Rideout and had purchased ten yearlings on credit.

"I'll take Marcus and Clancy over there day after tomorrow and herd them here, since you have the fences all checked and fixed."

"I saw a caravan of wagons this afternoon. Looked like a circus," reported Marcus.

Horace gave his brother a sideways look.

"We met them on our way in," started Papa. "It is a gypsy group. They're camped down by Jim Creek."

"Gypsies?" Mama said. "Jim Creek isn't too far away. Should I lock up the chickens and shut the barn tonight?"

"Wouldn't be a bad idea." Papa answered. "I think I'll take Whitey and ride down there after bit and check it out. They said they had tools to sell. I want to go see what they have. I could use a new ax."

Horace snickered. "I'll ride along with you, Hiram. From the looks of them, they have lots of good wares to sell."

Papa gave him a stern look then replied. "We'll leave in about fifteen minutes."

Clancy spoke up then. "Can we come, too? You know, I'd like to see them wares, too." He elbowed Marcus, who echoed the request.

Mama started to protest, but fell silent with one look from Papa. "It'll be fine," he told her. "Sure, you can come. We'll take the buckboard since it is four of us going."

Jesse looked up. "Four? I want to go. Can I Papa?"

"Not this time, Cowboy. Gypsy camps aren't for boys. They're for men."

"But Marcus and Clancy aren't men yet," Jesse argued.

"They might be before the night is done," Horace mumbled. Claire didn't think anyone heard his remark but her, and while she didn't completely understand what he meant, the same fearful feeling she'd had before returned.

Mama's eyes were angry, but she kept quiet and put her head down.

Papa stood up and put his napkin on the table. "We might be late gettin' back," he told Mama as he left the room.

Claire heard the buckboard leave while she was washing dishes. Mama was getting Jesse settled down and occupied in his room. The house was quiet when Mama joined Claire in the kitchen. The dishes were all washed. Claire was drying. Mama swept the floor and put a clean tablecloth on the old pedestal table.

"This house is hot," Mama said when she'd finished. "Let's go sit a spell on the front porch."

The family rarely used the front porch or the parlor. The kitchen and its back porch opened to the barnyard. The small parlor at the front of the house opened its door to the west. Claire sank down into one of the two old rocking chairs that adorned the covered porch, her mother took the other one. Both were quiet as the sun sank below the trees lining the corn field. Occasionally the floorboard beneath Mama's chair gave a little squeak. In the distance a dove cooed. They sat, enjoying the rest, until Claire began to see fireflies flickering on and off in the field.

Mama cleared her throat and reached into her pocket. "I know this wasn't much of a birthday for you."

Claire turned her chair so she could face her mother.

Continuing in a quiet voice, Mama said. "I am really proud of you. You are a hard working girl. You are a comfort to me and a great help. I love you very much."

Claire's eyes began to fill. Her mother didn't often talk to her this way.

Mama pulled her hand from her pocket and extended it to Claire. "This belonged to my grandmother. I don't know where she got it, but she gave it to my mother on her sixteenth birthday. My mother gave it to me the day I turned sixteen. Today, I give it to you." She handed a small grey box to her daughter.

Claire accepted the box and held it tight in her hand. She put her hand to her heart and gazed at her mother. "Mama, thank you so much," she whispered. Claire knew what was inside. Mama only wore it on special occasions, but in rare moments, like this one, Mama had shown her the few treasures that she kept tucked safely in a drawer. The grey box and the pin inside were one of the few treasures her mother owned.

Claire remembered her Grandma Lara, who had only come to visit them one time, when Claire was just ten. Behind closed eyes, her grandmother's face smiled at her as they played checkers on a sun dappled afternoon. Claire admired the quiet kindness in the woman's actions and the calm peace that seemed to surround her and those near her. With Grandma Lara there, her father had been docile and polite, and the lack of tension was a true holiday for everyone. What stayed with Claire most, though, even more than the hugs and the jovial checker games was the simple and sure love that Grandma Lara bathed her in. Her love was unconditional and unending, and Claire basked in it even though she didn't quite understand it. Claire considered that short visit the best two weeks of her life.

Mama's voice pulled Claire from the memory, "Do you like it?"

Claire released her grip on her memory and opened the box. Inside, on a piece of blue linen lay a flat, silver daisy about the diameter of a half dollar. Sixteen petals fanned out from the center. While much smaller than a real Black-Eyed Susan, the pin was a perfect replica of the flower, complete with intricate detailing. Claire looked closely. She could see the veins in the tiny petals and feel the roughness of the center.

"Thank you, Mama," Claire said again. "I do like it very much. It will always be precious to me."

"Lord knows there is hardly an occasion to wear it around here," Mama answered. "But I have high hopes for you. I pray

15

every day that you find a way for yourself in this world that does not include being secluded on a farm in South Dakota."

Claire searched her mother's face. She'd never heard her disparage her life on the farm.

Mama continued. "President McKinley has passed the Dingley Act to protect our factories and our country is getting stronger. America is growing. Maybe someday you will have the opportunity to go back east and see New York, or even visit the Hawaiian territory. There's a great big world full of opportunities that I didn't have when I was your age."

Claire settled back to listen to her mother, unsure which she would treasure more, the heirloom pin in her hand or this rare moment they were sharing.

"My papa left Mama, my sister Rebecca and my brother Zina at our house in Madison, Wisconsin and joined the Union Army. He served with the 2nd Wisconsin Volunteers. They were part of the Army of the Potomac and saw their first battle at Bull Run. Papa was on McPherson's Ridge at the Battle of Gettysburg.

"The regiment was sent home in July of 1864. I was five years old." Mama stopped, her eyes filled with the memory. When she resumed, her voice was quieter. "He lost his left arm, just below the elbow." Mama stopped again and smiled at the past.

"He looked so different. He'd grown a beard, and he had one partially empty sleeve. He wasn't at all what I remembered. The night he came home my mother rushed out to embrace him. They cried and held each other, then turned to us. Mama said, "Look children, your father is home!"

"I stayed back, but after Zina and Rebecca hugged him, he looked at me. I approached him, not altogether willingly. He hugged me and said, "What's wrong Dorinda?"

"His voice was familiar, soft and gentle, but his face and body were just so different that I blurted out, "Where's my other Papa?"

"That made him throw his head back and laugh. Then he scooped me up and danced around the yard with me. His laughter is what did it. I knew my Papa was home.

"By the time I woke up the next morning, he had shaved. I had no more doubts as to his identity. In the weeks and months that followed, I watched how he adjusted to life with only one hand. Many men who came back from the war with healing wounds or missing limbs grew mean and bitter. Some drank too much, or thought that the government owed them something. Not my papa. He had been a carpenter before the war. He made beautiful furniture. When he got back, he learned to hold the wood with his stump arm. For times when that didn't work, he fashioned a vise that would hold for him, and he went right on making tables and chairs and building cabinets for houses. He asked my mama to make a leather glove for his stump. He'd sit a nail against his gloved stump, then pick up his hammer and pound that nail in.

"I'm sorry you never met your grand-dad, Claire. He was a good, kind man."

They sat in silence. Claire pictured the reunion scene. She wondered what it would feel like to be held and cherished by a father. She looked at her mother in the gathering twilight, surprised to see that she was brushing away tears.

"Mama, are you alright?"

Mama reached over and took Claire's hand. She smiled a sad smile and took a breath. "I was seventeen when I married your father. My papa and Rebecca died the winter before that, during the yellow fever outbreak. Mama was so sad she had trouble getting up in the morning. It was a very hard time for us. Zina did his best to earn enough, but he was only eighteen. I kept the house, did the cooking. I tended chickens and we had a cow, so I sold eggs and cream to the neighbors to help out.

"I met Hiram at church. He was tall and handsome. His family was more well-off than ours ever had been. He was visiting an uncle who owned a shipping business in Madison. He was charming and generous. He talked with shining eyes about the farm he would own someday in South Dakota, it was still a territory back then. His dreams were so big and bright. In the weeks he was in Madison we saw each other, properly, of course, many times. We went for walks and had dinner together at his uncle's home.

"My mother's sister came to visit about that time. She lived in Milwaukee. She could see how badly Mama was doing and tried to convince her that a change would be good for her. Aunt Beth was married and had one child. Their home was big enough for Mama, but not for Zina or me. Zina didn't care, he was aching to go west. When Hiram heard about it, he never hesitated. He talked with my Mama and asked for my hand. She agreed to the marriage because she knew that Hiram's uncle was a prosperous and respected man.

I think she also agreed because she was too tired and sad to disagree."

Mama was quiet for a long time, and Claire wondered if she'd say more. They sat and watched night fall. The fireflies danced among the corn stalks. The wind barely whispered. They heard a thump inside the house, and Claire remembered that Jesse was still up. Mama remembered, too, and stood up to go inside and check on him. She hesitated, putting her hand on Claire's shoulder.

"Hiram asked his uncle for a job and Mama for my hand. No one ever asked me."

3

June, 1894
Atley farm - near Mitchell, South Dakota

Claire was sleeping fitfully in her stuffy attic room when the men returned. She heard them as the wagon approached. Pieces of a song drifted into her window. She couldn't make out the words, but could tell that Clancy and Marcus made up the choir. Claire moved the curtain slightly so she could look down on the yard. Papa drove the wagon into the barn and shut the door. Marcus and Clancy moved across the yard on unsteady legs. When they entered the house there was loud giggling and shushing each other. Papa and Horace followed them in, each a bit wobbly as well but much more quiet.

Claire got back into bed, tense and worried. Papa was a mean drunk, and Mama usually caught the brunt of his anger. She lay still, listening. For a few minutes there were many thumps and bumps. Something crashed and then there was silence for a time. She began to relax when she heard quick footsteps and then the sound of retching. That soon quieted and the house was silent. Claire finally went to sleep, grateful that Papa and the boys had come in without wanting to fight.

The farmhouse came to life the next morning a bit later than usual. Claire and her mother were up at the normal time, though. Mama went outside to gather eggs, asking Claire to watch the bacon as it fried. The coffee was perking. Unspoken between them was the understanding that Papa would be testy when he arose and everything needed to be done before he came in.

Claire was slicing the bread when she heard someone behind her. She turned to see Horace enter the kitchen.

"Good morning," she said calmly, though she didn't feel it.

"Would you like some coffee?"

"Yes, I would," he answered. She turned her back to him to retrieve a cup. A chair scraped behind her. She turned toward the coffee pot on the stove, surprised to see that Horace had not sat down but was standing very near her. Remaining calm, she poured the coffee and stepped backwards away from him, extending the cup between them. He accepted the cup with his left hand then reached across to pick up a spoon that was lying on the counter. As he moved, his arm brushed her bosom.

"I need something sweet this morning," he said. His voice was low and calm.

Claire's eyes grew wide and she tried to step away, but the chair was behind her. She froze, realizing that he had created a small trap for this purpose. Horace kept his eyes on her. She watched as he scanned her face, then dropped his eyes lower. Aware that he still held the boiling hot coffee, she tried to move sideways. He stepped forward slightly and she stepped backward. Their little dance backed her tightly against the counter with his body within inches of her in front.

He lifted his right hand and trailed a finger along her cheek. He hesitated and glanced at her face. She tried to keep her thoughts hidden and her face blank. She didn't want him to see her anger and fear. Then his finger moved down along the side of her neck to her collarbone.

"Brown gypsy skin is soft, but not as soft as yours," he began.

The back door creaked. Claire looked away from Horace to see her mother standing in the doorway. "Is that bacon burning?" she said as she crossed the kitchen. Claire jumped and turned to the stove. She was shaking and fighting tears, glad to have her back to everyone.

There was an awkward silence in the room. Dori planted herself directly between Claire and Horace, facing him with hands on her hips. "Breakfast won't be for another fifteen minutes or more. Horace, you have time to go unhook the horses from the wagon in the barn and give them hay. Someone forgot to tend them last night when you four came in."

He stood there, meeting her stare, considering. Finally, he turned and left the house, letting the door slam behind him.

Claire's tears were sliding silently down her cheeks as she finished moving the bacon strips from the pan to the platter. She was ashamed of what her mother had seen, afraid that she had done something wrong. Turning slowly, she put her head and eyes down.

"Claire." Mama's voice was just an urgent whisper. When Claire looked up, her mother continued. "I saw that spectacle. Has he done this to you before?"

"Yes, Mama. Yesterday morning."

Mama took a breath and reached for her daughter. She hugged her tightly and whispered, "Go upstairs now. Wash your face. Is that old carpetbag full of quilting material still in the attic space next to your room?"

Claire nodded.

"Good. Empty the material out of it into that old trunk in the corner. Then I want you to pack as many of your clothes and things as you can in that bag. When I call for breakfast, come down and pretend nothing ever happened. Leave the bag where you found it in the attic, do you understand?"

"Yes, I mean no, I…"

They heard footsteps in the hall. "Go now."

Claire turned and ran up the stairs. She heard Mama say good morning to Jesse.

All of Claire's clothes fit easily in the carpetbag. Claire looked around the room. The grey box with the daisy pendant was on the dresser beside her brush, comb and mirror set. Claire tucked them all into the bag and fastened it shut just as Mama called them all to breakfast. She returned the bag to the attic, wondering what Mama had in mind.

Claire slipped silently into the room. Jesse was bright eyed and smiley, *The only sunshine in the room*, thought Claire. Marcus and Clancey sat sullenly. Marcus had his head in his hands and was trying not to look at the food on the table. The back door slammed as Horace came in. Claire turned quickly to the counter so she could avoid looking at him, and picked up the plate of biscuits and the butter dish. With her head down, she approached the table, deposited the food, then took her place. Papa came in wordlessly and sat at the head of the table at the same time Mama put the gravy on and sat down.

Papa prayed, the same prayer as every meal, and when he finished, Mama began passing serving plates.

"I love biscuits and gravy!" Jesse announced.

21

Marcus groaned.

Horace snickered.

They ate for a time in silence.

Papa finally pushed his plate away and reached for his coffee. Mama rose quickly, retrieved the coffee pot from the stove and refilled Papa's cup. As she sat down, Horace lifted his cup up toward her. He was challenging her, making sure she knew her place in the family. Wordlessly, she stood again and, with a smile, moved around the table to refill his cup.

When she was seated again, Mama looked at her youngest. "Jesse, after you wash your face and hands, could you please go up to the attic. There's an old carpet bag up there that I filled with quilting material. I need you to bring it down here for me."

"Okay, Mama," Jesse answered. He got up from the table and went to the sink.

"Hiram," Mama cleared her throat and looked at her husband.

"No lectures about the boys coming in late last night, I hope?" his voice was cross.

"Not at all," Mama answered. She smiled at him.

"Good, because the boys work hard around here and they deserve a little fun and relaxing now and then."

"I understand. I do have something I need to talk to you about, though."

Uncle Horace pushed his chair back and stood up. He addressed Mama, standing across the table, looking down at her he said, "I have some pens and chutes to build if we are going to be ready for those steers to arrive tomorrow. I don't have time to stay and listen to questions about egg money or quilting. That is what you'll be talking about, isn't it Dori?" His voice was even and smooth, but his eyes were steel and fire.

Mama smiled back at him, "You are right, I know you men have important work to do, I just need to talk to your brother about being neighborly."

Horace seemed satisfied that Mama understood his unspoken threat, and looked at his younger brother. "Clancey, you and Marcus can help me build holding pens today. Get your hats, Boys, let's get to work."

Claire felt awkward being alone with her parents at the table. She rose as quietly as possible and began stacking plates and carrying them to the sink.

"Well?" Papa said.

"I need to walk over to the Foster's place today. She needs some material for a blanket she's making for the new baby that's coming. When her older boy stopped by here on Monday to get eggs, he said that Haddie was having a real hard time carrying this baby, and that she was spending a lot of time in bed. He'd been sent to ask if Claire could come and help them out. What do you think about that?"

Claire grabbed a tin bucket and went outside to the well. She could have just pumped water for dishes inside, using the small pump on the sink, but she needed to think, so she headed to the larger hand pump outside. Her thoughts flew. She had been by Mama's side for the entire time she'd talked with Mrs. Foster's son. There was no mention at all of Claire, nor of the Fosters needing help. Mama was lying to Papa. Instead of standing up for her and telling Papa about what Horace had done, Mama was trying to get rid of her. She slammed the bucket under the faucet head and began pumping water into it. *How could she? Does Mama think it is my fault? Did I do something wrong to make Horace act that way toward me?* Claire took deep breaths and tried to calm herself. She finished filling the bucket and lifted it. In her anger, the water sloshed and she ended up with water down the front of her dress and apron. Angrier still, she approached the back door just as Papa was coming out.

"You'll have to be more careful than that if you want to do a good job, Girl," he said. "Don't embarrass me to the neighbors."

Papa walked by her with a shrug of the shoulders, as if he expected her to do exactly that.

The kitchen was empty when Claire arrived. She poured half the water into the pot on the stove, then added a log to the firebox. While the water for dishes was heating, she cleaned off the table, returning the butter and jam to the ice box and stacking the dishes neatly by the sink. She swept the floor. The actions were routine, and she did them without thinking. She just kept turning the morning's events over and over in her mind. She hadn't done anything to invite Horace's manly attentions. She's hardly even spoken to him. *Have I made Mama angry at me?* The storm of thoughts continued. Claire went from angry to sad. She felt hurt and resentful for one heartbeat and then confused and afraid with the next.

When the water was warm enough to wash the dishes, Clair began. Mama came in, dressed in her nice dress. Without a word she tied on an apron and began drying. They worked together, as they had for so long, without a word. When everything was washed, dried and put away, Mama untied her apron and turned to Claire.

"I know you don't understand. I'm just asking you to trust me."

"Mama, I do trust you, but why do you want to get rid of me?"

Her mother took a shuddering breath and steadied herself. "Your Papa and his brothers are very close. Who will he believe if you have one story and Horace has another? For as long as Horace lives here with us, you aren't safe. I can't change much around here, and I can't leave, but I will do whatever it takes to see that you are out of harm's way. The Fosters are good people. You will be safe there."

"Mama, are you sure you aren't mad at me?"

Her mother's eyes welled up. "I am not mad at you. You have done nothing wrong. You are innocent and beautiful, and I want to protect you. I can't do that here, but I can get you away from the danger."

"But what about you? That leaves twice the work for you."

"It'll be fine, Claire. Don't worry about me. I'll get Jesse to help me some, and we'll be fine. This is a good chance for you."

Tears threatened both women. Claire watched her mother fight off her emotions and steady herself and forced herself to do the same.

4
June, 1894
Foster farm - near Mitchell, South Dakota

It had been a hot and humid day. Claire's hands and arms were tired from doing laundry – scrubbing and wringing out the family's clothes by hand then hanging each piece up on the line. She'd worked for the Fosters for three days.

After supper was cleaned up, everyone sat on the front porch to enjoy the cool evening breeze. Not wanting to intrude, Claire sat in the kitchen until Mrs. Foster called for her. "Claire, please come join us, we'd love your company."

Claire tucked a stray strand of hair back into one of her braids and went out onto the porch. Matthew, the oldest son, had a harmonica and was playing "Oh Susanna!" Lanky and lean, his blue eyes shone as his music filled the evening air. The two youngest girls, two-year-old Molly and seven-year-old Milly were playing on the floor with a set of rag dolls. All of a sudden, halfway through the song, the oldest girl, Marney jumped up and ran into the house. A moment later she was back, producing a jaw harp. She sat next to Matthew and added to his music. Though she was more than a year younger than Matthew, they were nearly the same height and stature. Claire smiled as she watched their blond heads bobbed in unison as they played. Soon, Mr. Foster added the words to the tune,

It rained all night the day I left
The weather it was dry
The sun so hot, I froze to death
Susannah, don't you cry.

25

Oh, Susannah,
Oh don't you cry for me
For I come from Alabama
With a banjo on my knee.

Mrs. Foster, her swollen feet propped up on a crate, clapped with the rhythm. When the song was done, the family laughed and applauded themselves. Claire spoke quietly to Mrs. Foster, "That song was written by Stephen Foster. Is he any relation to Mr. Foster?"

"Tell the story, tell the story to Claire," Marney called out when she heard Claire's question. "Papa, tell us the story of Stephen Foster!"

Mr. Foster smiled as Milly dropped the doll she'd been playing with, climbed into his lap and settled down. "Well, Claire, Stephen Foster was my great-uncle, though I never met him. He was my grandfather's youngest brother. They lived near Pittsburgh, Pennsylvania. There were ten kids in that family, and Stephen was the youngest. He always loved music, and even though he earned his living mostly by being a book-keeper for my grandfather's steamship company in Cincinnati, he loved music and writing songs.

"Stephen was a talented musician and composer. His best friend was Charles Shiras, a strong abolitionist. It seems that Charles' influence was pretty important to Stephen's songs and the way he thought. Even though they lived before the Civil War, many of Stephen's songs told stories from a point of view of respect and kindness toward people with black skin."

"What happened to Great Uncle Stephen?" asked Marney.

"You already know that, why don't you tell Claire the answer?" responded Mr. Foster.

Marney looked at Claire. "He had a bad fever and tried to get out of bed. He fell and cut his head and neck and died."

"That's really a sad ending," Claire whispered looking to Mr. Foster for some clarification.

Mr. Foster finished the story. "When he fainted and fell, his head and neck were both cut. He bled for quite a while before anyone found him. By then he was so weakened he just couldn't recover. He was only thirty seven years old. He had thirty eight cents to his name when he died. But, the good part of the story is that he left us so many songs that make us happy."

Matthew picked up his harmonica and started to play a new song. The rest of the family joined in singing and clapping.

The Camptown ladies sing this song,
Doo-da, Doo-da
The Camptown racetrack's five miles long
Oh, de doo-da day

Goin' to run all night
Goin' to run all day
I bet my money on a bob-tailed nag
Somebody bet on the gray.

"Claire, do you sing?" asked Matthew.

"I, well, I've never sung so that anyone could hear me before," she answered.

"You are welcome to join this motley choir any time you'd like," laughed Mr. Foster.

Matthew began "Camptown Races" again, and Claire shyly joined in. When they had sung it through twice, Matthew began a new song. Claire and the children listened as Mr. and Mrs. Foster sang "Amazing Grace". Mrs. Foster's high clear voice resonated with her husband's low gravelly tones, and Claire couldn't remember ever hearing that song more beautifully done.

Amazing Grace, how sweet the sound,
That saved a wretch like me.
I once was lost but now am found,
Was blind, but now, I see.

T'was Grace that taught...
my heart to fear.
And Grace, my fears relieved.
How precious did that Grace appear...
the hour I first believed.

Twilight was growing thick as the last notes hung in the air. Milly was asleep in Mr. Foster's arms, and Marney was fighting to keep her eyes open, her head resting in her mama's lap.

Claire walked over and took Milly from Mr. Foster and stepped toward the front door. As she cradled the child and started for the door, she heard Molly whisper as she rose to follow them.

"Papa?"

"Yes, Little Sweetie?"

"Can I sleep with the little grey kitty tonight?"

"No, that kitten isn't big enough to be away from its mama yet. You'll have to wait."

"Okay, Papa. Good night."

The toddler in her arms never awoke as Claire put her to bed. Marney and Molly joined them in the bedroom. Claire got both girls snuggled in with dolls and blankets and kisses on each cheek. A few minutes later, Claire tucked herself in. She looked around at the room she shared with the girls. "I'm sorry that you have to share a room," Mrs. Foster apologized on the first night, but Claire liked its coziness. Milly had a crib in one corner. Along the far wall was a small trundle bed where Marney and Molly slept. Claire's bed was a cot near the door. She had space underneath for her carpetbag. Mrs. Foster cleared two hooks for her behind the door so that she could hang up the dresses she owned.

After two weeks at the Foster's, life had settled into a routine for Claire. Keeping a close eye on the youngest Foster, Claire did her best to keep the family fed and the house clean. Molly shadowed her older sister, Marney, and both girls were happy to help Claire with anything she asked.

Claire dried her hands on a towel and leaned against the sink. "Miss Claire, can we go outside and play with the new kittens now?" Marney asked. Cleaning the kitchen after the noon meal went quickly when the girls washed, dried and put dishes away while Claire got Milly to sleep and then swept the floor.

"Sure," Claire answered. "You two are such good help around here, all our work is done until supper time. Go and have fun."

The girls were gone in an instant to the barn. The big yellow mouser who lived in the hay loft surprised the family a few days before Claire arrived with a litter of five kittens. Now that the kitties' eyes were open the mama cat allowed the girls to get close and play with her babies. Maybe she's glad for the help to keep track of them, Claire thought with a smile.

Life in this family is so much different than at home. Claire rested, leaning against the sink as she waited for the water in the teapot to heat up. She spent a lot of time thinking about the differences between the two households. The Fosters didn't have it any easier than her own family. Times were lean for all the farmers in the area. Mr. Foster only had twelve-year-old Matthew to help him with the milking and farm work instead of three nearly grown boys like Papa had. *Yet, they laugh and seem to enjoy being together.*

She thought about an incident the day after she arrived, when Molly and Marney smuggled the calico kitten into their bedroom before bed. Even though the girls tried hiding it under the covers, the baby's mews caught Mr. Foster's attention when he kissed them goodnight. Claire cringed as she remembered the tightness in her chest as she feared what he would do. Instead of yanking the girls from their beds and spanking them soundly as Papa would have done, Mr. Foster calmly but firmly demanded the girls get up and take the kitty back to its mother. Tearfully the girls complied. When they returned to the house, both girls stood silently in front of their father. He sternly explained to them that lying and disobeying were not tolerated, and that their punishment would be to stay away from the kitties for two days. He didn't yell and he never hit them, yet the girls were truly sorry and Claire knew that they had learned a valuable lesson. When she considered it later, she realized that she had learned a lesson as well. Not all fathers beat their children.

Claire smiled again at the kindness she was experiencing as she got to know the Fosters better. Her work was hard and the days were long, but she didn't mind it. She found herself looking forward to joining the family in the evenings on the porch after the kitchen was cleaned to talk or sing. She was slowly getting over her shyness, and had been the recipient of several comments about her pretty singing voice.

The teapot whistled Claire from her reverie. She poured the water into a china teapot and added a measure of tea leaves. Transferring the pot to a small tray she found in the pantry, Claire added two tea cups and the sugar bowl. Carefully, she carried the tray into the parlor. Mrs. Foster sat in the sunlight near the window, stitching up a hem on a dress for one of the girls.

"Claire, you are so dear!" she said when she looked up. "A grown up tea party, how delightful!"

Claire smiled and put the tray down on a small table beside Mrs. Foster, then sat in the rocking chair on the other side of it. "I hope I put enough tea in. We never have tea at home."

"My grandmother was English, so we drank tea all the time when I was growing up," replied Mrs. Foster. "I'm sure you did just fine."

She put her sewing in the wicker box next to her chair and reached for the tea pot. "My grandmum made sure that my sisters and I all knew how to make and properly serve tea. She said that every fine lady must always be the best of hostesses." She poured the tea for them, exclaiming about how perfect it was and how much she appreciated Claire's thoughtfulness.

Claire watched Mrs. Foster's every movement, noticing how she placed her finger on the lid of the teapot as it was poured, how she held the saucer with one hand and the tea cup gently with the other as she sat back and relaxed.

Mrs. Foster breathed in the aroma of the tea, then smiled. "My grandfather was a proper British gent," she started. "He often drank his tea by pouring a little bit of it into his saucer, then using a spoon to drink it like soup. He said that it cooled faster that way." She laughed softly at the memory.

"How are you feeling, Mrs. Foster?" Claire asked shyly.

"Claire, dear, I would love it if you'd be comfortable enough to call me Haddie. I love having you here. You have made things so much easier for me."

"Thank you," Claire replied. "I'd love to, Haddie." Claire tried it out. "But you didn't answer me about how you are feeling," she finished with a smile.

"I try not to think about how useless I am right now to my own family and how much I am beginning to resemble some of the milk cows in the barn," she laughed. "My feet are much less swollen than they were though, and I don't feel as tired and achy as I was feeling before you came and took over. I will forever be grateful to your Mama for bringing you to me."

Claire tensed. She didn't want to discuss her mother's motives for sending her to the Foster's home. She concentrated on her tea cup and didn't meet Haddie's eyes.

The silence stretched. Finally, Claire glanced up at Haddie to find the woman studying her. She smiled wanly and began to rise. "I better go check on Milly," she started.

30

Haddie put her hand gently on Claire's hand. "What is it Claire?"

Claire smiled again and tried to sound upbeat and calm. "I've just malingered long enough. The girls have been out in the barn for quite a while. I'll just look in on them after I check on Milly. You relax now and enjoy the rest of your tea. I'll come get the tray in a bit."

On her way to find the girls, Claire worried that she had been rude to Haddie, but when she went in to pick up the tray a few minutes later, everything seemed normal. Haddie was back to sewing when she came in. The girls were now in the parlor, playing with the kittens.

"I'm going to name this one Chester," declared Molly.

"How do you know it is a boy?" asked Marney.

"Because he is grey and grey is a boy color," she answered with authority.

Claire and Haddie met eyes over the heads of the girls. Haddie grinned and shrugged. "Don't keep those kittens away from their mama too long, girls. She's liable to get pretty cranky if you do."

"Yes, Mama, and Papa might get cranky, too."

Molly carefully put Chester in her apron skirt and wrapped him up. "Let's go," she said to Marney. "Would you like to play jacks with me after we take the babies back?"

"Sure!"

The back door slammed behind the girls a moment later.

"Claire, I'm thinking we are running low on a few things, and I know that William will be going to town in the next few days."

"I do know that the salt box is nearly empty."

"There are paper and a pencil in the top pigeon hole of my secretary desk in the front hall. Would you get them so we can start a list of things we need?"

Claire handed the paper and pencil to Haddie and sat down beside her. Haddie began the list, then shrugged. "Claire, this baby won't stop kicking me today. Could you take over the list?"

She handed the paper and pencil to Claire. Claire took them hesitantly.

Haddie settled back and said, "Oh, I know, we are going to need some talcum powder for the baby when it comes. Let's add that to list so we have it on hand when the time comes."

Claire stared at the paper. "Well, I..." Claire was mortified.

There was an awkward silence as Haddie searched Claire's face. Then, her eyes widened and she spoke quietly, "Oh dear. Claire, I'm sorry. I just assumed you could…" she broke off as she studied the stricken look on Claire's face.

Claire's eyes were down. The pencil and paper were in her lap. "Papa says that there's no reason to teach girls to read and write. He thinks that it's a waste of time because females can't think as well as men. Papa says that God made women to be submissive and to have babies, not to think about things better left to the men."

"I see." Haddie's voice was stern and tight. Claire looked up at her in surprise, she'd never seen Haddie angry before, but there was no mistaking that Haddie was furious. "I'm so sorry!" Claire began, "I didn't mean to speak out of turn."

Haddie's face softened. She reached out for the second time that day and put her hand over Claire's. "Don't misunderstand me, Claire. I am not upset with you. I mean no disrespect to you, but your father's pin-headed attitude makes me so mad I could spit."

Claire's eyes grew wide. Her bottomless fear of Papa was so ingrained that even miles away from him Haddie's words scared her.

Deliberately, Haddie smoothed her hair and then her dress, calming herself and returning to her previously calm mood. "I think there is only one thing we can do under the circumstances," she said finally, her voice light and lilting.

"Yes," answered Claire, "I guess that you will have to make the list yourself."

"This time, you are right," Haddie chuckled. She squeezed Claire's hand so that the girl finally looked up at her. "But now I know exactly what we are going to do! It will give me something to think about and something to feel like I am accomplishing!" Haddie's smile was big, and her eyes were twinkling.

"I don't understand," stammered Claire.

"My Dear, in the afternoons when you have a break from your work, and again in the evenings after the children are in bed, you and I are going to do something marvelous. We are going to open up the whole world to you. We are going to have you reading and writing before this babe is born!"

5

August, 1894
Foster farm - near Mitchell, South Dakota

Haddie began teaching Claire to read using four primers that she had purchased to teach her children. Matthew and Marney could already read quite well, and Haddie had just begun working with Molly when Claire arrived. Haddie and Claire quickly moved through the four volumes of William H. McGuffey's Eclectic Readers, beginning first with writing the letters and identifying the sounds each make. By the time they had completed the four primers, Claire was able not only to sound out nearly every word she encountered but was beginning to recognize many at a glance. Certainly there were afternoons when Claire was sure Haddie must think that she was too thick headed to actually learn to read. The woman's patience and encouragement pulled her through those frustrations. Claire was so grateful for the time Haddie spent with her and feared letting her down. Sometimes, she awoke early and crept into the kitchen to practice the previous day's lessons. Soon, Claire graduated from the primers and began, haltingly at first, to read on her own with the poems in Robert Louis Stevenson's Penny Whistles.

They fell into a comfortable routine. After the children were in bed, Mr. Foster, whom Claire now called William, sat at the kitchen table doing the books for the farm. Claire helped Haddie get comfortable on the settee in the small parlor, then made tea for all of them. Then she joined Haddie. Claire treasured the hour or two she spent with Haddie, their heads together over a book. When William finished his work at the kitchen table, he joined them in the parlor. Twice, he joined the lesson and read aloud.

Now they were working on *Treasure Island*. She read aloud as Haddie looked on. Claire read how Jim Hawkins, concealed in an apple barrel, overheard John Silver plotting a mutiny with other sailors on the Hispaniola. "Oh my," interjected Claire. "What an evil man. I knew that the captain shouldn't trust him!" Haddie chuckled.

"Congratulations, Claire, you are now officially a reader."

Claire smiled back. "What do you mean?"

"Lots of people can cipher letters and words, but they aren't really reading until the characters and actions on the page come to life. I can tell that Jim and the rest of the crew, including Silver, are real in your mind, and that tells me that my job as a teacher is nearly finished with you."

"Haddie, I'm sure I have a long way to go to read as beautifully and smoothly as you do, but I do thank you for this wonderful gift."

* * *

Claire had now been with the Fosters for nearly two months. The evening was sultry and hot. The girls had been irritable all day. Claire was tired and felt a bit grouchy herself. After supper was cleaned up and the dishes done and put away, Claire washed the girls' faces, hands and necks with a cool cloth and tucked them into bed. She read Stevenson's poem "The Lamplighter" to them.

My tea is nearly ready and the sun has left the sky.
It's time to take the window to see Leerie going by;
For every night at teatime and before you take your seat,
With lantern and with ladder he comes posting up the street.

Now Tom would be a driver and Maria go to sea,
And my papa's a banker and as rich as he can be;
But I, when I am stronger and can choose what I'm to do,

O Leerie, I'll go round at night and light the lamps with you!
For we are very lucky, with a lamp before the door,
And Leerie stops to light it as he lights so many more;
And oh! Before you hurry by with ladder and with light;
O Leerie, see a little child and nod to him to-night!

The girls were asleep before she'd finished. Claire closed the book and sighed. She watched the girls sleep for a few minutes, then walked softly to the parlor. Haddie was melted into the settee, her face a bit pale. Her eyes were nearly closed and her breathing was even. She looked up as Claire came in.

"Are they asleep?" she asked. Claire nodded and sat down in the rocking chair opposite the couch. "Claire, I don't know how I would have survived without you these past two months. I can't ever thank you enough for all the work you've done around here."

"It's me that needs to thank you."

"I've had so much fun helping you learn to read. You catch on so fast."

"Learning to read is the most wonderful thing that has ever happened to me, and I thank you for that. But Haddie, you've done much more for me than you know."

Claire hesitated, swallowing hard and wondering how she could thank this woman for being part of Mama's plan to protect her from Horace. Tears threatened, but Claire took a deep breath and steadied herself.

When she looked up, Haddie was watching her. Haddie smiled, then grimaced. She shifted positions and frowned more deeply. "Claire, could you help me stand up? I just can't get comfortable."

Claire stood quickly and reached for Haddie's hand. Using Claire's strength as well as her own, Haddie stood up, then doubled over. "That's what I thought," she said. "I think we might have a baby tonight."

Haddie straightened up and looked to see sheer panic on Claire's face. She reached for the girl and hugged her. "Don't worry, I've done this four times already. Each one gets a little easier." Still holding on to Claire, they headed toward the kitchen. William was just closing the ledger book.

"Hey Dad," Haddie said softly. "How about you take a ride and bring me a doctor?"

William stood up and embraced his wife. He saw Claire's nervousness and smiled. "It only took about four hours for Milly to get here, so I better get going. Do you need help with anything before I leave?"

Haddie answered him, "I think I will take a short walk around the yard while you get ready. Claire can walk with me. We'll see if these pains get stronger or go away so I don't send you on a goose chase."

Claire stepped up beside Haddie as William kissed her forehead then went out to saddle the horse. They walked quietly around the front yard, stopping every few feet for Haddie to breathe.

"What can I do?" asked Claire.

Haddie grimaced and bit her lip for a minute before answering. Sweat popped out on her forehead and upper lip. "I think I need to take a rest," answered Haddie finally. She leaned on Claire's arm as they slowly walked back inside.

Claire was thankful that she and Haddie had discussed what needed to be done ahead of time. She helped Haddie into the high backed oak chair that sat by the window in the bedroom, then she pulled the sheets and blankets off of Haddie and William's bed. She replaced them with the thick, brushed cotton blanket that Haddie had used to birth her other children, tucking the edges in all around. Then she added a light sheet on the top and two pillows. She kept an eye on Haddie as she worked, feeling more confident now that she had something to do. Her heart was racing, though, and she sent silent messages to William to hurry. Leaving Haddie sitting in the bedroom, Claire went to the kitchen. She put the teapot on one burner and a large soup pot full of water on another. She added kindling and stirred the coals in the firebox. Soon, the fire danced happily in the belly of the stove. Claire went to the cabinet by the back door and retrieved some clean rags that they had prepared last week.

"Can you help me out to the privy?" Haddie asked when Claire returned.

"I can just get you the chamber pot, if you'd rather not walk to the outhouse," Claire suggested.

"No, I think the walk will feel good, and the privy will be much more comfortable than that little pot," replied Haddie with a smile.

They walked slowly in the twilight arm in arm. Claire stayed close while Haddie was inside the privy in case she might be needed. She was just becoming concerned when the privy door opened and Haddie came out.

Her face was pale and her breathing a bit quick. "I'm not sure we are going to be able to wait for the doctor, Claire, I'm feeling a strong urge to begin pushing this baby out. I was hoping to spare you the details of birthing, but I think we might not have a choice."

Claire felt her fears growing like a burning darkness in the pit of her stomach. She swallowed hard and encouraged Haddie to lean on her as they made their way back into the house. Haddie sent Claire to the kitchen for a glass of water, suggesting she make herself a cup of tea. Claire realized that Haddie needed a moment of privacy to change clothes and prepare herself. She moved the boiling water to the back of the stove to stay warm while her tea steeped.

She picked up her cup then quickly returned it to the table. Her hands were shaking enough now that the tea wouldn't stay inside.

One look at Haddie when she returned to the bedroom told Claire that time was short. Haddie reached a hand out to Claire. The girl moved quickly to her bedside.

"What do I do?"

***

An hour later, Claire was back in the kitchen, sitting quietly at the table. Her hands had stopped shaking, and her breathing was normal. The baby had come so quickly that there had been no time to be scared then; it was only after the doctor had come and she'd returned to the kitchen that her eyes had blurred with tears and her hands trembled. She relived the moment that she'd seen the baby's head, had reached for it and supported it until Haddie's final push freed him and he entered the world. Her heart stopped then, until he finally squeezed his eyes tight and began to cry. She gently handed him to Haddie then reached for a cotton blanket to cover him. Haddie lay back on the pillows and smiled first at her newborn son, and then at Claire. It was then that they heard William's and the doctor's heavy boots on the wooden porch. Claire pulled the sheet over Haddie and turned. William nearly sprinted down the hall, stopping only when he reached Haddie's side. He touched her face lovingly.

"William, we have a new son," Haddie whispered.

The doctor stopped in the doorway and watched for a few seconds before he interrupted. "Looks like I missed the good part and am stuck with the clean up here." He ushered Claire and William out of the room.

Claire had heard women talk about birthing now and again. She remembered hearing her mother talk about women screaming and crying. She thought about how silent Haddie had been. Claire admired the woman's strength and determination, and her courage.

The doctor left instructions with William and Claire that Haddie should not be out of bed for three or four days, to give her time to heal and recover. As soon as the doctor left the Foster farm that morning, news began to circulate that the baby had arrived. By noontime, neighbors began to stop by, dropping off a pie or a casserole, or a small baby gift. They didn't expect to see Haddie or the baby, just to share their congratulations and good will with the family.

Within a day and a half, Haddie was chafing at the doctor's orders. "It was such an easy time, I feel fine." William finally agreed that she could move out to the porch in the afternoon of the second day.

Claire's mother arrived while they sat on the front porch. Haddie had just finished nursing the baby. Claire sat in the rocking chair, cuddling him as he dropped off to sleep. Dori stopped at the foot of the stairs. "I didn't expect to see you Haddie," she began. "I just wanted to drop off a little something for the baby and give my own girl a hug."

Haddie's smile was radiant. "Please come up and sit down. I'm going a bit crazy sitting around, a good visit is exactly what I need."

Claire handed the baby back to Haddie, then hugged her mama. Each time Dori had come to visit in the two months that Claire had been staying with the Fosters, she had hugged her daughter tightly when she arrived and before she left. She lingered a minute, looking carefully at Claire before she moved over to admire the baby and hand a small package to Haddie.

"Thank you so much, Dori," began Haddie. "You didn't need to bring us a present, the gift of Claire here to help me has been the richest blessing I could imagine."

Claire put her head down, uncomfortable with the praise. It made Claire feel guilty when Haddie thanked her for all she'd done. Haddie had no idea that the real reason she was here was to protect her from her uncle.

"What are you going to call him?" Dori asked as the baby snuggled deep into Haddie's arms.

Haddie laughed, "William and I can't seem to agree. The other four children's names all begin with M, and I'd like to keep that tradition going, but William doesn't like Mark or Manuel – which are the only M names for boys that I like. William likes Kendall or Russell, but those don't start with M. At the rate we are going, the poor boy will be talking before he has a name."

Claire got up and stood by Haddie. "Would you like me to go put him in the cradle for you?"

"That would be great. And would you mind making your mama and me some tea?"

"I'd love to," Claire answered. She tenderly lifted the baby from his mother's arms and started into the house. She stopped and turned to look at the women. "Maybe you could name him Marshall. That kind of sounds like Russell and Kendall, but starts with M."

"Marshall? Hey, I think I like that. Marshall. What a good suggestion, Claire, we'll have to see what William thinks of it."

Claire put the baby down in his cradle in Haddie's room then went to the kitchen to put the tea pot on to boil. She walked quietly out to the barn to look in on the girls and stopped at the clothesline to check the diapers she'd hung there this morning. Then, she made her way back to the kitchen to prepare a tray with tea and some cookies that another neighbor had left.

Carefully balancing the tray, Claire was halfway down the hall. She froze as she heard what Haddie and her mother were discussing.

"Haddie, I miss her so much, but I am frightened for her to come home. Claire is pretty and innocent. Horace is mean and selfish and sees no harm in taking advantage of any girl he can. I've seen him look at her like she was something to gobble up. I just don't know how to protect her."

"Can you talk to Hiram about your fears?"

"I tried once before the boys came to live with us, and it didn't go well. To tell the truth, Hiram sees things in a similar fashion to Horace. I suspect their Pa used to do unspeakable things to Hiram's two sisters when they started to grow up. I've always tried to keep Claire looking as much like a little girl as I can, even before Horace and Clancy came to live with us, to make sure she didn't catch anyone's eye. But she's really blossomed, and I can't keep her in braids and pinafores any longer."

"Dori, it seems that the only answer is to keep Claire away from home. We need to find another woman who needs someone to help out, and move Claire there."

"I've thought of that, but Hiram has been asking about when Claire is coming home, complaining that I'm not keeping up with my work."

Claire felt bad about eavesdropping, but she felt rooted to the floor. At first she was relieved to know that Haddie knew the truth, but she also felt ashamed at the same time. That Mama was talking about private family matters with Haddie was a surprise. As she listened, a wave of understanding enveloped her and she thought back to the morning of her birthday. Now she understood that her mother's insistence on braids and pinafores was an attempt to keep her looking more like a child in order to protect her.

There was a lull in the conversation. Claire cleared her throat and stepped onto the porch. She served the tea as her Mama and Haddie chatted about the baby, the girls and the weather. Dori stayed another half hour and then sighed. "I told your Papa I'd been gone only a short time, he'll be wondering where his supper is if I don't get home."

She congratulated Haddie again on her beautiful boy, then turned to leave.

"I'll walk with you a bit," Claire began. Then she turned to Haddie, "Will you be needing anything for a few minutes?"

Haddie chuckled, "Claire, you have ruined me with the way you have spoiled me! I'm fine, you go on and have some time with your Mama."

They walked in silence until they'd passed the gate. Claire was thinking about the differences between the Foster home and her own. "I'm proud of you, Claire," her Mama said, breaking the silence. "Haddie can't say enough about how hard you've worked for her and how you helped deliver the baby just like a midwife. She says she would have been lost without you."

Claire watched as the dust swirled around her shoes as she walked. "Thank you, Mama, I've tried to remember all you've taught me." Claire hated how awkward she felt talking to her own mother. *Why do I feel so much more comfortable with Haddie?*

"It sounds like she'll be up and around real soon, I'll be happy to have you back home."

"I've missed you, Mama. I'll probably be home next week."

When they reached the barbed wire fence that marked the end of the Foster's property, Mama stopped and turned to look at Claire. "Haddie says she's never seen or heard of anyone learning to read as quickly as you have. Says you can read anything you can get your hands on."

"Mama, reading is a whole new world. I sometimes get lost in the pages and feel so free. Haddie says that I can borrow a few of her books to bring home and read. You and I can read together."

Mama reached out and lifted Claire's chin, so that her daughter was looking at her. "Girl, your Papa isn't going to like it if you come home with fancy ideas or if he finds you with your face in a book. I can see that you've grown up quite a bit in the short time you've been gone, but don't think that anything has changed at the farm just because you have."

"Yes, Mama." Claire felt as if she were a balloon and the air had slowly begun to leak out of her.

"That William Foster is a progressive man, and he runs his household in his own way. Your Papa is a good provider and he has his own ideas, and you dasn't ever forget that, or confuse the two." Her voice was stern, almost angry.

"Yes, Mama," Claire said again.

Mama hugged her then, strong arms held her tightly for a few seconds, then relaxed. She turned and started down the road, then stopped and turned. "I expect I'll see you within a week. Laundry day will be Thursday, I could use your help."

She resumed her trek home, not looking back again. Claire watched her until she disappeared from sight around the bend. Her eyes filled with tears. Claire hadn't imagined the kindness in her mother's voice when she'd been talking privately with Haddie. She now understood some of the ways Mama acted at home. Mama told her that she'd done well and that she was proud, but then seemed angry. Claire was confused and hurt. Her mother was a puzzle she couldn't solve.

That evening, after she'd cleaned up supper dishes and gotten the older children to bed, Claire stepped outside. She leaned against the front gate and tried once again to understand her mother's words and actions. She remembered the worry in Mama's voice as she'd been talking to Haddie in confidence about Claire's uncle, and she heard the pride in her voice when they'd talked about how well Claire could read. Those tendernesses were shadowed by the harshness in Mama's voice as they parted on the road. *What did I do to make her angry?*

It was nearly dark when she heard the screen door slam behind her. "Oh here you are." William stepped off the porch, calling to Claire. He joined her at the gate, sighing. "It's a might cooler out here than in the house, isn't it?"

Claire smiled at him and murmured a quiet, "Yes, it's nice here."

"Claire, we were already indebted to you because of how you have taken such good care of us and been such a help to Haddie. Now, I owe you even more thanks."

Claire met his eyes. They were smiling and kind.

"Thank you for solving the problem we were having of naming our son."

For a minute Claire had no idea what he was talking about, then she remembered.

"Haddie and I have agreed that his name will be Marshall at your suggestion. Come on in the house," he finished. "Let's have a slice of that pie the Wilsons left this morning."

The kitchen was bright and cheery, and very warm in contrast to the cool darkness outside. Haddie already had three slices of pie dished out on the table. "Would you like a glass of milk?" she asked as Claire sat down.

"Yes, that sounds wonderful," Claire answered.

They enjoyed their treat in silence for a few moments.

"Did William tell you the news? We've named the baby," started Haddie.

"Yes, you've decided on Marshall?"

"Marshall Clark Foster." Haddie was beaming.

"That's a great name. Is Clark a family name?"

"No, that was William's idea. We want you to know how much we appreciate all you've done for us, but Claire isn't a very manly name, so we changed Claire to Clark, to honor you."

Claire was speechless. She stammered a few seconds before she could get out a thanks. Her mother's harsh words bashed up against the kindness and acceptance Haddie offered her.

6
Late August, 1894
Atley farm - near Mitchell, South Dakota

This has been the longest two weeks of my life thought Claire. Her arms ached from wringing out the clothes as she pulled them from the wash tub. Her hands were red and itchy from the lye soap she'd been scrubbing with.

Adding the last pair of pants to the basket of wrung out clothes, she straightened up and stretched, trying to relieve the tired muscles in her back and shoulders. She sighed as she looked at the sky. Clouds were gathering to the west, dark and looming. *I'll probably have to take these down off the line as soon as I get them up*, she groused to herself.

Claire felt as dark and gloomy as the western sky. She longed to hear laughter or a bit of music like had filled the Foster home, but there were none here. Of course, she'd never missed it before, but she missed it now. She picked up the heavy basket and made her way to the clothesline. She shook out each pair of pants, shirt and towel and pinned it up. Sweat trickled down her back. The air was heavy and the heat pushed down on her.

As she worked, she thought about her homecoming. They hadn't talked about it, but Claire could see that Mama was happy to see her and glad she was home. Mama hadn't argued with her the first morning when she'd come downstairs with her hair braided in one braid down her back and no pinafore. Instead, she hugged her daughter quickly, then handed her an apron to tie on. With that, both acknowledged that the ruse of dressing Claire as a child was beyond useful.

The August heat along with the added livestock kept the men working long days, so Claire was able to avoid Horace and her

43

Papa most of the time. In fact, Papa usually even took Jesse with him to the fields so Mama and Claire had been alone during the days much of the time. After supper each night, Claire finished the dishes and cleaned the kitchen floor, then retreated to her room to read for a few minutes while there was still light enough to see. Those stolen minutes were precious.

A movement by the fence caught her eye. Claire looked up to see Marcus running towards the farmhouse. He was dusty and disheveled. He stumbled as he came around the fence, but righted himself and kept running. As he approached the barn, he hollered for Mama. Claire dropped the last shirt back into the basket and ran toward the house.

Mama came out after Marcus' second call. "What is it?" she called back as he headed into the barn.

"Been an accident," Marcus yelled.

"Who is hurt?" Mama hollered back as she rushed to meet him.

"Jesse."

"Is he alive? Is he going to be alright?" Mama's voice rose in pitch with every question. She had gone pale.

Marcus pushed open the barn door and reached for the bridle for Whitey. Mama and Claire stood together at the door, watching him hitch Whitey to the buckboard. As he worked he explained that while the men were cutting hay in the lower field, "Jesse was standing on the back of the harvester. I don't know how it happened, maybe they hit a rock and it knocked him off his feet. He fell right in between the two canvases of the binder."

"Is he alive?" Mama asked again.

"I lit out of there right away, Mama. He was still trapped in there. I could hear him whimpering, so I know he was alive. Papa, Clancy and Horace were trying to figure out how to get him out."

"We're going to need bandages." Mama's face became a stone. She needed to think calmly. "Claire, go get some rags and put some water in a couple of quart Mason jars. Marcus, bring the wagon up to the house when you are finished, I am going with you."

Claire ran. Marcus worked as quickly as possible. Mama came into the house, grabbed two quilts and her sweater. Soon they were bouncing their way back to the field. Marcus yelled and snapped the reins to urge the horse to go faster.

Claire pictured the old 1882 twine binding harvester made by The Wood Company. Papa was so proud of that machine, even though it was second hand when he got it. He liked to brag how he owned one of the first harvesters equipped with an original knotter mechanism to tie the twine and bind the bales of hay. Claire knew that the canvases were thick and strong and nearly brand new.

When they arrived in the field, Papa and Horace were using a crowbar to try to pry open the arms that held the canvas. Both were sweating, Papa was swearing. Mama jumped off the wagon and rushed to his side. "Jesse, Jesse!" she yelled.

Papa looked up at her, the strain and frustration showing on his face. "He was crying until just a minute ago. Now he is quiet. I can't get him out!"

Horace rushed to the wagon, "Marcus did you think to grab a machete or knife?"

Marcus looked stricken, "No, I…" he stammered.

Papa swore again. He threw down the crowbar in frustrated agony then grabbed the top canvas with his bare hands. He gritted his teeth and tried to tear it.

Nothing happened.

He relaxed his efforts and took a deep breath, then tried again. Slowly, the canvas gave way with a groan and a low ripping sound. When the gap was about three feet wide, Papa dropped the canvas and reached in with both hands to retrieve his son.

Jesse was limp, like a rag doll. "Is he breathing?" Mama whispered.

Papa lay the little boy on the ground gently. In the silence that followed everyone willed Jesse to breathe and open his eyes. Claire saw his hand twitch first, then a moment later, he opened his eyes. Much later, Claire would remember that moment and think of the collective sigh of relief as a prayer of thanksgiving.

"Get him a blanket," Mama was the first to recover. "He needs a doctor."

Claire reached into the back of the buckboard, grabbed one of the quilts, and ran. Mama wrapped the boy up as Papa wiped the sweat from his forehead. "Horace, you stay here and see what you can do to fix this and finish the harvest before the rain comes. Clancy hurry on ahead and find the doctor, we'll bring him in to his office in town. Marcus, I'll drive while you hold the boy on the way to town."

"I'm going, too." Mama's voice was quiet and stern. Papa began to argue, but with one look at her face, he closed his mouth again and nodded.

Claire stood by the harvester, unsure of herself. Was it selfishness to worry about being here with Horace?

Mama climbed up into the wagon and Papa handed Jesse up to her. Then she noticed Claire. A look passed between mother and daughter. "Marcus, I'd appreciate it if you'd stay behind. Please walk back to the house with your sister. She's going to need help with tonight's chores.

Marcus was clearly disappointed, but didn't argue. "Yes, Mama."

7
Late August, 1894
Atley farm - near Mitchell, South Dakota

Claire felt as if one of the mules had kicked her in the belly as she watched the wagon move down the road and out of sight. Jesse was so small and pale. She trudged back to the house silently with Marcus beside her. Without talking, they started in on the chores. Trying to keep her mind off her brother, Claire sang softly as she worked. She was just finishing the last verse of *Amazing Grace* when Marcus joined her in front of the barn.

"That was real pretty," he said, "I know Jesse really likes that since you've been back home you've been singing to him when he gets in bed."

Claire's eyes flooded with thoughts of Jesse and with the kindness in her older brother's compliment.

Even though they knew it was unlikely that Papa and Mama would be back before tomorrow, Claire and Marcus finished all the chores keeping an eye out down the road for the wagon to return. Clouds were building to the south in huge, grey billows threatening and marching closer. The temperature rose as the wind died.

"It feels like nature is holding its breath, waiting just like we are," remarked Claire to Marcus as they finished feeding the pigs.

Horace and Clancy returned from the field at twilight, tired and hungry. Claire cooked ham and eggs with toast for supper. She was relieved when no one complained about having breakfast at night. Worry and hard work had succeeded in taming their disapproval. She was even more thankful when, after supper, Horace announced that he was going to bed early after such a hard day. Claire cleaned up the supper dishes and retreated up to her room. The night's stifling heat and mugginess were amplified in her attic space. She allowed herself the indulgence of reading and not worrying that Papa would see the light and holler at her for wasting the kerosene. She was working her way through Stephen Crane's book *The Red Badge of Courage*. Claire was happy to have such a popular book to read. Haddie sent it to her along with a shawl she'd crocheted as a thank you. Claire struggled with the story, there were many words Claire could only guess at meanings for. The subject was raw and violent.

She closed the book and went to the small, screenless window. She leaned out to try to catch a breeze as she considered the story. The main character, Henry Fleming, had run away from his first Civil War battle. Afterwards, he developed a desire for a wound to prove he wasn't a coward. Claire stared, unseeing, out the window and thought about Henry Fleming. Was he a coward? Were wounds the only tally of courage? Claire didn't consider herself a coward when she bowed her head and answered Papa with a quiet "Yes, Papa," instead of standing up for herself. Claire pictured Mama, eyes down but jaw clinched, letting Papa rant and rave instead of arguing back. *That wasn't cowardice, it was common sense,* Claire thought. Mama and Claire both had received "wounds" from Papa. Claire could make for herself a long list of bruises and welts from the back of Papa's hand or his thick belt. She unconsciously rubbed the small scar on her arm where Papa had thrown a crockery cup at her that wasn't clean enough. Those weren't symbols of courage, they were the result of not retreating quickly enough or of being too near when Papa's temper flared.

Claire sighed and leaned a little farther out the small attic window. Lightning flashed to the south, jaggedly disturbing the darkness of the night. The storm was closer now, and she longed for it to arrive and break the tension in the air, even if it meant enduring a wicked storm. She felt the wind stir as the storm approached and welcomed the coolness. Chuckling with a dry mirthless laugh, she connected the storm to her own life. She hated Papa's anger and meanness, but when his temper started to build it was like the storm, threatening and ominous to the point that when he did blow up and hit or punch or throw things it was a kind of grim relief. And, just like the aftermath of a summer thunderstorm, once her father spent his anger at the women in his home, the air would clear and there would be quiet and peace for a little while until the clouds began to build again.

The rain began with a few sprinkles that quickly turned into a strong shower. Claire could see that as the bulk of the storm moved east of them, they would be spared the full weight of the lightning and the downpour. Cool wind played with her thin curtains, made even more yellow in the kerosene lamplight. It lifted her hair from her forehead and cooled her. She pulled the shutter closed part way, turned off the lantern and crawled under the sheet, nestling into her bed as thunder boomed in the distance. She was worried about Jesse and Mama but allowed herself to close off those thoughts and sink into sleep.

Claire cooked a breakfast of pancakes and eggs. Afterwards, Clancy, who had returned to the farm late, and Horace were armed with a dinner bucket filled with cold sausage and thick bread slices, set out to check on the cows after the night's storm. Marcus left to do the chores while Claire tended the kitchen. She knew Mama would be tired and have her hands full with tending Jesse when they returned, so she put a pot roast in the Dutch oven on the stove and mixed up a batch of bread. While the bread was rising on the sunny window sill, she walked through the house, straightening and dusting.

She formed the dough into loaves and set them to rise a second time, then helped Marcus with some of the chores. He gathered eggs while she slopped the pigs. He was only a year older than she, but a head taller. She watched for a minute as he mucked out stalls. He was her quiet brother. He was nearly always kind to her now that they were older, and he went out of his way to help her and Mama when he could, without attracting Papa's attention. He, being male, was never on the receiving end of Papa's cold rage, but he seemed to suffer himself when Mama or Claire were hurting.

Taking a break, Marcus leaned on the pitchfork and smiled at her. "You look done in," he said.

"You do, too," she answered back.

"Do you think he is alright?" she continued.

"Yup, he's too ornery of a little guy to let a harvester beat him. There wasn't any blood, he wasn't cut anywhere. I think he was just shaken up."

"How did he not get cut by all the sickle blades that turn inside that harvester?"

"I was standing right beside Papa when he tore that canvas. Before he reached in and pulled Jesse out I saw that Jesse was holding on to a bolt that was sticking out. That musta kept him from being pulled farther in where the blades could catch him."

"Thank goodness for that."

Marcus grinned and started back to work.

Claire was on her way to check on the bread in the oven when she first saw the dust cloud that meant someone was on the road. She couldn't tell from that distance who it was, but crossed her fingers that her parents and little brother were returning.

Two golden brown loaves of bread sat on the sideboard with a flour sack towel lightly covering them when the wagon pulled into the yard.

Claire and Marcus waited outside to hear the news, but they knew it wasn't too bad when they saw that Jesse was sitting between Mama and Papa on the buckboard seat.

Papa got down from the wagon seat, then reached up for Jesse. He carried him into the house, leading the rest of the family in.

They were all talking at once. Questions and answers flew back and forth as they all settled into the kitchen. "That bread smells heavenly," Mama smiled at Claire.

"Sit down, Mama, and I'll get us all a piece of bread and jam. I've got coffee just percolating,"

Claire sliced one loaf of bread, added butter and jam to the table along with knives and plates while the coffee finished. She retrieved cups from the cupboard and put them on the table. Papa washed up in the sink while Mama took off her hat and brought Jesse a blanket for his legs. They all sat around the table as Claire poured the coffee from one of her Mama's prized possessions, a percolator patented by Hansen Goodrich in 1889. Goodrich lived in Illinois near a cousin of Mama's. Last year for Christmas, she sent the pot as a gift. Along with the percolator was a paper package of Maxwell House coffee from Tennessee. Claire thought it was funny that the package claimed that it was "Good to the last drop."

Papa blew on his coffee, then began his story. "We found the Doc at his office, and he went right to work checking Jesse out. Nothing is broken in his legs or feet, but he was complaining that there were 'flies buzzing' around his legs."

"They still are, but not as bad," interrupted Jesse.

"The Doc says that the tight canvases must have cut off the circulation in his legs, and that's what makes them feel like they're buzzing," continued Papa. "Doc says he needs to rest and take it easy on those legs, but that he'll be fine."

The family lingered over coffee and bread for a time, cherishing the fact that all was well instead of tragic. Papa thanked Marcus for doing such a fine job on the chores, ignoring Claire's contribution even when Marcus pointed out that she had done a lot. Mama softened Papa's slight, "This bread is real good, Claire, you did a good job on it, and that roast is smelling fine."

Claire smiled at her mother, noticing how tired she looked.

The family mood was broken when they heard Horace and Clancy ride into the yard. Papa got up, then, and put on his hat. "Let's go to work, Marcus," he said, and they were off, leaving Claire to clean up as Mama helped Jesse to the settee in the parlor for a nap.

8

Labor Day: September, 1894
Atley farm - near Mitchell, South Dakota

In 1887 Labor Day was established on the first Monday in September to celebrate the hard work of the American people and focus on tradesmen and labor organizations. In the nine years since it began, Labor Day had become a large celebration in Mitchell, South Dakota and many other small towns in the Midwest. This year, Labor Day was declared a national holiday by the U.S. Congress. Claire smiled as she bounced along in the back of the buckboard. The whole family was going to town to see the parade and enjoy a picnic at the Corn Palace on Main Street. Mama, Jesse and Papa sat side by side on the seat of the wagon. Claire, Marcus, and Clancy occupied the back bed of the buckboard while Horace rode Whitey alongside. Claire and Mama had worked for two days to prepare the picnic lunch that sat safely beside her in two large wicker baskets. At the back of the wagon bed was a roll of canvas. Claire didn't know why it was there, but didn't consider it too long.

The closer they got to Mitchell, the more traffic they encountered. Wagons created a parade of their own as families travelled to town to celebrate and enjoy a day of rest. Papa found a shady spot just on the edge of the Corn Palace grounds to leave the wagon. Marcus tethered the horses and put out some grain for them while Clancy and Horace unloaded the food baskets. They all trooped together across the thick grass to find a spot near the street.

Claire watched Jesse as he bounced along beside her. His face was flushed with excitement. He didn't seem to mind the small limp that he retained as a result of the harvester accident.

Soon, the family was settled on a large quilt, ready for the parade. By the time the parade began, they were surrounded by many farm families that they knew. Claire watched as Mama talked happily with Mrs. Reinholz and Mrs. Grosz. She didn't enter in, she just absorbed the excitement and warmth of the day filled with visiting and smiling.

The parade began with a color guard carrying the American and South Dakota flags. The crowd stood respectfully as the colors passed. Town men, who worked inside as shopkeepers and bankers were easily recognizable since their foreheads were the same color as the rest of their faces. Farmers and men who spent their days outside in the hot sun, sported tanned, ruddy faces with very white foreheads. With their hats off as the flags slowly progressed down the street, the differences were stark. Claire looked around and giggled to herself.

People remained standing after the colors passed as a large brown, riderless horse was lead down the street by a tall, thin man dressed in black. The pair was preceded by two children, also in black, carrying a banner that said, "In memory of Richard D. Welch". Mr. Welch was the mayor of Mitchell until he died unexpectedly in June. Claire remembered him as the fire chief for the town, and could picture him cutting the ribbon at the opening ceremony for the Corn Palace in 1892. Mrs. Reinholz, standing beside Claire, wiped her eyes when the horse had passed. "He was such a nice man," she remarked. "He did a lot of good for this town."

Next in the parade was a large, noisy brass band. They played John Philip Sousa marches as they stepped smartly down the street. Claire sat down beside Jesse and enjoyed the morning. Group after group of marching men streamed down the road. The Knights of Labor walked by, chanting about workers' rights and handing out salt water taffy wrapped in squares of waxed paper. Claire and Jesse enjoyed the treat as they watched the men pass.

The Salvation Army band marched by. Claire watched the bass drummer, a large man with a very red face, twirl his drum sticks between each beat. Right behind them came about twenty women, the first and only females in the parade, carrying signs and banners championing temperance and a ban on alcohol. Someone nearby in the crowd called out, "Go back to your husbands where you belong."

Another voice rejoined, "They're too ugly for husbands, especially sober ones!"

Other men joined in with insults as the women marched along. The exchange was like a small raincloud for Claire. No woman in the crowd defended the Temperance League members. Most sat quietly or became interested in fixing their blankets or wiping a toddler's nose. Claire retreated into herself and thought that the whole day was set aside to celebrate and admire labor, but not one entry in the parade showcased the work that women did in their homes. She knew that there was nothing she could do to change the situation, especially with her Papa.

The sun was straight overhead and hot by the time the parade was finished. The family joined the throng of others as they picked up their baskets and quilts and moved to the grounds of the Corn Palace for their picnic. Papa pointed out a shady spot beneath a large cottonwood tree. "You go put out our picnic over there. I'll be back in a minute."

Jesse helped Claire spread the quilt out, then ran off to play with some boys he spied trying to climb the tree. Claire and Mama emptied the basket and sat out the plates. When they'd finished, Claire sat back to survey the spread. There was fried chicken, potato salad and five-bean salad, deviled eggs, dinner rolls, a jar of pickled beets and another of dilled cucumbers, carrots and onions. Still tucked away in the basket were a peach pie and a cherry pie. Claire's mouth watered in anticipation.

Papa and the boys returned. The boys were carrying the roll of canvas Claire had seen in the wagon. They sat it down beside the quilt and fell ravenously on the picnic. Claire ate slowly, cherishing the day. She listened as her Papa and brothers bantered back and forth. She looked around at the families nearby. Toward the end of the meal, she was excited to notice the Fosters sitting under another tree nearby.

"I'm too full for pie, right now, Mama," sighed Marcus. "Everything was so good!"

"We'll wait for a while to cut the pie," replied Mama. "Let's rest and visit a bit first."

"I'm going to walk over to the saloon and get a drink," Papa announced.

Claire glanced quickly at her Mama. The happy smile that had adorned her face turned into a worried one. "I think the games will be starting soon, you always enjoy watching the boys in the three-legged races," she said quietly.

"Don't go preaching, Dori, I won't be gone long."

Horace cleared his throat, "I'll go with you, Hiram."

"Ma, can I go back and play in that tree with those boys?" asked Jesse.

"Stay where I can see you, please," was Mama's quiet answer.

Clancey punched Marcus on the arm, "There's a horse shoe tournament starting over on the front lawn of the Corn Palace, let's go!"

The women finished up repacking the leftover food and dirty dishes into the baskets, then they shook the crumbs off the quilt and spread it out again on the ground. They were just finishing up when Haddie appeared with baby Marshall in her arms and Milly trailing behind.

"I thought I saw you over there!" Claire jumped up to hug them. Then, they settled down to visit.

The ladies talked and talked, and this time Claire participated in the conversation. They discussed the little girls and how they were adjusting to their new brother. When they had caught up on all the family and community news, Haddie sighed, "Isn't this nice? Taking a day to relax and not work is such a treat."

"I can't remember the last time I sat for a whole afternoon," added Mama.

Turning to Claire, Haddie said, "It's too bad we don't live in England. We could be spending this afternoon watching tennis."

"I don't know what tennis is," Claire answered.

"I'm not sure of all the rules, either, but as I understand it, there's a small ball that two opposing players hit over a short fence between them. They score points when the other player can't return the ball. It is quite popular in England. This is the 20th year that the men held the championship at a place called Wimbledon."

"Men get all the fun."

"Actually, women play tennis, too. The women even have championship games at Wimbledon as well, though I don't think they've held them as many years."

Mama thought for a minute, "I don't know about tennis, but I do enjoy watching a baseball game now and then. Some of the ladies this morning at the parade were saying that a man named Big

Ed Delahanty scored four home runs in one game for the Philadelphia Phillies last month. I'll bet that was exciting to watch."

Claire's mood plummeted then, as she watched her father and Horace make their way towards them. Marcus and Clancy trailed behind them. Her father stumbled a little, then laughed and spat. There were several men with him that Claire didn't recognize.

Mama and Haddie didn't notice the group until they were very close. Mama looked up and whispered under her breath, "Oh dear," when she saw her husband.

Papa and Horace didn't acknowledge the women when they got close. They were bantering with the other men, loudly, attracting the attention of others.

"I tell you Hiram, you didn't rip the canvas of a grain binder with your bare hands if it was new. It must be old and rotten. It is too thick," asserted a tall man with a handlebar mustache.

"I brought it with me, Amos, because I figured you boys would doubt my story. Unroll that canvas, Marcus and Clancy and hold it up. I'll show you how rotten it is!"

By now there was quite a crowd gathered. Claire, Mama, and Haddie stood up and moved to the edge of the circle as others joined them. To Claire it was obvious that Papa had gone to the saloon, had a few drinks and began bragging about how he got Jesse out of the grain binder. Many men in the group were shaking their heads and pointing.

Papa looked over at Claire. "Girl, come here."

Claire was frightened of the loud group of men, but her father insisted she walk into the middle of the circle. She felt hot.

"Yes, Papa?" she said as she stood beside the man.

"You saw what happened when your brother was in the binder, tell these men what you saw."

"Well, when Jesse,"

"Speak up there," shouted a man from the back. "We can't hear you."

Claire's legs felt wobbly and she had to take a breath and start again.

"When I came up, Jesse was crying softly. Then he stopped. We all thought that he was dying, so Papa gripped the canvas with both his hands and just tore it into two, then he reached in and got Jesse out."

"See there, the girl isn't lying about this!" She quickly returned to her mother's side, reeling from being put on the spot in front of so many people, but also at the smile she'd received from Papa.

Papa looked around the circle of men and women who had gathered. "I'll bet anyone a dollar that you can't tear this canvas again!"

"I'll take that bet," answered the man with the mustache. He stepped up and grabbed the canvas with two hands. He smiled at the crowd and shrugged, showing his bravado. When he tried to rip the material, it didn't budge. He repositioned his hands and tried again. His face turned red, but the canvas didn't budge. There were cheers and advice yelled from the crowd, but to no avail, the canvas didn't tear. Finally, the man let go and stepped back.

"Hiram, I just don't know how you did it, but that was certainly quite a feat," he said as he pulled a dollar coin from his pocket. "Here's your dollar."

Papa laughed and pocketed the coin. "Anyone else want to take my bet?"

Two more men stepped up, and the crowd got louder and larger. In the end, four men tried to tear the binder canvas, and their four dollars were now safe in Papa's pocket.

Eventually the men drifted away. Haddie hugged Claire and her mother goodbye and returned to her family. Mama got out the pies and served them.

Claire took a bite of her cherry pie slice and looked up to catch Horace staring at her. She quickly looked down and busied herself with brushing crumbs from her skirt. When she looked up again he was talking to Papa.

As she finished her cherry pie, she thought about the three weeks she had been back on the farm since working at the Fosters. Horace stared at her often at dinner, and 'accidentally' touched her as he moved by her when they were with the family in the house. She tried to be very careful to always know where he was when he was around so that she could stay clear of him. Twice he managed to get her alone. Once he caught her in the barn. Claire had been pouring a bit of milk in a saucer for the barn kittens when Horace closed the barn door and leaned against it. The look on his face was hard and hungry. She looked frantically around for a way out or something to help keep him away from her. As she reached for a rake, Horace strided across the barn and confidently took it from her. Then he pinned her against the stacked bales of hay. He rubbed his body against her, holding her tightly by the shoulders. His face was close to hers. She tried to turn her head, but he caught her chin and made her look at him. His lips had just brushed hers when the barn door began to open and he released her. Claire had never been so glad to see Marcus in her life. She tore free of Horace and fled to the house. She wondered later what exactly Marcus had seen and what he thought.

Then yesterday, Horace caught her alone in the kitchen. Mama and Jesse were visible out the kitchen window, Papa and the rest of the boys were pitching hay in the barn. Claire was finishing supper dishes when Horace came in for water. Claire's heart raced, even though she was sitting on the blanket at the picnic when she recalled his lips on her neck and his hands rubbing her chest. She could once again feel the heat of his body as he pressed her from behind into the table. "You know what I want to do to you?" He whispered.

In her innocence, she didn't know what he had in mind, but instinctively she was frightened and knew that whatever he did would be awful. Tears slid silently down her cheeks.

"Stop."

She said it quietly, afraid. "You'll be begging me not to stop when I finally am able to teach you all about being a woman. But, sadly for you, I'm busy right now." He squeezed her breast, hard. She cried out. Immediately he spun her around to face him. He roughly put his hand over her mouth.

"Just remember, who will your dear Papa believe if you tell anyone?"

He released her then and was gone, leaving her shaken and sick.

"Claire, are you alright?" Mama's voice pulled her from the kitchen and back to the picnic. "You are pallid, do you feel alright?"

Claire took a ragged breath and forced a smile. "I'm just a little warm, Mama, I'm fine."

Mama continued to look with concern at Claire for a few seconds, then smiled.

9
Mid-September, 1894
Atley farm - near Mitchell, South Dakota

As fall progressed and evenings turned cooler, Claire began to feel more and more restless and worried. Winter kept the family indoors more and she feared that it would be harder and harder to stay out of Horace's way. The thought of being alone with him again made a panic well up inside Claire that she had trouble containing.

She found an old wooden chair in a far corner of the hay loft. She scrubbed the thick coat of dirt and neglect from it and carried it to her attic room. "There," she said aloud to the empty room. "You fit just right under that glass doorknob. Now no one can come in here without my knowing and approving of it." She wiped her hands on the back of her skirt and smiled to herself. She'd been afraid that Horace might sneak up to her room in the night and surprise her while she slept. With the back of the chair wedged under the doorknob she felt safe. *Now if I could just stay in here always and never go out.*

***

The first snow arrived with the month of October. The ground was covered with only an inch of snow, but the wind was whistling through the cracks around the windows in the kitchen and Claire felt cold in spite of the fire dancing in the cook stove. Mama got up and added a piece of wood when she noticed Claire shiver. "You've been even quieter than usual today. Are you coming down with something?"

59

"No, Mama, I was just thinking."

Claire knew that her mother had noticed the looks that Horace gave her, and she guessed that Mama was concerned, but neither of them had mentioned him since before she'd returned from the Foster's months ago.

Silence returned and both women focused on the sewing in front of them. They were working on blocks for a new quilt for Jesse's bed. Once a year, Papa allowed Mama to order material from the Sears and Roebucks catalog for shirts and dresses. Mama saved every scrap to use for quilts. For this quilt, Claire suggested they try a churn dash pattern like one she'd seen at Haddie's. She'd loved the way the rectangles and triangles fit together to create a picture frame kind of pattern. "They say that this outer part looks like a butter churn and the square in the middle is the butter", Haddie remarked, "but I don't see that at all!" Haddie gave a sweet musical laugh at herself. Claire cherished that memory, and chose this pattern in honor of Haddie's laugh.

"Mama, Haddie told me that some people think this quilt pattern was used to help guide runaway slaves north to freedom."

"Only the very brave would have taken the chance of helping a runaway slave before the war, Claire. I don't think many people, especially women, have that kind of courage."

"There were women during the war who acted as spies. That was brave."

"Is that something you read in one of your dime novels? Those things are full of all kinds of foolishness."

Claire didn't answer. She'd been surprised that her mother wasn't more receptive to her daughter's literacy. Mama hadn't been angry, she'd just matter-of-factly told Claire not to dally with books and reading when there was work to do. Claire took care to conceal the three Beadle's Dime Novels that Haddie had given her from plain view. Her mother knew she had them, she just tried to keep them out of sight and mind. Claire hadn't read about Civil War spies, but she had read about a brave girl in *Alice Wilde, the Raftsman's Daughter.* A second novel, *A Forest Romance,* told of girl characters being adventurous and exploring. The idea of women's bravery piqued her imagination late at night when she couldn't sleep. Claire knew her mother wouldn't understand, so she went back to her silent sewing.

The next morning dawned clear and cold. Claire was thankful that she'd added a layer of newspaper between her sheet and quilt to help keep her warm in the drafty attic. The wind died down in the night, leaving instead thick, icy frost on all the trees. Claire hesitated after dressing and braiding her hair to enjoy the view from her window.

Had she known that this was the last day of her childhood - her last day at home - perhaps she would have hurried downstairs to spend the few remaining quiet moments with Mama. Instead, she surveyed the farmyard, noticing that the unpainted fence, and ramshackle chicken coop. Even the sagging barn door looked almost pretty covered in ice and frost.

She watched Papa trudge toward the house from the barn carrying a pail of milk, then she quietly removed the chair from under the knob and stepped down the stairs and into the kitchen. Without thinking, she greeted Mama and then fell into the routine of setting the table and getting breakfast on. The boys came in, boots dirty, pushing each other and laughing. The smell of horses and manure mingled with that of hot biscuits and gravy. Mama hurried off to find Jesse as the others sat down.

The morning was so normal, Claire didn't pay attention until she realized everyone was looking at her.

Papa's irritation was fleeting and he started again. "I was at Franklin's Hardware yesterday and ran into George Behl. He was asking about you, Girl."

"Me?" stammered Claire. "I don't know George Behl."

"Of course you don't. He is a farmer from up near Aberdeen. He's a friend of William Foster, distant cousin, maybe. He'd been talking to Foster and his wife about needing some live-in help at their farm. I told him that since you was passable at the housework, and there weren't any gentlemen callers around here for you, I thought having you hire out with them was a good idea."

Papa smiled at her, and she felt that he was proud of her. She'd never seen that in his eyes when he looked at her before. She was shocked and said nothing.

"What kind of a man is he, Hiram?" asked Mama quietly. Claire glanced at her. Clearly, Papa's announcement was news to her, too.

"I just told you. He's a farmer from up near Aberdeen." Papa's voice grew a bit louder.

"I meant is he clean and respectable?"

Papa's eyes snapped as he answered her tersely, "Don't get all excited. He owns about a hundred acres of good corn, oats, and durum wheat fields. He speaks well for himself and had on a brand new pair of boots."

Marcus swallowed his last bit of biscuit and cleared his throat. "I met his oldest boy, a tall kid about fourteen years old. Name's Lucas. He told me that there are three little girls younger than him at home and their Mama is sickly. He seemed alright."

Papa nodded as if all was settled. "Behl is heading back to Aberdeen today. He'll be stopping here about nine to collect you."

"Hiram, so soon?" Mama began, her voice shaky.

"Don't get all weepy. It's just like when she went to the Fosters. She'll be back, I expect, in a few months." Dismissing the subject Papa turned to Horace, "I want to work on the windmill in the lower pasture today. We need to get it weatherized and ready for a hard freeze. Marcus and Clancey, I want you boys to finish the work on that wood snow fence north of the shed."

The men got up with scraping chairs and clomping boots. They donned coveralls, hats and gloves. Papa was half way out the door and turned back.

"Work hard, Girl, and do what you're told. Remember, being lazy reflects bad on all of us."

With that, he was gone. Claire couldn't move. Her whole body felt heavy and stiff.

"Mama?" Mama put an armload of dishes into the sink and turned around.

"He could be here any minute, and you can't keep him waiting. You should be proud. Your Papa has confidence in you to go so far away, and this gets you out of harm's way here." Her face was shielded. A mask with no emotion. Claire had seen it like this many times and knew it was how Mama got through difficulties, but it felt cold and unbending just the same.

"Mama, we don't know these people. We don't know anything about them. Maybe I'll be in more harm-"

"Hush!" Mama's voice was harsh. "You need to trust your Papa. He is looking out for you. Now, go get that small trunk from the storeroom and pack up. You can use the carpetbag, too if you need it. We haven't done laundry this week, so you will have to wear the dress you have on. I'll go get that blue print dress I never wear. It should fit you, and then you'll have two work dresses.

62

Don't forget to pack all your warm leggings and your jacket off the hook at the back door."

Claire made her mind turn off as she got up. There was no use thinking or crying or asking questions. She used an old rag to wipe out the dust from the trunk, then she laid in her dime novels, *Treasure Island*, and the other books Haddie had given her. She packed her clothes. She was nearly finished when Mama came up with two dresses. "I think this green dress of mine will fit you also, so pack it. I haven't gotten a chance to make you a dress from that pale pink we ordered, so these will have to do." Mama left, talking quietly to herself. Claire looked around her room. She didn't have many belongings, they all fit into the trunk. She stood there, frozen by the suddenness of events when Mama returned with her arms full. She put her load on the bed and began folding and organizing. She handed the items one at a time to Claire.

"You may need a sewing kit, so this little basket has needles and pins, thread and some scissors in it. Now here's some heavy stockings and an extra petticoat. I found this warm hat and gloves in case you need to work outside sometimes. Is there room in the trunk for this quilt?"

"Mama, I'm sure they have bedding there for me," whispered Claire. She felt overwhelmed with Mama's actions. *I am coming back, aren't I?* she thought.

"Claire, I've never been to Aberdeen, it is so far away. You might get homesick. When I married your Papa and moved out here, I made myself ill missing my mama. I remember how much it helped that I had a few familiar pieces of home with me."

Thinking about Mama's words, Claire looked at Grandma's mirror on the wall. "Do you think it would be alright if I took the mirror with me?"

Mama gazed at the mirror and her eyes filled up with tears. She crossed the room and took the mirror from the wall. She wrapped it carefully in the quilt and laid it in the trunk. She reached into her apron pocket.

"This Bible was my Grandma's. I want you to have it."

Mama placed the small volume in the trunk and closed the lid. She reached for her daughter and hugged her fiercely. Claire's tears began then, and she held on to her Mama, taking in her warmth, her smell. They could hear the squeak and groan of a wagon approaching the house and knew that they didn't have much time.

Mama let go of Claire and held her by the shoulders searching her face. "Beside your time with the Fosters, this is all of life you have ever known, and it isn't much. You aren't going to find anything here except more of the same. I love you with all my heart, and I want more for you than I have. I want you to make your own choices and find a man who will make you his partner. When you think about what a marriage should be, think about Haddie and William Foster, not your Papa and me."

Mama's words were scaring Claire, and she tried to interrupt.

"No, listen to me. Most of the time I convince myself that all is well, but we don't have time for anything but the truth right now. If the situation with the Behl's is good, stay as long as you can. Make friends with people there. If the situation isn't good, protect yourself. Keep your eyes open for other possibilities. You can read and write, you could be a teacher in a small school, you could learn to keep the books at a mercantile. I will miss you every day, but if you can, don't come back here – get yourself free and make a good life for yourself."

Mama stopped to wipe her eyes on her sleeve. Papa's voice echoed up the staircase, "Behl is here waiting. Girl, get down here!"

"Send me letters when you can, but send them to Haddie. She'll safeguard them and read them to me."

"Dori!" Papa's voice was stern.

With one last hug and a silent look, Mama turned and went down the stairs. On her way down, Claire heard her say, "She's going to need help with the trunk."

Claire took one more look around. She heard footsteps on the stairs and picked up her sweater. When she turned around, Horace was right behind her. He trailed his fingers over her cheek. "Too bad you're leaving," he whispered. "I didn't get to teach you all about being a woman."

Claire pushed him away from her and fled down the stairs. She heard him laugh, and the sound reverberated in her head, along with her mother's words, for miles and miles.

10
November, 1895
Behl farm - near Aberdeen, South Dakota

Claire wiped off the kitchen table, then rubbed her tired shoulders. Over a year had passed since she'd left her father's farm in order to provide help for the Behls. She sat to rest for a minute before checking on the children and thought about the family. George Behl was a kind man who treated his wife and children with care and respect. Claire watched him sometimes as he talked and listened to the children, and was touched by his obvious love for them. Felicia Behl was morose and distant to her family and even more so to Claire. She took very little interest in the daily functioning of her family. She insisted that the three girls, Jolene, Abigail, and Darcy come sit with her every afternoon for an hour or so. Claire assumed that they talked then, but she was never invited to join the closed-door ritual.

During the long ride to the farm when Claire first met Mr. Behl, he explained the family's situation.

"South Dakota became a state nine years ago this month. I bought a hundred acres of land and we moved here from Indiana about a year after statehood. Until then, I was a surveyor for the rail road. I'd done surveying in the Aberdeen area when all the railroad lines were coming in. We had three of our children then, and my wife hated that surveying took me away from home so long and so often. Land was cheap, I had savings enough to pay cash for these acres, and Freda, that's my wife's sister Mrs. Baxter, and her husband were already here. We moved with high expectations of raising our family out here in peace and contentment. We did just that at first."

"What happened?" Claire asked quietly.

"Several things, really. Farming is a fickle business. We had several really dry years that harmed us financially. Life became more and more difficult - for Felicia especially. The final blow to her health and well-being came two years ago when our fifth child was stillborn. She hasn't been able to get past the sadness of that."

Pulling herself away from that conversation a year ago, Claire looked around the kitchen and pictured the rest of the house. It was a large, two-story home. The children's bedrooms upstairs were full of light. The girls shared a room with cheery wallpaper of intricate vines growing on a trellis with pink flowers and blue birds. The sheer white curtains with the white furniture made the room light and happy. Lucas' room, while smaller and more serious with ivory walls and deep blue curtains seemed rich and comforting. The bedroom Mr. and Mrs. Behl shared had pale blue wallpaper with faint white stripes. The curtains were thick blue brocade that sealed out the light and made the room cave-like and sad.

The main floor of the house was finer than anything Claire had ever seen before. She loved the feel of the thick mahogany table and chairs in the dining room. The family, including Mrs. Behl, took all meals in the dining room so Claire made sure that it was spotless and shining. The matching side board held fine china and delicate cups and glasses that were never used but spoke of happier and more festive times. The parlor was furnished with Duncan Phyfe furniture. Claire was gentle as she polished the carved mahogany on the sofa's arms and back and carefully placed the two bolster pillows at each end. She oiled the tables and chairs in the parlor every week even though the family rarely used the room, carefully dusting the music box that sat on one of the round tables.

"Those vases are amethyst Bristol glass from England. Our father's partner sent them to Felicia in 1875. Do be careful with those," Mrs. Baxter cautioned Claire one Tuesday afternoon right after she'd arrived. "You could never replace them."

Claire looked around the kitchen. The room was large enough to hold a small table and four chairs in addition to the large cook stove with a large wood box beside it, plus a long preparation table. Last winter, Claire suggested that Mr. Behl install a series of hooks on opposite walls so that on snowy, wet days she could still wash laundry and dry it inside.

"What a clever idea!" Mr. Behl responded enthusiastically to her request. Within the day, the hooks were installed and Claire had enough rope to string three lines if she needed to.

Off the kitchen was a small room that had been used for storage and as a pantry. This room was now converted into a bedroom for Claire. Since it was a storage room there was no wallpaper here, but Mr. Behl whitewashed the walls. The room had a window facing south, giving it light and cheer while protecting it from the mean winter north winds. Claire was delighted when Mr. Behl and Lucas carried in a brass headboard and footboard. She scrubbed it and stood back to admire how the patina, while faded and dull, looked rich. Lucas came in the next afternoon with a small round table.

"Father asked me to bring this to you, Miss Claire. He said to ask you where you would like it."

"Lucas, it's beautiful. Are you sure it is for me?"

""Yes, I'm sure," he smiled.

***

Sunday afternoon, over a year later, found Claire sitting at that table, pen in hand.

November 15, 1896

Dear Mama,

By the time you get this Thanksgiving will be passed, so happy Thanksgiving! Mr. Behl told me that it's been 33 years since Abe Lincoln asked us to celebrate a day of Thanksgiving on the last Thursday of November, and I know that you work harder every year to make the meal special, especially without me to help. Mrs. Behl is quite infirm and I see her only at meals. She stays in her room mostly, so I expect that I will do my best at a big dinner for the family. I've learned so much in the year that I've been here. I'm confident that Christmas dinner will be much better than my try last year!

Most days are not very different from any other day. Four children sure eat a lot. I spend most of my days in the kitchen. I am thankful that Mrs. Behl's sister, Mrs. Baxter comes every Tuesday to bake bread for the family. I don't see how I'd have time to do all the cooking and laundry and also get the bread baked.

Mrs. Baxter isn't very warm. She hardly talks to me when she is here, though I tell her thank you again and again. I'm trying my best, Mama, don't you worry. I think you'd be proud of the pork chops I made yesterday. They turned out real good, Mr. Behl even commented on them.

I miss, you, Mama, and I hope that things on the home place are good. Please give Jesse and Marcus my hello, and Papa, too.

Haddie, hugs to you. Thank you for your letter I received last week. I laughed when you told about baby Marshall trying to help milk the cow. He's a born farmer!

> *Love,*
> *Claire*

Claire put the fountain pen down and flexed her hands. She loved Sundays. The Behl's, with Mrs. Behl wrapped in a thick woolen shawl, travelled first to church and then to Mrs. Baxter's home each Sunday when the weather was fair. They returned usually about sundown. The first Sunday she'd been there, Mr. Behl carefully explained that the family would be gone nearly all day and that she would have the day to herself. He was very kind, trying not to hurt her feelings that she wasn't included but worrying that she would feel slighted. Claire reassured him that she wasn't offended and looked forward to some time to read and write letters.

"You read? How marvelous!" he exclaimed.

"Haddie Foster taught me when I worked for them."

Mr. Behl smiled at her. "What kinds of things do you like to read?"

"Anything I can get my hands on," Claire admitted. "I especially enjoyed *Treasure Island*, and I borrowed *Journey to the Center of the Earth* by Jules Verne from Haddie and liked it very much. I brought a few books with me, though I've read them all at least once."

"There is a shelf in the parlor with some books on it. Help yourself to whatever you like. I am happy to share them with you."

"Thank you so much," Claire smiled.

Now it was Sunday afternoon. In the year she'd been with the Behls she had read all the books on the shelf, plus several more. Mr. Behl brought a book home from town quite often, then would mention that he wasn't going to have time to read it right away.

"You go ahead, Claire. I'll read it when you get done. Maybe things will slow down this winter."

Claire realized after a while that Mr. Behl was actually buying the books for her. His kindness touched her.

Despite Mr. Behl's kindness, working at the Behls wasn't easy. Mrs. Behl was a stranger, removed from life in many ways and very cold to Claire. The three young girls took their cues from their mother and didn't warm to Claire either. They weren't mean or disrespectful, but aloof. She was alone and lonely most of the time. She reread the letter she'd just written to Mama. *I didn't lie*, she told herself, *I just didn't tell all the truth, no sense in worrying Mama.* Mrs. Baxter did come every Tuesday to bake bread and also to criticize everything Claire did.

"I don't understand how you can work in a kitchen this disorderly," Mrs. Baxter complained this week. "It only takes a moment to dust off the shelves and put things away properly."

"Yes, Ma'am," Claire answered. It didn't do any good to try to explain or defend herself. She knew that the shelves weren't orderly, but Mrs. Behl insisted that her two older daughters help with the dishes, and no matter what Claire said, they put things away in a different place every time.

Unfolding a dish towel to put over the rising dough, Mrs. Baxter clicked her tongue and made a sound in her throat that sounded like a quiet growl. It was a sound that Claire was too familiar with. "Did you actually use lye soap on these towels when you washed them?" she asked with a sneer.

Claire folded the letter to her Mama and put it in an envelope. She wrote the address carefully on it and sighed. She felt trapped. Every week was the same – cooking, cleaning and laundry. She was worn out. *I need to count my blessings*, she thought. *I have a room to myself and no one leers at me or tries to touch me here. I have food to eat and a warm house to live in. Mr. Behl is very kind to me, and encourages me to read when I can. He even discusses books and the news with me sometimes. I have Sundays to myself. Stop complaining!*

The next morning, Mr. Behl mentioned at breakfast that he was heading into town. Claire stopped him as he put his hat on and prepared to leave.

"Mr. Behl, I have a letter here to mail to my Mama. Would you mind taking it to the post office for me, if it isn't too much trouble? I don't have any money to give you for postage, though."

"I don't mind at all, Claire, and postage is no problem," came his answer. "That reminds me, I need to send your pay for this month to your Papa."

"I beg your pardon?" Claire's head snapped up to meet his eyes.

"When I talked to your Papa and hired you on, your Papa suggested that I send your pay to him for safe keeping. He said he'd send you an allowance for what you needed." He searched her face and then added. "Were you aware of my deal with your father?"

Claire hesitated. She didn't know what to say. "Um, no sir, I thought that I was staying here and helping out in exchange for food and a place to stay."

Mr. Behl looked shocked and then angry. Quickly, as understanding came to him, he smiled at Claire. "I'm sure that your Papa felt that you wouldn't have any way to spend the $15 a month that I agreed to pay. I paid him in advance for the September when I hired you, and I've sent him $15 a month since then."

Claire felt as if she'd been slapped. She'd been careful not to impose on the Behls or ask for anything so that she wouldn't be a burden. Her shoes were nearly completely worn down and she'd patched her work dresses many times, trying to keep presentable. All along her Papa was collecting money without telling her.

"Yes, Sir," Claire squeaked out.

"I'll see you this evening, Claire. Is there anything else you need from town?"

"No," Claire began. "Well, the kitchen could use some more flour and coffee if you are going to the mercantile."

"I'll pick some up."

Their conversation replayed itself over and over in her head through the day. She tried to convince herself that her father was saving the money for her, but she knew him and his selfishness too well for that. The children were tucked into bed and the house quiet when Claire finally had a minute to sit down. She pulled the carpetbag from beneath her bed and retrieved all the letters she'd received from Haddie. There were thirteen letters and she knew them nearly by heart. She rifled through the envelopes and found the one she was looking for.

June 5, 1896

Dear Claire,

Today is your birthday, and I wish you the best of days. I wanted to send you a nice present, but money is tight here on the farm. I talked to your Papa about sending you some money for a new dress like you asked, but he says that since it is so dry, we have to save every penny to buy hay and grain for the cows. He hopes that they are fat and healthy for the fall auction. He added that he hopes you spent the $3 I sent you in March wisely.

I am tucking in a dollar from my egg money as your present. The next time you go into Aberdeen, buy yourself something nice and think of me.

Your Papa and Horace have a new venture. They rented the old Grisholm place down by Jim Creek. Mr. Grisholm fell from the hayloft and broke his leg so he can't farm. He's moved into Mitchell to stay with his daughter while he heals. Hiram and Horace rented the land from him and that includes the house. They bought a used tractor and some seeds. They've been staying up there for the past few days to get the wheat in. I'm not sure where they got the money — I think they must have borrowed it, but when I asked, Hiram just said I shouldn't worry about it.

We are all well here. I am working on a new quilt, but without your help, it is taking a long time.

Love,
Mother

P.S. Dear Claire, this part is from me. I wanted to wish you a happy birthday, too! You are never far from my thoughts. Your Mama looks good, though I think she is a bit thin. Jesse is nearly taller than she is now, and has been wonderful help to her around the farm. He is a sweet boy. I am adding another dollar to your mother's present. If you can find it, H.G. Wells' book —
which was published just last year is quite a story. It is called The Island of
Dr. Moreau. *Love to you, Haddie.*

Claire folded the letter carefully and returned it to the envelope. She wanted to rip it up and throw it away, but her mother's words, and Haddie's, were too precious to waste with her anger. She returned the packet to the carpetbag and slid it back in its place under the bed, all the time fighting tears of anger and

71

betrayal. All these months, all this time, her father was collecting money from her hard work and using it for himself without her or Mama even knowing it. Rereading the letter confirmed for her that her mother had no idea of the deal that Papa made with Mr. Behl. She wasn't part of Claire's deception. "He's lying to her, too!" Claire said it out loud.

Papa used my money to rent the Grisholm place and do more farming, but he didn't even allow Mama to send me money for my birthday or for a new work dress.

Claire was too upset to sleep. She paced her room, thinking, when a new thought came to her. Diving back under the bed for the carpet bag, she pulled out the letter she'd received in September.

September 16, 1896

Dear Daughter,

We have had such good fortune this month! Mr. Grisholm has decided to sell out and move permanently to town. With the money your Papa and Horace made from the calves they bought last spring, and with a good wheat crop from the rented land, they have given him a down payment and contracted to purchase the farm from Mr. Grisholm. Your Papa has gone into partnership with Horace, who is moving permanently to farm there. Clancey is moving, too. That means that Horace is gone from here. Maybe we will be able to have you come home before Christmas. Wouldn't that be grand?

Claire stopped reading. She paced for a while longer, then made a decision. She sat down at her desk, placed a piece of paper on the blotter and began writing.

November 16, 1896

Dear Haddie,

This letter is to you, not to my Mama. I hope that you will respect our friendship and not tell her or anyone about what I am going to say.

It was the middle of the night before she finished. She poured out her heart to Haddie, explaining what she'd discovered about her father's business deal with Mr. Behl and describing the bitterness she felt. By the time she completed the letter, Claire had changed from a naïve little girl into a new person. She knew now that she would never go home, and that whatever happened to her, she was the one who needed to make the decisions. Claire was convinced that her father was aware of Horace's unhealthy interest in her, though he did nothing to stop it. Her father used money she'd earned to help buy a farm for Horace. She grieved that she wouldn't be able to go home to her mother, but knew there was no way she could face her father, knowing that he'd used her and knowing that Horace was certainly aware of what he'd done. She wasn't a person or a daughter to her father, she was a tool. A means to an end. Horace's laugh on the day she left echoed again in her ears. She was furious, but recognized that there was nothing she could do about the past, but began to ask herself what actions she could take from now on.

***

Claire looked around at the beautiful day before her, only partly appreciating the warm sunshine and the budding roses that lined the fence near the clothes line. In the days since she'd realized the truth about her father and her life, she worked diligently to act as if everything was normal and fine. She found that she was able to focus on the tasks at hand and put her anger out of her mind. In the quiet moments when she considered it all, she realized that her Mama was her good teacher. *How many times was I angry and frustrated with Mama as she simply shrugged when Papa backhanded her, or yelled at her, or demanded the impossible? Now I understand, Mama, that in order to go on and not let him win, you let it go.*

Claire appreciated her Mama's strength and dignity, but chafed at the idea of forgiving him. In this way, Claire knew, she was different than her mother, who was able not only to go on but to forgive her father's meanness. "He's doing the best he can. He treats us the way he knows how, he isn't evil, it's just the way he was raised."

Any argument that Claire offered her mother when she said this fell on deaf ears. Mama was married to him and in her eyes it was her place to accept and forgive.

"You know that we don't go to church, but we are God-fearing people. The Bible says that women are to be submissive to their husbands and that children need to obey their fathers." Mama's words bounced around in Claire's memories, she heard them so many times when she lived at home that they haunted her now.

Realizing that she'd been standing idle instead of pinning up the wet clothes, Claire shrugged and then laughed quietly to herself. "I've perfected the art of shrugging off the bad," she said to herself. She pinned up another shirt as a thought flitted through her mind. She pictured again the character in *Red Badge of Courage* and revised her judgement of him. *Sometimes courage and good judgement is walking away or not arguing,* she decided. *But then other times, courage means doing whatever you have to.* All of a sudden, the soldier's desire for a tangible symbol of his courage, like a wound, made sense to Claire and she began thinking more earnestly about the choices she might have.

Two days more passed, and Claire's thoughts cooled from fury at her father to more practical matters. Every month her father received her wages. There was no use thinking about the money that Mr. Behl had already sent to Papa. That was spent and gone. Claire added it up. She'd worked for the Behls for a year and two months. In that time she'd earned and Papa had received $210, a staggering amount for a girl who owned one pair of two year old shoes.

In order to leave here, to start a life of her own choosing, Claire needed money. She needed to be able to pay to travel somewhere and to rent a room while she found herself an income. Claire considered living in a large city, working at a mercantile or teaching school. None of her dreams could begin without a little nest egg to get her started.

What Claire needed to figure out was how to approach Mr. Behl about giving her the money instead of sending it away where she'd never see it. She was frightened about what Mr. Behl might think if she asked. She was also frightened of what her father would do if his monthly bonus stopped coming. Would Mama suffer? Would he take his anger out on his wife? Would he demand she come home so he could sell her to someone new? She considered asking for just a portion of it, to buy needed clothes and supplies, but that wouldn't get her the savings she knew she needed, and Papa would certainly react to even a small reduction in his income. Fear paralyzed Claire. Days and then weeks went by. She said and did nothing to help herself, seething deeply at how her father was controlling her even from miles away.

11
December, 1895
Behl farm - near Aberdeen, South Dakota

"The wind is blowing hard enough to make the house shudder at times," Claire vented to the walls. "It's like the cold wants in." She grumbled as she cut up a chicken to fry. She kept the fire burning in the heating stove so that the shirts she'd washed this morning and then hung on the make-shift line in the kitchen could dry. Lucas was out in the barn working with his father. The girls were trapped inside while the snow piled up outside. They squabbled and argued throughout the morning. Claire knew that their crabby voices were probably filtering up the stairs to Mrs. Behl's room so she tried to find something to engage and placate them.

She succeeded in settling them down to draw paper dolls. *This peace is heavenly*, Claire thought. She finished cutting the chicken and began dredging the pieces in flour, getting ready to fry them. Already the potatoes were boiling. She hoped that a nice meal would settle everyone down and calm them.

Claire was just putting the chicken on a platter when Mr. Behl and Lucas came in. Cold wind assaulted Claire as they entered. She finished cooking and soon, boots, hats and gloves were set out by the stove to dry and everyone was seated at the table in the dining room. Claire made sure the family had everything and turned to go back into the kitchen to eat.

"Claire," called Mr. Behl.

"Yes, Sir?"

"I'd like to talk to you after we eat. Will you have a minute?"

"Yes, Sir, I'll just be in the kitchen."

"Great. I'll come find you when dinner is done."

Claire returned to the kitchen, concerned. The tone in Mr. Behl's voice was serious, and she wracked her brain for anything she might have said or done to upset him. From past experience she knew that a misspoken word to Mrs. Baxter or one of the children could come back to her later. Mr. Behl was never mean, but he could be stern when she made a mistake.

As it turned out, Claire was just finishing the last of the dishes after dinner when Mr. Behl found her in the kitchen.

"I planned to talk with you earlier, but then I remembered that I had to show Lucas what I wanted him to do in the barn," Mr. Behl explained.

Claire poured a cup of fresh coffee for him and put it on the small kitchen table. Then she sat down beside him.

"Claire," he began, "Have you given any thought to what you would like to do once you leave here?"

Claire looked up, frightened, "Mr. Behl, whatever I've done, I'll make it right," she announced.

"No, no," Mr. Behl answered. "I'm sorry Claire, I started this conversation badly. I've just been wondering why a smart girl like you stays in a thankless job like this one." He smiled at her to set her at ease.

Not waiting for an answer, he continued. "I actually have two things to discuss with you. The first is that every Sunday my dear sister-in-law," he rolled his eyes as he said 'dear', making Claire smile. Mrs. Baxter often spoke to Mr. Behl with the same condescension that Claire usually heard. "My sister-in-law brings up that she lives in a house large enough to accommodate my wife and girls and that she could give her sister much better care there than she gets here."

He raised his hand to stop Claire's question. "Claire, you are doing everything you are asked and everything necessary. This conversation isn't about you or what you do, it is about me and the care my sister-in-law thinks my wife needs."

Claire relaxed a little. She knew that Mrs. Baxter pressured Mr. Behl about moving to town. Mrs. Baxter was a self-possessed woman who saw very little value in thinking that was not her own.

"The truth is, Claire," continued Mr. Behl as he rubbed his hand over his eyes, "My wife is not getting better. I've had her to some of the best doctors in South Dakota and Iowa and though they find nothing physically wrong, she continues to be in pain and have no joy in her life. Up until now she has not given her opinion one way or the other about moving in with Freda, but just this week she did mention that maybe she'd like to try a change of place."

He sat silently, lost in thought. After a minute, he looked up at Claire and continued. "I want what is best for my wife, and for the girls, so when the weather warms this spring, perhaps by the middle of May, I will be moving them to Freda's house in town."

"Will you need me to stay on and keep house for you and Lucas?" Claire asked.

"One of the reasons I am waiting until May to move them lies in that question's answer."

He smiled at Claire's confusion.

"I'm not a farmer at heart. I loved surveying. I enjoyed the travel and being out. Lucas is old enough to learn surveying. I've contacted the railroad to see if they'd have a position for me and Lucas. They've told me that they want me to start the first of June. The family doesn't yet know it, but I am moving Felicia and the girls to Aberdeen , and Lucas and I are selling out here."

"I see." Claire put her head down. Panic nibbled at her insides. *I can't go back!*

"That brings me to the second thing I wanted to discuss with you." He paused. "Claire, I have done a lot of thinking since our conversation a few weeks ago about your pay. I sent a letter to William Foster, and yesterday I got the response from him that I guessed I would get."

Claire looked down at the table, suddenly ashamed that this man, whom she respected and admired, knew how her father did business.

"Claire, please look at me."

She raised her eyes slowly, afraid of what she'd see in his face. She studied him for a few seconds, surprised that there was no trace of pity or even disgust. She saw warmth and understanding. Tears threatened.

"Claire, in some ways and at some times we are reflections of our parents and of how we were raised. As we become adults, though, that reflection fades and we become ourselves. When I look at you, I see an upright and noble soul who works hard and diligently and who knows how to be a good person."

Tears flooded Claire's vision but not her hearing. Mr. Behl continued. "I do have to admit though, that I'm none too pleased with the certain knowledge that you and I both were dealt with dishonestly. We are, then, back to the question I started with. As I see it, you have quite a few options. So, what are you thinking you'd like to do when you are no longer needed here? "

Blinking, she took a deep breath and steadied herself. "I know that I can't and won't go back to my father's farm." She looked at Behl for reassurance. He nodded in agreement. At that moment, knowing she was talking with an ally, she felt lighter and braver. "Haddie suggested once that I could become a teacher since I read and write. The problem with that is that I don't know any arithmetic beyond a little adding. I'm not sure I'd like teaching, either. Since I've never gone to school, I don't know how it all works."

"I can tell you have been thinking about this."

"Yes, Sir. I have wondered about working in a store or an office, but I don't know."

"I'll tell you what. You keep thinking, and I will make some inquiries in town about possible opportunities. In the meantime," he reached into his vest pocket.

"I've decided that your father has received enough of your wages. I mailed him a letter this morning explaining that from now on I would be giving your wages to you directly." He extended a group of folded bills out to Claire.

Panic returned. She leaned back away from him, afraid. "Papa will be very angry, Mr. Behl. I'm not sure this is a good idea. Maybe it is better just to let him have it."

"You are worried about your mother?"

Claire hesitated. "Yes, Sir," she answered with a whisper.

"I don't believe in being deceitful, but, as Shakespeare points out in his play *Henry IV*, there are times when discretion is the better part of valor." His eyes twinkled as he finished the sentence.

Claire's heart pounded in her chest.

"What I told your father was that I had fallen on some hard times and would not be able to fulfill our contract fully. I assured him that you were a good, hard worker and that as soon as I was able, I would resume payments. In the meantime, I assured him that I was feeding, housing and clothing you well."

Behl could tell that he hadn't convinced her. "I also let him know that if he wasn't agreeable to this new arrangement, I would put you on a stage and send you home. Though, I may have stressed that if he wasn't agreeable to this I'd understand, though I couldn't pay for the price of the fare and he would have to send the fare for you to travel home."

Claire was impressed at how adeptly Mr. Behl defused the situation. Papa might still be angry, but he wouldn't want to pay her fare home. She relaxed.

Mr. Behl got up and reached for his hat. "Claire, I haven't discussed this with my wife or the girls. I want to wait until the time is closer. Please don't say anything to anyone about my plans."

"No, Sir, I won't," Claire responded.

He started for the door and then stopped. "You know, as a surveyor I worked with numbers every day. Mostly, I know geometry, but I also do know a little about book keeping. How about if you and I sit down after supper a few times and I'll teach you what I know?"

Claire smiled. "That would be a wonderful help, Mr. Behl. Thank you very much."

George Behl made his way out to the barn to check on Lucas and start the evening chores. He pitched hay and did the milking, all the time thinking about the letter he'd received from Bill Foster and wondering how a man like Claire's father could treat his own child like that. It was killing him to think about leaving Felicia and the girls with Freda. He loved his daughters and his wife. But after spending a year watching and getting to know Claire, then having his suspicions about her life confirmed, he became committed to putting away his own self-interests and doing the best for his children, even if that meant being away from them. In town, the girls could attend school and become part of the society, they could grow and meet new people. They would see that there are choices in life beyond being trapped on a farm.

12
May, 1896
Behl farm - near Aberdeen, South Dakota

Claire waved to the girls one final time as the wagon rounded the bend and disappeared from sight. The morning had been a flurry of last minute tears and laughs, searching for one last, lost item, and a round of hugs. Mr. Behl drove the wagon. Mrs. Behl sat, grim faced and silent beside him. The girls sat on a shelf of trunks, facing backwards and waving. The rest of the wagon was filled with boxes and cartons of their belongings. Lucas followed on his small grey horse.

Claire turned back to the house, stepping into the cool interior. She surveyed the parlor. Most of the furniture remained. Mrs. Baxter's home was already furnished and she decided that there would be no need and no place for the family's furniture in her house. Mrs. Behl spoke up only once, asking that her Bristol glass vases along with the table they usually sat upon be included in the move.

Claire made sure that the furniture was all dusted and in right order, then she made her way upstairs. The new owners of the farm were set to arrive in the morning, and Claire wanted to make sure that the house was perfect for them. She spent the rest of the morning beating the dirt out of the bedroom rugs and airing out the mattresses upstairs. She returned everything to its proper place, then dusted and swept. By the time she descended the stairs it was early afternoon.

"I deserve a rest," she told the quiet kitchen.

As she lunched on the last of Mrs. Baxter's bread and a small chunk of hard cheddar cheese, she pulled a letter from her pocket.

April 30, 1897

Dear Miss Atley,

*   I am looking forward to your arrival on or about May 16ᵗʰ. As we agreed, you will be provided a small private room above the store to accommodate you. After a period for training, your duties will include keeping records and working with me on the ordering of the inventory plus keeping the books for the store. In addition, at times you will be needed to help with customers in the store itself. For your work, you will be paid eight dollars per week.*

*   I look forward to meeting you soon.*
Yours truly,
Thomas Sweeney, prop.

Claire smiled. Thanks to Mr. Behl's advice and tutoring with figures, and through a connection of his at the railroad, she was moving to Rapid City. Claire thought about her conversation, over a month ago, recalling the pride and happiness on Mr. Behl's face as he talked.

"I have a little something for you," he began. He handed her an envelope then watched her face as she read the letter offering her a position at the Sweeney Hardware Store.

"I've heard good things about Tom Sweeney. He started his hardware store in Rapid City in 1878. From what I hear, the store is quite big and very successful."

Claire was speechless. She had been harboring fears of not finding a position other than housekeeping.

"Claire," Mr. Behl's voice was serious and she looked up and met his eyes. "I know it is a long way away. What do you think about that?"

Since their first conversation about her father in November, Claire and Mr. Behl had become quite frank with one another. "I was actually afraid that we'd find something too close. I don't want to ever run into my father. I miss my mother, but Haddie helps me keep in contact with her, so it is alright."

Claire rubbed her neck and looked around the newly abandoned kitchen. "This house is ready for its new family," she said aloud. "Now I can pack my own bag and trunk so that I am ready when Mr. Behl and Lucas return for me in the morning."

***

The sun had barely begun turning the sky from its inky black of night to a pale teal when Claire pulled herself out of her bed. Alone in the house, she hadn't been afraid but the excitement of what this new day would begin had kept her from sleeping well.

She stood in front of her grandmother's mirror as she put her hair into a bun at the nape of her neck. She stared at the girl there. On the first day she was in this room, she'd vowed never to wear her hair in two braids again. Since then, she'd experimented with different styles, using pictures from the Sears and Roebuck catalog to get ideas. Satisfied with her look, she carefully lifted the mirror from its nail on the wall and packed it into her trunk.

By the time she heard the sounds of the wagon entering the yard, Claire was ready to go. She looked around one last time to be sure the house was ready for its new owners and met Mr. Behl and Lucas on the back step.

"Did you get Mrs. Behl and the girls all moved in?" she asked as they shook the dust from the dry road off their hats and shirts.

"Yes. They seem to be pretty comfortable already," Mr. Behl answered.

"Pa, did you see that Mama smiled this morning at breakfast when Aunt Freda told her that some ladies were coming over today for tea?"

"Yes, I did see that, Lucas. I hope that is a good sign that the change will be good for your mother."

"Claire, are you ready for us to load your belongings? The train leaves Aberdeen at ten sharp, so we can't be late."

"Yes, Sir, I'm ready," Claire answered. "My trunk and carpet bag are just inside my room."

In just a few minutes, Claire climbed up on the seat of the wagon beside Mr. Behl. Lucas sat astride his horse, waiting for them to begin. In addition to her bags, the Behls added two large bedrolls and a canvas bag to the cargo in the back. Claire smiled, "You are travelling light."

Lucas answered her with a mixture of pride and trepidation. "Pa says we need to carry in one trip everything we need while we are surveying."

"Well, either you need to get really strong, or pack just the essentials," Claire teased.

Mr. Behl chuckled as they pulled out of the yard. He stopped the horses just before the bend and they took one last look. Claire realized that she felt more nostalgia leaving here than she'd felt leaving her own home.

They arrived at the station in Aberdeen about half an hour before the train was due. With all her earthly belongings on the platform beside her, Claire turned to Mr. Behl. "I can never thank you enough for all you've done to help me," she began.

"I am the one who needs to be thanking you," he answered. "I am well aware that ours was a solemn home to live and work in. Thank you for all the hard work you put in for my family."

They shook hands then, warmly. Lucas fumbled with a handshake and ended with a quick hug before he ducked his head. Claire watched them walk away, unsure if she'd ever see them again, silently thanking them for the escape they had provided and the opportunity in front of her. When the train arrived, a porter arrived at her side, "Do these go?" was all he said. Claire nodded her ascent and the man hefted her trunk onto one shoulder and moved off down the platform. Claire had read about people of color, but had never seen one. This man was very tall and broad shouldered with close cropped hair under his hat. His skin was a deep chocolate brown and Claire marveled at how rich it looked. She tried not to stare, but found her eyes returning to him as he worked to load the train's baggage car.

Soon, the conductor called "All Aboard!"

Claire stepped up on to the train and found her seat. She watched as other passengers boarded and got themselves settled. The train whistle blared as the cars jerked forward. Claire's pulse quickened with the newness of it all.

My life starts today, she thought. *Up until now, my whole life has been arranged or dictated by others. Today, I am in charge of me.*

Claire cleared her mind and let herself enjoy the view of the passing countryside. Farms and plowed fields seemed to fly by one after another. The conductor walked through the car after a while and checked passenger tickets. He was a white-haired man with a round, happy face and smiling eyes. He took her ticket, punched it with a small tool, then returned it to her. "Sir, can you tell me how fast the train is travelling?"

He stooped down and looked out the window. "Right now, we are close to our top speed of 50 miles per hour."

Claire gasped. "It is hard to imagine travelling at that speed."

"Yes, Miss, I agree. We won't stay that fast for long, though. This train will stop five more times between here and Huron, and it takes a few miles to both speed up and to slow down. The weather is good today, though, so we should be into Huron at 3:30, right on schedule."

"Thank you," Claire answered as he turned to the next passenger.

Claire was tired of sitting and happy to disembark the train by the time she heard the call. "Huron!" the conductor sang out as the train pulled into the station. She stepped down onto the platform and looked around, anxious and excited.

"Claire!" She heard her name and turned to the sound. In a second, Haddie was beside her, pulling her into a long hug. "I am so happy to see you!"

They stepped apart as a porter approached, carrying her trunk on one shoulder and her carpet bag under the other arm. "Where can I carry this, Miss?" he asked.

She took the bag from him. "Is it possible for that trunk to stay here at the station tonight? I am leaving tomorrow to travel west, and I don't need it tonight."

"Yes, Miss, I will put it in the baggage room. Tomorrow, you'll need to make sure someone loads it on your train."

"Thank you so much," Claire smiled, but the man kept his head down and didn't look at her.

She turned back to Haddie. "I can't believe you came to meet me here," she started. "I've missed you so much!"

Haddie hugged her again. "When we got your letter outlining your plan of spending the night here before you leave for Rapid City, William suggested that I come. At first I thought it would be impossible for me to do, but he assured me he could take over the household and stay with the children for the one night I will be gone, and then he pushed me out the door!"

Haddie linked her arm through Claire's, "I feel free and young like you today, Claire," she said. "I've already checked into our room at the hotel. Let's go drop off your bag and walk a little around town."

"I love that idea," Claire agreed. "I enjoyed being on the train, but it is really nice to be walking around and not swaying back and forth."

The hotel was only a short block from the depot. The ladies soon found themselves in their room. Haddie watched Claire as she freshened up. Claire caught her stare in the mirror and turned around.

"Is something wrong?"

"Not at all," Haddie responded. "I'm just relishing how you've grown."

Claire put her head down.

"I picture you when you first came to stay at our house. You were a little girl, shy and unsure. Now, two years later, you are a woman – and a very pretty one at that!"

Claire smiled. She finished tidying her hair and sat down on the edge of the bed. "Thanks to Mr. Behl, I've managed to save up what feels to me like a lot of money. The only clothes I have are homemade. I don't think anything I have is suitable for working in a store. I've never owned a dress I or Mama didn't make. I was hoping that while we are here in Huron you will go shopping with me. I feel uncertain what to do and I don't know what to buy. I do know that I need to have nice clothes to wear to work when I get to Sweeney's Hardware. Will you help me?"

Haddie stood up. "I would absolutely love to!" she answered. "I had about two hours after I got settled here in the hotel before your train arrived. I walked through two dress shops and saw several dresses that would be perfect."

Haddie and Claire spent the rest of the afternoon buying Claire five new dresses. They ate supper at the hotel restaurant and then returned to their room. Haddie had on her nightdress and was sitting up in bed as Claire brushed out her hair.

"I can't believe that I spent twenty one dollars today just on me." Claire exclaimed. "But I got so many pretty things."

"I know it was hard for you to do, Dear, but you only bought what you really needed. I especially love the crème silk and rose faille dress."

Claire smiled and turned to look at Haddie. "It is like I was just born today. I didn't even know what the word faille meant this morning, and now I own a dress made of the soft textured silk."

"I think I understand what you are feeling. I remember feeling similar on the day I realized that I was carrying Matthew. Knowing I had a babe inside changed the entire world for me. It was like the world tilted a little on its axis that day and life was never the same."

Claire put her hairbrush down and snuggled herself into bed next to Haddie.

"How did Mama look when you last saw her?"

Haddie thought for a minute. "She seems fine. She may be a little thinner than she was, and a little greyer, but she seems fine. I'm sorry I couldn't figure out a way to get her to come with me."

"It would have been nice if she could have come. But, I don't want Papa to know anything about me from now on. When I was little, I thought all fathers acted the way he does. I thought that all men were the bosses and all girls and women had to just take it. Mama says that the Bible says that's so. I say if it says that, then I don't want anything to do with the Bible." As Claire spoke, the anger built. "I hate him, Haddie. I hate him for all the times he hit me and Mama and the way he doesn't even feel bad about it afterwards. I hate him for Horace, too. I heard Mama try to warn Papa about Horace coming to live with us, and he knocked her into the wall."

Haddie put her hand on Claire's arm. "How your father treated you and your mother is wrong, and you have a right to your anger. But be careful, Claire. Once you let hate start, it can grow like a wildfire."

"I know all men aren't like Papa," Claire answered. "I have seen how William treats you and your children. I watched how patient and kind Mr. Behl is to his wife, even when she didn't respond well to him."

"That's right. There are many examples of men who are kind and good in this world. Don't forget that."

"I won't." Claire was quiet for a few minutes. Haddie reached over and turned off the kerosene lamp bedside the bed.

"But I also won't forget or forgive him, Haddie."

13
July, 1896
Rapid City, South Dakota

"It is so hot I can't breathe," grumbled Lucy. "There isn't one whisper of air moving outside, and this store is like an oven!"

Usually Claire didn't listen to Lucy's griping. It was always too hot or too cold or too busy or too slow with Lucy. She was never happy. Today, though, Claire agreed and felt grumpy herself. She closed the ledger book with a loud thud and rubbed her tired neck. Sweat trickled down her back. She checked the clock on the far wall, it was 4:15. She had another hour and forty five minutes in the work day. Tom made sure that his employees arrived promptly at eight o'clock and worked until six. She'd eaten lunch at noon with Lucy, sitting at a small table behind the sales counter, but that seemed ages ago.

"I'm finished with my books for today, Lucy. Is there anything I can do to help you?"

"Well, if you are certain you have time, you could straighten out the shelves. Pay special attention to the nails and screws up near the front. Some little boys were in here earlier with their Pa, and I think they were playing in the bins."

Claire was happy to be standing, doing something that she didn't have to think much about. Beginning at the wall to the left of the front door where they kept mining supplies, she walked slowly, replacing and organizing the shallow pans, sluice boxes and rocker boxes that prospectors used for placer mining. Next came small hand tools and supplies for underground mining. She worked her way down the shelf, straightening the chisels, bits, and sledge hammers. There were many tools that Claire couldn't identify and had no idea how they were used, but she knew that the store sold a wealth of mining supplies. Rapid City was called the gateway to the Black Hills since gold was discovered in the mountains in 1876. Two years later Rapid City was founded by some discouraged miners. They'd been unsuccessful at finding gold, and realized that they could easily earn the gold of others by providing supplies and comforts. Tom Sweeney explained the history of Rapid City to Claire when she began working for him.

"Most prospectors never make a profit," he told her with a smile. "But selling tools and supplies to every man who gets gold fever is a pretty good living."

She finished with the merchandise on the wall and turned to the shelves along the first aisle. This brought her facing the rest of the store and gave her a good view of the wide room filled with aisle after aisle of hardware. The store not only catered to miners, but also had large stocks of farming and building equipment to keep up with the demands of a growing city and the farms nearby.

The small bell above the door jangled. Claire looked up from a bin of nails to see two young women enter the store. She had seen them before, both in the store and at the café where she sometimes ate Sunday dinner. Mostly hidden behind the display of nails, Claire watched them. *They are so beautiful*, she thought. The blond was short, shorter than Claire. Her dress, a deep blue brocade with velvet piping on the sleeves and bodice, fit her tightly to show off her figure. Unlike Claire's modest dresses with high necklines, this woman's dress had a neckline that dipped in a smooth oval, showing her delicate collar bones. It was accented with a large cameo pendant. Her hair was pulled up away from her face with a ribbon and cascaded to her shoulder blades in the back in a mass of curls. Her friend was taller and thinner. Her light brown hair was twisted into a knot at the top of her head. Framing her face were tight curls. This girl's dress was red silk, tight at her waist and even lower cut than the first. Her purse was a round velvet bag that swung carelessly from a strap around her wrist.

The women walked side by side towards the counter at the back of the store speaking quietly to each other.

"May I help you?" Lucy growled as they approached the counter. Her disdain for the women was clear.

"We are here to pick up an order for Jack Clower," began the blond. "Jack said that Tom told him they'd come in."

"Let me check." Without another word, Lucy disappeared into

the back room. Claire watched as the tall one made a face at the retreating Lucy. Her friend laughed.

In just a minute, Lucy returned with a package wrapped in brown paper. "Here you go. Shall I put this on Mr. Clower's account?" Lucy wasn't even trying to hide the sneer in her voice.

"Yes, please. I also need a short length of rope, maybe 10 feet long, and something to hang the rope with. We need to fashion a clothes line inside our room."

"I'll get you the rope," Lucy answered. Then she called out, "Claire, in the bin about halfway down to your right are some eye screws. Pick two of the larger ones and bring them here, please."

Claire found them easily, chose two that seemed the right size for a clothesline and carried them to the counter.

The blond girl reached for the screws. "These are exactly what I want. My daddy made a clothesline for my Mama using exactly this kind of hardware." She looked at Claire and smiled.

Claire smiled back.

Lucy coughed and said, "That will be forty two cents. Does this go on Mr. Clower's tab?"

"Oh, no," came the answer. "I am paying for this myself." She reached into the small blue bag hanging from her wrist and pulled out a roll of dollar bills. Claire was impressed at the size of the roll, but spun around quickly to return to her work so she wouldn't be caught staring.

The women finished their transaction and turned to leave. As they passed near Claire, the blond girl stopped. "Thank you again," she said, looking Claire in the eye. Then they were gone.

Lucy started in as soon as the door was closed. "Those hussies! They should be ashamed of themselves being out in public."

Claire didn't quite understand Lucy's reaction to the women, but she also didn't want to get Lucy started on a tirade so she kept quiet. She went back to sorting, thinking about them for the rest of the afternoon.

***

Claire looked out at the street below her boarding house window and remembered how much she enjoyed her Sundays off when she worked for the Behls. Here, it was different. She felt her loneliness like a shawl on her shoulders. Returning to the desk in her room she shrugged.

"No matter how many times I count this, it is still not enough," she said to herself. Spread before her on the desk was one dollar and fifty four cents, all in change. It was all the money she had.

When Tom Sweeney offered her the job in Rapid City, the eight dollars a week he offered to pay her seemed like a fortune. That was before she'd seen the room he had for her. It was a cramped attic room above the store with only a cot to sleep on, no windows and only a curtain for a door. In addition, the privy was outside in the back of the store and there was no source of water for a bath. Claire slept there for two nights, then found that she could rent a room at Mrs. Payne's boarding house just two blocks away for fifteen dollars a month. Mrs. Payne provided clean towels and sheets weekly, a clean room for bathing and a private room with a bed, desk, two-drawer dresser and a window. She also fixed breakfast every morning and dinner every night except Sunday.

For her lunches, on Saturday mornings every week Claire went to the mercantile and bought a loaf of bread, some hard cheese and twice she'd bought an apple as a treat. "Lunches cost me a dollar a week. Add that four dollars to the seventy-five cents Sunday dinners cost at the café each week, and I have two dollars left for everything else I need." Claire stood up and paced across her room a few times. "Winter is coming and I don't have a coat or any boots. Where am I going to get money to buy one?"

Frustrated and lonely, Claire paced the room twice more. She considered possible remedies. She could skip lunches and Sunday dinners, that would add to her savings so that she could buy a coat, but in the long run she felt trapped. She could see no end to her money troubles. Discouraged, she decided to take a walk.

Out on the streets of Rapid City, Claire found no relief for her dull mood. She watched a couple stroll arm in arm laughing and talking together. On the other side of the street she watched two boys about Jesse's age playing mumbly-peg in the dirt.

She walked for quite a while and eventually found herself near the café. Her resolve to skip the meal was melted as her stomach growled. It had been a long time since breakfast.

She always hated walking into the café alone. She tried to find a table in the corner. Today her heart sank as she looked around. There was one empty table in the middle of the room, all the rest were filled. She started to turn around and leave when a voice to her right caught her attention.

"Hey, look, it's the girl who was nice to us at Sweeney's the other day. Honey, would you like to sit with us?"

Claire looked around and realized that the voice came from the pretty blond girl she'd seen in the store last week. The girl motioned for her to come over.

"Come on, there's another chair right here," she said, scooting her chair over to make room. Claire approached the table, surprised and pleased at the invitation.

"Don't you hate eating alone, Estelle?" the girl said.

"I do, I feel like everyone is watching me," came the answer.

Claire smiled and sat down. "I usually try to sit in the corner where no one will notice me," she added.

The blond put her hand out. "My name is Lela and this is Estelle. It's nice to meet you."

"I'm Claire," she answered.

"We've seen you in here a couple of times, but you're always alone."

"I've only been here for a few weeks. I don't know anyone here."

"Well now you know us!" Estelle answered.

The waitress came to them then. "Hello Ladies. Our special tonight is meatloaf and mashed potatoes for a dollar. We also have shepherd's pie for seventy five cents."

Estelle and Lela both ordered the meatloaf.

The waitress turned to Claire. "How much would a bowl of soup be?" she asked.

Lela interrupted. "Oh, Claire, don't bother with the soup, have the meatloaf, my treat." Claire was so surprised at the girl's generosity she didn't know what to say.

Turning back to the waitress, Lela added, "Make it three meatloaf dinners and all three of us will also have a piece of your terrific cherry pie for dessert!"

"I'll get it right out to you," answered the waitress as she walked away.

"Thank you," stammered Claire. "That is very nice of you."

Claire enjoyed the meal and the conversation. As they chatted, she found out that Estelle and Lela grew up near each other in central South Dakota and had moved to Rapid City almost a year ago. They traded details of farm families, brothers and sisters. "We both had to get away from that little town and those little minds," Estelle explained.

By the time their slices of pie were eaten, their friendship had begun.

"We each found ourselves really respectable jobs," added Lela. "I worked at the Pennington County Bank and Estelle worked at the bakery across the street. We shared a room at the boarding house across from the fire station."

"Do you have the same jobs now?" Claire asked.

The girls laughed at the question. "Honey, I suspect you are finding the same thing we did. Those jobs might be appropriate for respectable ladies but they don't pay you enough to live on."

"I do admit there isn't much extra left at the end of the month," Claire stammered. "So, where do you work now?"

Lela and Estelle exchanged glances. "We work at Big Jack's," Estelle answered.

The blank look on her face told the girls that Claire was unfamiliar with the landmark.

Lela continued. "Big Jack Clower owns and runs the largest saloon in Rapid City. We work for him."

"I see," said Claire, though she wasn't exactly sure that she did.

"Did you notice how that lady at the counter at Sweeney's acted towards us?" asked Lela.

"Yes, but she's grumpy all the time, so I wouldn't take it personally."

Lela laughed out loud. "Claire, you really need to live in the world more. She was rude to us because she doesn't approve of us. We sell drinks and take care of customers at the bar. To most respectable women, we are trash. Fallen women."

"Soiled doves," added Estelle with a giggle.

"Shady ladies." They both laughed, while Claire felt a mixture of horror and surprise.

"Little do they know that we have more money than some of them will ever see in a lifetime."

Claire now understood. They wore the beautiful dresses and expensive jewelry. Their lovely faces and hair were intentional to attract customers and keep them happy.

"You look a bit peaked," volunteered Lela. "Are you embarrassed now that you agreed to be associated with us?" She smiled but her eyes showed a hint of hurt.

Claire took a breath and decided to be candid. "I am not sure how I feel. I admired how pretty you are when you came into the store last week, and I admire you now. You have been gracious and kind to me, and I am grateful to feel that you've become my friends."

"But you don't approve of us now that you know how we earn a living," Estelle's voice had a hard edge to it.

The waitress returned then with the bill. Lela opened her bag and paid the tab, then the three women got up and moved outside in silence. "It was nice eating with you, Claire," said Lela. "See you around."

Claire stood mute for a minute as the two began to walk away.

"Wait," she called after they'd taken several steps. She caught up to them and the three faced each other on the boardwalk. "You are making the assumption that I don't approve of you because I told you I didn't know how I felt. That's unfair."

Lela and Estelle looked shocked. "Are you saying you do approve?"

Claire took a breath and something inside of her cracked. "All my life I had men dictating my every move. I had a Papa who'd rather hit than talk and who valued his boys and brothers over his wife and daughter. I've met a few very nice men, but mostly I've met men who think more of their horses or dogs than of women. Now I meet you. You sell drinks to men and look pretty for them and I wonder if you aren't worse off than I was when my papa knocked me around. This has nothing to do with approving or disapproving."

Claire was shocked at the words that had tumbled out. From the looks on their faces, Estelle and Lela were shocked as well. Claire felt her heart pound three times before anyone moved. Lela smiled. "Well now," she said reaching out to wind her arm first through Claire's and then Estelle's. She began walking. After a few steps she continued, "I can see how you might think that cozying up to strange men, drinking with them and putting up with their advances may be a kind of slavery. I'll admit to you, for some of the girls it is exactly that."

Estelle joined in, "Lela and I aren't like that, though. We don't do it because we want the attention or crave any kind of love or affection."

"We know that the men who come in are using us," Lela continued. "They want their needs met and don't care one jot about who we are, any girl will do. What they don't know, though, is that we are using them, too. Estelle and I have a plan. We want to move back east and find respectable, loving husbands who have more money and dignity than any hardscrabble farmer in South Dakota. We want nice houses and fine families. To do that, we need money. So, we work here, smiling and charming men from their dollars, then we stash those dollars away at the bank. The way we are going, it will take us another two years for each of us to have enough money put away so that we can leave it all behind and start over."

Claire smiled. "I like how you are thinking," she said. "It makes a lot of sense."

Looking around, Claire suddenly realized that it was nearly dark. "I have to go," she said. "Mrs. Payne has a curfew for the girls who board at her house. She demands that everyone is in before dark."

Lela laughed again. "She wants to make sure you stay respectable and proper, and away from the likes of us!"

The three laughed together then parted. "Do you have every Sunday off?" Lela asked.

"Yes."

"Good, then let's meet next Sunday and spend the day together."

"I'll see you next Sunday after breakfast. Where shall we meet?"

"How about in front of Sweeney's?"

"Alright. I'll see you next week." Claire smiled and waved as she hurried off.

14
August, 1896
Rapid City, South Dakota

"What are we going to do today?" Lela asked as Claire approached her. "Last week's picnic was such fun, but it looks like it is going to rain, those clouds to the west are pretty dark."

"Where's Estelle? Is she meeting us later?"

"No, she wasn't feeling well," Lela put her head down and avoided Claire's glance. "It's just the two of us."

"I'm sorry! Is she alright?"

"She will be, she just needs some rest."

"Are you sure?"

Lela let out a sad laugh. "Our dear Estelle always worries about getting fat. A few months ago she ordered a special concoction to help her lose a little of her curves."

"Has it made her sick?" Claire was concerned.

"Well, actually, they were tapeworm eggs."

"What?" Claire's voice was louder than she'd intended.

"Yes, many of the girls take them. You really do lose weight when you have a tapeworm. But after a while, you have to get rid of them."

"How?" Claire wasn't sure she wanted to know the answer.

"A little arsenic does the trick, but it makes you feel pretty lousy for a few days. Our Estelle took her cure last night, so she'd be ready to work on Monday. Jack hates it when we are sick."

"That frightens me. What if she takes too much?"

"I told you, the girls at the saloon do this all the time. She'll be fine by tomorrow, don't worry." She shrugged, then smiled.

"What would you like to do?" Claire faltered.

"Honestly, I'm tired today. Yesterday was really busy and I didn't get a lot of sleep last night."

"I wish I could invite you to come back to my room and relax," started Claire.

"Oh, I can just imagine the look on Mrs. Payne's face when I walked in the door." Lela's laugh was without mirth. "She'd have a fit."

"Estelle and I share a room, so we'd disturb her if we went there, but we have a small sitting room at our place, Claire, if you'd be comfortable with that?"

Claire hesitated. They both knew that she stood to lose her room at the boarding house and probably her job if Mrs. Payne or Mr. Sweeney got wind of her association with Lela and Estelle. For the past month, as their friendship grew, they had been very aware that they needed to be discreet. Both Lela and Estelle dressed plainly on Sundays so they wouldn't draw attention, and the friends usually walked to the woods on the outskirts of town to enjoy their day off together.

"Lela, I'm sorry, but I better not."

Lela smiled. "I understand. You have a lot to lose."

Sprinkles of rain began plopping on the boardwalk. Lela looked up and sighed. "We're going to get wet, I better go. I'll miss you today," she added.

Claire was sad to think of her Sunday alone after the pleasant afternoons she'd spent with the ladies. She shrugged and gave Lela a quick hug. "Let's meet next week," she said as the rain picked up.

"Oh, wait!" Lela called as Claire turned to go. She handed the girl something rolled into a tube. "Here's a copy of last month's *Good Housekeeping* magazine. I've finished reading it, and I brought it for you."

Claire took the tube. She didn't know what *Good Housekeeping* was, but the kindness in Lela's voice was unmistakable. "Thank you!" she called as they both ran in opposite directions.

By the time Claire shut the door to Mrs. Payne's boarding house, she was soaked. No one was in the hallway, so she wiped her feet and made her way up to her room. She stopped at the top of the stairs and looked back, making sure that she wasn't leaving wet prints on the hard wood floor, then she went into her room.

Still a bit breathless from the run in the rain, once inside her room she tossed the tube Lela had given her on to the bed. Then, she slipped off her dress and hung it up to dry. She stepped out of her shoes and peeled off her stockings, reaching for a towel to dry her face and hair. Rain pounded the roof over her head. Claire moved to the window and looked out on the small alley behind the house. Lightning flashed, followed quickly by the slow rumble of thunder.

She brushed out her hair and ruffled it so it would dry, then she looked around her room, feeling lonely and grumpy. "A whole day alone," she grumbled. Then she spied the magazine on her bed.

Good Housekeeping: A Family Magazine, she read on the cover. "Conducted in the Interests of the Higher Life of the Household June, 1896"

Claire picked up the magazine and sat down on the bed. She pushed the pillow against the headboard and made herself comfortable, tucking her chilled bare feet under her. She turned the page and read a poem called "Old-Fashioned Roses". Totally enthralled, Claire devoured the pages. She read poetry and fiction along with articles about home keeping, entertaining, and child rearing. Her mouth watered as she read recipes for salads made with lobster or oysters even though she had never tasted either. She pictured herself, in a home of her own, making a "Convent Salad" for her family:

"Slice boiled potatoes while yet warm, mix with them a sliced cucumber, some minced onions, with a small sprig of tarragon. Add salt, pepper, oil, vinegar and sour cream, mixed with a well-beaten egg. Serve direct from the ice chest."

The rainy afternoon was lost to Claire as she immersed herself in the magazine. Each of the journal's forty-eight pages had two columns of information and entertainment. She found a remedy for sunburn. *"The mixture of equal parts of Vaseline and olive oil is a quick remedy for skin burn, whether from March winds or August sunshine."* Toward the back, she was delighted to find two pages of book reviews. One piqued her interest, a non-fiction book called *A Woman's Part in a Revolution* by Mrs. John Hays Hammond. The review explained that the revolution in question was one in South Africa. Claire only knew that it was far away, she had no idea where. One line caught her attention, though, "A woman's part in a revolution is a poor part to play. There is little hazard and no glory in it."

Claire sat and thought about that. Her life had borne out the truth and the fiction of the thought. "But there is hazard in a woman's life," Claire told the quiet room. "And certainly there is no glory in it!"

When Claire finally looked up from the magazine, the afternoon was waning. She walked to the window to see that the rainclouds were retreating, as was the sun. The sky to the west was clear. The sun, a shining yellow ball, slipped beneath the horizon as she watched.

Claire's stomach growled. She sighed and turned to find her pocketbook. In it, she knew, was fifteen cents. She didn't have enough for even a bowl of soup at the café. She reached for the last crust of the loaf of bread. It was dried and crunchy, but it was all she had. Lela's words came back to her, "I understand, you have a lot to lose." She considered those words. *Oh yes, I couldn't possibly give all this up*, she thought. As she swallowed the last of the bread, her stomach growled again.

***

"What time is it, Claire?" Lucy called her out of the balance sheet she'd been absorbed in. Claire looked up at the William L. Gilbert mantle clock on the fireplace behind her.

"It's five minutes after eleven," she answered. *Oh dear*, she thought. *It isn't even lunch time on Monday and I'm tired. This is going to be a long day.*

Lucy went back to shelving the new tools that arrived Friday on a freight wagon from St. Louis. Twelve minutes later, she called out again, "Claire, what time is it?"

"Lucy," Claire smiled. "It is eleven seventeen. What are you waiting for?"

Lucy walked closer to Claire's desk and smiled. "Remember I told you about a man I met at the church picnic a month or so ago? He and I have been talking after church since we met, and yesterday he asked if he could come and visit with me during my lunch today. He'll be here at noon. Mr. Sweeney already told me that I could have a full hour today for lunch."

Lucy was nearly vibrating with excitement. Usually, she was solemn and kept to herself. She was efficient and polite with customers, but also reserved and not overly friendly. Claire giggled to herself as she listened to Lucy wait on the next customer in the store. She chatted amiably with a wizened old farmer about yesterday's rain and the blight on his tomatoes. *Lucy has talked more in one morning than in all the other mornings combined,* Claire thought.

The bell above the door jingled precisely at noon. A tall, thin man came into the store. He fidgeted with the bowler hat in his hand as he made his way to the back counter. Claire took a minute to size him up before he saw her. His suit was a fashionable three-pieces. The vest was a bit darker brown than the jacket and trousers. His hair was mousy chestnut color, cut short and thinning a bit on the top. His white shirt was crisply starched with a square collar and a pale blue four-in-hand tie. His shoes were old, but polished to a nice shine. He looked nervous, approaching the counter quietly. Lucy had been in the back room. She saw him as she came out from behind the counter. Both froze and looked at each other. Lucy smoothed her dress, then her hair.

"Good afternoon, Miss Lucy," the man said quietly.

"Hello, Robert," Lucy answered with a smile. "Claire." She turned to the desk at the side of the counter. "Claire, this is Mr. Robert Murphy. Mr. Murphy, our bookkeeper, Claire Atley."

Claire greeted the man and they exchanged pleasantries for a few minutes.

"Claire, will you watch the counter while I'm gone? Mr. Sweeney said he'd be back close to noon to take over for you. I'll see you at one o'clock."

Claire watched them go. Her mind split into two factions. One part of her was happy for Lucy and a bit jealous that she had a suitor. The other part of her, the cynical, hardened part, wondered how long it would be before proper Mr. Murphy would turn Lucy into a frump who lived only to please him.

The bell jingled her out of her thoughts. Two men entered the store. The first man was tall and barrel-chested. The other man was younger. His dark brown hair tumbled into his eyes as he removed his hat. What caught Claire's attention was the sky blueness of those eyes. Both men were dirty, covered in dried mud and darker stains that were probably grease. Claire was used to miners in the store. Usually, a group came to town for supplies, a bath, and a night or two of drinking before they headed back up to the mountains and their gold claims.

The tall man came to the counter, greeted Claire, and handed her a list. "We want to leave in the morning, Miss. Do you think you can get this order together by then?"

The other man walked around the store as she dealt with the spokesman. Claire scanned the list, noting that these men had some items on the list that she wasn't familiar with.

"I am confident, Sir," Claire began, "that we can fill most of these items for you by tomorrow. I am not sure about the sulphuric acid and chloride of lime, however."

She looked up to see the man's scowl. "I wrote to Tom Sweeney a month ago telling him I'd be in for these supplies," he boomed. "He damn well better have these in!"

"Gray, that's no way to talk to a lady." His voice was deep and quiet, filled with calm authority. Claire looked up to see his blue eyes watching her over the nail aisle.

The tall man released a breath in exasperation. "Beg your pardon, Miss," he mumbled.

The doorbell jangled and Claire looked up. Her boss, Tom Sweeney, took two steps into the store and then recognized the man at the counter. "Well, Grey Madison, you old son of a gun! Are you making a killing up in the Galena Mining District?" The tension in the room burst like a soap bubble as the two men shook hands.

"Glad to see you, Tom," Madison smiled. "This little lady was just giving me a heart attack telling me you might not have the chemicals I need to chlorinate the gold ore we're getting."

Sweeney smiled. "Grey, go easy. This is my bookkeeper, Miss Atley. She is terrific with numbers but doesn't usually mind the store. Claire, this is Grey Madison, an old miner friend."

"How do you do?" Claire asked politely, wishing she could just melt into the floor. Madison's behavior had frightened her, and she kept her hands clasped behind her back so they couldn't see that she was shaking.

Sweeney continued to banter with Madison, and nodded slightly to Claire. Relieved, she excused herself then returned to her desk, opened the ledger book and picked up her pencil, acting as if she were working. It took a few minutes for her nerves to calm. She tried not to listen as the men discussed the process of chlorination that Gray and his partners were using.

"Tom, this is my engineer, Daniel Haynes. Haynes here is new to the area, he just came up from Cripple Creek, Colorado."

The men shook hands. "You from Colorado, then?" asked Sweeney.

"No Sir, I'm originally from Iowa. I went to school in Colorado and got my first mining job in Cripple Creek."

"How are you liking the Black Hills?"

"They are a new kind of challenge. I like the stability of the rock, it makes for safer shafts, but it's frustrating having the gold so encased."

"The gold they are getting from the Homestake Mine is good quality and easy to extract from the quartz it veins in." Madison added. "The gold we are getting in Galena is good gold, but it is refractory, meaning it is chemically bound to the rock around it. We've been having pretty good luck using chlorine gas made from sulphuric acid and chloride of lime, but it is a hard process," Madison explained.

"I've been hearing about a chemist who is experimenting with cyanide to break the gold out of its bonds, but I don't think they've perfected that process yet," Sweeney answered.

"There's got to be a better way, I just don't know what it is."

Sweeney clapped the man on the back. "Gray, don't worry. Go get yourself a room, a bath and a meal. I'll have your order ready by eight o'clock in the morning."

Their voices were lost as Sweeney walked them to the door.

Claire was adding up a column of numbers when she noticed Mr. Sweeney standing nearby. She looked up to find him watching her. "You're doing a good job, here, Miss Atley."

"Thank you," Claire answered.

"If you ever get an order that you don't know all about again, just say that I'll take care of it, don't tell anyone we might not have it. It will save you some worry. Let me take the fire from someone's temper."

"Yes, Sir. I am sorry about that."

"No need to be sorry, you did nothing wrong. I'm just giving you some advice for next time." Sweeney smiled at her and Claire relaxed.

15
October, 1896
Rapid City, South Dakota

The wind was howling as dark clouds scudded across a steel colored sky. Claire was thankful for the warmth the scarf and gloves that she wore gave her. She loved how soft they felt against her skin, and she smiled when she thought about how attractive the scarf looked, even over her old, tattered coat. Immediately the smile was replaced as she remembered that now, because of her purchase, she had fifteen cents to last her a whole week. *And I still need a pair of boots for the winter!*

She put her head down as a new gust of frigid air whistled around the corner. She'd only been waiting to meet Lela and Estelle for a few minutes, but she was already cold. She stomped her feet for warmth as her friends came into view.

They greeted each other with quick hugs. "Claire, it is freezing out here! I know you've hesitated about it before, but let's go back to our room. I put together a picnic lunch for us and left it there. I have a copy of a Vogue magazine – the New York fashions in it are startling!"

Claire hesitated only for a second. She had spent too many Sundays alone and hungry, plus she was cold. She smiled her assent and they set off.

"We'll go in through the alley door, no one will see you this time of the day," Estelle reassured her.

A few minutes later the three sat facing each other. Lela sat on a small, narrow bed that was pushed up under the single, high window in the room. Estelle's bed was against the adjoining wall, creating an l-shape. In the corner was a short, square table that the two shared as a headboard. Claire looked around as Estelle hung up their coats and Lela put a short log in the firebox of a small heating stove in the opposite corner. The room had blue flowered wall paper and pale blue curtains on the window. There was a large armoire next to the door. A blue, green and yellow braided rug lay in the center of the room. The overall effect was homey and feminine.

"This is very nice," Claire said.

"You sound a bit surprised," laughed Lela in response. "Did you expect it to be seedy?"

"Yeah, maybe you pictured it with red velvet and thick brocade."

The girls were teasing her, but she was embarrassed, anyway. She stammered. "No, I…"

Lela laughed again. "Claire, relax. These are our private rooms. We don't work in here."

Even though they had been friends for several months and had spent many Sundays together, they rarely discussed the work that Lela and Estelle did at the Saloon. It had seemed to be an off-limits topic. Claire assumed that her friends understood that it made her nervous, so they steered clear of the topic.

Soon they were sitting on the floor, looking at the fashions in Lela's magazine, laughing and chatting. Lela turned the last page and closed the book. "I have three other issues. We can look at those later. I'm hungry, let's eat!"

Estelle grabbed a pink shawl and spread it out on the floor over the braided rug while Lela retrieved a basket. They sat down and soon the floor between them was filled with bread, cheese, a bunch of grapes, and some fried chicken. Estelle reached back into the basket and added three hard boiled eggs and some dill pickle spears wrapped in waxed paper.

"This is a crazy feast," giggled Lela. "The cook lets us just clean out any leftovers from the ice box and the pantry on Sundays, so we never know what is going to be available."

"It's very nice that they let you just raid the kitchen on Sundays," remarked Claire. "There is a lot of food here."

"The cook gets a day off, too, if she makes enough so that there are leftovers on Sunday. Big Ed says that his girls need to be healthy and round, so they make sure that we have good provisions."

"He sounds like a nice man, even though…," Claire cut herself off. She didn't want to sound judgmental.

Estelle shrugged. "Claire, Lela and I were raised in homes probably similar to yours. Go to church on Sunday, pray at meals. My mama read the Bible to us and always stressed that I needed to be a 'good girl'. But what did being a 'good girl' do for her? At forty-five years old she looks, acts and walks like an old woman. Her hands are scarred and gnarled, and she is broken down and unhappy."

"My ma did all those things, too. She made us go to church, she read us the Bible, then snuck drinks of moonshine whiskey through the day when she thought no one was looking. My pa talked about being holy on Sundays, then added a little sand to bags of wheat he sold to our neighbors to make them heavier." Lela's voice was filled with quiet emotion as she continued. "When Ma died three years ago with her liver all ate up by the drink, she left six kids and a dirty house. Pa went out less than a month later and found himself a widow only six years older than me to marry. I looked at her pretty face and soft hands, knowing what they were going to look like in a few years, and decided that I wasn't going to stay around and watch. More importantly, I decided that if that was what life was for 'good girls', then I was going to make a new kind of choice."

They were quiet for a few minutes, enjoying their lunch quietly.

Claire broke the silence. "But what is your life like, now? You have pretty clothes and enough to eat. You have this nice room. But what is the tradeoff? Is what you do for this worth it?"

Lela finished chewing and cleared her throat. "When you start with Big Ed, all you have to do is be friendly with the customers and bring them drinks. You flirt a little and sit and talk, mostly. We are forbidden to drink any alcohol. They give us juice or tonic water so that we look like we are drinking, too. Most of the men that come to the saloon are miners. They've been up in the hills working. Most of them are disappointed and tired because mining is hard work and not very many actually get rich. They are lonely and need to talk. So, we provide them some light conversation and a pretty face to look at."

"It is pretty fun, really. You meet some interesting characters," added Estelle.

Lela laughed. "Remember that old guy who came in a week or so ago?" Estelle nodded and laughed. Lela looked at Claire and continued the story. "He looked to be about ninety years old. He told me I looked like his 'dear, departed wife' and then called me Sally Ann the rest of the night. All he wanted was a whiskey and to hold my hand. Then he left me a five dollar liberty head gold piece."

The girls laughed together. They shared several vignettes of customers they'd met. Claire thought the most interesting was an old Indian man who came in about once a month. Estelle described her encounters with him. "He never speaks to me, beside a low mumble that I can't understand. A small woman with dirty black hair always comes with him and stands just inside the door. She never sits and she never speaks or looks around. He comes in, motions for one drink, then points at me. At first, I didn't want to go, but Ed told me that he's harmless; he's been coming in for years. So I go and sit beside him. Every time, he reaches out and touches the lace on my sleeve. He drinks his drink while he rubs the lace between his fingers. Then, he gets up and leaves. The woman follows him out. That's it."

The girls regaled Claire with a few more stories as they finished their picnic.

"Yes," Claire said, haltingly. "But what about, well. What about your other duties?"

"Big Ed never makes you go upstairs with a customer at first," answered Estelle. "It is your choice when you start that."

"I don't understand, then. Why do you do it?"

Lela's answer came quickly. "For the money. Working in the saloon gets you $10 a week plus any of the tips that the men give us. Ed takes out five dollars for our room and board, so that leaves only five dollars a week pay. He also gives us twenty five dollars a year for clothes. When I was only in the saloon, I earned about five dollars a week in tips, but that wasn't enough. I've told you, Estelle and I have plans. We aren't going to do this our whole lives. This is a means to an end."

"So then, um, going upstairs pays well?"

"The house pays us a dollar for every trip upstairs. Then, usually the men give you a little something if they've had a good time. I usually make an extra twenty dollars a week."

"That's a lot of money," replied Claire. "But, well, is it awful?"

Lela smiled. "No, it isn't awful. Well, sometimes it is, but most times it isn't. Some of the men are actually pretty attractive, and I can enjoy it. Other times, I just think about what I am going to do when we move back east until they finish."

"Hey," Lela jumped up and moved the basket. "I want to try that hair style we saw in the magazine. Claire, come sit in this chair and let me experiment on you."

The rest of the afternoon flew by. Claire admired a dress ad at the back of the magazine she was holding. She took a relaxed breath and stood up, stretching.

"Oh dear, look outside!" said Claire as she looked out the window. "It is snowing. I better get going."

"I hate for you to leave," answered Estelle, "we've had such a nice day."

"I hate to go, but I better. Thank you for the fun picnic."

"Your hair looks great, you should wear it that way tomorrow."

"I think I might," Claire answered as she wrapped her scarf around her head.

Later, in the quiet of her room, Claire stared out the window and replayed the day. She kept coming back to their conversation about working at the saloon. She looked around the austere, lonely little room and compared it to the warm, homey feeling of her friends' room. Polite society, ladies like Lucy at the store or the farm wives that she met at the mercantile, judged Lela and Estelle. They looked down on them and considered them 'shady ladies' and 'fallen doves'. Claire knew them, though, and knew that they had good hearts and the same desires and dreams as everyone else. She also knew that they seemed much happier and comfortable with themselves than any other women she'd ever met, except maybe Haddie.

Thinking about Haddie reminded her that she hadn't gotten a letter from her since the end of August. She lifted that letter from her table and re-read of Haddie's concern that several people around Mitchell had come down with yellow fever.

You probably don't remember the last time we had a plague scare around here, you were too young. But once a fever starts in a community, people get frightened. A yellow fever outbreak in Philadelphia in 1793 killed nearly ten percent of the population, and just a few cases can cause people to panic. Just a little over twenty years ago, yellow fever killed about a quarter of the people living in a small town in Louisiana and a few years later it killed about twenty thousand people in the Mississippi River region. Some doctors are saying that maybe we get yellow fever from mosquitoes, but others think that people spread it.

We've had a few cases and already there is talk of quarantines and people are staying home unless they must go to town. People aren't shaking hands or spending time together. Church services are pretty empty and the Presbyterian Church just cancelled their August Picnic. Don't worry about us, though, I saw your Mama last week and she and the family are fine. I stay home most of the time and you know that your Mama rarely gets off the farm. It has been a wet summer, though, so I make sure that if the children go out in the evening they wear a long sleeved shirt. I also made a 'potion' of lavender, peppermint and lemongrass that I rub on them. You should hear William tease me about my witches' brew, but he also says it seems to work.

Claire sighed and flopped down on her bed. It just didn't seem as if anything in the world was right. She hated the snow and cold that swirled outside her window. Her room felt cold, especially since she had no stove merrily burning in the corner like Lela and Estelle had. She shivered, though she wasn't sure if it was that cold in the room or if worrying about her Mama and the Fosters was the real cause. The kerosene lamp sputtered and drew her attention.

"Oh drat!" she said aloud. The lamp was nearly empty. Mrs. Payne had begun charging her a nickel to fill it, saying that she used too much kerosene with all her reading late at night.

Claire quickly changed into her nightdress and climbed into her bed. She put out the light. Sleep didn't come for a long time.

16
Late October, 1896
Rapid City, South Dakota

Claire frowned at the column of numbers. Every time she added them, she came up with a different answer, and none of them matched the sales receipts book. She was irritated. Lucy, on the other hand, bounced around the store humming a quiet tune and greeting customers with a cheer and happiness that made Claire want to scream.

There was a lull between customers, and Lucy was resting her elbows on the counter, looking at something intently, humming an upbeat tune and tapping her foot. Claire looked at the numbers again, slapped her pencil down and mumbled, "I don't see why Mr. Sweeney can't buy us an arithmometer." She stood up and walked to the counter.

"What is an arithmometer?" asked Lucy, looking up. Claire could now see that her coworker had a magazine open to a page of wedding dresses. Lucy and Robert Murphy had set a wedding date for early spring.

"It is a mechanical calculator that would help me add up these cursed numbers," Claire answered. "There are actually several kinds of adding machines available. I saw a deColmer arithmometer in a business catalog last month, and it would be the best help I could have today."

"Are you still worried about your family?" Lucy's voice was soft and soothing.

"Yes, I've written four letters, to my Mama and to our neighbor Haddie, and I haven't gotten a response. I just wish someone would let me know what was going on."

"I'm sorry, Claire. I wish I could do something to help."

Claire mumbled her thanks and then excused herself to go use the privy. She really didn't need to go, she just needed a few minutes by herself. Her money troubles mixed with worry about her family and the Fosters weighed her down. *Add that to the fact that I dread coming in to work each day because it is so routine and mundane,* Claire thought. *I'm trapped!*

A few minutes later, Claire was back at her desk. She took a few breaths and started in on the column of numbers once more. She didn't look up when the bell above the door signaled someone was entering the store. She knew that Lucy was still at the counter.

"Oh, good morning, Mr. Sweeney," Lucy called out.

"Good morning, Lucy. How is business today?"

"It's been pretty slow. I've sold only six dollars' worth of merchandise so far."

"It's the time of the year. All the miners hole up during the winter, nearly no one works when the snow flies in the Black Hills."

"Yes, Sir," answered Lucy.

Sweeney came to stand between Claire's desk and Lucy at the counter. "I need to talk with you both." His voice was quiet and serious. Claire put her pencil down and turned to face her boss. Lucy rested her hands by her sides and leaned against the counter.

"The financial panic back east in 1893 didn't really reach us out here, especially because of the gold that they were pulling out of the mountains, but this recession our country is in has been creeping this way, and I'm afraid that it is finally reaching us. I don't expect it to be as bad here as it has been in the east, but we are feeling the pressure of inflation and higher prices."

Lucy nodded her head, though Claire was quite sure she hadn't understood a thing Mr. Sweeney just said. Claire read the newspaper when Mr. Sweeney left it on the counter, so she was a little familiar with what he was referring to.

Sweeney continued. "With the winter slow down and the recession, I need to do a little cutting back. Starting tomorrow, I am going to cut back your hours. Lucy, I'd like you to come in at the regular time of eight o'clock. Claire, I'd like you to start at ten. It is usually pretty quiet in the early afternoons, so you can get the bookwork done while you are both here. Then Lucy can go home at four o'clock and Claire can help customers and close up."

"Yes, Sir," Lucy said again.

Claire had a hollow pain begin in the pit of her stomach. "Mr. Sweeney, what about our pay?"

"The reduced hours will change your pay, Claire. You will work ten hours less per week, so I think it will be fair if I pay you six dollars a week instead of the eight you have been getting."

"But," started Claire.

He interrupted her. "If you need to move back into the room upstairs instead of staying at the boardinghouse, I will understand and approve. I expect that this will only last through the winter, things will look up again in the spring."

The front door opened and three men walked in. Mr. Sweeney looked up and smiled. He took two steps then stopped. "Ladies, I understand that this is a hardship. But the recession is taking its toll on all of us." He walked away, greeted the men and began to chat.

Lucy patted Claire's shoulder. "It'll be alright, Claire, it is only for a little while."

Claire turned back to her desk, willing herself not to cry. She took a deep breath and began to add the column again.

Later, Claire and Lucy ate their lunches in silence as the clock ticked. Mr. Sweeney was in his office in the back, visiting with the attorney that worked next door. The girls heard their deep voices and an occasional burst of laughter. Claire finished the cheese she'd brought and folded up the small piece of wax paper to use again. The store door opened and shut. Lucy hastily cleaned up the remains of her lunch and dusted off her skirt then headed for the counter. Claire turned to begin working on the inventory ledger.

"Hello, Mr. Smithfield," Lucy called. "How are things at the post office?"

"Quite well, Miss Wills."

"What can I help you with?"

"I came to see Miss Atley, actually," he replied.

Claire looked up to see the postmaster at the counter, a letter in hand. Her heart missed a beat as she moved toward the counter. When Mr. Smithfield saw her, he nodded politely. "Miss Atley, I know that you've been waiting to hear from someone back home. I received this letter this morning and didn't want to wait for you to be able to come and get it." He extended the letter out to her.

"Thank you very much," Claire replied. "I appreciate your kindness."

"You are welcome." He turned around and headed for the door.

Claire was frozen. A quick glance at the envelope told her that the letter was from Haddie.

"Lucy, would you excuse me for a few minutes?"

"Sure. Why don't you go in the upper room so you can read your letter in private."

Claire whispered a thanks and moved toward the stairs. She stopped at the top stair, sat down and carefully opened the envelope. Her hands were shaking as she read.

My Dearest Claire,

I am certain that you have been worried sick waiting for news from me, and I am sorry that I haven't written earlier. This is a hard letter to write and will be a hard letter to read. The yellow fever plague has run its course and there haven't been any new cases in the area for at least two weeks. Milly and Molly both fell ill about a week after I wrote you. I guess my 'potion' didn't work. They were so sick. The fever made them both delirious. After a few days they cooled off, but then Milly's fever returned. She turned yellow, her eyes, her skin, even her finger nails were yellow. She is better now, but the doctor is fearful that it has done permanent damage to her liver and kidneys. She has trouble eating and is quiet and withdrawn. The rest of my family is fine, even Molly, though I feel drained.

I hadn't heard anything from your folks for weeks. A few days before the girls got sick I sent Matthew over with some extra cream I had and to check on them. Matthew came back saying that everyone was healthy, and that your Mama sent the message not to worry about them. Then the girls got sick and I had my hands full.

I hate writing this to you, Claire, and I wish I could tell you in person and hug you. Your Mama passed away about two weeks ago. Marcus tried his best to care for her, but your Papa was sure that she'd be fine, so he didn't send for the doctor. Marcus and your father had a huge fight over it in the afternoon after they buried her. He was pretty busted up, with a black eye and a cut lip from the fight. He's asked to stay here and work for William, saying that he won't go back.

William went over the next day, hoping to get Hiram to come talk to Marcus and patch things up. Instead, he found Hiram drinking heavily and packing the wagon. He said his plan was to meet up with his brothers and go out to California. He had little Jesse doing heavy work carrying supplies while he cussed and stormed. William calmed him down some and then was able to talk your Papa into letting Jesse come to our house.

I know this is a lot to take in. Marcus is angry down deep, but he is putting lots of effort in his work for William and seems to be working it out in his own way. He sleeps in the barn, William and he cleaned out the old tack room and created a room for him. I actually saw him smile yesterday. Jesse is fine. Our children are happy to have a new 'brother', and he's moved into Matthew's room. I've started teaching him how to read and write. I've included him in the children's lessons every night. I invited Marcus to join us as well, and while he doesn't participate, he sits in the room often and listens.

Yesterday William and Marcus went to town. They heard from Mr. Grisholm that Horace and Clancy have reneged on their deal to buy his place and that they were behind on payments to him. The rumor in town is that they and Hiram left town on Monday, telling people that they were headed for California.

Marcus and Jesse send their love. Marcus asked me to tell you that they buried your Mama under the pine tree by her garden. He has her mantle clock and a lock of her hair for you.

You are in my heart and prayers,
Haddie

Claire stared at the letter, not seeing and not feeling. She didn't cry and she didn't feel sad. She had no idea how long she'd sat there with her mind and emotions blank. Eventually she became aware that Lucy was standing at the bottom of the stairs, calling her name softly.

"Claire, what can I do? It was bad news, wasn't it?"

Claire looked at Lucy's furrowed forehead and appreciated her more in that moment than she ever had. She took stock of her emotions, feeling almost as if she was a casual observer standing removed from the Claire that was sitting on the stairs. *I should be grieving,* she thought. She tried to smile at Lucy, and stood up.

"My Mama died, Lucy," was all she said as she started down the stairs.

Lucy's eyes welled with tears. "Oh, Claire, I am so sorry!"

They returned to the back counter of the store.

"Do you need to go home? I have some money if you need to buy a ticket."

"Thank you – that's so kind of you, but no," Claire answered. Then she whispered, "They buried her in a beautiful spot and she doesn't need me there. No one does."

Lucy hugged her, then stepped back. "I'll tell Mr. Sweeney what happened, if you'd like. Do you need to take some time for yourself?"

Claire took a breath. She felt so tired and heavy inside. "I'll be no good here for today. I think I will just go for a walk, if you'll talk to Mr. Sweeney for me?"

"Of course," Lucy answered. Claire quietly gathered her pocketbook, scarf and hat. She stopped and turned back to Lucy. "Thank you," was all she said, then she walked quietly out.

The air outside was cold and jarring. Claire began walking, not heeding where she was going or who she passed. The sky was a bluish grey, the clouds formed a bowl over her head that let in a muted light but no warmth. Sunday's snow lay in a crust beneath her feet, though she didn't register how it crunched under her footsteps. She walked on.

As evening approached, the temperature dropped and hovered near bitter, but she didn't notice for a while. Finally, with the cold air clawing at her cheeks, she stopped and looked around. She was on a familiar path on the outskirts of town. She'd been here on a picnic with Lela and Estelle last month. They'd laughed and teased each other as they ambled to a stand of trees just over the ridge and then finally headed home. Today the laughter was silent but the wind wasn't. Gusts pushed at Claire as she stopped and looked around, finally realizing that evening had come.

"What am I supposed to do now?" she asked the cold. Knowing she wasn't going to hear an answer, she looked within. *I should be crying*, she thought again. *I should be sad.*

Should. She hated that word, a word she'd often heard from her mother. "We should be thankful for what we do have." "You should be patient with your father, he's doing the best he can." "You should be more lady-like." "Don't be mad at him for this bruise, I should have been more careful." She realized that her mother had lived her life on shoulds.

She stood, taking in the rugged mountains in the distance and watching lights blink on in the windows of houses at the edge of town. She scanned the sage brush prairie nearby. She smelled a mixture of pine and sage along with wood smoke.

She realized she was relieved. Her mother was out of danger. Her father couldn't hurt her, couldn't hit her, couldn't cause her pain and worry ever again. *She is free from 'should' and 'must' and the hardness of life and from him,* Claire thought. *Marcus and Jesse are also safe and tucked into a family that will show them what a real family can be.*

She understood, then, that while she would miss her mother, she couldn't and wouldn't grieve for her or for the family she'd grown up in. Her mother's passing was a blessing for them all. *I'll never have to see Papa – no,* she thought with a force that came from the very core of her, *I will never think or refer to him as that again. I'll never have to see Hiram or his horrid brothers again. Mama will live in my mind and memories, but Hiram and Horace and Clancey are dead.*

She was cold. Her toes were numb. She shivered once and turned around. As she began the walk back into town Mr. Sweeney's words from earlier in the day - before the letter came - returned to her. She just couldn't imagine how she'd make it on reduced hours and only six dollars a week. She was barely making it through each week on eight.

As the twilight increased, so did the wind. It slapped at her cheeks and whipped her skirt around her legs as she walked. She felt the wind burning its cold into the skin on her face. At the same time, coldness was burning inside her. Any tiny speck of sadness was replaced with heart-freezing anger. *Mama was trapped by his mean, quick fists and her own illusions. She called it love, but it was fear. Mr. Sweeney thinks he has me trapped. He thinks I'll do what I should and stay willing and loyal even though he cuts my pay. But I'm not trapped and today, all my illusions are dead.*

Instead of turning right when she got to Main Street and going back to Mrs. Payne's, Claire turned left. She walked west, with ever increasing resolve and assurance, past several store fronts. She stopped to check her reflection in the glass window of the mercantile. As the piano played an upbeat tune she took the scarf off her head and smoothed her hair. She hesitated only for a breath at the door before she pushed herself into the brightly lit saloon called Jack's Place.

17
April, 1897
Rapid City, South Dakota

At Lela's urging, Big Jack hired Claire. "You look a little scrawny," he teased her that first night. "Get yourself some nice dresses that will show off what you've got and we'll start you in the saloon." He walked with her to the kitchen and introduced her to the cook. "Myra, we're taking this stray in. Get her some money for clothes and find her a room."

The room Myra found for her was at the top of the building. Living in the attic again gave her new home a kind of familiarity to the farm and she liked the space. She was also thankful that the space was too small to share. The narrow room held a single bed and a small dresser. Estelle and Lela helped her find a cheerful yellow and orange quilt in the storeroom to use as a bedspread and she bought a short length of material in pinks, yellows and oranges that she made into a curtain to cover the single, high window. There was no wallpaper here, but the off-white walls along with the warm colors of the quilt and curtain made Claire feel as if she were harbored in a safe cocoon.

Her new friends also helped her get ready for her first shift. Lela knocked on her door then came in with an armful of dresses. "We went through everyone's closets and found these for you," Estelle explained.

"The girls wanted to welcome you, so we all pitched in to find a few things to get you started," added Lela. "We didn't really think your other clothes would work out."

"Wear this one," Estelle handed her a crimson velvet frock. "It will look better on you than it ever did on me."

They helped her get dressed then sat her down to fix her hair. Watching intently in her Grandmother's mirror, Claire sat nervously as Lela twisted her long hair into a bun, adorning it with a matching red feather. Then, Estelle stepped between Claire and the mirror to apply some rouge and green eye shadow. "Here, just finish up with this lipstick and you'll be all set."

Claire hesitated. "I've never used lipstick, how do I do it?"

The girls laughed merrily and helped with the finishing touches. "There," Lela said as she stepped back to admire their handiwork. "You look beautiful."

The room grew suddenly quiet. "Um, is it ok if I take a minute before I come down? I, I need a bit to myself."

Lela patted her arm as Estelle smiled and turned to go. "We understand. Just relax and smile a lot. We'll be right beside you tonight to help you figure it all out."

The door closed gently and Claire was alone. She put her head down and tried to calm herself. She felt like crying, but was afraid for her makeup. Needing something to do, she looked at the dresses that the girls had left on her bed. She picked up each one, shook it out and hung it on the pegs along one wall. Then, she turned and met herself in the mirror.

What she saw surprised her. She looked so different. An old memory surged up and she pictured the two gypsy women she'd seen that day so long ago. Often she'd recalled how exotic and somehow frightening they'd looked to her then. The face she studied now had an exotic look as well, but her eyes held unmasked fear. She thought of her mother then. *What would she think of me now?* But no sooner had the thought registered in her mind she pushed it away. *No. Mama was frightened of Papa and that made her a victim to her life. I can't be that. I refuse to be afraid. This is where I am and who I am today. I am choosing this.* Claire closed her eyes and breathed deeply. Finding a strength deep inside. When she blinked and met the woman in the mirror, she thought she detected a change.

***

She was nervous the first few nights, unsure of herself. With Lela's encouragement and Estelle's help, she began to notice the admiration and approval in the eyes of the men she talked to, and that helped her confidence grow. The other girls welcomed her, trading tricks for fashion and make-up, and soon Claire found that she enjoyed the interaction with the men who came into the saloon.

One evening in December, when it was snowy outside and there were only a few men at the bar, the piano player, Tucker, began to play "Oh Susanna". As she wiped down an empty table, Claire began to sing along. She sang quietly as she worked, and only realized during the last chorus that nearly everyone in the bar had stopped talking and was listening to her. The song ended and several men clapped. Big Jack, ever present and watchful behind the bar, called to her, "Hey Scrawny, sing another one."

Claire blushed and tried to ignore him, but the men clapped again, so she moved over toward the piano. Tucker smiled at her and asked her if she knew "Daisy Bell". Claire nodded. She'd heard him play it many times in the past two months, then added, "I'm not sure of all the words."

"No problem, just read them off the sheet music." He showed her the lyrics, then began playing. He nodded to her to help her get started.

There is a flower within my heart
Daisy, Daisy!
Planted one day by a glancing dart,
Planted by Daisy Bell.
Whether she loves me or not,
Sometimes it's hard to tell:
Yet I am longing to share the lot
Of beautiful Daisy Bell!

Daisy, daisy,
Give me your answer do!
I'm half crazy, all for the love of you!
It won't be a stylish marriage,
I can't afford a carriage,
But you'll look sweet upon the seat
Of a bicycle built for two!

Her voice was shaky at first, but she concentrated on Tucker, the piano and the words in front of her so that by the end, her voice was strong and confident. She looked up as Tucker played

118

the last chord and was greeted with smiles from the customers and Big Jack at the bar. A few called for more, but Claire just waved, picked up the bar rag she'd been using, and headed for the kitchen in the back.

Later, as she helped dry the dishes in the kitchen, Big Jack pulled her aside. "You've been holdin' out on me, Scrawny," he said with a smile. "From now on, I'd like to have you do a couple sets of singing with Tucker. I'll pay you an extra five dollars a week for two half hour sets. What do you think?"

Claire felt warm and panicky. She stammered and tried to say no, but Jack just patted her shoulder. "Talk to Tucker and set up some time for the next couple days to rehearse. See how it goes, then decide." He winked and walked away, leaving Claire with a pounding heart.

The next morning, Lela was sitting on Claire's bed relaxing and chatting. She'd been upstairs with a customer when Claire sang, so Claire filled her in on what happened and what Jack offered her later.

"I just don't know, Lela, I don't especially like having people watching and listening to me, it makes me uncomfortable. I'm really not that good a singer."

"Claire," Lela's voice was serious. "Jack certainly thinks you have a beautiful voice, and you just told me the customers enjoyed your song last night! Also think of this, you have been hesitating and finding excuses and so far Big Jack hasn't pushed you about taking customers upstairs. That's a big part of our job here, though, and he's going to lose his patience with you."

Claire sighed. The idea of being with a customer haunted Claire. She really didn't want to take that step but knew that she'd have to, and soon.

"Maybe, if you are singing every night, Big Jack won't make you go upstairs."

Claire thought about her friend's idea, and hoped she was right.

***

By mid-April, Claire was confident and comfortable with her life. She sang five nights a week along with sitting with customers and helping serve drinks and clean up. She teased with the regulars and listened to the stories the miners had to tell when they were in town. She relished her Sundays off. She still spent them with Lela and Estelle most of the time. Now that the weather was warming up, they were able to take walks, and they'd had a picnic just last week, soaking up the spring warmth and feeling renewed with the budding trees and flowers.

Claire finished singing her first set of the evening then retreated to the kitchen for a drink of water. She sat at the small table with her shoe off, rubbing her sore toes. Lois plopped down beside her. "My feet hurt, too! It is so busy out there tonight!"

They chatted for a minute. Lois smiled and left quickly when Big Jack came into the kitchen. Claire put her shoe back on, finished her water, and turned toward the saloon doors. "Wait a minute, there, Scrawny," Jack called to her.

Claire turned and waited. Jack approached her with a smile. "You are doing a good job out there."

She smiled and said a quick "Thank you."

"You've gotten yourself an admirer, a high roller poker player that I've known for years."

Claire met his eyes and waited.

"He's asked to take you upstairs. I told him you'd be available after your second set of songs."

Claire felt the panic rising. She tried to cover it, but Jack missed very little when it came to the bar and the girls. He softened his voice and stepped in. "I know it will be your first, and I told O'Reilly that. He's a good guy. His wife died several years back, and he needs a little companionship. He'll treat you right, and I'll expect you to treat him right in return." There was understanding in his eyes, but also a hardness that let her know there was no sense in arguing.

"Yes, Sir," Claire answered.

"Good." He smiled at her and walked away.

The rest of the evening was a blur caused by her nerves and fears. Later, she'd not remember what she sang or even have a clear picture of her partner's face.

The women at Jack's were a tight group, though, and as soon as they knew Claire was going upstairs, they stepped in to help and prepare her. Lela gave Claire some last minute advice and tips, then smiled. "You'll be fine. I know Mr. O'Reilly. He's very thoughtful. Don't worry."

That night, afterwards, the veteran, Mabel, pulled Claire aside.

"Here, take this and use it tonight before you go to bed."

"What is it?"

"Mix the powder with some very cold water and rinse yourself out well. It will keep you from getting pregnant."

The total confusion on Claire's face let the woman know that she needed to explain farther, so she put her arm around the girl's shoulder and ushered her into her own room. Claire was embarrassed, yet the woman's matter of fact attitude and directions helped her to hear Mabel's advice and coaching. After fully explaining how the douche needed to be used, she advised Claire to invest in a womb veil.

"I don't understand," was all Claire could whisper.

"I know, Darlin'" Mabel patiently answered. "A womb veil is a disk made of rubber that you put inside. It makes a barrier between your womb and the outside, and it will keep you from having a child. I use one, and I also use these powders I just gave you just to make sure."

"Where do I get one?"

"Well, since the Comstock Laws were enacted, birth control is illegal, but there are lots of places that you can order one from. Here's a catalog. Look in the back and you'll find a womb veil and some preventative powders. I'd suggest making sure that you order a veil made of Goodyear rubber. Those are the best from my experience."

Claire appreciated the care that Mabel took with her and the information. She ordered what she needed right away, and was relieved when her order arrived and she could begin using the products.

Life settled into a routine. Claire concentrated on how much she enjoyed singing, her growing bank account, and the comfort of her friends. She found that with practice and deliberate effort she could successfully navigate her way through her trips upstairs with customers by smiling and then thinking of other things. *It isn't really much different than what I did to survive Hiram's tirades,* she realized. *In many ways it is easier and most of the time it is much less painful.*

18
June, 1897
Rapid City, South Dakota

"Happy Birthday!" Lela smiled and held out a medium-sized round box tied with a bright pink cloth ribbon. "We know that your birthday isn't until Sunday, but since tonight is Friday night, we knew we'd all be here, so we decided to celebrate your birthday early!"

Estelle, Mabel, and Lois stepped into Claire's room behind her. "Open it," prompted Estelle with excitement. "We all pitched in on it."

Claire held the package in her hands and looked around her. The women settled themselves on the bed and floor of her room, smiling and bantering with one another. Claire felt, for the first time in her life, as if she truly belonged.

She untied the ribbon carefully then held it up, "This will look so pretty in my hair. It will match my pink and red dress."

She removed the lid from the box. A small hat lay on tissue paper. The deep green taffeta spoon hat was decorated with paler green silk leaves and crushed black and grey ribbons surrounding a yellow daisy of silk. The daisy reminded Claire of the daisy pin, now tucked safely in her bottom drawer, which her mother gave her on her sixteenth birthday such a lifetime ago. Tears suddenly filled her eyes.

"Thank you so much," she said as she ran her fingers over the shiny fabric and delicate flowers.

"Put it on!" the girls prompted. Claire blinked twice and recovered her smile. She lifted the bonnet out of the box and sat it on her head at a playful angle, then wrapped the ribbon under her chin. She tied it on the side of her face near her ear.

"What do you think?"

The room was filled with delight and compliments. They chatted amiably for several minutes, then Mabel, stood up and smoothed her dress. "Well, ladies, it is nearly time to go to work."

There were a few groans and sighs, but soon everyone was up, smoothing skirts, adjusting bosoms and checking hair in Claire's mirror. "I need to finish dressing," said Claire. "I'll be down in a minute."

She shut her door and leaned against it for a minute. Claire allowed herself a moment of missing her Mama as she looked around her room. The window let in the last of the sunset in front of her. Along the left wall of her cocoon were pegs on which her dresses and hats hung. Claire smiled at the pretty wardrobe, a rainbow of colors bringing cheer to the drab tan walls. She admired the many nice 'work dresses' that occupied the first pegs but her favorites were the two on the end. They were dresses she rarely wore, but that were suitable for a real lady.

She could hear the piano playing downstairs and knew she needed to go. She sat on the bed and quickly pulled on her stockings and shoes then took a final, quick check in the mirror. She smiled at the woman looking back at her. Many nineteen year olds back home were married with one or two children. Claire smiled at herself, thankful that she wasn't in that trap, and then turned and flounced downstairs.

The bar was surprisingly full even though it was early. Claire came down the stairs and began talking with two men sitting at the bar. They were regulars, farmers from nearby. She asked about their crops and cows, then listened. Over the months, she'd learned that more than anything else, most of the men in the bar were lonely and just wanted someone to listen to them.

A rowdy group came in the door a few minutes later. They sat at a table near the back by the piano. Mabel moved towards them, greeting and smiling. Claire watched for a minute. Judging from their clothes, they were miners. Soon, another group came in and Claire turned her attention to them. These were cowboys, dusty and rough. All four of them had jangling spurs on their well-worn boots. They found a table on the side. Claire walked over and asked what they were drinking. A minute later she was at the bar, filling a tray with steins of beer for them when Lela came to stand beside her.

"I need two whiskeys, Jack," she called. To Claire she said, "This could be a wild night. That group near the front looks like they could be trouble. Lois and Estelle are sitting with them. They seem like they are ready to blow off some steam. I hope we don't have a fight tonight."

"I agree, they do look pretty rough. Good luck to us all!"

They parted, each carrying drinks and wearing smiles.

The miners near the piano quieted down as Claire began singing. She started with "Maggie Murphey's Home" by William A. Pond. The crowd clapped along with her as she worked her way through five songs, ending with "Tra-La-La-Boom-De-A". As she sang, she noticed the men around her. Two of the miners looked familiar, though she couldn't place from where. One was tall and built stoutly. Mable, sitting on his lap, looked small in comparison. He was drinking fast and talking faster. The other man sat with half a drink in front of him. Though he was smiling and taking part in their discussions he somehow seemed removed from them a bit. It wasn't until her second set, when he looked up at her with intense blue eyes that she realized she had seen him at the hardware store last fall.

The night drew on. It was warm in the bar, all the doors and windows were open to let in the night air. Claire sat with three men at a side table, business men travelling north. All three had been in the bar about an hour. They were dressed in expensive trousers and jackets. After a couple of drinks, one loosened his tie, the other two doffed their jackets and hung them over the backs of their chairs. She got them all a fresh round of drinks, then sat down.

"I'm glad that McKinley won the presidency and has taken over. With a Republican president and majority in the Senate, he should be able to get a lot done. I'm worried what would happen if William Jennings Bryan got his way and took us off the gold standard."

"I agree," answered the man across the table from him. "Bryan's idea of bimetallism and including silver with gold to back our money system doesn't make sense to me, especially for foreign trade."

The third man added, "McKinley suggested some good changes to Congress that helped the country begin recovering from the Panic of '93. That's what made me like him from the start."

A loud voice interrupted their conversation. "You Republicans are ruining this country!"

Claire and her three tablemates looked up to see one of the cowboys standing behind them. As he continued, two of his buddies joined him.

"William Jennings Bryan should have won that last election. He has the working stiff in his mind, not the rich easterners like McKinley!"

Claire got up smiling. She moved closer to the loud cowboy, trying to deflect his anger. Big Jack talked with all the girls often about how their intervention could quickly defuse a fighting drunk if they caught it quickly.

This time, it didn't work. The cowboy looked at her with disgust. "You were sitting with these guys, you must be a Republican whore!" He pushed her.

Claire wasn't expecting the power he used and she tumbled into a table. Drinks sloshed then crashed to the floor. Claire, unable to get her feet under her, twisted and tried to grab the side of it, but the table tipped and fell over, taking her to the floor with it. Above her, fists were flying. The businessmen, unused to needing their fists to solve conflicts, were easy targets for the cowboys, but others quickly jumped in. Claire rolled over onto her hands and knees, keeping her head down, and trying to unwrap her skirt from her legs so she could stand and get out of the fray when the cowboy who'd pushed her took a roundhouse punch. His spur caught her hand as he fell backwards over her, slamming into the table and knocking her flat.

The fight didn't last long. Big Jack and Tucker started grabbing the cowboys, pulling them apart and throwing them out the door. Others separated the last of the combatants and calmed them down.

Claire's head hurt and her dress was dirty and torn. By the time she was back on her hands and knees trying to get up, hands were on her shoulders helping her.

She stood up finally, meeting blue eyes.

"Are you alright?" he asked, concern on his face.

She smiled, "Yes, I think so." She pushed her hair from her face and took a breath.

"You're bleeding," he said, taking a blue bandana handkerchief from his pocket.

She smiled again and pressed the cloth against her hand. "It doesn't look too bad," she answered. Then, Lela was beside her, joined quickly by Big Jack.

"You ok, Scrawny?" he asked.

"I think so," she answered. "I just need to clean up a little."

Jack thanked the miner for his help, then started righting tables and chairs. He motioned to Tucker, who headed back to the piano. The miner backed up as Lela guided Claire to the kitchen. She pulled out a chair for Claire, then hesitated. "I better get back out there," she said. Claire nodded as Lela turned to go. Within minutes, sounds from the bar indicated that things were back to normal, minus the rowdy cowboys. Everyone was settling in. Claire could hear the din of voices and piano through the kitchen door.

Myra reached for a metal box in the pantry. "An old friend gave me this kit a while back," she explained as she opened it. "It is from a company called Johnson and Johnson. They make first aid kits for the railroads, and the old railroader got me one after he was involved in a bar fight here." She chuckled at the recollection. She pulled out some gauze and tape and wrapped Claire's hand. The cut was about two inches long, and not seriously deep.

She flexed her hand. "Thank you," Claire said as Myra finished. Claire looked at the bandana lying in her lap. She rose slowly and made her way back out into the barroom. The room was considerably less crowded. The table where the blue-eyed minor sat was empty. Lela walked by with a tray of dirty glasses.

"They left a few minutes ago," she smiled and winked. "He was very handsome." She grinned again as she passed Claire.

Jack was behind the bar. When he saw Claire, he came over. "You sure you are alright?"

"I'm fine, just a bit shaken up."

"We're doing fine here. Go ahead and call it a night." Claire nodded her thanks and turned towards the kitchen. "Hey, you did a good job of trying to stop that. Those cowboys were looking for trouble."

"Thanks, Jack," Claire responded.

Back in her room, Claire slipped off her dress, then inspected it. She had a small rip by the hem that she knew she could fix so it wouldn't show. She laid the dress aside, resolving to mend it on Sunday. Then, she poured some water into a basin from the pitcher she'd brought up with her. She washed her face and neck, enjoying the freshness of the water against her skin.

A few minutes later, cool in her plain cotton nightdress, she pulled the covers back on her bed. She noticed the bandana on the floor and picked it up, picturing the kind and caring face of the minor who helped her.

***

"Good morning, Miss Atley." The bank teller was always polite, but his stiff, terse tone let her know that while he was happy to take her money, he didn't approve of her. Claire was used to it. She heard the same tone from most of the ladies in the mercantile. They happily rang up sales and ordered dresses or hats for her and the rest of the girls, but they were never over-friendly.

Lela and Estelle laughed at them and wore their work dresses when they went shopping or were out in town. Claire tried to fit in. She didn't want to be hypocritical, but she didn't want to antagonize anyone. Today she wore a high-necked white blouse trimmed with rows of lace down the front with a short black open jacket. The wide black belt over a plain grey skirt accented her small waist. If the people in town did not already know where she worked, they would have smiled and nodded to her, but knowing she lived and worked at Jack's Place made them look away instead.

Claire smiled at the balance in her passbook when the teller handed it back to her. She had no idea what she wanted to do with the money, but every week she added to the total and felt a little more confident that she was on the right track. She thanked him and turned to go, nearly bumping into the customer standing next in line.

"Oh, I am so sorry!" she began, then looked up.

They both stood for a moment, surprised. When he spoke, it was with a deep, quiet voice, "How are you this morning? How is your hand?"

"It is fine," she said, looking down at the bandage. "No problem."

"Next," called the teller.

He hesitated, then said, "This will only take a minute. May I buy you a cup of coffee at the café?"

"Well, yes, well, I'd like that."

"I'll meet you outside." He waited for her nod, then turned to the teller.

Claire walked slowly out of the bank and stood in the sunshine on the boardwalk. She couldn't deny that she was attracted to the man, but she also knew that very few men were interested in a serious romance with a saloon girl. Claire heard Lela's voice in her head, "The only reason a man tries to see a working girl outside of work is to try to get it for free." Claire tried to still her thoughts and quiet the voice by looking around. It was a beautiful morning, the sky was clear and deep blue over head with only a smattering of clouds floating by. The street was busy with horses and people. A team of four large draft horses pulling a freight wagon full of supplies lumbered by. Then, a man on a bicycle zipped past. The Pennington Bank Building behind her was one of the newest and finest buildings on the block. Across the street was Jack's Place. Tucker was sweeping the boardwalk out front. Her eyes moved farther down the street where she could see a large watering trough for thirsty teams of horses to stop and rest. Claire concentrated on the hustle and bustle, trying to quiet the butterflies she was feeling, when she felt a gentle hand on her arm.

"Thank you for waiting."

"It's such a pretty morning," Claire answered shyly. "I'm enjoying this summer sunshine."

"I don't see a lot of sunshine," he admitted, "I spend a lot of time underground." They began walking toward the City Café around the corner in the next block. He released her arm, but walked closely. Claire sought frantically for something to say. Finally she offered, "Is it scary, being down in a mine, knowing you have tons of rocks and earth above you that could cave in?"

"Oh, I guess it was at first, but you get used to it." He smiled, "Is it scary putting up with drunk cowboys and miners?"

They both chuckled.

They crossed the street and walked about a half block when he touched her arm again and stopped to face her. "I don't know where my manners are. My name is Daniel Haynes." He held out his hand. She took it and answered, "I'm Claire Atley. It is nice to meet you."

"I am pleased to meet you, Miss Atley. I felt terrible last night when we left before I knew you were fine."

"No harm done. The cook helped me with this bandage, a bit

overdone actually."

They entered the café and found a small table on one side.

Conversation lulled as the waitress greeted them and then quickly brought them each a cup of steaming coffee. As Claire stirred sugar into the brew, Daniel began the conversation anew.

"Are you from Rapid City, Miss Atley?" She appreciated his formal tone.

"No, I was raised on a farm in southeastern South Dakota. I've been here for a little over a year. How about you? Where are you from?"

Daniel took a sip from his coffee then answered, "I was raised in Iowa in a little town just west of Des Moines called Adel."

Claire sipped her coffee and met his eyes. Encouraged, he continued. "My dad is a farmer there. Some boys go fishing with their dads on Sunday afternoons," his voice held a warm chuckle. "My dad and I used to go out to the Raccoon River and pan for gold."

"Gold panning in Iowa? I thought that was only for California and here in South Dakota."

"There isn't much there, and what is there is called flour gold. The flecks are so fine they are nearly powder. Some people think that the gold comes from deposits in Canada, so by the time it makes its way all the way to Iowa it is finely ground."

"Did you ever find any?"

"Gold? Not much. I think Dad has all we ever found in a small glass jar in his desk."

"It sounds like you are close to your father. How about the rest of your family?" Claire realized that she wouldn't mind sitting here all day listening to Daniel talk. He had an easy, comfortable manner. *Don't let your heart get involved,* she told herself.

"We are a close family. My mother is a terrific cook and a seamstress – she makes clothes and quilts. I have two older sisters. Both are married. One, Addie has two boys and lives in Denver. Her husband is a banker. Then there's Irene. She is married to a farmer outside of Adel and has a baby on the way. What about you?"

"Mama passed away last fall."

"Miss Atley, I'm sorry."

Claire smiled weakly and continued, "I have two brothers who are still in South Dakota." Claire concentrated on keeping her voice steady and tried to steer the conversation away from her. "How did you end up here?"

Daniel chuckled again. "My grandfather Haynes was as English gentleman. I never met him, but he left me some money for my education. I'm sure it was because of the gold fever my dad and I shared, but when it came time to go to college, I decided to pursue mining. I made it into the Colorado School of Mines, graduated in '93 and got a mine engineering job in Cripple Creek."

"Is that in Colorado?"

"Yes, Cripple Creek is a mountain town, rough and even wilder than Rapid City. It sits pretty near Denver, but high up in the mountains near Pike's Peak."

Daniel noticed that Claire's cup was empty. He motioned to the waitress and she came over. "Can I get you anything else besides coffee?" she asked as she refilled their cups.

Daniel looked at Claire. "Are you hungry?"

"I ate breakfast at, um, I have already eaten, thanks, but if you are hungry go ahead."

He looked at the waitress and smiled, "I'm fine with just coffee." She nodded and walked to the next table.

They sat in silence for a minute, then Daniel said, "I've been talking about me this whole time. Where did you learn to sing? Have you taken formal voice lessons?"

Claire stammered, suddenly uncomfortable. "I haven't had any voice training, but thank you for saying that. I haven't been to school at all. I worked for a family one summer who liked to sing sitting on the porch after supper, and I learned some songs from them."

"I really enjoyed listening to you last night."

Claire searched Daniel's face. She expected to see insincerity somehow revealed in his look, but all she could discern was kind openness.

The café door opened, and one of the men who'd been sitting at Daniel's table last night entered. Claire watched as he looked around, then started towards them.

"I should have known you'd be here with a cup of coffee and a skirt," he teased. He tipped his hat and winked at Claire then turned to Daniel. "Gray is ready to head out, he's looking for ya'."

Claire could see a muscle in Daniel's jaw tighten. He responded quietly, "I'll be right out."

The man grinned and walked away. Claire smoothed her skirt and returned her napkin to the table. When she looked up, Daniel was studying her.

"I apologize for Harley's rudeness, Miss Atley," he began. "I'm sorry also that I need to go. I have enjoyed talking with you." He reached into his pocket, then placed some change on the table.

Claire fidgeted. The moment of comfort and ease was gone. "Thank you, Mr. Haynes, for the coffee and the company. I liked talking to you, too."

She stood, and he turned quickly to slide her chair for her. They zig-zagged through the tables and were soon on the boardwalk outside the café. Daniel turned to her. "I won't be back into Rapid City for at least a month. I hope maybe I can see you then." It was a sentence with a hint of question in it.

"I'm at Jack's Place six nights a week," Claire replied weakly.

He studied her face for a moment, tipped his hat and smiled, then strode off. Claire watched until he rounded the corner and was gone. She stayed rooted to the boardwalk. *Don't start,* she told herself. *He was being kind. You are not anything but a diversion to a college-educated man like that.* Claire took a deep breath and squared her shoulders, willing herself to put him out of her mind. She headed towards the mercantile to complete the errands she'd planned for the morning.

19
August, 1897
Rapid City, South Dakota

Sharp flashes of lightning followed quickly by loud, pounding thunder brought Claire out of a sound sleep. At first, she lay, unsure of what awakened her. Then, her room was suddenly lit by another nearby bolt and a second jolting boom. She arose and stood at her window. The light show continued and rain began to drum on the roof above her. The storm was strong and vibrant in its violence, and its free fury excited her. The beating of the rain turned louder, and Claire could see white hail jumping on the ground below each time the lightning illuminated the town. Her window was open only a few inches, but the air that blew into the room was chilly, a blessed relief from the summer heat. She pushed the curtains open then climbed back into her bed, leaning against the wall so that she could continue to watch the storm.

Her thoughts turned to the letter she'd received from Haddie. Thankfully, everyone was well. Haddie's letter was filled with news of the children's antics and the funny things they'd done through the summer. Claire was relieved to hear that Jesse was happy and well. Marcus though, Haddie wrote, was not as satisfied with life at their home.

For quite some time, Marcus has been restless. He has worked hard for William, and is always kind to the children and helpful with me, but he just isn't settled here, so it was no surprise when he asked to speak with William and me after dinner last week. He has been considering joining the Army. He's heard that President McKinley is worried about how small our army is, and Marcus is considering joining up. He wanted William's opinion. He says he hasn't made any decisions yet, but I think by next summer, we will be seeing him go.

Claire was thankful that Marcus had William's wise advice. She tried picturing her gentle brother as a soldier, and knew that the strength he had from growing up on their farm would serve him well. Lightning stabbed the darkness of her room again and Claire jumped. It took longer for the thunder to crash, though, so she knew the storm was moving off. Claire thought again of Haddie. She treasured the letters that she received, and sometimes ached to see her friend. At the same time, she knew that she'd built a terrible wall between them, one that Haddie had no idea was there. *Each time I sit down to write to her, I think that I will tell her about working at Jack's, but I can't. I haven't exactly lied, I just haven't told her the truth. I've told her about the money I am putting away, but not how I've earned it, I just can't face losing her friendship and I know she just wouldn't want to have anything to do with a 'strumpet'.*

Claire shifted, putting her head back down on her pillow and pulling up the quilt. The storm was in the distance now, and in the new coolness in her room, she slept.

***

Each day, the girls in the house rotated chores, helping Myra in the kitchen or joining with a crew to do laundry and cleaning. Saturday was Claire's kitchen day and she was peeling potatoes for Myra. Estelle sat beside her on the back porch. Both held pans of peelings on their laps and paring knives in their hands, working quickly and enjoying the sunshine. They'd been chatting and laughing together when they heard Lela's voice in the kitchen behind them.

"She's on the back porch," Myra answered.

The screen door squeaked as it opened. "Oh, there you are." Lela greeted them. The girls turned to say hello. "Claire, I have something for you." Her voice was a teasing sing-song.

"What?"

Lela held out an envelope accompanied by a small nosegay of wild flowers.

Claire looked at the surprise and sighed. Estelle giggled and commented, "Another love note? Is that the third one, or the fourth?"

The girls continued their kind ribbing as Estelle and Claire scooted apart to make room for Lela on the steps. Claire took the flowers and card.

Claire looked at the little bouquet, carefully constructed with the stems wrapped in a small blue doily and tied with a blue ribbon.

"Those are really pretty," breathed Estelle, a bit jealous.

"Open the card!" Lela encouraged again. "What does it say this time?"

Claire shrugged again. She'd received three other notes from Daniel Haynes in the past two months. They each had been kind notes saying that he was working and not able to come to town, but that he was thinking of her.

They giggled together as Claire carefully opened the envelope and retrieved a small note. The handwriting was exacting and flowing.

I have thought about you every day. May I take you on a carriage drive on Sunday afternoon? I am finally in town and staying at the Harney Hotel.
Warmly, Daniel Haynes

Claire was stunned. Estelle voiced what Claire was thinking, "Maybe he is just a nice guy who wants to get to know you."

Lela's laugh was harsh. "Estelle, what are you thinking? What would a respectable man do with one of us? He just wants a romp in the hills for free."

"He just seems so nice," argued Estelle. "He's acting like my brother-in-law back home acted when he was courting my sister." Claire put up her hand to quiet them. Claire's mind was blank for a few seconds as she read his invitation twice more. Lela and Estelle were silent for a few seconds.

What if Estelle is right? She asked herself. She raised the flowers to her nose and breathed their gentle scent. *Be realistic, Claire, no educated man wants you for anything but temporary companionship.*

"I think you should at least give him the benefit of the doubt and accept," Estelle added quietly.

"No, I can't," Claire began.

"Why not?"

"Estelle, look at me. I am a prostitute! I sing in a bar. I serve drinks and kisses and much more to men I don't know - for money!"

"What does that have to do with anything?" Estelle asked.

"He's educated. He's a gentleman. He can't want me!"

"Now you are thinking clearly," encouraged Lela. "We've seen this happen more than once, Estelle. Some sweet-talking man comes in and fills one of us with hope then disappears."

"But clearly, he is interested." Estelle pointed to the letter.

Claire looked down again at the paper in her hand. "He just wants to hire me for the day."

Estelle let out an exasperated breath. "Claire, if he wanted to 'hire you' he'd be sending money to Big Jack, not flowers to you! Wake up, Girl, he is asking you to spend the afternoon with him, not service him!"

Claire shook her head. She'd spent a month carefully convincing herself that he had just been kind when he bought her coffee and that Lela was right about the notes. "I'd love to believe that a man could be interested in me under these circumstances, for something other than his urges, but I know too much about men. They satisfy themselves with women like us, then go home and father children and pay for china and build homes with delicate, pure girls that they consider possessions. I have no intention to allow a man like that to play with my heart and emotions. He knows what I am, he'll never see me as anything else."

Claire handed the bowl of peelings and paring knife to Lela and stood up. "If you'll help Estelle finish here, I will go put an end to this."

Safely back in her room, Claire held the flowers once more to her nose and wished it were real. Then she dropped the nosegay in the trash basket and sat down.

Dear Mr. Haynes,

Thank you for your invitation and your recent notes, however, I will not be available this Sunday, or any Sunday, to take a drive with you. Please do not contact me again.

Claire Atley

Before long, Claire handed the envelope to one of the young boys who helped Tucker clean the saloon. "Johnny, I've got a nickel for you if you'll deliver this note to the Harney Hotel for me."

"Sure, Miss Claire, I'd be happy to," he responded. She smiled and turned around. *There, that's the end of that,* Claire thought as she headed back to the kitchen.

***

A few hours later, Claire made her way downstairs, surveying the crowd of men at the bar as she descended. The saloon wasn't very full yet, but she knew it would be crowded before long. Summer Saturday nights were usually rowdy and loud.

She was barely in the room when she heard Jack call her. Claire approached her boss at the bar, "Yes, Jack?"

"There's a gentleman in room three upstairs waiting on you."

"Now?" Usually Jack waited until after her second set of songs before sending her to work upstairs.

"Yeah, he was insistent that it was you and now. I told him that would cost him extra and he didn't hesitate. Get on upstairs," he finished with a shrug of apology and a crooked smile that said 'Business is business.'

Claire shook her head and climbed the stairs. Outside room three, she smoothed her dress and hair, then knocked quietly and entered the room.

Room three was directly over the bar on the east side of the building. It was sparsely furnished with a brass bed left of the door, its headboard against the hall wall. A kerosene lamp gave off a weak, flickering glow from a small round table flanked by a straight-backed wooden chair in the right corner. A window, framed and covered by red velvet curtains, was directly opposite. Her client held the curtain to the side, while looking out the window.

"Good evening, how are you?" Claire made sure her voice was light and happy even though she was not pleased that she had to be there. Not waiting for a reply, she turned toward the bed and reached over to turn down the spread. Big Jack insisted that the bed be made after each use, explaining that turning down the bed each time adds to "arousing the passions" of the customer.

"Miss Atley."

Claire froze. She knew the voice, and in that split second she knew that while she'd tried to convince herself that Lela was right, she had truly harbored the hope that she wasn't. Now, she had no hope left.

Forcing her best smile, Claire turned to Mr. Haynes. *No, he's just a client!* She unbuttoned the top button of her dress.

"Stop," he said.

"Okay," she answered coyly, "if you'd rather do it."

"No, wait." He crossed the room and stood in front of her.

"I don't want you," he began. Then, he grimaced and put his head down. "That didn't come out right."

He gestured toward the chair. "Would you please just sit down and talk with me?"

His request put her off balance. Claire didn't understand his discomfort or his desires. She hesitated and he added, "Please?"

She crossed the small room and sat down. He paced the room twice, then turned to her. He ran his fingers through his hair and took a deep breath.

"This was the only way I could think of to get you alone to talk to me after I got your note this afternoon. Miss Atley, I am interested in you, and I'd like to see you and get to know you. That morning we met at the bank and had coffee together has stuck in my mind for the past two months."

"Mr. Haynes, I am happy to just talk if that is what you want, but please be aware that Big Jack expects me to be downstairs in half an hour to sing, so if talking is what you need to get started, then we need to hurry it along." She tried to make her voice even and business-like.

"You have misunderstood me. Maybe this was a terrible idea." He paced the room again. "I am trying to tell you that I don't want to hire your services, I want to court you."

She stood. Claire fought a raging battle with herself. She wanted him to be sincere. The naïve girl in her wanted a happy ending and a knight in shining armor. Experience and sound logic wouldn't let her cling to hope, though. She was instantly angry to be in this situation.

"Mr. Haynes, you seem like a nice man. You seem gentlemanly, successful and you have a good job. I am certain that when you decide to settle down and start a family, it will not be with a dance hall girl. You can't possibly think that I believe you'd be willing to introduce a soiled dove to your family for example, or that polite society will welcome one. Therefore, courting is a waste of time. I'm not sure what you are playing at but I want no part of it."

The expression on his face stopped her. It was a mix of grief and desperation.

"The lady I take home to meet my family will be accepted no matter who she was or is, just because I care for her." His voice was quiet and calm. "My family and society are important to me, that is true, however, they are not the first consideration right now. You are. I am not asking you to marry me, though I wouldn't rule that out. All I am asking is for a beautiful woman to take a drive in the country with a man who is interested in her."

He stood firm, searching her face. He locked his eyes on hers and continued, "I promise to treat you as a lady. Please, I just want to get to know you."

She hesitated. Her anger dissipated and was replaced by a cautious hope. She took a deep breath and allowed her pulse to return to normal. "No matter how lady-like you treat me and how genteel this Sunday drive is, I am still a working girl. You can't change that."

"I know. I also know that there is a lot about me that you don't yet know and that might just horrify you. We all have a past, Miss Atley and we all make choices that we have to live with. I'm in no position to judge anyone, and for sure not you."

He grinned at her then, boyish and jovial. "Can I pick you up at eleven tomorrow morning? Please?"

"This could be against my better judgment," she smiled back. "But yes, you may."

20
August, 1897
Rapid City, South Dakota

"You are not serious!" Lela shook her head but also smiled.

Estelle playfully pushed Lela's shoulder as they sat together on Claire's bed the next morning. "He sounds really sweet and honest."

Claire held up a blue dress, one of her conservative frocks. She'd just told her friends about the scene in room three. Estelle was sighing, letting her romantic nature effuse the room with hope. *Even Lela,* thought Claire, *is hoping for the best for me today.*

"I like that one," Lela pointed at a hunter green dress hanging on the last peg. "You could wear the hat we gave you for your birthday with that one."

Claire reached for the dress and held it up. This was her favorite. It was very simple. Its only decoration was black piping at the edge of the bodice front. It made her feel pretty.

"I think you are right," she agreed and slipped the dress on over her petticoat.

Lela helped with her hair and then both girls watched Claire tie on her hat.

"I hope you have a nice day, truly." Lela hugged Claire then held her by the shoulders. "Just be careful. Take care of yourself."

"Oh, Mom," teased Estelle as she took her turn and hugged Claire.

"Don't worry, I will," Claire answered. The girls watched her walk down the stairs and out the front door.

Daniel was waiting for her when she exited the small alley beside the bar. He was leaning against the hitching rail, when he saw her. He straightened up and came to meet her.

"Have you been waiting long? Am I late?"

"No, I was early," he admitted. His chuckle lightened her nerves. He guided her to a black Columbus Phaeton carriage then helped her up. As he turned to check the harnesses she rubbed her hand over the soft, deep red velvet upholstery and looked at the fringed canopy overhead. Claire was impressed, she'd never ridden in a phaeton.

"This is a beautiful carriage," she remarked when he joined her in the seat and had the horse moving down the street.

"I agree. It was a surprise that the livery had this and allowed me to rent it for the day," he smiled.

The day was clear and bright, the light breeze kept them cool as they travelled east out of town toward the foothills. Their first attempts at conversation were stilted and stiff. Then, Daniel began to talk about working at the Galena Mine. He told Claire about a small cave in.

"This happened just last week?"

"Yup. I'd been down in that room earlier in the day, and told the foreman to shore up one of the vault ceilings. I told him I didn't like how much crumbling there was. He's an older guy, been around mines for lots of years. He's made it clear that he doesn't like taking orders from me."

"Why not?"

"I'm young and he thinks he knows it all because he's spent more time underground than I've been alive." Claire enjoyed Daniel's chuckle and his humble way.

"What happened?"

"The shift was changing and the rest of the men were climbing ladders to the next level up. Chuck, the old guy, and I were the only ones left down in that vault. I heard a pop and a part of the ceiling started sloughing off. We ran for the closest overhang and waited it out."

Claire gasped and shivered. The idea of being hundreds of feet under the ground was terrifying to her. Hearing about the ceiling breaking off and falling in made her heart race.

Daniel smiled at her reaction and went on. "The dust settled in just a minute or so, and when I flashed the light on the tunnel leading out, it wasn't there. That's when the fun started."

"What do you mean? It sounds horrid."

"I've studied the rock formations in that entire shaft. There wasn't any rumbling that would have signaled a large cave in. Everything told me that this was just a minor pile up of rocks by the entrance, I knew it wasn't deep and that all the slag in front of the exit tunnel was small. I knew we were going to get out without much trouble, but old Chuck, he panicked."

"But I thought he had a lot of experience. Didn't he see and hear the same things that you did?"

"You know, being underground can do strange things to a man. Cave-ins are scary, and they can mean instant death or long, agonizing days in pitch dark waiting for someone to get to you. You never know how one will affect you. Just now I made it sound like it didn't bother me, and that isn't true. My heart was pounding and I had to fight my fear. But they trained me in school to make my mind be in charge, so I was fine. Next time it could be different. This time, though, for whatever reason, Chuck's fear overtook him for a bit. He was crying and screaming and throwing rocks to reopen the tunnel."

"What did you do?"

"I just stayed out of his way for a few minutes while he spent himself. Pretty soon, he calmed down some, and I got in beside him and started helping clear the way. It wasn't fifteen minutes before we felt the air of the tunnel coming in around the rocks and we knew we were nearly out."

"Were there men working on the other side?"

"No, they'd already cleared the ladders. It was such a small slide that they didn't hear it from above."

"You could have been down there a long time and no one was coming to help?" Claire shivered again.

"They would have figured it out when we didn't come up in another thirty minutes or so, but we were on the top by then."

"So, how is Chuck?"

Daniel smiled again. "That's the best part of this story. When we got to the top, we were both covered in mine dust, and the men could see the tracks of Chuck's tears on his face. One of the other guys made some remark at Chuck about it. Chuck sort of stammered a bit and I just answered that it was hot, sweaty work getting us out and that Chuck had led the way. The guys all nodded and let it go. As we left the mine, Chuck shook my hand and thanked me."

"I'll bet he won't give you a hard time anymore."

"Well, the next day, he was his normal, wise-cracking self, but he made sure that his crew shored up that ceiling like I'd asked him to."

They rode along in comfortable silence for a few minutes.

"Have you ever been to Canyon Lake before?" he asked. They had entered a thick stand of evergreen trees at the base of the foothills. At the next bend, they could see a calm lake surrounded by trees.

Daniel stopped the phaeton and climbed down. Claire drank in the rich greens of the trees and foliage mirrored in the silvery glass of the lake. No one was in sight, and the peace of the place permeated her thoughts.

***

"I miss you," whined Lela, only half kidding. "We used to have such fun on our days off, and now you are gone every Sunday with *him*." She emphasized 'him' and scowled.

Claire turned from the mirror and looked at her friend. Lela was sprawled on the bed, looking at the latest Vogue magazine.

"I miss our Sundays, too," she started.

Lela looked up and laughed. "No you don't. And it is okay. I'd rather be with a handsome suitor myself."

Claire turned back to the mirror and began pinning her hair up into a loose bun. "We'll have lots of Sundays together soon, when the weather turns bad," she remarked.

"If you think a little snow is going to keep that man away from you, you should think again."

Claire finished with her hair and sat on the edge of the bed. "Lela, these past four weeks have been beautiful. Daniel is so polite and he treats me properly. For a few hours once a week, I forget about the bar and singing and, well, all the rest. Daniel has never broached the subject with me."

"You've stolen his heart and he doesn't want to let anything get in the way."

"I haven't stolen anything. This has to be a diversion for him, and that is all."

"It isn't just a diversion for you, though." Lela's words hung heavy in the air. She was right. Claire had worked really hard in the past month to remind herself that her relationship with Daniel was too good to be true. She'd concentrated on enjoying each day they were together without counting on the next one, but still, she knew that she wasn't succeeding in keeping her emotions in check.

Tears threatened as the two women sat together. Finally, Claire took a deep breath and reached for her hat. "Well, when this all comes to an end, I will still have you."

Lela reached for Claire's hand and squeezed it.

There was a knock on Claire's door. "Your beau is waiting out front," Ethel called, then giggled. All of Jack's girls knew about Daniel and teased Claire, though they were careful to keep the information from Big Jack. They all knew he wouldn't sanction a relationship with a customer.

"Thanks!" Claire called back. With one more squeeze from Lela, she headed for the door. "Don't forget your coat – it looks like it could be chilly today."

Daniel beamed when she rounded the corner and came into sight. Claire was amazed anew that she could have that effect on him.

"The phaeton wasn't available today," Daniel apologized. "This little buggy was all they had." The small gig had one bench seat perched between two wheels. One roan horse stood pawing the ground, waiting for them to get settled.

Claire heard disappointment in his voice and met his eyes. "It's alright. This will be fine."

"I'm afraid you'll get cold without a top to cover us. I did get an extra blanket for our laps." He took her hand and helped her into the carriage then searched the skies. "Those clouds could turn to snow this afternoon," he worried.

He made sure she was settled, then snapped the reins gently and made a clicking sound to get the roan started. "I thought maybe we could go back out to Canyon Lake today. We haven't been there since our first day together, and I thought being in the trees might make it a warmer day."

"That sounds lovely," Claire answered. She glanced at Daniel. His jaw was set and his smile was not as bright as usual.

They travelled out of Rapid City and took the fork toward the lake. "Daniel, you are very quiet. Is everything all right?"

He took her hand. "I'm fine. It has been a long week with long hours." He hesitated. "I have a lot of things on my mind."

"If you would rather not go today, I would understand."

Daniel twisted in the seat so he was facing her and held her hand a bit tighter. "There is nowhere else I ever want to be than with you." His eyes widened and he looked a bit surprised at his own words. He continued, "I'm just irritated that it is chilly today, and I want you to be comfortable."

They lapsed back into silence. Despite his words, Claire worried that Daniel was tiring of her. *If I were a real lady, he wouldn't have to take me to the country to spend the day with me.* She told herself that he had to be ashamed of her and their relationship.

When they arrived at the lake, Daniel helped her down, then picketed the horse. She walked to the lake's edge and stood, absorbing the beauty and peace. The lake sat tucked up into the base of the foothills, a little higher in altitude than the town. Fall had arrived here, bringing with it a splash of yellow and orange to the aspen trees to complement the deep greens of the lodge pole pines. Some of the grasses and short plants were already fading into brown. The water, though not as calm and glass-like as the first time she'd seen it, reflected the colors of the trees and the steel blue of the sky.

"I saw a picture of a painting by a man named Monet in a magazine," Claire said when Daniel joined her. "He uses vivid colors and paints landscapes in France. I wonder what he'd think if he saw this."

"It is beautiful," Daniel answered. "I have often thought it would be gratifying to be able to paint and share the beauty of the mountains."

He took her hand and they began walking. "Tell me about your week," Claire said quietly.

"It was just a week," began Daniel. On past Sundays, Daniel gave Claire detailed accounts of the workings of the mine. Today, he seemed to have little to say and little to tell. Claire's fears rose, and she became more and more convinced that Daniel was tiring of her and their outings. Again, they lapsed into silence. They walked for nearly a quarter hour without talking.

"Let's sit down and rest," Daniel offered finally, indicating a rocky ledge with a large boulder at the lake's edge.

Claire watched him as he stared out at the lake, the muscles in his jaw flexing. "Daniel, what is it?"

He turned to face her. "Claire, I live all week in anticipation of

Sunday. When something happens in the mine I think, "I can't wait to tell Claire about this." The days drag starting about Wednesday because it feels like forever before I can see you again."

"But you are unhappy today."

"Yes, I am a little. You see, I spend all day on Sunday talking. I've told you about my family, my schooling and about my job. I have such a wonderful time. But then, when I leave you on Sunday evening and make my way back up to the mine, and as I go through my week, I realize that we don't talk about you. I know nearly nothing about you. When I ask you a question - about how you grew up for example or how your week was, you deflect it and we end up talking about me."

Claire felt shaky inside. "But you are interesting, I'm not," she whispered.

He took her hand, rubbing the back of it with his finger. "You are interesting to me, but you won't let me in. I've been thinking about this all week. I am wondering why you don't talk about yourself."

Claire didn't know what to say.

Daniel let the silence stretch for a few seconds, then added, "Maybe you don't want to tell me because you aren't very interested in me."

Claire felt as if he'd slapped her. She tried to take a breath but it caught in her throat. Daniel looked up at her, and searched her face.

"Daniel, I work in a dance hall. I get paid to be nice to men, to drink with them and flirt with them. I entertain them by singing and," she hesitated then decided it had to be said. "And, I entertain strangers by having relations with them for money. We can't continue pretending that you are courting me and ignore what I am doing the other six days of the week!"

Daniel's smile was soft and a little sad. "Claire, have I not made it clear to you that I know what you do and I don't care? What you do isn't who you are." He chuckled. "You're right though, I don't really think I want to hear the details of your week with other men at the saloon, but I do want to know *you*. I want to know about your family and what brought you to Rapid City. I long to know your dreams and plans."

Claire looked down at their hands. His was tanned and

calloused. Hers small and pale. "What if you don't like what I have to tell you?"

Daniel stood up suddenly and paced a few steps out and back. He ran his hand through his hair and flexed his shoulders in a familiar gesture. Claire steeled herself for what she imagined was coming.

He stopped and faced her, then reached for her hand and pulled her up to stand facing him. "You are stubborn and maybe a bit dense, Miss Atley." He smiled at her confused expression.

"I am in love with you, completely and forever. There is nothing that you can say or do to change that fact. All I am asking is for you to let me in. Let me know all about you." He blew out a breath, relieved to have finally said it.

Claire blinked twice, absorbing his words. She'd been so sure he would finally reject her that she had trouble taking it in.

Daniel misread her hesitation. He ran his hand through his hair again and stared out at the lake. "Of course, if you don't feel the same as I do, I understand..."

"I love you." Her words were quiet but assured.

He stopped. Then he pulled her to him and held her.

Time started again, and he finally released her. "It's such a relief to finally be able to say it out loud." He grinned at her. "Maybe, just because I can, I will say it again. I love you."

Claire let the words seep into her.

"I want to know all about you, but I can tell there are things you don't want to talk about."

The fear returned again, a little less formidable. "What if you don't like what you hear?" she asked for a second time.

"I can't imagine you could tell me anything that would dim my feelings for you. If our love is to grow, you need to trust me."

Claire studied his face. "Trust is hard for me. I only know two men I have ever trusted."

"Tell me about them."

They sat back down on the boulder, and Claire talked with Daniel about Mr. Behl and how devoted he was to his family. Then she told him about William and Haddie. She described watching how William treated his children and wife, and how kind he was to her while she lived with them. Daniel listened silently and watched Claire's face light up as she described their home.

"It's the kind of home I would love to have. One where the

husband and wife are equal and respect one another. One where all the children are considered important and precious."

Daniel's shoulder was warm against hers, his hand covered her own. The warmth and steadiness encouraged her. "Claire, your description of their home sounds like the one I was raised in. But, it wasn't like yours, was it?" His voice held a mixture of sadness and understanding.

Claire took a breath. "No, not even close. My father valued his sons and his two brothers who lived with us. My mother and I, being female, were of little consequence. He believed himself well within his rights to treat us and control us in any way he wanted." She inhaled again, and then went on, describing in general terms how her father's anger was easily raised and the result.

"You never felt the desire to fight back?"

"It wasn't an option I thought existed. Looking back, I understand now that it wasn't just my father who believed that my mother and I were inferior and in need of 'guidance' as he'd sometimes call it. My mother allowed it and taught me to accept it because she believed it as well."

Claire was quiet for a while. The muted sounds of the chilly day filled the silence between them. By the time Daniel left Claire standing alone in the late afternoon gloom, watching him drive away, Daniel knew about Claire's family and most of the story of how she ended up in Rapid City. She left out mentioning her uncle and his advances. Trust was growing inside her even as the fears continued to gnaw.

21
Early November, 1897
Rapid City, South Dakota

Lela walked ahead of Claire and Estelle as they strolled down the busy boardwalk. It was nearly noon, and the girls were out for a walk. The day was beautiful for November. "The sky is so blue today," remarked Claire. "The sun isn't warm like summer, and the air has a bite to it, but it's a gentle day for November."

Estelle and Lela looked at each other and giggled.

"What?" asked Claire.

"Next you're going to start spouting poetry, that's all." Lela answered.

"The more time you spend with your Mr. Haynes, the more like a poet you sound!" added Estelle.

Their light-hearted teasing prompted Claire to giggle along with them. "I have changed, for certain, as a result of Mr. Haynes' attentions. Why, even what I read has changed. I used to love adventure stories like those of Jules Verne or Robert Louis Stevenson. Lately I've been reading romances. I've just finished *Pride and Prejudice*, and right now on my night stand is a collection of poems by Emily Dickinson."

"You make my case for me!" laughed Estelle.

Lela stopped suddenly and the girls renewed their laughter when Estelle ran into her.

"What are you doing?" Estelle teased. "You are causing a log jam on this thoroughfare!"

"I just wanted to stop and read this poster. I was hoping it was a travelling show coming to town, maybe a circus or a play."

They stood for a moment, reading the colorful broadside.

"Rats," remarked Lela. "It's only a stupid revival meeting coming this Sunday. Nothing fun."

"I went to a revival with my mother once," Estelle turned to her friends with her eyes wide. "I watched a man who couldn't see be cured by the preacher. I was pretty little, and that preacher scared the daylights out of me with all his yelling and shouting about the end of the world and how everyone was going to burn in hell. I had nightmares for weeks." She shuttered and resumed her walk down the street.

"It's going to be slow at Jack's for a week or two." Lela commented as she and Claire followed Lela. "Nothing like guilt to keep men out of a bar for a few days. The good thing is, it won't last. It never does."

"Have you ever gone to a revival?" Lela asked Claire.

"No, I'm not even sure what one is exactly. Are they like a church service?"

"More like a snake oil show," replied Estelle.

Lela frowned a bit at Estelle and then answered Claire, "There are revivals that are good. Famous preachers like Billy Sunday or Dwight Moody had revival meetings and talk to people about God and being saved."

Claire wanted to ask what that meant, but before she could speak Estelle jumped in. "Travelling tent revivals like this one are all the same. There's some good gospel music to get the crowd warmed up and then some man with a loud voice yells and screams about repentance. He scares people and tells them they have to come up and dedicate themselves to Almighty God. Then, they sell you a Bible, take down their tents and go on to the next town of suckers."

Lela's voice was quiet. "Don't you believe in God, Estelle?"

"I don't know about that at all. I just know I won't waste my Sunday on a spectacle."

"How about you, Claire, do you believe in God?" Lela was serious.

"My Mama used to quote the Bible saying it gave my father permission to treat us however he wanted and that our job was to honor him for it. If that's what God is all about, then I want nothing to do with him!"

***

149

Claire was awake early Sunday morning. Lela's prediction had come true, the saloon was nearly empty Saturday night and the men who were there were subdued. Jack sent over half of the girls, Claire included, to their own beds early. For once, Claire wasn't tired on Sunday morning. Instead she was up early, humming a quiet tune. She treated herself to a hot bath and spent extra time on her hair. Instead of putting her hair up, then adding a hat, Claire decided to try the grey snood she had purchased at the mercantile. It took her a few minutes to get her long hair to behave inside the mesh bag of the snood, but she finally was satisfied. Adding two extra hairpins to hold it securely in place, she stepped back to survey the look. It matched her grey frock perfectly. Standing before her in the mirror appeared a demure and classic figure full of respectability and refinement. "If only I really was," Claire whispered to the girl.

She had at least an hour before Daniel would arrive. Sometimes he came down from the mine on Saturday for supplies. Claire liked those times because they could have more time together on Sundays. Most of time, like today, she knew that he would travel both ways. That meant he would be in town sometime after 11 o'clock. Once when Daniel was having a beer at the saloon with several friends she heard them teasing him. "Haynes, I've never seen a guy work as hard for as many hours as you do. You put us all to shame."

Daniel's face reddened a bit as he answered, "I was hired to do a job, and I take that seriously."

Claire sat at her table and picked up the thin volume of Emily Dickenson poems that she'd checked out from the small library in town. She opened the book and re-read a poem she'd read several times.

> *"Hope" is the thing with feathers -*
> *That perches in the soul -*
> *And sings the tune without the words -*
> *And never stops - at all -*
>
> *And sweetest - in the Gale - is heard -*
> *And sore must be the storm -*
> *That could abash the little Bird*
> *That kept so many warm -*

I've heard it in the chillest land -
And on the strangest Sea -
Yet - never - in Extremity,
It asked a crumb - of me.

She read it twice, once silently and the second quietly aloud. She liked the poem. It described perfectly that small place inside her that allowed her to believe that Daniel really could love her and that the life she now led could change into something else, something better.

Time passed slowly, and Claire was looking out her window, drumming her fingers on the sill when a quiet knock and Ethel's voice let her know that Daniel had finally arrived.

She grabbed her bag and her woolen wrap and flew downstairs.

"Daniel, are you well, you look wrung out this morning." They stopped outside so that Claire could adjust her wrap, tightening it around her to fight the cold air. He had embraced her, chastely, and held her hands for a moment before leaving the parlor. She was concerned about the weariness in his eyes.

"I am fine, just tired. We've begun a deeper shaft in a new direction. I'm the engineer in charge of that shaft, and I've been worried about some of the shale I am seeing not being stable enough to hold up. Management isn't keen on the amount of bracing timbers I've ordered, so I've been in long discussions all week full of tension. Balancing the cost versus the safety of a project always makes for heated debates." He smiled. "Don't worry, I'm well."

She breathed a small sigh of relief, placated but not wholly convinced.

"It's too cold to spend the day outside today. Let's go to the café and have breakfast, and decide what to do that won't include freezing." Daniel put his hand at the small of her back to guide her. When they were alone at the lake or walking in the forest, they held hands, but in town, they knew it wasn't proper. Even so, Claire ached to slide her hand into his as they moved down the boardwalk.

The café was half filled. They were right between the morning breakfast rush and the after church lunch crowd. Claire ate two pancakes and some sausage, then sat back with a cup of tea to watch Daniel consume pancakes, eggs, bacon, and sausage.

"Have you eaten at all this week?" she teased.

"I left early this morning. Breakfast is my favorite meal of the day and it's been a long time since last night's dinner. I sure hope you can cook, I look forward to having you make pancakes for me every morning for the rest of our lives."

Claire was in the middle of a drink of tea as he spoke. She nearly choked as she forgot how to swallow in favor of listening to his words. She coughed and sputtered while Daniel grinned.

"Daniel, really!" was all she could say when she regained her breath.

"I know that we don't often talk about the future, Claire, but you have to know that I think of it all the time. Those thoughts get me through the day sometimes."

Claire was embarrassed and wasn't sure what to say. Daniel grinned again, then changed the subject. "Let's plan today. I have a meeting with the management at nine o'clock in the morning. With as cold as it is, I'll need to start back earlier than usual."

Claire's disappointment showed in her eyes and shoulders, but she kept her voice light and happy. "There isn't much indoors to do here. We could go back to the parlor and play checkers or Parcheesi. I'm sure the girls wouldn't mind having you there."

"It's too bad that there isn't a play or a travelling show in town today. You look too pretty not to show off in town."

"Thank you." Their eyes met and held.

"I saw some broadsides posted as I rode in to town, have you seen what they are advertising?"

"They are for a revival meeting today at one o'clock at the Baptist church."

"A revival meeting?" Daniel paused looking thoughtful, then continued. "We've never talked about your faith or mine. Do you believe in God?"

"I don't really know if there is a god or not, but if there is, I'm pretty sure I have no use for him. My father prayed over each meal we ate, thanking God for our blessings, but he certainly wasn't thankful to the hands that worked hard to make the meals. Mama had a Bible she could barely read that was her mother's. My brother sent it to me after Mama died, but I've never read it. I've looked at it a few times, but I have trouble with the language in it."

She stopped and dropped her eyes. "Mama always justified not standing up to my father's fists and mean words by saying that the Bible says that women are to submit to men. I just can't trust in a god that would not only allow that but dictate it."

Claire fidgeted with her tea cup, then her napkin. Finally she raised her gaze to Daniel's face. He was studying her.

"I grew up in a home that loves Jesus. My father is the head of his household, but that doesn't include treating my mother with anything but respect and love. We went to church every Sunday – but not out of obligation or to show off to the town like some folks do. My mother still sings in the choir, though her voice has become a bit tinny as she grows older. God was a real force in my life." He stopped to gauge how Claire was receiving his words, then continued. "When I was about twelve I received Jesus as my savior, but in the years since I went away to the Colorado School of Mines, I sort of dropped off and have not been to church or thought much about God."

"I don't know what that means," Claire said, then clarified, "I don't understand receiving Jesus as your Savior."

Daniel pulled his pocket watch from his vest. "I'll tell you what. It is a quarter to one. Let's walk down to the church and slip in the back. We'll listen for a while and you can see what it is all about. Maybe that will answer some of your questions."

Claire wasn't convinced. "Estelle says that revivals are like travelling medicine shows that sell lies and try to take your money."

"That's true of some," Daniel agreed. "If this is like that, we can leave anytime you want. I'll even encourage us to leave if what they are saying isn't true as I understand it. Many revivals, though, are set up and run by people with true faith who just want to share that with others."

Claire hesitated, but she knew that it was too cold to take a long walk, and the parlor at the house wasn't the best choice.

"Okay," she said at last. "As long as we spend the day together, I'll be happy."

Daniel left money to pay the tab on the table and helped Claire with her wrap. They silently walked toward the church, about three blocks away. About half a block away from the church entrance, Claire stopped.

"Will they let me in?" she asked.

"Why wouldn't they?" asked Daniel.

"You know. Jack's girls are not usually welcomed by polite society, I don't want to make a scene or embarrass you, or myself."

"You can never embarrass me," he said it simply and truthfully. "The Bible, and especially Jesus, had a lot to say about 'holier than thou hypocrites', and none of it was positive. Churches don't usually stop people at the door. If that actually happened, the seats would all be empty. I'll not promise that some old biddy won't look at you sideways, but I'll be beside you. I think you can stop worrying."

Daniel's words were confirmed when they approached the door. A gentleman stood at the threshold, shaking hands and welcoming everyone. His smile was warm and his handshake strong as he greeted the pair. Claire stopped for a moment while Daniel helped her remove her wrap. Then an usher showed them to seats about three-quarters of the way back on the left side aisle. The usher smiled at her as he turned around, giving Claire a bit more confidence.

The room seemed huge to her. It had high ceilings with exposed oak beams. There were six regular glass windows along each of the side walls. Between them on the walls were pictures. The closest one was of a man with longish hair wearing a long sheath and standing amidst some snowy white sheep. Daniel followed her gaze then whispered, "That's Jesus. The Bible calls Him the Great Shepherd because he cares for His people like a shepherd looks after his sheep."

Sounds of calm piano music began and she raised her gaze in search of its source. The breath caught in her throat as she took in the view of the rest of the room. Multi- colored light streamed in through a tall stained glass window above a weathered cross at the front. Claire had read about stained glass windows, but had never seen one. She'd read the word 'transfixed' in a book before as well, but until this moment she had never experienced the awe that would cause someone to not be able to look away. Fully lit by the afternoon sun, colors in the patterned glass seemed to dance from the window and to all parts of the room, casting an ethereal glow over the entire scene.

All the pews were full when a man in a dark blue suit stood up and walked to the center of raised dais.

"Welcome, Friends. God's blessings to you today. I'm the regular pastor of this little church, and my name is Mark Crosby.

Thank you for coming today. Let's pray."

The congregants all bowed their heads. Claire looked at Daniel. He sat with his head slightly bowed and his eyes closed. Claire mimicked him and listened to the man's words.

"Father God, we are all sinners and we all need You. Be in this house with us today. Touch our hearts and teach us Your lessons. Guide this service to be for your glory only, not man's. Amen.

When he finished, he sat down, replaced by a choir of four men and four women. They led the group in singing several songs. The first was familiar to Claire, and she hummed along quietly. She remembered how Haddie and William Foster sang *Amazing Grace* together that night so long ago when she lived with them.

When the choir finished, Pastor Crosby returned. He made several announcements about Bible study groups and a pot luck supper coming up, and invited everyone to attend.

"Now I'm going to ask Brother James and his wife Sister Mildred to come and bring us a song. Now this song is probably familiar to you, but do you know the story behind it? A man named Horatio Spafford lost every material possession he and his family owned in the Chicago fire. Then, he sent his wife and daughters to England to start a new life. Spafford himself had to stay behind to finish up some business. But, Folks, there was a collision at sea, and his beautiful daughters drowned, only his wife was rescued. Now you and I – we'd maybe get mad at God for the hard things He put us through. Maybe we'd turn bitter and reach for a bottle of whiskey or some other diversion to help ease our pain. That would be a pretty human thing to do. Not Horatio Spafford, though. Spafford loved the Lord and knew that He loved him back. Spafford trusted the Good Lord's plan for his life even though he didn't agree with it or understand it. In his grief, he got on another ocean liner and made the voyage to meet his bereft wife. When the ship passed the site of the collision – Yes, the very site of the death of his daughters - Horatio Spafford wrote a song. He wrote this song."

A middle aged couple rose and came forward. The piano began, and they sang. At first, the high bell-like soprano mixed with rich baritone impressed Claire, but soon she began to attend to the words they were singing as well.

When peace, like a river, attendeth my way,
When sorrows like sea billows roll;
Whatever my lot, Thou hast taught me to say,
It is well, it is well with my soul.
It is well with my soul,
It is well, it is well with my soul.

Though Satan should buffet, though trials should come,
Let this blest assurance control,
That Christ hath regarded my helpless estate,
And hath shed His own blood for my soul.
It is well with my soul,
It is well, it is well with my soul.

My sin—oh, the bliss of this glorious thought!—
My sin, not in part but the whole,
Is nailed to the cross, and I bear it no more,
Praise the Lord, praise the Lord, O my soul!
It is well with my soul,
It is well, it is well with my soul.

For me, be it Christ, be it Christ hence to live:
If Jordan above me shall roll,
No pang shall be mine, for in death as in life
Thou wilt whisper Thy peace to my soul.
It is well with my soul,
It is well, it is well with my soul.

But, Lord, 'tis for Thee, for Thy coming we wait,
The sky, not the grave, is our goal;
Oh, trump of the angel! Oh, voice of the Lord!
Blessed hope, blessed rest of my soul!
It is well with my soul,
It is well, it is well with my soul.

And Lord, haste the day when the faith shall be sight,
The clouds be rolled back as a scroll;
The trump shall resound, and the Lord shall descend,
Even so, it is well with my soul.

The sanctuary was quiet when they finished and sat down. Claire wondered if she'd ever heard anything so beautiful. It crossed her mind that she'd like to sing it herself, though she doubted she could ever make it as lovely.

The man in the blue suit came up again. He thanked the couple for their music then introduced a man he called "Brother Tyler". Claire didn't understand the significance, but according to his introduction, "Brother Tyler came to Jesus under the watchful eyes of Pastor Dwight Moody. Under Pastor Moody, and at the Moody Bible Institute, Brother Tyler heard God's calling to be a preacher." The introduction continued as the accomplishments and accolades of the man were listed. The list meant little to Claire, but from the nods and smiles of those around her, she could tell that others were impressed.

When Brother Tyler finally replaced the pastor on the stage, the room was silent. He eyed the crowd, walking once, then twice from one side of the front to the other. He waited, letting anticipation build. Claire expected his voice to boom out loudly, but when he finally did speak, his voice was gentle and confident. "Jesus loves you."

He waited again for a few heart beats, then continued. "If you hear nothing more from me today, hear this: Jesus loves you and wants you to believe it and love Him back." That's the simple Truth of the Gospel and the simple Truth of God."

During his sermon, Claire frequently was confused. She didn't understand all the references to Bible passages or the mention of people or stories, so the man's points became muddled for her. She heard the sincerity in his voice and saw the nods of agreement from the crowd, but couldn't understand how the Maker of the Universe could love her. As best she could make out, the people Brother Tyler was using as examples were fine, good people. David, he said, was a warrior and a king who defeated God's enemies. Of course, Claire thought, God loves him. Peter was a fisherman who walked away from everything to be with Jesus. He was good and faithful. Of course Jesus loved him. She listened as the preacher described how Jesus willingly died a cruel death to take the punishment for sin so each person didn't have to.

She began to feel weary and could tell others were starting to be tired of sitting as well. The sunlight through the glass began to fade as the sun moved through the afternoon. The sermon was beginning to wind down. Claire's attention was caught again.

"Let's be very careful, Brothers and Sisters. We can't forget that we are all sinners and that Jesus died on that cross for each of us. It doesn't matter if you have lived a perfectly upright life or you are at the bottom of the barrel. Jesus died for you. Remember the story in Luke chapter seven, Friends. A prostitute, yes a prostitute came to see Jesus."

Claire began to panic. She was instantly frightened that somehow this man had identified her and was going to embarrass her in front of everyone. Daniel reached over and squeezed her hand. Searching his face, she saw a smile. He wasn't afraid or angry. The gentle pressure of his hand helped calm her as the sermon continued.

"That woman was fallen. We'd all agree she was far from good, and most of us here would be as horrified as the Pharisee if we were invited to dinner with the likes of her. But – and here's a big piece of information – but just look at what Jesus did. He noticed that woman's heart. He saw when she kissed his feet and washed them with her tears and He tells the group, "Her sins, which are many, are forgiven." He goes on then to say to her, "Thy sins are forgiven, Thy faith hath saved thee, go in peace."

"Brothers and Sisters, make no mistake, sin is sin and that woman was deep into big sin, but Jesus saved her and forgave her. A lie is a sin and so is murder. Stealing is a sin, and so is cheating. The Bible doesn't say that a little sin will get you into just the warmish part of hell, it says any sin separates you from God and separation from God means an eternity in the lake of fire. It's all or nothing folks, and Jesus' love doesn't choose the nicer ones over the really evil ones. We are all evil.

"Now I'm going to ask the piano player to come and start playing. I'm going to pray, and I'd like to invite you to come. We all need Jesus, we all need to give our hearts to Him, we need to admit to Him that we are sinners and need His death on the cross to save us. All it takes, Folks, is a prayer from your heart and you can know that your sins are washed away and you are perfect in God's eyes.

Claire wanted to get up right then and run down the aisle. She wanted to talk more with Brother Tyler about the prostitute who Jesus loved. She wanted to ask if He could love and forgive her, too. Her thoughts swirled, wondering if it could be true that she could be washed clean but still doubting. The preacher called God 'our father in heaven'. How could God be a father who loved her when her own father didn't? No, it just wasn't reasonable to think that there was hope like this for her.

Claire put her head down, but kept her eyes open. She watched a young man, one she thought she recognized from the saloon, timidly walk up the center aisle, his fingers fidgeting with the hat he held in his hands. When he arrived at the front, one of the choir members stepped up to him. They moved together off to the side, both of them kneeling down to talk quietly.

Behind her, Claire heard the loud whisper of an older woman. "I've been so mad at God for taking Walter and leaving me a widow, I'm so sorry, Jesus!" The woman stood and made her way to the front. Another choir member, a woman in a pale blue dress, stepped forward and moved to the side with her. Several more people made their way to the front as the preacher continued to pray aloud.

Daniel's hand still covered hers, warm and comforting. She looked at him. His eyes were closed, a tear wobbled its way down the side of his nose. His lips moved wordlessly and Claire realized he was praying. Fear assaulted her. She felt it physically. *He's asking for forgiveness for being with me*, she thought. She tried to slide her hand out from under his. His grip tightened and he opened his eyes. Smiling, he lifted her hand and caressed it carefully in both of his. The gesture along with the warmth in his eyes put her fears at bay.

The pastor completed his prayer and called for the choir. The congregation stood and sang a song. Claire wondered about the words, "When the roll is called up yonder I'll be there." Was it possible she could be on that roll?

22

Early November, 1897
Rapid City, South Dakota

Daniel and Claire shuffled down the aisle toward the back and through the double doors with the rest of the crowd. Pastor Crosby stood at the top of the stairs, shaking hands with each person as they left. When it was their turn, he reached out and shook Daniel's hand, then Claire's. "Are you new to our community, Friends?" he asked, looking at Daniel.

"Not exactly," answered Daniel vaguely.

Still holding Claire's hand in his, he met her eyes. "My wife leads a Bible study on Tuesday mornings here at the church if you are interested."

"I don't think I'm ready for a Bible study yet, Sir, I still have too many questions." Claire surprised herself with the bold answer, and dropped her eyes.

The pastor patted her hand and let go. "If I can help with those questions, I'd be happy to meet with you."

Claire kept her eyes down, mumbled a quick thanks and let the crowd move her away from the man.

By the time she and Daniel were back on the boardwalk it was late afternoon. The temperature was even colder and snow was threatening. Claire felt off balance. Her previous picture of God was that of a larger, meaner version of her own father, angry and strict – waiting eagerly for her to make a mistake and ready to punish. She had trouble grasping this new vision of God as One who loved and cared for her no matter what. They walked in silence, unmindful of where they were going, just walking.

After several blocks, Daniel finally spoke. "I'm wondering what you are thinking."

Claire stammered a bit, trying to frame into words what she was feeling and where her thoughts were taking her. She had so many questions and doubts, and Daniel patiently answered them as best he could.

"I'd be interested in hearing what was in your mind right before the service ended." Claire carefully asked.

Daniel looked a bit sheepish and dropped his eyes. "You saw my tears. Not very manly, right?" He grinned shyly.

"I just am not sure what they meant – were you asking forgiveness?" She stopped and faced him, "About me?"

Daniel's face registered his shock. Then, he broke into a broad smile. "No, you stubborn girl, I was thanking God that He brought you into my life. I'll admit, I have fallen away from my faith, and going today reminded me of that. I felt guilty and sad that I haven't been walking closely in God's path and I prayed for forgiveness and help to change that, but at the very moment we looked at each other back there, I was thanking Him for you."

Claire smiled weakly and they resumed walking. Finally Claire whispered, "I have so much to think about."

"I wish I was going to be in town to help answer your questions this week, but honestly, it's already past when I should have left for the mine."

Claire sighed and nodded. "Did you leave your horse at the livery like usual?"

"Yes."

"Then I will walk you back there and see you off."

"I have time to take you back to your place," Daniel answered.

"It's fine, I don't mind."

***

Claire awoke early. She'd had a fitful night. Pulling the curtain back, she saw the snow swirling. The brisk wind had already built a drift about five inches deep along the wall across the alley. Daniel came into her mind, and she worried about whether he made it back to the mine safely or not. She thought about praying for him, but shrugged and told herself that God didn't want to hear from her. She paced and fretted. Spying her trunk, she dropped to her knees and opened the latch. Her mother's Bible was tucked under a quilt on the left side. Retrieving it, she closed the lid and sat on her bed. For close to an hour she thumbed through the book, stopping at random places. Eventually she found the book of Luke, then chapter seven, the story the preacher talked about. She read the passage several times and finally slammed the book shut in frustration.

"Thee, thy, Pharisees, bidden. Why can't they just speak plainly?" Her irritation made her pace the small room a few more times. Finally, she began dressing and decided that even though it wasn't her day to help in the kitchen, she might as well go help Myra.

By the end of the afternoon, Claire had snapped at Lela, spilled her soup at lunch, and nicked her finger as she pared potatoes.

"You've been nothing but a flibbertigibbet all day," scolded Myra. "How about I send you to the mercantile to pick up some eggs for tomorrow's breakfast and let you get some air?"

Claire hesitated and looked down at her dress. Usually she didn't go out in her 'work dresses'. Today she was wearing a red velvet and satin frock with a low neckline that accented her cleavage. It was her most daring dress. She'd already applied rouge and some pale blue eye shadow as well in preparation for the night.

Myra's patience was thin, her tone waspish, "Maybe I could send the footman instead, Your ladyship."

Claire smiled, trying to make peace. "I'm sorry, Myra, of course I'll go. My coat is upstairs, I'll just be a minute."

She hustled up and grabbed her woolen wrap, pulling it around her shoulders tightly as she returned to the kitchen.

It only took a few minutes to walk to the mercantile, but by the time she arrived, she was cold. The wind, filled with stinging snow, brutally whipped around her so that her hood wouldn't stay up and the edge of her wrap flapped uncontrollably. She pushed on the door of the mercantile just as someone on the other side opened it. Off balance and disheveled, she tripped on her way in. Strong hands caught and steadied her. The door closed behind her and in the calm, she looked up to say thanks. Her eyes met the large brown eyes of Pastor Mark Crosby.

He stepped back and recognition showed in his eyes. "Hello there, how nice to see you again so soon." His voice was warm and so was his smile, but even as he said the words Claire watched him take in her hair, her painted face. She looked down and realized that the wind hand moved her wrap to reveal her outfit and neckline as well. There was no mistaking what she was.

"Excuse me, Pastor," Claire said. She put her head down and moved sideways to sidestep him.

"I didn't catch your name yesterday." Claire looked up and met his eyes, not believing that he'd want to spend any more time with her than necessary. *What would your congregation think?*

Stammering, she answered, "Claire Atley, Sir."

"Well Miss Atley, I am pleased to make your acquaintance." He extended his hand.

Claire froze, unable to believe that this man, this pastor was really offering to shake her hand right here in public.

He waited with his arm extended, kindness and warmth seemed to radiate from him, and Claire shook his hand.

An older woman in a black hat and coat pushed open the door and entered. Instead of using the interruption as an excuse to make his getaway, the pastor motioned Claire to the side, out of the way, and then smiled.

"How are you coming on getting your questions answered?" he asked.

"I can't believe, with all the people at the revival yesterday, that you remember our conversation, Sir," Claire answered.

She couldn't meet his eyes, but there was a sweetness in his voice when he replied, "Do you have time to go get a cup of coffee at the café to warm us up? We could start on those questions then."

Her mind tumbled. "I, well, I have to get this errand done and get to work – ah." She stopped, flustered and embarrassed.

Pastor Crosby touched her gently on the arm. "I can see this isn't a good time, and maybe you'd be more comfortable in a more private place. My wife and I live just next door to the church. It's the small grey house just north. Would you be available to come tomorrow morning?"

Unexplainable tears stung Claire's eyes, and she raised her chin to search his face. She had all intentions of saying no, but there was no condemnation or mockery in his face, just openness. She thought then about Daniel. She answered quickly, before she changed her mind. "I'd like that very much. Could we meet about ten o'clock?"

Smiling broadly, the pastor nodded. "I will look forward to it very much. See you then."

He smiled again at Claire, then settled his hat securely on his head and was quickly through the door.

Claire stood a moment, taking a breath to remember what she'd come for, then moved to the counter to make her purchases.

The next morning was bright and sunny. Though there was still a skiff of snow on the ground, the air was warmer and the wind had subsided. Buoyed by the memory of his welcome at the revival, and the gentleness he showed her yesterday, she told herself that meeting with Pastor Crosby was not going to be a disaster. She didn't expect him to be mean and judgmental, and decided that if he was, she could just leave.

She needn't have worried. The pastor and his wife welcomed her without question. After introductions, they ushered Claire into a large, cheery kitchen. Sunlight streamed through a south-facing window adorned with yellow gingham curtains tied at each side with a large bow. Pastor Crosby seated Claire at the table while Mrs. Crosby retrieved a coffee pot from the stove. It was a large, shiny, potbellied cook stove with silver trim. It was larger than any Claire had seen before, with added doors and compartments she couldn't identify.

"That's a beautiful stove," Claire commented.

Pastor Crosby laughed and his wife shushed him. "That stove is one of my most prized possessions. My father and mother gave it to us when we moved out here three years ago. Mark began a love-hate connection to it when he had to move it."

"Only because it is so heavy," he retorted in mock irritation.

"It is called a "New Household Range", his wife continued. "The back of it has a water tank attached, so I always have hot water for the house."

She placed a bowl filled with biscuits, some butter and a jar of jam on the table, then sat down. As they ate, Pastor Mark explained that they were from Ohio.

"Our children, we have two boys and a girl, were all grown up with families of their own. I'd been at First Baptist Church in Erie County, Ohio for twenty five years, we've been married thirty one years, and I was feeling restless."

"We started praying about it, and God sent us here," his wife finished.

"I don't think I understand. Did God actually talk to you?" asked Claire.

"I didn't hear an actual voice, no. But when a person prays with an open mind and seeks God's guidance, it's funny how things just open up and the path becomes pretty clear."

He went on to explain how not long after they started praying about a change, they received a letter from an old friend telling how the church in Rapid City had lost its pastor and was having trouble replacing him. Then, one of their sons got a job as an engineer for the railroad here.

"After a few weeks, it just seemed like we were being told to move here, so we did," he concluded.

Mrs. Crosby cleared the table and refilled their cups. Pastor Crosby reached behind him for his Bible, and their discussion continued. At first, he asked Claire questions about her family and how she grew up. Claire hesitated. She was so used to dodging questions about her life on the farm that she began to evade his queries. Then she stopped. Something about this couple made her trust them. After a pause, she shared a bit about her life on the farm, leaving out any mention of Horace but explaining her father's violence and intolerance.

Pastor Crosby only nodded his head, his kind eyes encouraged her that she'd made the right choice. Then he moved to questions about Claire's understanding of God. He was patient and kind as he explained and answered her questions and doubts. Mrs. Crosby was mostly quiet, but did add once in a while to help Claire understand.

"So, you see, God made it really easy for us to be saved. Jesus became a man. He felt what it was like to be human. He had troubles – troubles with friends, with family, with money. I can't think of one kind of human experience he didn't have. God isn't mean, but He is pure and fair. Fairness means that when someone sins, there is a price to pay. Right here it says that the wages of sin – any sin – is death. Jesus came to earth as a man so that he could stand in our place when it came time to pay those wages. All we have to do is believe it. Accept it. Take Jesus into our lives and ask for forgiveness."

"I don't mean to argue with you, Pastor Crosby, but you know what I am. I work at a saloon. I've... I've been with many men."

"Miss Atley," Mrs. Crosby took Claire's hand and held it in both of hers. "Sin is sin. You've sinned, no doubt, but so have I and so has Mark. Remember on Sunday when Brother Tyler said that there isn't just a warm spot in hell for those who have only sinned a little?"

Claire nodded.

"The reason for that is there isn't anyone who has just sinned a little."

Pastor Crosby spoke up. "Would it help to know what Jesus himself said about a woman who had been with many men?"

Claire nodded again, unable to trust her voice.

The pastor opened his Bible and rifled through pages until he found what he wanted. Then, he slid the book to Claire and asked her to read aloud. The story was of a woman who had been caught in the act of adultery. The townspeople wanted to stone her and brought her to Jesus. Claire cleared her throat and continued to read.

"But Jesus stooped down, and with his finger wrote on the ground, as though he heard them not. So when they continued asking him, he lifted up himself, and said unto them, He that is without sin among you, let him first cast a stone at her. And again he stooped down, and wrote on the ground. And they which heard it, being convicted by their own conscience, went out one by one, beginning at the eldest, even unto the last: and Jesus was left alone, and the woman standing in the midst. When Jesus had lifted up himself, and saw none but the woman, he said unto her, Woman, where are those thine accusers? Hath no man condemned thee? She said, No man, Lord. And Jesus said unto her, Neither do I condemn thee: go, and sin no more."

"The next part is also very important, Miss Atley." Pastor Crosby slid the Bible to himself and said, "Jesus went on to say, "I am the light of the world: He that followeth me shall not walk in darkness, but shall have the light of life."

"When you give your heart to Jesus and ask for his forgiveness, He takes away all your sins and frees you from paying your debt to God for them."

Mrs. Crosby quietly spoke. "I love Psalms 103 verse twelve. It says "As far as the east is from the west, so far hath he removed our sins from us." That means they are gone."

The room became very quiet. The mantle clock ticked comfortingly, a piece of wood shifted in the stove. Claire felt calm for the first time in days. She took a deep breath and looked first at Mrs. Crosby, then at the pastor. "Will you help me pray?"

All three of them wiped their eyes a few minutes later.

"Thank you, Mrs. Crosby," Claire said when the woman refilled her coffee cup.

"Dear heart, I think we can dispense with the formalities. Please call me Catherine. May I call you Claire?"

"Yes, I would love that."

"At church most people call me Pastor Crosby or Pastor Mark. Privately, I'd be pleased for you to call me Mark."

"Thank you so much. Thank you for your kindness to me. It still seems impossible how you've welcomed me here, even though I understand that I'm forgiven by God, it will take a while to take it all in."

"I certainly understand."

They sat in amiable silence for a few minutes. Claire lifted her cup for another sip of coffee when Mark spoke again. "Claire, now that you are a believer and a follower of Jesus, I am wondering what you'll do about your job?"

Claire stopped with her hand, mid-way between her mouth and the table. "Oh dear, I, well, I. I don't know." She said finally. Her cup found its resting place on the table. She put her hands in her lap.

The silence stretched.

"Pastor Mark, I understand that some of my duties are sins, and I'm sure you know what I mean. But is it a sin for me to sing at the saloon or serve drinks to the customers as long as I don't do, um, the other things?"

He considered his answer carefully. "I don't think the Lord wants you to remain in that environment long term. Singing a few songs and serving customers isn't a sin exactly, but men's hearts, when they go into a saloon, aren't set on righteous things, and there is a lot of sin there because of that. Each action separately, having a drink, meeting friends, listening to music, those aren't sinful acts. Put them all together with all the rest that goes on, and you find that a saloon isn't a place that honors God. Even if you only serve a man a drink, your presence there might make him sin in his heart, and God doesn't want us to cause others to stumble."

"But Pastor, what am I to do? I don't have anywhere else to go."

"Well, we are going to pray about it. We're going to ask God's guidance and that He show you what to do."

They clasped hands and prayed.

The mantle clock chimed as Pastor Mark said amen.

"I've taken up too much of your time. Thank you so much for everything, but I'd better go."

"Do you have a Bible to read, Claire?" asked Catherine as they stood at the front door.

"Yes, but when I try to read it, I get confused."

"I have two suggestions, Dear. First, before you start reading, always pray that God allow your mind to understand. Second, I'd love to meet with you for a Bible study, would you be willing?"

"I'd like that very much, Catherine, yes."

"Wonderful. How about we meet on Thursday morning?"

"That sounds great. Would about ten o'clock be alright?"

"Yes, Dear. Come here and we can pray and study together for an hour or two before Mark comes in for lunch. In the meantime, let's all be praying for God's leading for you."

23
December, 1897
Rapid City, South Dakota

Claire sat on her bed and looked around her homey space, thinking back to the first day she had spent together with Daniel after she'd become a believer. He'd been so excited to hear of her decision to accept Jesus as her savior, and he shared how he'd been praying for her since the revival had reignited his heart. She remembered the excitement in his eyes as they discussed it, but watched them cloud over as she began sharing with him new details about her life on the farm. "I want you to know everything about me, Daniel. I don't want any secrets between us." She told him then about her Uncle Horace, and how he had treated her.

When she finished, his fists were clenched. "I'd like to meet this uncle of yours," Daniel's voice was sharp and his blue eyes blazed after she'd recounted how Horace trapped her in the kitchen and grabbed her breast. "To do such things to an innocent girl, and his niece no less, shows him cowardly and twisted in the head. I'd like to meet this guy someday and teach him a lesson."

Claire shivered. "I hope to never see him or his brother – my father - ever again," she whispered. "Catherine says that eventually I will need to work on forgiving him and my father, but I can't imagine that."

Daniel softened his voice when he realized how upset she was. "He can't hurt you now. No one can for as long as it is in my power to be next to you and protect you."

Once her story was clear to Daniel and they had no more secrets between them, Claire began to feel more secure in her feelings for him and his for her. She strained at the idea that he could care for her, a sullied dance hall girl, but when those fears crowded in, she reminded herself of the forgiveness Christ had given her and how she was clean in His eyes. It became easier, then, to believe that Daniel could forgive her as well, especially when she could see the depth of his love in his eyes when he looked at her. He was always careful to treat her as if she were a lady, without any sarcasm or mockery. Slowly she began to believe that it may be true.

She struggled with trusting him. Except for Mr. Behl and Mr. Foster, the men she knew devalued, ignored and abused the women in their lives. She'd heard too many men at the bar talk about the 'little missus' at home as they climbed the stairs with her. She'd watched her own father be kind and thoughtful to Mama one minute and cruel and hard fisted the next, while all the time keeping her nearly a prisoner on the farm, demanding she meet all his needs as he could come and go as he pleased. She thought back to the gypsy caravan and understood anew what her father and brothers had been doing with the gypsy women. Claire's mind reeled with the contradictions between what she had lived and what her heart and Daniel's actions were showing her. Daniel's eagerness to talk through her fears and reassure her amazed her.

Catherine became a strong friend for Claire. She listened patiently as Claire shared her fears and insecurities. They spent a lot of time in prayer together. After their Thursday meetings, Claire always felt stronger.

Knowing that she needed to make some serious changes, Claire continued singing and working in the bar while she prayed about what to do. She knew that Jack had seen her talking with Pastor Crosby in front of the mercantile one morning. She guessed that he was aware that she had started attending church because he'd twice remarked that she was out early on Sunday morning. He didn't argue with her, though, when she told him a lie that that she was having some problems with her female parts and couldn't work upstairs for a while. She felt guilty for her untruth, but didn't know what else to do.

She'd tried to talk to Estelle and Lela about becoming a Christian, but they weren't very receptive. Any time she tried to bring it up, Lela quickly changed the subject. Claire kept her thoughts to herself more and more.

**

Early morning frost glistened on fallen leaves, creating a sparkly blanket of mottled yellow, orange and tan under the trees. Accompanied by Lela and Estelle, Claire made her way along the boardwalk on Main Street. They went first to the bank. Claire stared for a moment at the balance the teller had just written in her passbook. Fourteen hundred and twenty three dollars in her account! The budget she'd devised when she started work for Jack was paying off. She faithfully deposited most of her earnings each week, leaving herself an allowance that provided enough to make her comfortable but not extravagant. The extra earnings she received from Jack for singing and the tips she garnered from the customers along with being careful had caused her balance to grow more quickly than she'd anticipated.

"Christmas is three weeks away, have you gotten Daniel a gift yet?" Estelle asked.

Claire shrugged and frowned. "I haven't. I want something special, something that he can use, but I just don't know what."

"Does he have a pocket watch?"

"I've thought of that, but he has one that his mother gave him along with a beautiful chain and fob."

"How about a knife?" suggested Lela. "He could use that, and have it with him always."

The friends left the bank and headed towards Tom Sweeney's hardware store. Normally, Claire avoided her old workplace. Even though Mr. Sweeney was always cordial when she saw him, she felt uncomfortable around him. She knew that he had a nice selection of knives, though, so they headed in that direction.

"Claire, have you heard about the new dressmaker shop that's opened just around the corner here?"

"Yes, Ethel mentioned it to me."

"I want to go in and look around. Now that Lela and I each have our nest egg built up, we need to start thinking about respectable clothes. I hate the way that new clerk at Sweeney's looks at us like we are going to give her some sort of disease just by breathing."

"I understand. You two go ahead to the dress shop. I'll see you in a few minutes," Claire answered. She crossed the street and continued straight ahead while the other two turned to the right.

The familiar bell jangled as Claire stepped into the store. Lucy married last summer, and Mr. Sweeney replaced her with an older woman with a pinched, sad face. There were three men, miners from the looks of them, at the counter. Claire quietly moved to the side aisle where she knew she'd find what she wanted. There were three nice knives in the glass case.

The men completed their purchases, and finally the clerk approached Claire. "May I help you?"

Ignoring the edge in the woman's voice, Claire looked up and smiled.

"Yes, please. I'd like to look at these three knives."

The clerk sighed and slid open the back of the cabinet. She handed Claire the knives, one at a time. Claire looked them over. She didn't really know much about knives. Her hesitation clearly was annoying the clerk. A noise at the back of the store made both of them look up. Mr. Sweeney appeared at the counter. He smiled briefly at Claire and said, "Miss Atley, it has been a while since I've seen you. You look well."

"Thank you," Claire answered. "Good morning, Mr. Sweeney. How is Mrs. Sweeney?"

"She's well thank you."   As he approached the counter, the clerk moved away.

"I'll just go work on the new arrivals," she mumbled as she left.

"Are you needing a knife?"   Mr. Sweeney, always the salesman, asked.

"Yes, but I'm afraid I don't know much about them. This is a gift, and I'd like it to be useful and last a long time."

"That one might be your best bet." Sweeney pointed to the second one. "That one was made in Switzerland by the Elsener Company. It is equipped with a spring inside that allows the blades and tools to come in and out easily. This model is called the 'Officer's and Sports Knife.' It has two blades, a corkscrew and wood fiber grips. "

"I like the handle on it. It feels good. Will this knife last a long time?"

"That handle is oak. These knives are very sturdy, they were originally intended for the Swiss Army. I expect a fellow would have a hard time wearing this knife out."

"Thank you for your help, Mr. Sweeney. I will take this one."

"You're welcome, Miss Atley. It's good to see you again. I'll have Victoria wrap this up for you."

Claire left the store with a smile. She was confident that Daniel would appreciate the knife and thankful that she had the money to buy it.

On Thursday evening, snow flurries arrived and the wind picked up. Claire began to fret that Daniel wouldn't be able to come to town for their Sunday together. She bowed her head and whispered a short prayer. It was a comfort to know that God could and would hear her prayer even though she was wiping spilled whiskey off the bar.

Lela touched her on the arm as she walked by with a tray of full beer mugs. "Daniel is in the kitchen asking for you. Myra isn't happy that he's there, so you better come quickly."

Suddenly frightened, Claire smoothed her hair, left the rag behind the bar and entered the kitchen.

Daniel was standing at the back door. His hair was rumpled and his face flushed.

"Daniel, are you well? You look feverish."

"I'm fine," he answered, "but I need to talk to you right away."

Myra brushed past Claire and growled, "This is a kitchen. Customers should be out front. Don't you have work to do?"

"Can we go somewhere private?" Daniel's tone was urgent. Claire was at a loss. She was supposed to sing in just a few minutes, and since Ethel was sick with a cold they were short handed.

He took her hand. "Claire, this is important. I'll go to the café and wait for you. Please get away as soon as you can." He smiled and squeezed her hand.

"Ok, I'll be there right away."

The door slammed after him, leaving cold air where he'd been standing.

Claire took a breath and returned to the bar. Jack had just sat a glass of whiskey in front of a large man with a tall hat. He turned to her as she walked the length of the bar.

"I hear you have a visitor back there. Is he the female troubles you've been having lately that have kept you from working?" His voice was light and teasing but his eyes were hard.

Swallowing hard, Claire ignored his question. "Jack, I need to leave the saloon for a while. We aren't very busy, I'm sure that Lela can cover for me. Do you mind?"

"Yeah, I mind. You're supposed to be singing." He grabbed her arm. "I've got paying customers here that need attention and you've been somewhere in the clouds lately."

He wasn't hurting her, but his touch frightened her.

"Jack, please," she whispered. At that moment she wasn't sure what she was pleading for. It could have been to leave and see Daniel but it was also for him to let go of her and not hurt her.

They stayed like that for a few pounding heart beats, then he let go of her. "Damn," was all he said.

Claire fled the scene. She ran up to her room and grabbed her wrap and a hat and was quickly out the door.

The café was nearly empty when she arrived. She found Daniel easily and joined him at the table. He stood when she approached, smiling shyly.

"Daniel, you're frightening me, are you alright?"

"Yes, I am. Really, I am better than alright." He helped her with her chair, then sat opposite her. He leaned forward and continued.

"You may not remember, but on one of our outings I told you about a man I'd worked with. His name is Haggarty. He's an Englishman who came to America for adventure."

Claire nodded tentatively. "I think I recall a little of that."

"I met him in Cripple Creek. When I left, we corresponded some. I lost touch with him for a while, but a letter from him finally found me about a year ago and we've written back a forth a few times. He's been prospecting in southern Wyoming."

"So he found gold?"

"No, he's found copper. Gold is pretty rare in Wyoming, but it seems that there is lots of copper, and that's worth a lot of money, too. It is often easier to mine, so the return on your investment is greater even though the copper sells for less."

Claire became impatient. "Daniel, this is interesting, but Jack wasn't very pleased about me leaving and I need to get back."

"I'm getting to the point, Claire. I got a letter from Haggarty this morning. He's staked a new claim on the Continental Divide. All the assay reports agree that this is a mother lode for copper – a really rich deposit. He's sunk the first shaft and wrote to offer me a job. He wants me to sign on as his chief engineer."

Claire's heart began to pound. She'd never considered losing Daniel. She took a labored breath. "When are you leaving?"

"What?" he stopped and met her eyes. "Claire, *I am not* leaving, I hope *we* are."

Claire didn't understand. She was stuck on the idea of Daniel not being in her life. He rose then, and came around to her side of the table. He pulled something out of his pocket as he kneeled down beside her.

"This isn't a very romantic evening, and this certainly isn't a ring to be too proud of, but Claire, I want you to marry me and come to Wyoming with me." The ring he held out to her was a plain gold band. Claire stared at it, then at Daniel, not quite taking the situation in.

Daniel felt desperate that she'd somehow say no, so he continued making his case, "You and I have both been praying for God's guidance for you. I've been praying as well for guidance about us. I've known for a long time that I wanted you to be my wife. I just knew that there was no place for you to live near the mine except an isolated cabin. That would be torture for you. I've been waiting to see what might happen. Now this."

He stopped for a breath, then charged on. "This is the perfect answer. If you'll have me, we can get married right away. We can leave here and never look back. It will be a fresh start in a new place."

Claire sat stunned, saying nothing. She didn't move. Her thoughts were slow and foggy.

"Claire, please say something. I'm getting a cramp in my leg being crouched like this and people are beginning to stare." His blue eyes twinkled as he teased her out of her panic.

"Daniel, are you sure you want to marry a dance hall girl?"

"Former dance hall girl, don't you mean?" He chuckled. "Claire, I love you, please say yes."

"I love you, too, Daniel." She didn't hesitate again, "Yes."

"This isn't an engagement ring, so I'll wait to slip in on your finger until we say our vows, alright?" She nodded. Daniel tucked the treasure back into his pocket and regained his seat across from her.

"I had time to construct a plan while I rode down from the mine. How about this? I'll go and rent you a room at the hotel for a few days. I need to go back up to the mine. I'd already told the foreman that I thought I'd be leaving. I'll go up in the morning, get my last pay and clear out my room, then I'll be back here tomorrow night. You can go back tonight to Jack's and gather your things. I'll meet you in the back and help you move to the hotel.

Tomorrow, while I'm gone up the mountain, you can talk to Pastor Crosby and see if he'll marry us."

Daniel sipped at his coffee, smiling. All at once he became serious. Reaching across the table for her hand he asked, "Will there be trouble at the saloon? Will Jack let you go? I can go with you to make sure there isn't trouble."

"I think he suspects already. When I left just now he wasn't happy, but something he said tells me he is expecting it. He's a pretty decent man. I think it will be alright."

Outside the café they stopped. He took her hand and kissed it gently. "How many belongings do you have that we need to move to the hotel? Should I bring a freight wagon?"

Claire ignored his teasing and answered, "I have a trunk and a bag, but I'm not certain everything will fit into just those." She began to feel rattled.

"Don't worry. All we need to do is get your belongings to the hotel, then we can purchase as many trunks or chests as you need before we leave."

Claire sighed. "I love how matter of fact and calm you are. It helps me stay calm. Right now I'm not sure if I want to cry or scream out our happy news to the heavens."

He chuckled then. "I'll see you in less than thirty minutes out in the back."

They parted then, and Claire walked toward the saloon. She felt no regret at leaving, but the quick pace of the changes made her feel off balance. Instead of going around to the back entrance the girls usually used, Claire stepped through the swinging front doors. The tinny sound of the piano coupled with the deep sounds of male voices and laughter were a comfortable background for her spinning thoughts. Jack had his back to her as she approached the bar.

"Jack, may I talk to you privately?"

He looked up and frowned. "Can't leave the bar. What do you need to say?"

Claire stumbled through thanking him and then explaining that she was leaving. Jack was never physical with his girls, but she'd seen him lose his temper with customers a few times. By the time she'd finished, her heart was pounding.

"I knew it." He started. "I knew that miner would be trouble for you the first time I watched him look at you. You've been spending a lot of time with him, and at that church down the road, so I knew it was a matter of time."

"You aren't angry at me?"

"Hell, Scrawny, I am angry that I'm losing the best singer I've ever had in this place, but I'm happy for you. I've always known that this wasn't really the life for you, just a bump in the road."

She hugged him, then, and made her way upstairs. She looked around her room. First, she removed the frock she'd been wearing and hung it on a peg. She ran her hand over the velvet and satin, thankful that she could literally hang up this life and walk away. She slipped a grey twill dress on, then began to pack. Carefully, she took her grandmother's mirror from its nail on the wall, wrapped it with a quilt and packed it into her trunk. Lela and Estelle appeared in the open doorway. "Is it true? You are leaving tonight?"

Claire filled them in on the details.

"I won't be needing these work dresses," Claire announced. "Will you take them?"

Lela laughed. "I'm too big on the top for most of them, but I'd love your velvet skirt."

"That leaves most of them for me!" laughed Estelle. Then tears ran down her cheeks, "but I'm sure going to miss you."

"Not for long," Claire reminded them. "You've been planning to leave in the spring anyway, to go back East."

Claire finished packing. The three of them worked together to carry the trunk down the stairs and set it outside. On the next trip down Lela carried the carpet bag and Estelle struggled with an armful of dresses they'd wrapped in an old sheet. Daniel pulled up, driving a small buckboard. He loaded the trunk, then relieved Estelle of her burden and laid it on top. Claire arrived then with a smaller bag, which Daniel fit in along the side.

His voice was low, "Is everything thing okay?"

Before she could answer, Jack appeared in the doorway. Claire felt Daniel tense beside her as Jack boomed, "I'm not very happy with you, Haynes."

Jack stepped up to Daniel, then, and extended his hand. "I wish you both the best. Take good care of her, you hear?"

Daniel's shoulders relaxed as he shook the man's hand. "I will."

Jack turned to her. "Claire, here's what I owe you for this week, plus there's a little more as a wedding present."

Claire was taken aback. She took what he handed her and stuffed it in the top of the carpet bag, then stammered a thanks as Jack turned around. Passing Lela and Estelle he growled, good naturedly, "You two have work to do."

The three women hugged and said goodbye.

24
December, 1897
Rapid City, South Dakota

"Catherine, I don't know how I can ever thank you for all that you and Pastor Mark have done for Daniel and me."

Claire sat at the kitchen table in the Crosby home. Catherine smiled as she put the finishing touches on the cake she was frosting.

"We're just so happy for you, Dear." She put down the butter knife she was using to add frosting to the cake and stepped back to survey her work. "The white cake recipe was my mother's, and the chocolate icing recipe comes from my grandmother. I'm glad you've written them both down to try again another time." She chuckled. "Do you know that the ancient Romans used to crumble a kind of wedding cake over a bride's head for good luck and to please their gods?"

"I'm so glad we've let that tradition go," laughed Claire.

"Traditions are important, though. I'm so glad you and Daniel agreed to allow us to make your wedding a little more elaborate than you'd originally planned. As a married couple, you need to make your own traditions, and this is a good start."

"We didn't want to make a fuss or inconvenience anyone. We thought just meeting you here, or maybe at the church and saying our vows would be easiest."

"Easiest, maybe, but not as memorable," smiled Catherine. "As it is, the only 'fuss' was cooking dinner and baking a cake. I'd have cooked dinner anyway, and you helped with the cake, so it's been no trouble at all."

Catherine refilled their two tea cups and sat down across from Claire. "How are the rest of your plans going?"

"Well, I think." answered Claire. "Daniel got back into Rapid City late yesterday afternoon. He went to the court house and got a marriage license, then sent two telegrams, one to his parents in Iowa to tell them the news and the other to his sister in Denver.

"First thing this morning, he got a reply that surprised him. Addie, Daniel's sister, lives in a large house and has invited us to stay with them. She says she has plenty of room for us all, and this will be perfect for them to get to know me."

"How do you feel about that?"

Claire lowered her head. "I'm frightened beyond words." She said finally.

Catherine patted her hand. "It will be fine. All any family wants when someone marries is to know that the match will make their loved one happy. It is impossible to be in a room with you two more than just a few minutes before it's clear the bond between you is strong."

"I hate that I'll start my relationship with Daniel's family with a lie."

"I don't believe that withholding your recent history or being vague about what you did here is a lie. Remember, you are a forgiven, pure child of God because of Jesus. I don't think God will condemn you for leaving the past behind and starting again. East is a long way from West."

"I hope you are right. Daniel and I talked about this at length yesterday afternoon when he showed me the marriage license."

"Speaking of that, your groom will be waiting for you at the church in just two hours' time. What do you have to do to get ready?"

Claire stood up. "I need to go." She felt rattled again. "I want to go bathe and dress, and also finish packing. Our train leaves for Denver tomorrow morning at ten o'clock. We found a second trunk the perfect size for all the rest of my clothes and belongings, but I haven't filled it yet."

***

Three surprises awaited Claire on her wedding day. The ceremony was planned for five o'clock, Claire knocked on the kitchen door of the parsonage about twenty minutes before five. Catherine greeted her with a warm hug. "You look beautiful," she announced. Claire had chosen a dress she'd bought several months ago but had never worn. Made with pale peach polished cotton with small posies, the dress' neckline was a demure scoop in the front. The back was adorned with a small bustle of gathered lace. The lace repeated at the cuffs.

"Thank you," Claire answered as Catherine continued.

"Did you have this made for you? The bodice is a perfect fit, and shows off what a thin waist you have. The modified mutton sleeves give just enough gathering to be interesting without overtaking the rest of the dress."

"I ordered it out of a magazine, never guessing it would be my wedding dress."

Catherine stepped closer and examined the pin Claire wore. "This is pretty."

"It was my mother's. She gave it to me on my sixteenth birthday."

"What an intricate design. Is this a daisy?"

"Mama called it a black-eyed Susan. They were her favorite flower. I think maybe they were her favorites because of this pin. The pin itself was handed down to her from her grandmother."

"What a perfect heirloom to wear today, Dear."

Changing the subject, Claire lifted her skirt to show a pair of shoes. "I found these yesterday when we bought the trunk."

"I saw those at the mercantile. They're the beaver and fox leather ones, aren't they?" Claire nodded. "I thought so. I love the nine little buttons up the side."

Claire giggled. "I had to buy a new button hook, and these gave me a time since they are new. I almost thought I'd have to give up and wear my old shoes."

"Well, they look wonderful. I love the chignon style for your hair, too."

"I don't have a hat that matches this dress, do you think it's alright without?"

"Yes, you are the perfect bride." Catherine retrieved a box from the counter. "Daniel is already at the church. He stopped by a few minutes ago and left this for you."

Claire peeked into the box and removed the tissue paper. "Where did he get these in the middle of December?" she asked aloud as she lifted a small bouquet of fresh white daisies and yellow roses. "What a wonderful surprise." Claire put her nose to the bouquet and inhaled the aroma of the roses, lingering over the sweetness of the gift. Then she noticed what held them and received the first of three special surprises of the day.

"Catherine, look at this."

"Oh, Claire, what a beautiful gift."

Claire rubbed the silver, ornately filigreed tussy-mussy as a tear made its way down her cheek. "I don't deserve any of this," she whispered. "I don't deserve to be this loved and this happy."

Catherine hugged her tightly. "Maybe you deserve it more than most because of everything you've been though." She stepped back and looked at Claire. "Now, dry those happy tears. We need to go over to the church, it's time to meet your new husband."

Claire hiked up her skirts to protect the hem from the dirt and walked across the yard and into the church. She waited in the foyer for a minute until Catherine made sure everything was ready. "I'm going to go sit down. Then it will be your turn to walk down the aisle. Daniel and Mark are already at the front waiting for you."

Claire stood in the silence alone. She smiled when she looked down and realized her hands were shaking. Still new to praying, she breathed a sigh filled with thanks and pleading, then she stepped out into the doorway.

She expected the church to be empty. Her second surprise, then, was to see Lela, Estelle, and Ethel seated on one side of the church and three men seated across the aisle. She made her way to the front, where Daniel took her hand.

***

They stood at the altar after being pronounced husband and wife. Estelle and Lela came up, enveloped Claire in hugs and wished them both good luck. "We have to go, Honey, but I am hoping you write to us," Lela fought tears, "You know where we are, at least until spring."

"I will write, as soon as we have an address."

With one more hug, they were gone. Claire joined Daniel, who was talking with two men. "Claire, do you remember Grey Madison and Charlie Farley? I worked with them at the mine."

The group chatted for a few minutes, mostly concerning mining. Soon, the men made their farewells and left after additional congratulations and back slaps.

182

Pastor Mark stood with the third man Claire had seen when she came down the aisle. "Catherine went on ahead to finish up supper, but take your time here. I'll go see if I can help her."

"I can come help," Claire began.

"Oh, no you can't, this gentleman is waiting for us." Daniel grinned.

"Waiting for us to do what?" Claire began, then she saw the man lift a large camera onto a tripod. "You hired a photographer?" Claire's third surprise, then, was this.

Daniel took her hand in his. "I will remember this day and how beautiful you look forever, there's no doubt of that. But, I wanted to be able to share our wedding with family and friends. Mostly, I wanted to make you know that I'll do anything for you and I will cherish you every day for the rest of our lives."

"That sounds like the completion of our wedding vows," Claire whispered.

***

They boarded a Northwestern train the next morning. Claire waved until she could no longer see Catherine and Mark on the platform, then settled into her seat.

"We could just take the Deadwood stagecoach into Cheyenne," explained Daniel, "But I've ridden that route, and it is miserable. Plus, with our extra baggage, there would be a problem. So, we are going to make this an adventure and travel twice as far as a crow would between Rapid City and Denver."

"Why twice as far?"

"Train routes between here and Denver are not direct. We have to zig zag a while."

"What's our first stop?"

"The Chicago & Northwestern train we are on will take us south to Chadron, Nebraska. There, we change trains and directions, going southeast to Omaha, still on C & N. We'll stop in Omaha and rest for a night in a hotel room, then we'll board a Union Pacific train on the transcontinental route to Cheyenne. Once we get to Cheyenne, it's a hundred miles south bound for Denver."

"Will we change railroads again in Cheyenne?"

"No, it will still be the Union Pacific, they have a spur from Cheyenne to Denver."

Claire knew that the trip would take three days, so she tried to relax and enjoy the journey. She was enthralled for much of each day with simply holding Daniel's hand as he sat beside her watching the countryside pass by. The evening they spent in Omaha was a treat. The room they secured was richly furnished and welcoming. After a relaxing dinner, they strolled along a boardwalk at the edge of the Missouri River.

A bench along the walkway beckoned them, and they sat to watch the boats on the river and enjoy the night air.

"Daniel, in all the excitement of the wedding and leaving, I never gave you your present."

"You are the only present I ever want," her groom answered her with a crooked grin.

"Don't be corny. You gave me that beautiful tussy-mussy for my bouquet and a wonderful wedding. I love the portraits of our special day. But I never gave you your present." She reached into her bag and drew out a small package wrapped in brown paper and bound with course string. "It isn't a very pretty package, but I hope you like it."

Daniel took the gift and opened it slowly. He broke into a huge smile when he'd uncovered the Swiss army knife. "Did you get this at Sweeney's?" he asked.

"Yes," she answered not sure if his question meant he didn't like it.

"I saw this there. In fact, I looked at it several times. I really wanted it, but thought it was too expensive. Thank you!"

He kissed her gently then opened and closed each blade on his new knife. "What I like most is that you gave it to me, but what I like next is that it will be easy to keep this in my pocket for whenever I need it."

***

Their travels were an enjoyable honeymoon. Yet, the closer they got to Denver the more worried Claire grew about meeting Daniel's family.

"What are you pondering?" Daniel asked as they pulled out of

Cheyenne. He rubbed her cold hands between his own and waited for her answer.

"When I left the farm and took the train to Rapid City, I was starting over. I remember feeling so excited that I could make myself into someone new and leave the old behind. It's funny that I'm doing that again, I'm just nervous about it. What I am leaving behind is shameful, and I am afraid someone will find out and I will embarrass you."

Daniel tucked his wife safely under his arm. His embrace and his words comforted her, "My Darling, I could never be embarrassed by you. We've talked about this before and you know how I feel. Nothing will change that, especially what someone else thinks."

"I know that," Claire responded, "but I still worry. What if your sister and her family don't like me?"

"You worry too much, they will adore you."

***

Daniel's prediction turned out completely true. Addie and Paul and their two boys welcomed Claire with open arms. Within just a few days, Claire considered Addie a dear friend, and her confidence grew. After two weeks, Daniel left his wife in the happy company of his sister, and travelled to the wilds of Wyoming to begin his new job. Claire missed him, but settled herself into a routine in Denver, helping Addie with the housework and exploring her new surroundings.

One morning as they were finishing breakfast, Addie told Claire about her plans for the day. "I hope you won't get too lonely today. Once a month I meet an old friend for a long lunch. I'd love to invite you, but this is a long standing engagement that we both have agreed will be just for the two of us to spend time together alone."

"Oh, I don't mind," Claire answered as she finished her coffee. "I'm just jealous. I have a dear friend that I'd love to have lunch with, though I haven't heard from her in a long time."

"Do you write to her?"

"We used to write very regularly," Claire answered. "But then we just fell out of the habit I guess."

"That's sad. I wonder if you could reconnect with her now? I'd miss Sophia so much if she weren't in my life."

Claire shrugged noncommittally then asked, "Would you like for me to watch the boys for you?"

"Thanks for offering. No, both Jeremiah and Richard have made plans to go home after school with buddies from their class, and I should be home before they get here. You have the day to yourself."

When Addie left, Claire looked around. At first, she was happy to be alone. She straightened up the room she and Daniel shared, then settled into a chair to read. Within an hour, though, she was restless, and began thinking about Haddie and their lost friendship.

Haddie's last letters had gone unanswered over a year ago. Claire couldn't bring herself to admit to Haddie that she was working at Jack's, but she didn't want to lie to her either. In the end, it was easier to grieve the loss and not respond.

She wondered if she could just write now without explaining all that had happened in the interim. The depth of her loneliness for a confidante and the breadth of her care for Haddie prevailed. Claire sat down at the small desk in her room and began to write. When she finally folded the pages and stood from the table, the sun was making its way towards the Rocky Mountain horizon in the west. Claire completed the envelope and slipped the pages in along with a silent prayer. It felt good to tell the truth. It felt good that Haddie would know not just that she'd worked as a harlot in a dance hall, but that she was also now a follower of Jesus and a new wife. Claire wondered if Haddie would forgive her, and hoped that she would.

25
Late January, 1898
Denver, Colorado

Claire looked out the parlor window and studied the Rocky Mountains. The tops of the peaks were hidden by greyish-white cloudswirls. The air outside the window was cold and damp – snow was on its way. Claire thought about Daniel, far away in Wyoming. She was settling in with Addie and Peter, but long afternoons afforded her time to think and worry.

The front door slammed. The scuffling and noise told Claire that her nephews were home from school. Their arrival always brought a kind of sweet chaos to the otherwise quiet house, and Claire smiled. She enjoyed the boys.

"Aunt Claire?" Jeremiah walked through the house calling her name. "Aunt Claire?" Disheveled and still holding his school bag, the tow-headed boy appeared in the parlor doorway.

"I'm right here," Claire smiled warmly at the boy. "Is everything alright?"

"Yes, Ma'am. We stopped at the post office on the way home, and this came for you."

Claire stared at the return address. Haddie. Claire couldn't wait to open the envelope, but was frozen with fear at the possible rejection that it held.

"Thank you," she answered finally. "You are a terrific mailman."

"You're welcome. Where's Ma? I'm hungry!"

With that she was again alone in the parlor. Not knowing what the letter held, Claire decided to go to the privacy of her bedroom before opening it.

A few minutes later, after greeting Richard and checking in with Addie, Claire sat on her bed and quietly read the letter.

Dearest Claire,

I can't begin to tell you how happy I am to get your letter. I've prayed for you every day, not knowing what had become of you. Let me say this right now at the beginning so you have no fears. There is nothing you could ever do that would make me not care for you. I am so sorry that you've had to face the things you have. I can't imagine how desperate and alone you were when you were forced to make the decisions you did. It makes me sad that you felt you couldn't come back here. Please know we would have welcomed you back here and taken you in, but I understand you needed to walk your own path.

I wish you all the love and blessings in the world on your marriage. Daniel Haynes sounds like a wonderful, hardworking man, and someone that you deserve. I will be mailing you a little wedding gift in the next few weeks, so look for it soon. Claire, I am so thankful that you know the Lord. I won't need to worry about you as much now that He and Daniel are with you.

I will write more and catch you up on all the news here in a day or two, right now, William is waiting for me to get this in an envelope so he can leave for town. I made him promise to wait so you'd get my answer right away.

Love and prayers,
Haddie

Claire's face was wet with tears, and she found herself thanking God for His forgiveness and for Haddie's.

Within a week, Claire received both another letter and a box holding a beautiful tablecloth from Haddie. She'd answered them with another long letter, thanking Haddie and updating her friend about her new life in Denver. While she was still lonely for Daniel, and she couldn't wait to show both letters and the gift to him, her blossoming friendship with Addie, the hustle of their household, and her joy at reconnecting with Haddie made the days pass happily.

***

Claire stretched and snuggled closer to her husband as the sky lightened. He'd shown up unexpectedly last night just before dinner looking tired and drawn. It had been six weeks since he'd left, and while Claire liked being with Addie and her family, the time passed slowly. She felt more and more as if her life was holding its breath waiting to begin.

She concentrated on his warmth beside her. Daniel was clearly happy to see her, his embraces has been fierce and strong. She'd caught him studying her when he thought she wasn't looking at dinner last night. Yet, something in his actions kept him somehow distant and a little impatient with her at times. As she listened to him breathing, she thought again about his waspish answer to her at dinner the night before.

"Addie, these fried potatoes are great. I like the onions in them."

Addie smiled. "Thank you, Peter, I thought you'd like them."

Peter turned to Daniel, "What brings you to Denver, is this just a social call?"

"Hardly, right now there is no time for socializing up there. Before I go too far into the mine, I want to talk with an old teacher of mine at the School of Mines. Ed Haggarty agreed we needed to get someone else's opinion, so he suggested I come spend a few days with Claire and see what I could find out."

"How long are you home for?" she asked quietly.

"Now don't get all teary already. I just said, this is a work trip. In the morning I need to go up to the school and see if I can find some answers."

His tone and his words stung her again as she nestled next to him. She replayed the scene in her head several times, finally deciding he was tired from the trip and nothing more.

Daniel insisted that Claire accompany him when he went to Golden City to meet with his professor and she was happy to comply. They rode the train into the foothills, then walked from the station to the school. Daniel didn't seem hurried or tense this morning, and as they strolled around the campus, Claire watched the pride in his eyes as he showed her around, introducing her to old teachers and acquaintances. When the time came for his meeting, she waited for him in a common area in one of the buildings, happily reflecting on the beautiful turn her life had taken.

"How'd it go?" she asked when he returned an hour later.

"Very well. Professor Jacks, he's in charge of the engineering classes, agreed with me and my plan for opening up Rudefeha. He was really complimentary about my drawings and plans, and told me he couldn't have done a better job himself!"

"Congratulations," Claire said. She loved the way his blue eyes sparkled with the knowledge of his former mentor's approval.

"We had a good meeting, and I feel ready now to go back and get started."

"I'm not sure why you weren't confident."

"It is just such a huge responsibility. If I choose for a shaft to go in the wrong direction, or if I don't respect the rock formations and have the men tunnel where the mountain is unstable, not only will the mine lose money but lives could be lost. I've never been in charge of a whole project before. It makes me sleepless many nights, Claire."

They walked around the campus for a bit longer before starting back to Denver. Daniel showed her the Jarvis Hall Collegiate School building, explaining that it was the first building on campus.

"Imagine, the first year, 1883, they only graduated two men. Now, the classes are full. Professor Jacks even told me that they have a woman student who will graduate in May of this year."

"Wow, a woman engineer. She must be really brave to take this on."

"Yes," Daniel agreed. "She has to be pretty tough as well, to put up with the attitudes of some of her classmates."

"Not everyone is welcoming her, then?"

"From what Jacks told me, she'd had a really rough time. My hat is off to her and her tenacity to keep coming every day despite the mean spiritedness she's been subjected to."

Claire smiled at her kind and accepting husband. She considered for a moment how her father would have reacted to a woman at college, especially a mining college. She shook her head to dispel the thought.

Claire brushed her hair in front of her grandmother's mirror as Daniel got ready for bed that night. "What shall we do tomorrow?" she asked.

"Well, now that I have a confirmed plan for the mine, it is time to get back up there."

Claire turned to face her husband. "You aren't leaving right away are you? I thought you said Mr. Haggarty told you to take a few days with me."

Daniel's edginess returned. "Claire, you know I miss you, but I've got a job to do. There are men up there waiting for me. I can't be cooling my heels down here while time is wasting."

Claire stared at him, his words stinging her.

"The train leaves at noon. We have all morning to spend together." He folded her into his arms, then, and kissed her neck. "I know you are disappointed, but it's my job."

Claire told herself she understood. She packed away her hurt and hugged him back, thankful for the time they did have together. At noon the next day she found herself standing on the platform, waving as the train chugged out of the station. She held on to his promise that they'd be together again soon, and returned alone to Addie and Peter's.

26
February, 1898
Denver, Colorado

"It's hard to imagine I've been here so long." Claire was brushing her hair in front of the mirror while Daniel finished dressing. The morning had broken clear and crisp.

"The time has gone fast, I agree. Especially when I've been gone so much of it."

"Surprisingly, I really haven't minded most of the time." She turned. "Of course I missed you and I'd rather that you'd have been here the whole time, but Addie has been so kind."

"She likes you very much, but then, I told you she would." He pulled her in for a lingering hug.

"You got in so late that we didn't talk last night."

Daniel nuzzled her neck. "I wasn't interested in talking last night."

Claire giggled. "No, neither one of us was. But this morning, I do want to hear about the mine and how things are going. I also need to talk to you about something important."

"The first thing you need to know is that your time, our time, here is about up. Ed let me know that he's done sending me to recruit and order supplies, and he's ready to have me at the mine full time."

"Things are going well, then?"

"Ed has had nine men up there working all winter. It's been a hard go. You will be astounded at how rough that country is. The mountains are doing their part to keep us out."

"What do you mean, exactly?"

"Well, the mine is just down a short ridge from the Continental Divide. The snow is fifteen to twenty feet deep in the canyons. On the tops and sides of the slopes the snow is thin or there is just bare, frozen ground because the wind howls up there like a banshee."

"I want you to keep talking, but we need to go down to breakfast."

Addie, Peter, Jeremiah and Richard were around the table when the couple came in. "There you are," Addie greeted them, "I wasn't sure if you'd heard me call a few minutes ago, and I didn't want to disturb you."

Daniel gave his sister a peck on the cheek then helped Claire with her chair.

"We've already said the blessing, Uncle Dan," Jeremiah offered. "Ma made pancakes."

After a few minutes of passing and arranging, talking and jostling, the family settled in to eat.

"I was just filling Claire in on the progress at the mine," Daniel began.

"I'd certainly be interested in that," replied Peter with a smile, "since my bank owns shares in this operation."

"I was just trying to describe how rugged and inhospitable the land is up there. The snow is deep and the wind blows fiercely. The first hurdle we have to deal with is getting a road cut from the valley up to the mine. The land is steep and rocky to the extent that right now it takes two days for a man on a horse just to get there. They've brought supplies up so far with mule teams and freight wagons overland, but the kinds of equipment we need to actually start mining in earnest needs heavier wagons and larger teams. For that, we need a road."

"For that, you'll have to wait for the snow to melt, won't you?" asked Addie.

"Yes, for some parts of the road. A group of men has already been out on snowshoes and skis marking out the path. As soon as the snow allows, they'll get crews in there to work on it. Finishing the road is a real priority. Even when it is done, though, it will probably take three days at least for heavy loads to make it up to the mine. They will need to use fifteen- or twenty-animal teams to move the heavy supplies. And that's to cover only about twenty miles."

"What have the men up there this winter been doing? Are they producing any copper?"

"That's a good question, Claire," answered Daniel. "Right now, the men are clearing out and enlarging a cavern just inside the entrance to the mine. This copper vein is going to be a deep one, so Haggarty and his partners have plans for a small gauge train inside the mine to carry the ore out. The men have been pretty much living and working in that cavern. Right now, they have it about the size of the inside of the church sanctuary, which is about as big as it needs to be. When I get back there, my first job will be to start exploring, taking samples and testing the rock formations in that cavern to see where the first shaft needs to go and in what direction."

"Are all four of the partners up there this winter?" asked Peter.

"No. The only one there is Haggarty. I'd expect Ferris to be around a lot, but the other two are just money, not miners."

"Uncle Dan?"

"Yes, Jeremiah?"

"When we visited you at your mine in Colorado, that mine had a name."

"The *Mary Kathleen*!" added Richard.

"Anyway," Jeremiah continued, elbowing his brother for good measure, "does this mine have a name?"

"It does. It's called the *Rudefeha Mine*."

Richard scoffed, "That's a silly name!"

"It does sound a little strange. The name is a combination of the names of the men who are partners in the deal."

"I don't get it."

"Well, there's J.M. Rumsey, Robert Deal, George Ferris, and Ed Haggarty. If you take just the first two letters, Ru, de, fe, and ha, it creates the name *Rudefeha*."

"You've known one of the partners for years, correct? Do you know the others?" asked Peter.

"I've only met George Ferris once. He lives in Rawlins, about forty miles west of the mine. Deal and Rumsey are ranchers. I've never met either of them. Ed Haggarty and I are old chums from the *Mary Kathleen*."

"He's British if I remember correctly. What's he doing in Wyoming?" Peter continued.

"He's from a seaport town in northern England. He left England in 1885 needing some adventure and worked his way across the west. He ended up working in Cheyenne for the Union Pacific. He told me that he hated Cheyenne and its wind, so when he read in the *Rocky Mountain News* about gold mining in Colorado he packed a bag and moved to Cripple Creek. He talked himself into a job at the *Mary Kathleen* based on his experience with coal mining in England, and got put on the same crew as me."

"Ma, can we be excused and go outside?" asked Jeremiah.

"Wash your face and hands first, and stay in the yard, please."

"Yes, Ma'am." The boys bounded out of the room.

"So how'd he find the copper in Wyoming?" Claire asked. She and Addie had been listening to Daniel as they cleared the table and refilled coffee cups.

"Ed's never been one to sit still long. He was in Cripple Creek less than a year. I think he left not long after I went to the Black Hills. He moved a couple hundred miles west and north, into the Wyoming mountains of the Sierra and Snowy Ranges. Last summer he was in the Sierras prospecting. Bob Deal has a sheep operation up there, and Haggarty was living at the sheep camp and lending a hand to the herder while he combed the mountains for signs of copper."

"That sounds like a lot of work."

"He'd become very interested - while he was in Colorado - with learning how to find ore deposits. He made friends with some prospectors and a few miners and started grilling them for information about identifying rock formations and other signs that different ores were present."

"You mean like finding gold or silver?"

"Yes, exactly. He knew people had staked copper, silver and gold claims in southern Wyoming, and he started looking."

Addie sat down and sipped her coffee. "How long did he search before he was successful?"

"Rudefeha is actually not his first find. He staked a claim in the Seminoe Mountains. He sold that one pretty quickly, but I hear it made a nice return at least at first. Then Haggarty moved on to the Sandstone Area and staked three more. He sold those, too. He told me they just weren't big enough."

"Will he stay around for this one, or sell out soon?" Peter's frown let Claire know that he was thinking about his bank's investment in the mine.

"From what I can see, this find is a rich one. All the signs point to a huge, though deep, deposit of fine grade copper. If Ed's been looking for a big one, he's found it I'm sure."

Peter checked his pocket watch, then pushed his chair back. "I need to get to the bank."

"What are your plans for the day, Daniel?" asked Addie.

"Mrs. Haynes and I have a full day ahead." He smiled at his wife across the table. "I told Ed that I'd be up at the mine by the end of the month. Between now and then, we need to buy what we need to set up a home in Encampment and get ourselves moved."

"I knew this was coming, but I hate to see you go. I've loved having you here!" Addie's heartfelt announcement touched Claire.

After breakfast, Claire and Daniel sat in the parlor together, making lists of supplies they needed to buy before they left and planning the move.

"Maybe I need a list of all our lists," teased Claire as she put down her pen and sat back in her chair. They both sat quietly for a few minutes, surveying the lists of things to do and things to buy.

"Claire, before breakfast, didn't you say you had something important to talk to me about?"

"With all the excitement of your news, I totally forgot," answered Claire. "Yes, we do need to talk about something."

Claire retrieved a letter from her skirt pocket. "This is my latest letter from Haddie."

"I'm so glad you have reconnected with your friend. But that doesn't tell me why you are so serious." He looked out the window.

"I have an idea. Since we've been sitting here most of the morning would you like to take a walk and talk about it?"

Claire glanced out the window. The February sun was bright, reflecting the snow on the Rocky Mountains to the west. "The sunshine does look inviting. Yes, let's walk."

They donned their coats and hats, let Addie know they'd be back in a bit, then walked down the sidewalk hand in hand. Daniel stayed silent, letting the warmth of the sun's rays warm his back while Claire gathered her thoughts.

Finally, Claire began. "In this latest letter, Haddie mentions that my little brother Jesse is having a hard time."

"What kind of hard time?"

"He mostly is just quiet and sad most of the time, but sometimes in the last few months, he's turned angry and been difficult. He's treated Haddie's girls meanly at times. He asks Haddie often about Papa and when he will go live with him."

"Have you ever exchanged letters with Jesse?"

"I've written twice since we got here, and he's answered twice. His letters are worrisome to me, because talks about Papa and what he will do when Papa comes to get him. Daniel, I just can't let that happen."

Daniel stopped to face his wife. "Claire, what can we do to help?"

If Claire hadn't already loved Daniel, she'd have begun in that moment.

"I wonder if we could offer Jesse a place with us? I am not sure at all how to deal with an eight-year-old boy, but maybe just knowing we want him will help."

"That's a huge responsibility to take on and you know it will be more on your shoulders than on mine because I'll be working."

"Yes, I do know that, and I don't want to force you into taking this on."

"You do really well with Jeremiah and Richard, and they like you a lot."

"I love them dearly, but they are happy and well-loved boys. I don't know if I can help Jesse feel loved after Mama dying and Papa leaving him, especially if Haddie and William aren't being successful, but I've been praying about it ever since I got this letter and I think it is the right choice. If you agree."

"I agree," Daniel answered without hesitation. "You've told me before that Haddie thinks he feels like an outsider in their family no matter what they do to fold him in. Maybe he needs to be with his own flesh and blood."

"I will write to Haddie and see what she thinks. If she agrees, we can make plans for him to come to Encampment. Thank you, my Love."

"In the meantime, we need to proceed with our plans for moving. The house I rented in Encampment has an extra room I thought we could use as storage. We can turn that into his bedroom, the place will be big enough for three."

***

Four days later, Claire found herself turned in her seat waving goodbye to Addie, Peter and the boys. She sat beside Daniel on the spring seat of a large buckboard wagon. "I can't believe we got ready and are leaving so quickly," she said as she faced the road ahead.

"I'm pleased, too." Daniel captured her hand and held it tightly. Now that the four horse team was moving at a steady pace, he could hold the reins with just one hand. "We're a good team."

"I'm sorry we aren't travelling by train this time. It would be so much easier for you. We could have loaded the wagon on a train here and then gone to Cheyenne. But then we would have had to change trains there for one headed to Rawlins. In Rawlins we'd have had to backtrack in the wagon for two days."

"But isn't this route going to take us four or five at least?"

"Yes, but we'll have a hotel each night instead of sleeping out from Rawlins to Encampment, which would be very uncomfortable this time of year since there is nothing but sagebrush. Besides, this trip, though longer, will be full of beautiful scenery."

"If our backsides survive," Claire teased as they rumbled over a bump. "I'm glad you've found us a place already, so we don't have to be concerned about that."

"Claire, I know it isn't the best situation. I don't want to be away from you, but there is nowhere for us to live up near the mine. Right now, the men are living in the main mine entrance. When the snow melts, they'll move into tents until a bunkhouse can be built. Encampment is about fifteen miles away, but it is the nearest town to the mine."

"I understand that. I'm disappointed that I won't see you every day, but we'll manage. Do you think there will ever be a way to have a house close to the mine?"

"I don't know. It's so unforgiving up there. But, if the copper is there in the amounts I expect, the mine will attract people and surely towns will be built. As it is, some little towns or way stations are going to have to crop up along the road up to the mine. There at least needs to be places to eat and sleep along the way up."

"In the meantime, I will be in Encampment and you'll come home every week?"

"I hope so, at least every two weeks for a few days."

The day plodded on with each step of the horses. Claire and Daniel talked about their plans for the future, near and far. They marveled at the beauty of the Rocky Mountains to the west and the plains stretching east. The first night of their journey found them in Fort Collins at a small but clean hotel.

They set off early the next morning. Claire's back was stiff from the buckboard seat, but after watching Daniel stretch, she decided he must feel the same, so she didn't complain. While he checked the horses' lines and hooves, she lifted the heavy canvas tarp from the back and searched in one corner of the wagon. Triumphantly, she pulled out two pillows. She tucked the tarp carefully back into the wagon and carried the pillows to the seat.

"These should help," she said with a smile as Daniel climbed up.

"Hey, this is a great idea!" He shook the reins and they were off.

***

Boredom and weariness had ridden with them for miles. Claire was so tired when they arrived in Laramie two days later that she didn't even eat dinner. She enjoyed the vast valley that harbored the little town, but was achy from jostling along. "If it were summer, we could go over this mountain range ahead of us. There's a decent road over the Snowy Range, and it is beautiful up there, but it would take us a week," explained Daniel. "On this trip, we'll stay in the flats as much as possible, and go through a place called Woods Landing. There's a saloon there that's reputed to be pretty wild.

"Back when the transcontinental railroad was being built, these mountains were alive with men cutting trees to be used as ties. They'd drag the lodge pole pines down to Woods Landing and then float them in the Laramie River back to saw mills in Laramie. From there, they'd get loaded on the trains and taken to the end of the tracks."

"There's nothing about this country that's easy, is there?" remarked Claire.

***

Claire had been dozing, leaned against Daniel's shoulder. It was a testament to her complete fatigue that she could actually sleep on the trail.

She sat upright. Taking her hat off, she smoothed her hair and rubbed her neck. Daniel leaned over and kissed her cheek. Finally, after it seemed they'd been travelling forever, hope dawned.

"Claire, do you see that mountain peak over there?" He pointed ahead and a bit west.

"I see two right together," she answered.

"Right. The bald one is called Bridger Peak. When you stand on Bridger Peak, you think you're on the top of the world. The Rudefeha mine is just off that ridge a short distance to the northwest."

"So are we close to Encampment?"

"Yes, we'll be there in a few hours." He pointed again and helped Claire pinpoint the ridge that lies just above the town.

"The Grand Encampment is an old town and a new town," Daniel explained.

"I don't understand."

Daniel nudged her and smiled. "There's a lot of history there. Trappers and traders – real old mountain men - used to meet for a rendezvous every summer and they called it The Grand Encampment. That's where the name came from. Then, ranchers moved in, fighting warring Indians and the remote conditions to start ranches. This area, like around Woods Landing, was huge for supplying ties for the railroad, it still is in fact.

"The new part started just last summer when a man named Tom Sun surveyed and laid out the streets for the town. He works for a group of businessmen who are promoting the area. They were interested before Ed staked the Rudefeha claim, but now they are moving in high gear. There are four of them plus a man named George Emerson. He is the energy, and probably a lot of the money, behind it. I've known him since Cripple Creek. He's not one of my favorite people, but he gets things done. He lived in Denver before moving to Encampment and still spends a lot of time there."

"You've mentioned him before. Have you seen him lately?"

"We did talk about him at breakfast a few weeks ago. You and Peter were discussing an article about Rudefeha in the *Rocky Mountain News*."

"I remember now, it was a wonderful article written by Grant Jones."

"That's it."

Claire looked around, surveying all she could see of her new home. As the sun began to crawl towards Bridger Peak, they crossed a bridge over the Encampment River. The river wasn't very wide, maybe thirty feet, but it was lined on both sides with tall cottonwood trees.

"Is this Encampment?" Claire asked as they passed a small trading post.

"No, that is the Swan post office." He pointed uphill. "There's where we're going."

Just as he spoke, they cleared a stand of bare trees hugging the river. Claire got her first view of Encampment. Directly ahead of them was a sagebrush-dotted hillside that ended with pine covered foothills. Nestled in the elbow created there were a collection of wooden houses and buildings. The late afternoon was still, enabling the smoke from each home's chimney to climb straight up into the crisp blue sky.

Claire felt something like panic as she surveyed her new home town. Most of the buildings were rough-hewn boards with no paint. The streets were wide avenues of dirt and mud, rutted and full of puddles. A small dust devil swirled in front of them as they progressed, kicking dust into her face. She reached up to hold her hat in place.

"It doesn't look like, much, I know." Daniel held her hand as they approached. "It's growing, though, and if you hate it here, you could always move back to Denver."

"I wouldn't ever see you then!" Claire argued. "I'm sure I'll like it here just fine." She hoped her voice sounded more brave than she felt.

One of the horses nickered and tossed his head as they pulled in front of the livery. Clearly, this was the main street and business area. Claire looked around. Along the boardwalk were several store fronts boasting the assay office and a law office as well as the livery. The other side of the street looked like a mirror image. At the end of the block was a saloon. Claire could hear laughter and music drifting out through the open window.

Daniel stepped down, then reached up for Claire. A dusty young man with a beat-up hat walked out of the livery to meet them. "Evening, Cody," Daniel greeted him.

"Evening Mr. Haynes. Glad to have you back. Mr. Haggarty was down this week, he left this mornin'. He was askin' about you."

"Well, we're here now." Daniel introduced the man to his wife, then arranged for him to unhitch the wagon and take care of the horses. "I'd appreciate it very much if the wagon could stay in the barn tonight. Is there room?"

"Yes, Sir," Cody plopped his hat back on his head and took the lead horse by the halter. "There's plenty of room tonight, don't worry. Everything will be safe and dry until you come for it."

Daniel smiled. "That should be tomorrow pretty early. Thanks, Cody."

Cody led the horses and wagon into the barn after Daniel grabbed their two travelling bags from under the seat. "Now, Mrs. Haynes, let's find a place to lay our heads."

They walked to the end of the block and turned onto Freeman Street. Claire was a bit surprised to see street signs in such a rough little town. Ahead of them Claire read a tidy sign "Bohn Hotel and Restaurant".

***

Before she opened her eyes the next morning, Claire stretched. Her back and legs were stiff and sore, but the feather bed and soft sheets caressed her. She lay on her side, her arm across her husband, her head on his chest. For a moment, she didn't know where she was and didn't care as long as he was breathing beside her. Then she remembered.

She'd been surprised at how nice the hotel interior was compared to the rough look of the outside. It was apparent that Daniel had made arrangements with the proprietress, Miss Mary Bohn in advance. Claire took an hour or so for herself, and after a long relaxing bath, they enjoyed dinner together in the small dining room off the lobby. The staff was efficient and made Claire feel welcome. They'd taken a short walk after dinner and Daniel pointed out a few of the city's features so that she could begin to know her way around. After her initial horror at seeing Encampment for the first time, by the time they went to bed, Claire felt much more comfortable.

Claire stretched again and opened her eyes to find Daniel studying her.

"Good morning," he whispered.

27

May, 1898
Encampment, Wyoming

"Rejoice in the Lord Always: and again I say, Rejoice." Claire read the verse from Philippians several times. She looked around her house and smiled. *I know I have so much to be thankful for,* she thought. *This is small, but it was warm when the April snows fell, and it is safe.*

She sat by the only window in the parlor, tucked into a wingback chair they'd brought with them from Denver. Addie was making room for new furniture in her upstairs sitting room and offered the chair and a matching sofa to her. The chintz flower pattern was a little faded for Addie's tastes, but Claire thought they were lovely. She smiled, remembering how a trip to a large furniture store in Denver had netted them the three cherry wood end tables that completed the room.

She sipped her coffee, but put the cup down when she realized it was cold. Outside the window the muddy street reminded Claire the kitchen needed sweeping and dusting needed done. It had been just over three weeks since Daniel had last been home, and she wasn't sure when he'd be back. *Who knew that sixteen miles could be such a long way?* She sighed.

She thought with sadness about the argument they'd had when he was last home. It started innocently.

"When do you think the mine will be up and running enough that you'll be able to come home more often and stay a bit longer?"

"Claire, mining is tough work. Every day is a new challenge when men's lives are on the line. The deeper and farther in we go, the stiffer that challenge becomes. What are you talking about, really?" His voice had a hard edge.

Normally, Claire sidestepped him when he was surly, but she felt grumpy at knowing he was only planning to be home two days this time, and his answer set her off.

"What am I talking about? Well let's see. The first day you are home you are grouchy and tired because you usually work even longer than your normal twelve hour days to prepare to be gone, then after just a day or so home, you start getting that faraway look in your eyes that tells me your thoughts have gone back to work without your body."

"Gee, Claire, that's not true."

"Yes, Daniel. It is. You can be gone three or four weeks at a time. If you come home for three days, I get one tired day, one nice day and then one when you are distracted."

"That's just not true." He was yelling and so was she.

"The worst part is that I sit here alone, trying to fill the hours, knowing that when you are home you'd rather be there. It's a quandary to be jealous of a hole in the ground!"

Tears escaped as Claire recalled the fight. Daniel looked wounded at her words, but couldn't see her perspective. She tried, even three weeks later, to understand his dedication to work. She did love and respect him for how hard he worked, but continued to struggle with feeling like the mine was her rival.

A while later, Claire returned the broom to its spot behind the door and surveyed her work. The house was clean, the bed made, everything dusted and primped. It was barely after ten thirty. *What am I going to do with the rest of the day?* Claire thought. *I know I am supposed to rejoice in the Lord always, and I do. But the days are so long here by myself.*

She considered walking up to Main Street to the small market, but she knew she did that too often and tended to buy things she really didn't need. She'd already finished the dime novel she'd bought just last week, the laundry and ironing were done, there wasn't any sewing or patching to do. Irritation began to nag her. *Where was Daniel? Why didn't he come home?* She realized she was pacing. Then she asked herself, *What if he doesn't love me anymore? What if he has been killed?* Claire stopped herself, "This is silly," she told herself aloud. "This is what happens when you have too much time on your hands. Find something to do!"

She grabbed her coat and hat and fled. As she walked, she thought about her life. She'd never before been alone. At the farm, she couldn't be idle for fear of her father. There had always been chores to do. At Jack's she'd had more free time during the day, but there was always someone around to talk with. This life was different.

She let her thoughts wander as she walked east towards the outskirts of town. Encampment was a bustling place. Since the town was surveyed and planned last year, assorted homes and businesses were being built. Some were close to the center of town, but in other places a house stood alone with nothing close by. Now that the weather was warming, the snow melt caused the Encampment River to run high and fast. As she got closer to the trees signaling the river, Claire could hear the shouts of men. Curious, she headed in that direction.

Claire found a spot near the riverbank up on a small rise. She watched as six or seven men, standing on the river banks and using long poles, yelled at each other to coordinate efforts to sort out a jam that had occurred when two logs got themselves sideways to the others. Before long, the jam was cleared. The flotilla of logs and parade of men continued its way downriver. The water rushed quickly, so it didn't take long before the men were out of sight. These were the tie hacks she'd heard about. Tie hacks, which is what the locals called lumberjacks, scoured the foothills for timbers for the mine and local buildings as well as ties for several rail lines being built in southern Wyoming.

I'll have to describe what just happened to Daniel in my journal, she thought as turned back towards town. Then she had another thought. *The river will be a fun place to bring Jesse when he arrives. He'll be interested in this.*

Claire thought about Haddie and the plans they were making. Haddie and William were sad to see Jesse go, but agreed with Claire that joining her could be the key for him. As she continued her walk, Claire thought about the letter she'd received last month. Haddie described Jesse's excitement when they'd talked with him about moving to live with Claire and Daniel. Then, Jesse added a letter of his own thanking her and promising that he'd be "The best brother you ever had!"

Initially, Claire worried about how Jesse could make the trip. Both couples agreed that he was too young to travel so far alone, but they didn't know who could travel with him. After a few weeks of prayer and consideration, William found out that a friend of his

206

from Mitchell was planning a trip to San Francisco. Arrangements fell into place rapidly when the man agreed to escort Jesse as far as Walcott Junction, the closest stop on the railroad to them. Daniel could meet the train there, then he and Jesse could ride together back to Encampment. Her brother's arrival was less than a month away.

The next morning, Claire set out to do errands in town. "Good morning, Claire," Mary Bohn was sweeping the boardwalk in front of the hotel.

"Good morning," Claire answered as she covered the distance between them. "How are you?"

"I'm well, thank you. I don't see Mr. Daniel with you, has he gone back up the mountain?"

"Sadly, yes. I haven't seen much of him lately. The weather around here amazes me. Even though it is May, it seems like every time he tries to come down either there is a snowstorm or some problem at the mine that keeps him away. By the time he did come down the last time, I was nearly frantic worrying and missing him."

"I've heard talk of plans for a telegraph line from here to the mine. That would be good."

"I can't tell you how much I'd appreciate that," nodded Claire. "It's the not knowing that's hard."

"It's all hard, Claire, make no mistake. Every woman in this town who has to stay here and wait either prays too much or drinks too much!" Mary paused then changed the subject. "Have you heard the latest news from the mountains?"

"Not recently. What's happened?"

"Old Alkali Ike showed up in town yesterday. He spent about an hour talking with me and that couple who are staying here on their way to Montana. He sang us a new song and danced a jig for us."

"He sounds like quite a character."

"Yes, he is a good entertainer and though he's a bit odd, he's harmless. The other news is about James Graham. A month or so ago we had a report that he'd been doing some claim jumping up in the mountains and that he'd been lynched."

"Yes, I'd heard that. It was awful."

"Well, it turns out it wasn't true. Mr. Graham is alive and well."

"How did the story get started then?" Claire wondered.

"I don't know exactly. Mr. Graham is an attorney, and it sounds like maybe he was doing some inquiries for a client about a claim. How news of his lynching came about is anyone's guess. The *Encampment Echo* has confirmed that he is alive and well, though." The ladies chatted and laughed together for a few more minutes, then Claire continued on to the market.

"Good morning," Claire smiled as she entered the store.

"Good to see you Mrs. Haynes," responded the clerk, a middle aged matron with a kind smile.

They chatted for a few minutes. It seemed that Alkali Ike had stopped in here as well.

"I need a few things. Here's my list." As she handed the paper the clerk, she noticed the *Denver Post* on the counter.

"It's hard to believe that America is at war," she said, shaking her head.

"They are calling it the Spanish-American War. President McKinley tried to negotiate peace, but I guess Congress had no other choice than to declare war once the Spanish sunk the *Maine* and then declared war on us."

"I think you are right," answered Claire. "With 260 men dead and an American war ship lying on the bottom of Havana harbor, I don't see there was much choice."

Claire read the paper's front page article as the clerk gathered her order. When she returned and began wrapping the items in brown paper and string, Claire continued the discussion. "It says here that as of May first a large Spanish fleet has arrived at a harbor in the southern part of Cuba. Naval and ground forces are planning their response. It's all so terrible."

Claire fished a dollar bill and some coins from her purse to pay for her purchases.

"Thank you very much," she said and turned to go.

"Oh, wait! I nearly forgot. You have a letter." She reached behind her and retrieved a thick envelope. Claire saw Haddie's neat writing and her return address before she had it in hand. Claire tucked the letter into her purse and headed for home.

Later, she sat at the table to enjoy a 'conversation' with her friend.

Things are quite dull and normal here. It was a nice, wet spring so William's crops are growing well. Our children are all fine. Marshall is a beanpole, very tall and thin but always into mischief. A young family moved into your old place. I've only met them a couple of times but they seem nice.

Jesse seems like a different child now that plans are solid for his trip to you. I think you are right, much as we tried, he's not felt as if he fit in here. There were times when I'd notice that he'd call William 'Pa' like the rest of the boys do, and we certainly didn't mind, but then he would catch himself and stop. From the first letter I got from you after you and Daniel married, he began to share a barrage of memories about things you and he used to do. He got tears in his eyes when he talked of how you sang to him and read to him after he'd gotten caught in the grain binder. Even in this crowd, he tended to be sad and lonely a lot of the time. At eight years old, he still reminds me of a little old man. I've grown to love him very much, and I hope he knows that. I'll be sad to have him leave, but I am certainly happy you two will be together. I can't think of anything better for him.

As you know, Marcus left here about ten months ago to join the army. We haven't heard much from him, just a couple of postcards, but two weeks ago we had a letter from him. He volunteered and was chosen for an elite group of horsemen led by Teddy Roosevelt, the former secretary of the Navy. It is a cavalry unit that Roosevelt himself nicknamed The Rough Riders. They have been training in San Antonio, Texas, learning to shoot from horseback and maneuver together. He writes that they expect to leave Texas for deployment to Cuba by the end of May. I am enclosing his address, though we know that will change, and I have already written to him with your address. It sounds like he'll be in the thick of this war with Spain, but he assured me in the letter that they were highly skilled compared to the Spanish, who don't even have ground forces in Cuba.

Haddie ended her letter with a bit more news about local farmers and with love and best wishes. Claire read the letter twice more before returning it to the envelope. She sat for several minutes, thinking about Haddie and her family and praying for them and her brothers. Smiling, she pulled paper and pen out of the small chest in the corner of the kitchen and sat down to write, first to Marcus and then to Haddie.

***

Claire stood in front of her grandmother's mirror the next morning wearing her plain grey dress and holding a small, brimless hat trimmed with grey and black satin ribbon and small dusty rose colored silk flowers. The hat fit nicely over the low bun she'd twisted her hair into. Her small house shuddered as a wind gust attacked it from the east. Being the first of June, the air was fresh, not too cold and the sun shone brightly into her window, but the wind was gusty and unpredictable. *I'll need two hatpins to keep this toque from flying right off my head and down the street,* she thought as she worked to secure it. Finally satisfied at its look and security, Claire carefully tucked the two letters from yesterday into her small handbag and set out for the market.

About a block from her little house, Claire passed a large freight wagon parked in front of a large clapboard house. As she passed, a tall man dressed in a three-piece suit stood on the house's ample porch talking to two local young men. Claire could hear the man giving directions for unloading the wagon. With his prompting, they pulled a tarp off the wagon. Claire was surprised to see that tied on top of the wagon was a large brass bed that still sported sheets and coverlets. The sight was odd, and Claire wondered if someone had slept the night perched up there. Sitting off by herself at the other end of the porch was a young woman. Glancing only, so she wouldn't be thought rude, Claire noticed that a woman sat on a straight backed chair with her arms crossed in front of her and an angry scowl on her face.

Few people were out on the boardwalk when she reached the market, but inside there were several customers. The store was very small, and the variety of items for sale was limited. There were only two shelves in the common area to shop from, and most of those items were tools or livery supplies. Claire stood in line behind two older matrons she'd never met before as the clerk waited on a rough-looking man with mud on his boots.

"I hear they have come from Denver to open a mercantile," the taller of the two ladies in front of Claire said.

"It would be nice to have a large store to shop from," ventured her companion, "But I'm not sure about that outfit."

"Charlie says the woman didn't want to come. Said he heard the man teasing her about carrying her out of the house still in the bed. Seems that she refused to get up on moving day, so he had his men carry her out, bed and all!"

"Can you imagine?"

Their conversation was interrupted as the clerk turned to help them.

Later, as Claire left the store with her purchase of eggs and a spool of thread, she thought about the woman she'd seen on the porch. Claire had been happy to leave Rapid City and her old life behind to come to Encampment for a new start. She felt sorry for anyone who didn't want to come here. When she passed the house, she noticed that the wagon was now nearly empty, only a few boxes remained. The woman was no longer outside.

Claire spent the first part of the afternoon patching a pair of trousers Daniel had brought home. He'd caught the pocket on something and the fabric was torn. She bit the thread in two then surveyed her work. Satisfied, she folded the trousers and put them in Daniel's drawer. She rubbed her neck and looked around, recalling a conversation she and Daniel had the morning he left for the mine.

"I worry about leaving you here all alone. I hate that I'm up there so far away from you." Claire thought of the love in his touch as he reached for her hand. "I love you, even though you think I work too much."

"I worry more about you. I don't understand mining a great deal, but I know you are in danger."

"Not as much as you'd think, really. Please don't fret. I think one of the reasons Haggarty made me such a generous offer to be the on-site engineer was because he'd seen how careful I am to create a safe mine. There are lots of engineers who give in to owners and miners who want to hurry to the ore and don't pay enough attention to making the shafts sturdy and safe."

"Just be sure to come home to me," Claire continued.

"Honestly, Claire, I worry about leaving you here. I've been thinking about something you said yesterday about not having much to do to fill the hours of your day."

"Some days do really drag on and on."

"Would you be happier in Denver? I'm sure that Addie would love to have you stay with them, or we could rent a house close by. It would be company for you."

"I'd be so far away from you, we'd be apart even more than we are now." Claire began. "Thank you for offering, and thank you for suggesting it, but I think I'll be fine. It's just taking me some time to get my balance. Please don't misunderstand this, I certainly don't miss being at Jack's, but I do miss having girlfriends to chat with. It was fun to have Lela and Estelle to pal around with. I'd love to find a friend or two here, but I'm not sure how to go about it. Anyway, in just a few weeks, I won't be alone. We'll have Jesse here."

Claire sighed in her remembering. Daniel had no suggestions for her about how to meet new friends. In all her trips to the store and her walks through Encampment, Claire hadn't met anyone who struck her as a possible friend. Most folks she'd met were like the two gossips she'd listened to at the store. The ratio of men to women on this Wyoming frontier left her with few options.

The mantle clock struck one. Claire sighed again. The long afternoon stretched in front of her. She stood at the window, when the latest letter from Haddie caught her eye and gave her an idea.

Two hours later Claire found herself standing in front of the white clapboard house. The wagon she'd seen this morning sat empty. The house was quiet. Claire smoothed her hair and adjusted her hat then knocked at the screen door.

Soon, the woman Claire had seen briefly on the porch came into view. She smiled tentatively and opened the door.

"Hello," Claire began. She felt shy and awkward, but forged on. "My name is Claire Haynes, and I live just around the corner. I'm not the greatest of bakers, and I've never tried this recipe before, but I've baked some oatmeal nut bread to welcome you to Encampment."

Tears filled the woman's eyes. She took the cloth-wrapped bundle automatically as Claire handed it to her, fighting for composure. Finally, she smiled.

"My name is Ella Parkison, and you are an angel."

"Far from it," laughed Claire.

"Please come in," Ella stepped aside while she held the door. "I have just managed to clear the kitchen enough that we might be able to find a place to sit." She led Claire down a narrow hall toward the back of the house and the kitchen. Ella picked up a bowl that had been resting on one chair and moved it to the counter by the sink. The room was small and cluttered with boxes and items that hadn't yet been put away, but the braided rug on the floor and the well-oiled pedestal table helped it to already feel cozy and welcoming.

"I just made myself some tea, would you like some?"

"I'd love it," Claire answered.

28
July, 1898
Encampment, Wyoming

Clare was too anxious to sit down, but there was nothing left to do. She'd checked the storage room they'd converted into a bedroom at least four times. It was small, but with a fresh coat of white paint on the walls and ceiling and a green curtain over the high window, Claire and Daniel were satisfied that it would be a nice room for a boy. Claire liked the bed and dresser they ordered from Denver. She'd covered the bed with a light green blanket from Parkison's General Store. Just two days ago Claire spotted a small writing desk at Jameson's hardware that she couldn't pass by. Now, the desk and its matching chair, already equipped with paper, pencils and a new fountain pen sat in a corner of the room, just waiting.

Waiting. Claire paced inside for a while, then moved outside. She pulled a weed from the front flower bed, then tried to sit down. She knew that Daniel had planned to leave the mountains to be at the train stop in Walcott Junction at three in the afternoon day before yesterday to meet Jesse's train.

"I'll see how tired the boy is when he gets off the train. There isn't anything in Walcott except a café. We'll eat if he's hungry, then leave. I'll be sure to have a bedroll and a horse for each of us, and we'll stop at dark. Those eighty five miles will take two days of riding, so you can expect us accordingly. If we get a good start on the first day, that should put us into Encampment sometime in the late afternoon the second day."

"It's after two o'clock! Where are they?" Claire stewed, pacing and fidgeting for nearly an hour longer when she finally heard a commotion outside.

"Hello the house!"

Claire flew off the porch, reaching the travelers just as Jesse pulled his foot from the stirrup. She folded him into a hug. He hesitated for just a second, then his arms circled her waist in a tight embrace. Brother and sister stayed that way for nearly half a minute, not talking, just breathing. Finally, she loosened her hold and stepped back. Daniel encased her in a hug from behind as she studied her brother in front. He was taller than she'd expected, and he was thin and wiry. His hair, the same color as her own, was a bit shaggy underneath a dusty brown wool cap. His eyes, brown just like hers, hinted at a sadness his smile was trying to hide.

"I thought you two were never going to get here!" she chided with a smile. "What took you so long?"

"Claire, Daniel is the best!" Jesse's voice was still that of a little boy, now loud and excited. "We were getting tired and sore so we stopped at a place by the river where the water is hot, and went swimming."

Daniel filled in details as Claire smiled. "It's the mineral hot spring near Saratoga."

"We sat in the hot water for a while, then jumped into the cold, cold river." He stopped and looked at Daniel. "Was it the North Platte River?"

Daniel smiled, "Yes, that's right."

"Anyway. We swam, then let the sun dry us off. I've never had such fun!"

Jesse continued to talk, nearly without a breath, about their trip. Daniel listened as he worked to remove the bedrolls and saddle bags from the horses, then interrupted the narrative.

"We need to take the horses up to the livery for the night. Claire, will you walk with us?"

"I'd love to."

As they walked, Claire asked about the train trip.

"Oh, it was alright. William's friend Mr. Adams wasn't very talkative, and he read a newspaper or a book nearly the whole time. There were only adults on the train and they kept quiet, so I just spent the whole trip staring out the window."

"You certainly brought more than what was in the saddle bags with you. Where are your things?"

"Haddie sent me with a whole trunk full of stuff. She made sure I had five pairs of britches and nearly a dozen shirts, mostly hand me downs from Matthew, that she patched and hemmed. But then she packed up my quilt and some books and things for you."

"Where is the trunk?"

"Oh, Daniel talked to a man at the station about bringin' it. Claire, you should have seen that guy! He was as gruff as an old grizzly bear. He had a team of six white horses pulling a freight wagon loaded way high. When we were standing talking to him, another man came up and started teasing him. It seems that a few months ago, the driver was delivering some freight in Saratoga and threw a lighted dynamite stick into the river there. They were laughing about how it rained fish."

"Can you imagine?" Claire looked at Daniel for confirmation of the story.

"Everything Jess here is saying is the truth. The man's name is Jack Fulkerson. He runs a freight outfit. He delivers all around here, including dynamite and supplies up to the mine. I've met him several times. He's quite a character."

Jesse continued, "He loaded my trunk on the back of his wagon and set out. You know what?"

Claire smiled and shook her head.

"He doesn't sit on the wagon while he goes. He rides the horse closest to the wagon on the left hand side and he only holds the reins for the lead horse. I can't believe anyone could control a rig like that."

Jesse talked about Fulkerson for the rest of the walk to the livery. The siblings waited for Daniel outside in the shade. "You sure seem interested in horses and wagons," Claire observed.

"I truly love horses, Claire. Papa's horses were old and mean but William treated his horses kindly, and they were gentle. One of my jobs there was to feed the horses every day and muck out the stalls twice a week. I didn't mind that job a bit."

"You like horses so much you even liked cleaning the stalls?" Claire was teasing as she asked.

"The girls left me alone when I did it, and I liked that too."

Daniel rejoined them, then, and Claire let the subject drop. She wondered about what he meant.

***

That night in the quiet of their bedroom, Claire finally had a few minutes alone with her husband.

"You've spent more time so far with Jesse than I have. What do you think?" Claire asked.

"He seems alright. I haven't seen anything that isn't just like any other boy."

"He likes you a lot, it's clear," Claire smiled. "In the next few days it will be fun to establish a routine around here. I thought maybe tomorrow we could go for a picnic by the river."

"Claire, I need to leave first thing and go back to work."

"What? No! You just got here. You can't be home half a day and go back to work!"

"Claire, I have been gone from the mine for four days going to Walcott and then home. I need to get back."

"Daniel, please. You work all the time. Can't you take an extra day or two?"

Daniel's voice was impatient. "I know you miss me, and I miss you, but people are depending on me and I need to work. I don't want to fight about it, please."

"Well I need you, too." Her words came out whiny and she instantly wanted them back. Her irritation grew. "I never get the chance to depend on you. You are always there."

Daniel's eyes snapped up and locked on hers. They stood there, both angry.

After a few moments, Daniel shrugged. "I do need to get back. I know you are disappointed. Let's don't fight. I'll be back down more often, I promise." He held out his arms.

Claire wasn't satisfied but knew there was no point in continuing the argument. She loved how persistent and focused Daniel was about everything he did, but she didn't think she'd ever feel kindly toward the mine.

Sighing, she stepped into his arms and tried to let it go.

Daniel left his augmented family the next morning for the mine. In the next few days, Claire and Jesse fell into a comfortable routine. Claire wanted her brother to have chores around the house, but guessed that household duties wouldn't really interest him. Jess was drying dishes beside her on his third evening there.

"Aw, Claire, I don't mind much drying dishes with you. I used to do it for Mama. It was a quiet time for us to be together. Mostly, Papa had me out in the yard, taking care of the chickens and pigs."

"Maybe we should get some chickens for you to raise," suggested Claire, though the thought of having chickens made her shiver.

"If you want to, I'll take care of them, but I'm not real fond of chickens. They can be pretty mean."

Claire laughed. "Honestly, I hate chickens."

Jesse looked relieved. "I wouldn't mind having a horse. I love horses."

"I'm not sure our neighbors here in town would appreciate a horse. The horses you and Daniel used to come home from Walcott are ours, but when he's home they have to board at the livery."

"I s'pose that's true. It's kind of hard to get used to living in a town."

"I wonder if Cody down at the livery ever needs help with the animals there?"

Jesse's eyes lit up. "Do you think I could ask him? I could work for him all day, and he wouldn't even need to pay me!"

Claire smiled. "I don't think you are old enough for a full time job yet, but maybe we can work something out with him. Anyway, starting in the fall, you'll be spending your days at school.

"School? I don't need to go to school!"

"Yes, you do. Don't worry about that now, though. How about tomorrow you and I walk over to the livery and see if Cody could use your help sometimes?"

Jesse shrugged at the mention of school, but agreed easily to Claire's plan.

By the next afternoon, Jesse was a hired hand at the livery. He helped Cody with the afternoon chores of feeding, mucking stalls, and cleaning saddles and tack for a couple hours most days. Each evening when he came home, he had stories and descriptions of the stock and the people he'd met. His pay was twenty cents a week, and he was jubilant.

Claire decided that Jesse's assigned chores at home would include cutting the grass in the summer and shoveling the walks in the winter as well as making sure she had firewood in the house for heating and cooking. He accepted the shoveling and wood patrol jobs easily, telling her he was happy to continue drying dishes as well. When she first talked with him about keeping the grass around the house mowed, he was downcast. "Papa didn't like how

I use a scythe. He cussed me about how uneven my cuts were, said everything looked choppy and bad when I was finished."

Claire studied the slump of his shoulders and the droop of his head, then answered softly. "My friend, Mrs. Parkison and her husband, have a wonderful Budding Lawn Mower. It has a blade that rotates while you push it, and it makes their grass look like something out of a painting." She smiled. She had Jesse's full attention.

"How about you and I go over there and see if we could work out a deal with them?"

Jesse interrupted Claire. "I'll bet if I offer to cut their grass, they might let me use it to cut ours!"

Their visit with Ella the next afternoon was a profitable one. Ella was delighted to meet Claire's brother. After politely having tea and cookies with the women, Jesse shyly brought up the idea of mowing their grass. Ella answered that she wasn't in a position to strike a deal with Jesse. "Mr. Parkison is pretty proud of that mower, you'll have to talk to him."

Jesse thought for a minute, then turned to Claire. "Claire, could we go over and meet Mr. Parkison at the store later?" Claire was impressed with his zeal.

Ella smiled, also impressed, and offered the boy his first look at the mower, sending him out to a small shed behind the garden. He happily excused himself. When he was out of earshot, Ella asked Claire how he was doing.

"I think he likes it here. He seems to be relaxing and settling in. Sometimes he looks really sad, but he doesn't ever say much. Once in a while something slips out, mostly about missing Mama." Claire stopped there, uncomfortable sharing more of their family woes. She guessed that there was more to the story, but Jesse closed down or changed the subject anytime Papa came up.

Life settled into a comfortable routine. Claire and Jesse enjoyed each other and got along well. They both looked forward to when Daniel came home. It was an adjustment for Claire at first to share her husband with her little brother, but it was clear that Jesse was awed by his brother-in-law, and benefitted from the time he spent with him, so Claire willingly gave up a bit of her precious time with Daniel for Jesse.

***

218

The loose bun Claire had twisted her hair into early in the morning had partially come undone, her face was red and covered with a sheen of heat and worry, her dress and apron were coated with flour and several unidentifiable spots. The kitchen mirrored its mistress. Dirty bowls, pots and dishes filled the sink and counter. Daniel stood in the doorway smiling.

"You should take that goofy grin off your face and do something helpful," Claire teased with a slight edge in her voice. She felt crabby though she was trying not to be.

Daniel rolled up his sleeves and started washing dishes.

"I haven't ever given a dinner party before, and I'm so nervous." Claire stood beside him, now, with a dish towel at the ready.

He handed her the first pot. "It is going to be great. Everything smells delicious. Don't worry."

They worked in silence for a few minutes. As she dried each pot or dish, she went over her plans. The roast with carrots and potatoes was in the oven and nearly done. The bread she'd baked this morning was sitting on the cutting board ready to slice. She had cucumbers from the garden marinating in vinegar as a salad. The pie she'd baked while the bread was raising was golden brown, waiting for its debut as dessert.

Daniel pulled Claire into a tight hug. "I love you, you know," he whispered. His wife's disheveled hair tickled his nose.

Claire didn't respond. She just soaked in his embrace and words. She relaxed against him and let the tension flow from her neck. Daniel had been home two days and had promised to stay two more. Claire was ecstatic, even if a main part of the trip was work related and Daniel had been in meetings each morning.

Daniel continued, "It was nice of Mrs. Mullens to invite Jesse to her house tonight so that we could have company."

"Yes, it worked out well. Her grandson is here visiting, and it's been fun that Jesse and he became friends. They'll have a good campout tonight in their back yard, and we can enjoy an evening to ourselves."

"We have about an hour before our guests are due to arrive. I'll finish cleaning this kitchen if you want to go get ready."

"I don't deserve you," Claire answered. They stood together a minute longer, then she handed him her dish towel and left the room.

By the time their first guests knocked on the door, Claire was dressed, her hair was fixed and smooth and the kitchen was clean.

"Daniel, you remember Ed and Ella Parkison," Claire hugged her friend then turned to Daniel. The two men shook hands.

"Your home looks lovely," Ella smiled at Claire. "The daisies are so cheery." Daniel's final kindness after he finished the dishes was to cut some daisies from the yard and put them into a milk jar. The table was too small for the bouquet, so they sat on one of the side tables in the parlor.

The foursome talked about the hot weather and lack of rain for a few minutes when the second couple arrived. Claire had met Ed Haggarty several times, but this was the first time he'd been a guest for dinner. Daniel made introductions, as Ed and Ella had never met him, then Haggarty introduced his companion.

"Everyone, this is Miss Edith Crow. Her family ranches cattle just northeast of Encampment."

Claire brought in a tray with glasses of lemonade for everyone, then sat on the sofa next to Ella. The ladies listened as the men chatted about the stock holders meeting that they were out of the mountains to attend. Eventually, the talk moved to other current events and finally to grain prices in the valley.

Claire surveyed her parlor. Ed and Ella sat next to her on the sofa. He wore a rich, three-piece blue silk suit with a fine gold chain leading into his watch pocket. As he conversed with the men, his voice and demeanor were confident and self-assured. He talked with authority about the local economy and the expected growth of the Encampment region. It was clear he was a man used to being listened to, and for good reason.

Ella's pale blue silk dress complimented her husband's suit. She sat straight and tall, but even so she looked small and somehow fragile beside her tall, barrel-chested husband. Ella's dress had a lace collar buttoned at the neck and cuffs. She wore no makeup or jewelry, and only a small, plain hat.

Miss Crow sat quietly in the wing-backed chair. Her rose-colored cotton dress may have been handmade and it fit her perfectly. It showed her round, womanly figure. She wore a small hat that had a nosegay of flowers and feathers along the thin brim, pinned fashionably on the side of her head.

Claire's eyes and attention returned again and again to Ed Haggarty. He sat in one of the two kitchen chairs, pulled in to the parlor to accommodate the party. His hair was short on the sides and longer on the top, but parted on the side and slicked down with what Claire guessed was Macassar oil. She thought she'd gotten a whiff of its coconut oil and ylang-ylang when he kissed her cheek in greeting. Ed's tall, lanky frame and thin mustache somehow gave the impression of youth, though Claire knew that at thirty two he was a few years older than Daniel. He wore a white shirt and vest with no jacket. His pants were clean, but well-worn above a pair of scuffed boots. In comparison to Ed Parkison, Haggarty was completely underdressed and perhaps even a bit shabby, yet his humble confidence and quick smile were so ingratiating and genuine that Claire felt he'd never seem out of place whether at a bar or at court. Of course, his English accent commanded attention partly because of its novelty, but also because Haggarty only spoke when what he had to say was important.

"You own more than one mercantile, am I right?" Daniel was addressing Parkison.

"Yes, right now we just have one in Denver and one here, though I am negotiating for a new building to house a third store in the southern part of Denver. That area is growing so quickly, there's a need for another well-stocked mercantile."

"We're certainly glad to have the Parkison Store here in Encampment," ventured Edith. "It's such a relief not to have to wait months for things we need."

"I'm so glad," Parkison responded. "We're trying to get our inventory up to meet the community's needs."

"Well," added Claire, "I think we need ice cream."

The group chuckled as Ella elbowed her husband in mock irritation. "I've been telling you that since we got here."

"My dear wife has a soft spot for ice cream and hasn't given me a moment's peace about it since we arrived here. I am certain she instigated this line of discussion," he smiled at her then put on a grim frown at Claire. The group chuckled again. "Actually, I have been negotiating with a local man to build an ice house and harvest ice from the Encampment River this coming winter so that we have a sure supply for next year. If that deal works out, then next spring we will put in a small ice cream counter at the back of the store."

Ella smiled triumphantly while the ladies congratulated her.

Claire rose. "Daniel, if you will get the chairs replaced around the table, it is time to eat."

At the end of dinner, Ed Haggarty groaned. "Mrs. Haynes, this meal was fitting of Prince Edward's palate. I've eaten a right bit more than I should have I think."

Claire beamed as her guests echoed the compliment. "It's such a nice evening, Daniel, if you'll move a few chairs out to the porch, we can enjoy the evening air and I'll make some tea and coffee to go with our dessert."

A few minutes later, Claire joined the group outside. "Mr. Haggarty, we've not talked about your endeavors in the hills. How is work on the mine going?" asked Parkison.

"It goes well, I think. On the 25th of August, just last week it is, we blasted into the main cavern where we thought the copper vein was going to be. Thanks to Danny here, we uncovered a thick, rich vein starting at about thirty feet."

"That's good news for you."

"Quite so. The night before the blast I had dreams we'd come up with nothing, so I was never so happy to see that ribbon of copper."

"So mining will start in earnest now. When do you expect to start hauling ore out?"

"It's not as easy as that, I'm afraid. We have a bit of a problem with water in the mine that we have to deal with."

Daniel shrugged. "Listen to the master of understatement. That 'bit of a problem' is to the tune of fifty to a hundred gallons of inflowing water each hour. It turns out that the mountain houses copper and an underground spring at the same spot deep inside."

"Oh my," said Claire. "How can you resolve that?"

"We'll have to build a whim," stated Haggarty. He forged on, realizing that only Daniel knew what he was talking about. "A whim is a kind of pulley system. To start, we'll use horses to power it, but should be able to change it to steam power quite soon. The idea of a whim is that it has a vertical shaft that goes 'round and 'round. On one side a series of ropes and pulleys allows buckets to descend into the mine shaft while at the same time another set on the other side is ascending. It's an efficient use of power and t'will get the better of the water that is percolating into the mine."

"So you've built and used a whim before, huh Haggarty?" asked Parkison.

"Ay. I was raised in Cumberland, England. Now Cumberland has two claims to fame. One, 'tis a seaport. And two, 'tis a coal mining community. My da and all my uncles were coal miners. I did a bit of helping in the mine as I was growing up."

"I'm not sure we are actually going to have to build the whim, Ed." Haggarty's head snapped toward Daniel at his comment.

"That's a fine piece of information, Danny. What are you thinking?"

"I talked to a hand from the Peryam ranch today outside the stockholder's meeting. He thinks that the ranch has a whim, and from the sound of it, that could be the answer to our problem. I'll go over tomorrow afternoon to the Peryam place and see if they'd be willing to part with it, then we could get Jack Fulkerson to haul it up."

"I'd like to go with you. That would save us a lot of time and money."

"There's one other smaller problem we have to solve before we can start mining," Daniel addressed the whole group. "Last winter, the miners just lived right in the mine. This summer we've been in tents alongside the site. Once we start pulling the ore out, we'll work year round and there's no room for men to live in the mine. We've got to get bunkhouses built for the miners."

"How many miners are up there?" asked Ella.

"Right now we have eighteen. I'm advertising for about nine more men. I'd like to have twenty-seven when we start hauling it out."

"When do you expect that to be?"

"I predict that we'll have our first load on its way to Fort Steele by mid-October. Once we are selling the ore and seeing a return on the investments, then we're also going to have to find a different way than by wagon to get the ore to a smelter. Those mountains are treacherous in the summer and impossible to navigate in the winter."

"Daniel, isn't getting wood for the bunk houses something you've been working on since you came back to Encampment?" Claire asked.

"Absolutely," he replied. "I just today firmed up the deal for enough timber to be cut and delivered so that we can get started on a large bunk house and mess hall."

"Who'd you end up hirin', Danny?" asked Haggarty. "I know you talked to several people."

"I've signed a contract with Art Jameson's son Nathan. Jameson started the hardware store in town after he hurt himself as a tie hack, he passed on just last year and his wife, son and daughter took over the store. His son is a hard worker. He's putting together a crew of twenty young ranch and farm hands to get the job done fast."

Edith addressed the other ladies, "Have either of you ever met Lillian Jameson? She is Nathan's mother."

Ella shook her head. Claire responded, "I've met her at her store a few times, but we haven't talked really."

"You would like her so much. I come in to a Bible study at her house on Thursdays each week, we'd love to have you join us."

29
September, 1899
Encampment, Wyoming

Dear Haddie,

I can't believe that I've been in Encampment for well over a year. In some ways it seems like this has always been my life, in others it seems like we just got here. I was glad to get your last letter. I'm so thankful that William is recovering from the accident and will have only a few lasting effects. Falling off the hay wagon and breaking an arm sounds so painful.

Daniel is at the mine for about a week at a time, then comes down and spends a couple days here. He usually works a few hours a day while he's here, either ordering supplies or meeting with someone or other. The mine itself is doing very well. The main shaft is over eighty-five feet deep – I can't imagine being that far underground, but Daniel says that whether he's five feet or five hundred feet down, it makes no difference to him because if a rock caves in and hits you, you're just as dead at either level. I am just not convinced or comforted by his line of thinking. The vein is over seven feet wide. Daniel tells me there's enough copper for the mine to produce for at least fifty years. Right now there are over 250 men working in the mine and they are shipping 80,000 pounds of ore by wagonload to Colorado each day.

There have been so many changes at the mine, it is hard to keep up with them all. First, this Spring James Rumsey sold out his interest in the mine for $1,000. I can't write down what kind of a fool Daniel claims Rumsey was for selling out so cheaply.

Then, in June, Ed Haggarty came to dinner and told Daniel and me that he was selling out to George Ferris. I don't think Daniel was surprised. Ed seems to like the thrill of the find more than the drudgery of the mining. I've heard he got $30,000 in the buyout, which is a lot better than a thousand but nothing compared to the riches that are in that mine.

The worse thing and the biggest shock came just two weeks ago. George Ferris, the only remaining original partner and owner of the mine was killed. He was at a place called Snowslide Hill on his way back to the mine from his home in Rawlins. The road is very steep there. Apparently something in the load he had on his wagon shifted on the slope and the wagon flipped over. It crushed poor Mr. Ferris to death. His beautiful wife Julia is doing her best to take over her husband's interests. The mine has been doing so well with Mr. Haggarty's mining knowledge and Mr. Ferris' ambition and good business leadership. We just don't know what will happen now that they are both gone.

Ella Parkison has become a dear friend. You got me started by teaching me the basics of quilting, and I practiced with Mama. Ella is very skilled, so she is helping me to piece and stitch some intricate patterns for quilts. We have many nice afternoons sitting at her home or mine with needles in our hands. Ella's husband Ed owns and runs Parkison's Mercantile. It's a huge store that even has an ice cream counter in the back.

Mostly my days are very busy. It's a good contrast to when I first got here and had nothing to do. I'm so happy to have Jesse here, he is a dear boy and lots of good company for me. He's started back to school, and though he was very hesitant at first, he seems to be settling in. He also helps out at the livery most afternoons. I think I told you he worked out a deal with my friend Ella's husband to use their grass mower. He mows their yard to pay for using the mower to do ours. He's very industrious. The sadness in his eyes is gone most days. Every once in a while something will remind us of the farm, and he gets quiet for a while, but he recovers his smile much more quickly than he used to.

I've told you about our Ladies' Bible study. We meet once a week at Lillian Jameson's house. Her daughter Abby joins us and so does Mr. Haggarty's lady friend Edith Crow. Ella comes sometimes, but not every week. We've just added another member. Her name is Mary Nell Baker. Her husband is a miner at Rudefeha, so we two have a lot in common. I've just found out that she knows how to tat, and I would love to learn, so we've made plans to start lessons next week.

Claire put down her fountain pen, wiggling her fingers and shaking out her hand, relieving the tension of writing so much. As she finished the letter and readied the envelope, her thoughts turned to last week's Bible study. The discussion had been about forgiveness.

"I know that I struggle with forgiving God for taking Art when he was still so young," admitted Lillian. "I love God, and I trust Him, but even after nearly two years, I think I'm still mad at Him over it."

"I don't have too much trouble forgiving God," Edith admitted, "But then, nothing really bad has ever happened to me. What I have trouble with is forgiving others when they aren't even sorry."

The group agreed with Edith, and they spent a lively few minutes discussing whether or not someone should be forgiven without there being an apology first. Finally, Mary Nell spoke up, "Well, as I read the Lord's Prayer, Jesus tells us to pray to God to ask forgiveness by saying 'Forgive us out debts as we forgive others'. That scares me. I have trouble being forgiving, but I sure want my Lord to forgive me. So I think we need to forgive others whether they ask or not so that God will forgive us the same way."

"You know, though," Edith began after a few moments, "I think it is easier to forgive some things than others. I mean, little things should be forgiven and forgotten right away, but big things, like robbing a bank or killing someone, shouldn't be forgiven as easily."

"That's a good point," added Mary Nell. "It seems like there are some things that are just too black and deeply bad to forgive."

Lillian turned to Claire. "You haven't said much this morning, Dear. What do you think about all this?"

Now, even though it was days later and she was alone at home, Claire's heart pounded as she remembered. She'd felt so exposed and afraid right then. To answer Lillian, she'd responded that since she was such a new Christian, she just didn't know, all the while inside her head she was screaming: *Would these friends ever even talk to me again or welcome me in their homes if they somehow found out my buried past?*

She put the letter to Haddie on the kitchen table and wandered absently around the small house, tidying up as she went, but still lost in thought. I gave my life to Jesus, and the Bible promises that I was washed white as snow. That is perfect forgiveness. That means that in God's eyes, I am clean. But to the world, to Edith Crow or Mary Nell, maybe my sins are so 'black' that maybe they shouldn't be forgiven.

***

227

She was beginning to get used to having Jesse gone to school during the day. By the afternoon, Claire had finished all her chores. She tucked her tatting shuttle and ball of thread along with the letter to Haddie she wanted to mail into her market basket and looped her arm through the handle. She checked her hair and hat in the mirror on the way out the door. It was a beautiful fall day. The sky was a clear azure blue. Her eyes lifted to Bridger Peak over the tops of the buildings around her and she whispered a quiet prayer for Daniel's safety in the mine.

Thinking of Daniel at the mine instead of home was much easier now. She gave Jesse and Ella some of the credit for that, they were a blessed diversion for her loneliness. Mostly, though, she was thankful that the strength of their marriage had carried them through that rough patch. After a series of running arguments and heated yelling matches between them, Daniel finally began to understand Claire's feelings of jealousy about the time he spent away from her and had worked hard in the past months to come down the mountain more often, and to be sure to let her know how happy he was to have her to come home to.

Claire missed Daniel terribly while he was gone, and was secure in knowing that he missed her, too. She was thankful that she was more independent than most of the wives she knew. She smiled as she thought about the plan she and Daniel had worked out to help with the absences. They'd been in Denver at the beginning of the summer. Daniel had to go pick up some parts and invited Claire and Jesse to accompany him. Riding the new stagecoach to Walcott Junction, then the train to Cheyenne and finally on to Denver, they were met at the station by Addie and the children. Claire thoroughly enjoyed staying once again with Addie. Jesse became instant friends with Jeremiah and Richard. The adults didn't see much of the boys during their visit except at meal times. They spent most of their time in the back, playing in a fort that Peter built for the boys. They even slept out there several nights.

One afternoon Claire and Daniel went on a 'date' to the Denver Dry Goods Store. Advertised as the largest department store west of Chicago, the couple spent a large portion of one afternoon wandering through the lavish displays. In the book section, Daniel ran his hand over the smooth leather binding from one of the displays.

"That's really a beautiful volume, what is it?" Claire asked.

"It's just a writing journal filled with blank pages."

They stood a minute longer, admiring the selection on the table, then Claire had an idea. "Daniel, if we each had one of these, then every night we are apart we could write to each other. That way you'd know and I'd know that our last thoughts of the day were of each other."

Daniel considered her words and then answered. "That's a good idea. Then, each time I come home, we could trade. Then when I leave again, not only could we write our thoughts, be we could read what the other had written the week before."

Claire warmed to the idea immediately. "I'd always have a bit of you with me and I'd be with you."

They ended up buying four volumes that day. Since then, the ritual had become an important one for both of them. Each night before turning out the light, Claire read a day of Daniel's previous week and then added about her day and thoughts at the end.

Claire smiled again as she thought about the journals. She'd been surprised at first with how eloquent Daniel's entries were. He spent a lot of time describing how things looked and felt at the mine and the surrounding mountains, so that even though she'd never been up there, she felt familiar with the area. The journals afforded them a way to discuss issues and share ideas. Lately Daniel had also begun adding his personal daily prayer list to the bottoms of his entries. Claire loved it and was touched by how deeply he thought about things and how insightful he was about life.

Claire blinked her eyes as she realized she was almost at the post office already. She passed the W.C Henry Insurance office, then ducked into the narrow wooden post office building. "Good morning, Mr. Macfarlane," she said as she entered.

"Good morning, Mrs. Haynes. It's nice to see you."

"I still can't get over how wonderful it is having a real post office here in town, I'm so glad you're here."

"Thank you, Ma'am. Yes, we've made a lot of progress with the system in the short time since we opened and I became postmaster."

"I have a letter to mail."

"That will be two cents, please. I also have a letter that arrived for you this morning."

Claire exchanged Haddie's letter for a thin brown envelope, thanked Mr. Macfarlane again and left the store. She stopped for a moment and looked at the return address. It was a letter from her brother Marcus. Claire wanted to tear it open right then, but decided she'd rather savor the first communication with her brother since she'd left home. She tucked it into her basket, then turned left and headed toward Mary Nell's house.

The afternoon flew by as Claire concentrated on learning how to turn a tatted picot stitch. She'd been working on a length of lace edging, and was finally feeling comfortable with the stitches.

"That looks really pretty," said Mary Nell as Claire began collecting her scissors and returning everything to her basket. "You are catching on quickly. I had the worst time mastering connecting two picots together, but you picked it right up."

"I think you are a good teacher," Claire answered. "When do you expect Paul to come home again?"

"He only left on Tuesday, so it will be at least a week. He gets so tired of making the long trip all the way down here just to spend a night or two with me. He's been talking about a small settlement just down from Bridger Peak. It's called Battle."

"Yes, I've heard of it."

"Paul says it's getting to be a real town. People began moving up there last winter, and there's a mercantile, a saloon, and a boarding house. There's even a butcher shop. Paul just talked to someone about renting a little cabin. I think I'll be up there, closer to him, by summer."

"It would certainly be nice to be closer, and have a full time husband around," Claire agreed.

By the time Claire got back home and finished warming supper for herself and Jesse, the sun was down, the sky a soft, dusky indigo. Jesse went to bed soon after, tired from his busy day. She sipped the last of a cup of tea and then opened the letter she'd been anticipating all day.

Dear Claire,

I hope this letter finds you well. Actually, I mostly hope it finds you. By the time I could write you, the letter from Haddie had been through a lot, so I'm not sure I can read your address.

I am well. I returned from Cuba in August of last year, and believe me

230

when I say that it was h--- there. We were trained as a cavalry unit, but then they shipped us out to Florida. There was some sort of trouble about command and orders, so they only put some of our unit on a ship to Cuba with even fewer of our horses. That ship ride, which was pretty rough, turned us all into an infantry unit whether we wanted to be or not. The biggest battle I saw was what we called the battle of Kettle Hill. I'll never forget how Teddy Roosevelt, our commander, led us in that charge a'waving his hat with one hand and holding his pistol in the other. He led us up that hill shouting and cheering. Bullets pelted us like a spring rain in South Dakota. After that, we lay siege to the town of Santiago and it didn't take long for those Spaniards to give up.

We arrived back in New York from Cuba. I don't remember the first few weeks being there, though, because I caught malaria during the trip back. It took me about three months to start feeling better, and I'm just now back to feeling strong and weighing what I did before. I was too sick to stand at the disbanding ceremony in September of last year, but Colonel Roosevelt came by the hospital and shook each man's hand who'd fought with him. I felt really proud that day.

I wandered around New York for a while after I came out of the hospital. I worked a couple of security jobs. I've been working now for about six months for the Pinkerton Detective Agency. Right now I'm with a detail of detectives in Nevada. We're trying to hunt down a train robber named Butch Cassidy. So far, we are always a few days behind him.

Haddie says you are doing well and that you married a good man. I am glad to hear it. I know that you had a hard time of it growing up. Pa was never fair to you or Ma, and I regret that I never stood up for you. Last time I saw Pa, he and Horace were headed to Alaska to get rich on the Klondike, but I don't know if they really went. That was about three years ago. I lost all respect for him, and my eyes were opened about what kind of a man he was in the last weeks before Ma died. He could never think of anyone but himself.

When this job is done, I'd like to come visit you now that I know where you are. It will be hard to get a letter to me as we travel around a lot, but I'll try to write again sometime soon.

Love, your brother
Marcus

Claire wiped the tears from her cheeks and returned the letter to its envelope. She bowed her head and prayed for Marcus as twilight waned and darkness fell outside.

30
December 31, 1899
Encampment, Wyoming

"You look so beautiful tonight," Daniel stood at the front door, holding Claire's coat, staring unashamedly at his wife.

Claire met his eyes and smiled back. "This is going to be a fancy dinner party, are you sure I look alright?" She turned to the mirror, but ended up looking at Daniel in its reflection instead of herself. She'd spent the last two hours getting ready. She knew that the teal silk skirt and jacket flattered her. The matching hat accented her dark eyes. She was satisfied with the chignon style of her hair. No matter, she still felt nervous tonight.

"Yes, there's no doubt you will put everyone else to shame."

"It's just that there will be so many important people at this dinner, and many I've never met," Claire began.

Daniel interrupted by drawing her safely into his arms. "It's the last night of this century. Don't spend another minute being nervous. Let's go celebrate and enjoy." He kissed her sweetly.

"Jesse, old man, are you about ready to go?"

"Yes, Dan. I'm ready to walk out the door as soon as I grab my ruck sack."

"Are you sure you'd rather spend New Year's Eve with your buddies instead of going with us?"

"And get all dressed up in a stuffy suit like you?" Jesse shot back.

Daniel laughed and slapped the boy on the back. "Can I come with you instead?"

The little family continued the teasing as Daniel helped Claire don her coat. They walked together in the crisp night air for two blocks. Standing in front of the Smithfield house, Claire hugged

232

her brother tightly. "Happy New Year," she said as he pulled away.

"Happy New Year!" he called as he mounted the steps and knocked on the door. Mrs. Smithfield waved as Jesse disappeared inside.

Encampment sported thirteen saloons and three hotels. The Bohn Hotel stood out among them all as the most upscale. Claire was impressed at the festive decorations in the large dining room that housed the party. As Daniel and Claire entered the large room, the host of the evening, Willis George Emerson grabbed Daniel's hand in a hearty welcome.

"So glad you are here, Mr. Haynes," Emerson boomed. "It's been a while, and who is this priceless young woman on your arm?"

Before Daniel finished introducing Claire, the boisterous Emerson kissed her on both cheeks and tucked her hand under his arm. Over his shoulder he said to Daniel, "I'm just going to steal her for a minute, Haynes, to introduce her to some others."

Claire looked over Emerson's ample frame to catch Daniel's slightly irritated frown before she was guided to the other side of the room.

A few minutes later Daniel arrived back at Claire's side with two crystal glasses. "I thought perhaps you'd enjoy a sherry before dinner," Daniel winked at her. Emerson noticed Daniel's arrival and began a second round of introductions. "Mr. Haynes, this is Mrs. Abigail Gillingworth, from Denver. Her husband and I are associates. We initially read law together in Chicago, and both of us then relocated to Denver. Gillingworth is that tall drink of water in the corner over there." Indicating the next person in the circle, Emerson continued, "This is another of my associates, Mr. Barney McCaffrey. He's just become one of our new mine investors. He hails most recently from the mountains above Denver, though we've worked together both in Kansas and in Chicago."

Daniel and the man shook hands and exchanged pleasantries for a few minutes, Claire sipped her sherry. McCaffrey was a large, bullish man with curly hair and a handlebar mustache. Something in his look spoke of shiftiness and Claire instantly distrusted him, though he was gallant and polite.

Soon, Mrs. Gillingworth excused herself and moved off to another group as Daniel, Emerson and McCaffrey discussed the mine.

Claire, happy to be out of the conversation and out of the limelight, studied the room and its thirty or so occupants. There were many familiar faces. Mr. and Mrs. Mullens stood near the door talking with Mr. Henry from the insurance agency. Ella and Ed Parkison chatted with Lillian Jameson in one corner. She recognized Mr. Macfarlane from the post office, standing quietly off to one side talking with a white haired woman with kind eyes. Claire assumed this was Mrs. Macfarlane as the two looked equally uncomfortable in this setting and stood close together as if needing protection. Claire felt a camaraderie with them and their discomfort.

Claire noted several other faces that were familiar and many who were not. As she looked around, Claire's attention turned to a man standing at the bar. He threw back a small shot glass of what Claire assumed was whiskey based on its clear, honey brown color, then nodded at the attendant for a refill. Claire tried not to be obvious, but continued to watch the man. He was about the same height as Daniel, with a thin build. Claire admired his handsome features, his dark eyes and hair, his high cheek bones. He was dressed richly in a black three-piece suit that fit him well. His shoes were shined to a fine gloss and he looked the part of a refined, educated gentleman. Something about him belied his ease and wealth though, and Claire wondered if it was her experience at Jack's, that hinted to her of some underlying darkness in this man.

Mr. Emerson interrupted Claire's thoughts with a raised voice welcoming the guests. "I am so glad to have you all here to celebrate the end of the year and ring in the promising and exciting new twentieth century.

"The growth of our Grand Encampment is just beginning. As the new century unfolds, I predict we are going to see our humble little town become the Pittsburg of the West, garnering the attention of the nation and world for the riches of copper. People everywhere are going to know about our beautiful home and clamor to come and be a part of it. We are going to have a front row seat to watch this area boom, prosper, and bring us all money and happiness." The guests applauded as Emerson paused and looked around.

"And now my friends, let's feast. Let's make our way to the tables and enjoy this wonderful evening. Thank you again for coming. And may I be the first to wish you the grandest of happy New Year's."

Daniel appeared at Claire's elbow and jovially clinked his glass gently against hers. He leaned in and winked at her, then quietly said, "He's certainly a charismatic character, isn't he? I'm not sure why, but I have trouble putting my trust in that man."

A few minutes later Claire and Daniel found themselves seated at a richly set table. Claire was pleased to have Daniel on her left and Ella Parkison on her right. Ella and Claire admired the decor. The candles and lanterns glowed a soft golden onto the starched white table linens. There were golden chargers underneath the plates. "It's been a long time since I've seen a table set this finely," remarked Ella.

"Goodness," added Claire, "I hope I know what to do with all these forks and spoons."

The seat directly across from Claire remained empty for a few moments as the guests sorted themselves out. Someone finally pulled out the chair and Claire looked up from her discussion with Ella to see the handsome man she'd noticed at the bar. He seated himself, then looked across the table and smiled. He rose slightly again and reached for Daniel's hand. "My name is Grant Jones."

Daniel made introductions for Claire and the Parkisons then asked Jones, "You are from Denver, Mr. Jones?"

"I live there now," he answered. "I'm most recently from Chicago."

"I enjoy reading your articles in the paper, " remarked Ed Parkison, who was across from Ella and right next to Jones.

Claire knew his name sounded familiar when he was introduced, now she placed from where. She'd read his name and articles many times while she lived in Denver.

"Thank you for saying so."

The group chatted for a few minutes, when Ed Parkison turned in his seat, "Mr. Jones, how long have you been a journalist?"

"I graduated from Northwestern College in Illinois, then wrote for the *Chicago Herald*."

"How'd you end up in Denver, Mr. Jones?" Claire asked.

"That's a convoluted story." He smiled at her shyly then continued. "Emerson over there was a lawyer and politian in Chicago, but he's also done some writing."

"He's published a novel, right?"

"Yes, two actually. He's got *Gray Rocks: A Tale of the Middle West* and *Winning Winds*. I met him when he hired me as an editor for *Grey Rocks*."

Daniel nodded, then asked, "How long have you been in Denver?"

"Not very long. I did some high profile news coverage, like at the last Republican nominating convention, while I was writing in Chicago. Then I decided I needed a change. Old George sent me a letter, telling me how much fun he was having in Denver, so I moved there about six months ago and began writing for a variety of papers in Colorado and also for Omaha, Chicago and Kansas City."

Claire kept silent, but she noticed that Jones' hand was a bit unsteady as he lifted his glass. *When he smiles,* she thought, *the smile doesn't reach his eyes.*

The meal was wonderful. The food was rich and fine. When the meal finished, the guests moved back into the main hall, where a three-piece band was set up. Claire and Daniel danced and laughed.

"My feet are tired, let's find a spot to sit," Claire finally admitted. They were happy to find two empty chairs next to Ed Haggarty and Edith Crow. Ed was explaining how he had been enjoying his 'retirement' after selling out to George Ferris.

"I don't like to sit still long. I've been lendin' a hand out at Mr. Crow's ranch. I've learned a bit about repairing fences and breaking up ice at wind mill water troughs. I've also been keepin' an eye out for signs of copper float in the foothills."

"So you've been riding out doing some new prospecting, then?" Daniel teased.

"I can't seem to break the habit," Haggarty laughed.

Waiters began circulating amongst the revelers with flutes of champagne. Daniel pulled out his pocket watch and told the group they had only five minutes left of the nineteenth century.

Anticipation grew and the group became quieter. People began to stand, and rejoin spouses and friends. George Emerson began the countdown at twenty seconds and everyone joined in with energy and glasses held high.

At the stroke of midnight, Daniel kissed Claire tenderly, then touched a tear with his fingertip where it trailed down her cheek.

They seemed alone in an envelope of silence despite the uproar around them.

"What is the tear for, my Love? Is something wrong?"

"No, Daniel, it's just that everything is so right."

31
April, 1902
Encampment, Wyoming

"Is there anything more I can do to help you get ready before the baby comes? You don't have long now." Claire asked Ella as they sat on the Parkison's back porch soaking up the April afternoon sunshine.

"No, I think I have everything in order. I expect my mother to be here within the next few days. She'll stay until I'm up and around after the birth."

"Some women these days actually go to the hospital for birthing, but you are planning to stay here, right?" Claire held up the quilt block she'd just completed. It was only her second block for a double wedding ring quilt she'd decided to try.

"I'd hate being away from home. And anyway, the hospital here in Encampment is not completed yet. All hospitals are for the sick or injured. Having a baby isn't an illness."

"I agree," answered Claire. "If Daniel and I ever are blessed with a child, I'll want to be at home also." They continued to chat, with Claire telling Ella the story of helping Haddie bring baby Marshall into the world.

"You never talk about your youth," remarked Ella.

"I don't have a great deal of happy memories from my childhood," Claire evaded. Changing the subject Claire began a new topic. "I miss Edith Crow – I mean Haggarty. How long are she and Ed planning to stay in England on their honeymoon?"

"I don't think they actually know. He'd been away for so long with only limited contact with his family, so I think they had to wait and see how things went once they got there."

"Theirs was a beautiful wedding," Claire sighed. "I loved it when her father walked her down the aisle. I'd never been in the Episcopal Church here. It was much bigger than I'd anticipated. They made it so festive with all the toile bows and bright colored ribbons."

"The wedding was beautiful. It seems like our little town is growing up. I hear they are making great progress on the construction of the Opera House down on Main Street, but with this big belly I haven't been up to walking there to see it."

Claire's gaze started on Ella's middle, then came to rest on her eyes. "It looks nearly done from the outside, though I think it's a bit funny that they are calling it the Opera House when everyone knows it's just going to be a meeting house for the town. I can't imagine Caruso ever coming here to sing for us."

"Did you hear that he's actually made a recording of his singing? They say that it won't be long before people can buy gramophones and hear people sing or talk anytime they want to."

"I just can't imagine that," Claire shook her head. The women sipped their tea in quiet for a few moments. Claire changed the subject when she spoke again. "Did I tell you I got a letter this week from my brother Marcus?"

"No, I hadn't heard that. It was so nice to meet him last year at Christmas when he stayed with you. He's such a nice man."

"Yes, he's done very well for himself. The Pinkertons kept him travelling. He asked to transfer back to the east coast and the president's protection detail. Marcus served under Teddy Roosevelt in the Spanish-American War. Now that Roosevelt is president after President McKinley was shot, Marcus wanted to be back there."

The women continued to stitch and talk as the sunlight moved across the floor of the covered porch.

Finally, Ella put her needlework down stood up. "At this point, it doesn't matter what I do, everything is achy. My back hurts today, I think I overdid while hanging out the wash yesterday."

Claire dropped the quilt block into her basket and stood as well. "I'll go so you can rest. You have time for a little nap before Ed gets home from the store, don't you?"

"Hmm, that sounds like a really good idea. When do you expect Daniel home again?"

"Not until next week sometime, and then only if it hasn't snowed up there. This time of year everything is so muddy, it is hard for him to come down."

The two friends embraced and said goodbye. Claire walked happily towards Main Street on her way to the mercantile. She missed Daniel when he was gone, but their marriage, at four years old, was strong and stable. Claire had Jesse plus a nice group of friends to help her fill up lonely hours. She'd created a routine that kept her busy and satisfied most of the time.

The sun warmed her, and she whispered a prayer of thanks for the life she was living. The afternoon was drawing to a close by the time she finished her errands down town. Claire stopped in at the livery to see if Jesse was ready to come home, and after a short wait while he finished hanging up some tack, the two started for home.

They turned the corner that brought them only two houses from her own. Daniel's horse was tethered in the front yard.

Claire began to run, convinced that something was wrong. Jesse jogged beside her. She burst into the front door, looking and calling for Daniel.

"Are you alright? What's wrong?" she asked when she found him in the kitchen.

He laughed and hugged her. "I'm fine."

"You should have seen the look on your face when you started running, Claire. I thought your skirt was on fire." Jesse teased her.

"You gave me quite a scare."

"Why does anything have to be wrong, you worrywart, can't a guy come home?"

Claire relaxed and laughed, his easy answer calmed her fears. "You can come home every day as far as I'm concerned."

"Well, that's exactly what I came home to tell you. Or ask you, I guess."

Despite Claire's barrage of questions, Daniel would say no more until they were sitting together at the table with a cup of tea. When they were settled, he began.

"You may have heard me talk about a fella we have working at the mine named Dillon, Malachi Dillon."

"Yes, I think so."

"Anyway, Dillon has worked in several mines, and he was down in the hole with us for a while, then he transferred up to the mess hall when it was completed. He has some experience with restaurants, so he ended up organizing and supervising the meal service for the miners. Personally, I think he didn't like the hard work of the mine, but he's done a good job.

"Well, for several months, he's been hounding the shift bosses up there to let him open a saloon next door to the bunkhouse. I've agreed with the management who have told him no. The last thing I need on a shift is a drunk miner, and I'm sure that's what would happen if they had easy access to alcohol up there.

"Dillon has been adamant about it, though, and tempers got a little hot. When the bosses told him again last month that they were all in agreement that he could not sell liquor at the mine site or anywhere near it, Dillon quit, packed his bags and cleared out. We thought we'd seen the last of him."

Claire refilled Daniel's cup and returned to the table.

"Turns out," Daniel continued, "Dillon didn't leave the area at all. Instead, he did some scouting around and then ended up staking several claims about a mile down the valley from Rudefeha."

"Is he going to mine for copper there?"

Daniel grinned. "No. There's no copper where he staked. It's a nice little valley, protected like a bowl with tall peaks all around. It's pretty flat for being in the mountains, and Haggarty Creek runs though the edge of it. It's a perfect place for a town."

Claire was confused at what Daniel was getting at, but then understanding dawned as he continued. "I don't know if you remember me telling you this, but it was Dillon, Jim Rankin, and Charles O'Connell who actually started the town of Encampment as we know it."

"I thought George Emerson started the town."

"That's what he tells everyone, but Dillon, Rankin and O'Connell actually had it started before Emerson showed up in 1897. Anyway, Dillon has experience with laying out a town and has contacts with surveyors and developers. He's already lined up a crew and they've begun building the saloon and boarding house. He's marking out streets to build a full-fledged town, and it's just one mile from Rudefeha."

"How do the mine bosses feel about that? How do you feel about it?"

"At first I was mad that he figured out a plan to get his way about opening a saloon, but then I realized that it meant we could build a cabin up there and I'd see you both every day. Claire, what do you think? Are you willing to give up living in Encampment and try an adventure in the mountains?"

Claire hesitated and Daniel grabbed for her hand. After a minute, she admitted, "I'm fearful about it, I've never been up there at all," She hesitated then added, "But Mary Nell says moving up to Battle was a wonderful decision for them. She loves the mountains and is very happy. Do you think others will move their wives, too?"

"I know it. I've talked to several, and they've already talked to Dillon about buying plots of land in his city. Dillon gave Harv Whitley a price for a cabin site that is very reasonable."

"When is all this going to happen?"

"I expect, if you are willing, we can be up there and in a cabin within the next two months."

So began a flurry of activity. That afternoon, Daniel and Claire met with Nathan Jameson at the hardware store about building their cabin. He was already committed to helping with the saloon and boarding house, but he got Daniel in contact with another man, Robert Simons, who agreed to build it. Daniel left for the mountains the next morning with the intent of purchasing a tract of land from Malachi Dillon before he next came down.

By the end of May, the cabin in Dillon was nearly complete. Claire looked around the small house that had been their home in Encampment, now filled with a jumble of boxes and packages, and sighed. The thought of being close to Daniel and seeing him every day made her heart soar. On the other hand, she'd never lived in the mountains before, and the thought of being enclosed by dense trees, the threat of bears or mountain lions, plus the winter snows made her nervous. She worried about how they'd manage and how Jesse would continue his schooling.

Now that everything was ready, she tried to relax. All she had to do was wait. She expected Daniel this evening or tomorrow. He'd arranged for a couple of miners to come down with him to help load up their belongings and haul them to Dillon, the name of their new home town.

To his credit, Jesse was positive about the move. At first, he didn't want to leave his job at the livery, but soon became excited about living near the mine up in the mountains. His attitude helped Claire's excitement grow.

"Claire, my room is all packed up, including the bedding. I'll just sleep on a bedroll until we move." Jesse lumbered into the kitchen, laden with a box. He added it to a stack in the living room then plopped down on the chair beside her. "You asked me to remind you that we still need to go over to the schoolhouse."

"I was just thinking about that. Mr. Drake spends time each afternoon at the school house, getting ready for next year I suppose. Let's walk over there now and see if we can find him."

Soon brother and sister were climbing the stairs to the Encampment School house. Claire knocked. A deep voice called "Enter!"

Mr. Drake greeted the pair when he looked up from his paper strewn desk. "Well there, Jesse. Come to say goodbye?"

"Yes, Sir. And to thank you for all you've taught me."

Claire tried to hide her surprise at Jesse's classy response. The threesome chatted for a few minutes, then Claire got to the point.

"Mr. Drake, there isn't a school up in Dillon, and I was hoping that you might be willing to give me some advice about how to keep Jesse moving forward in his studies."

The teacher rubbed his chin and then adjusted his glasses. "I've been thinking about that same thing. You aren't the first student, nor the last, that I am losing to the new towns in the mountains. I have been thinking about how our school down here might help young scholars up there." He stopped, adjusting his glasses again.

"Jesse, if I loan you a set of books for your next grade, will you promise me to work at them, then return them to me and trade for the next grade?"

Once again Claire was surprised by her brother's answer. "Oh, yes Sir! I'll make that promise."

"I was hoping you'd say that. Then here's what we'll do. I've got you a stack of materials right here. With all the development up on the Divide, mail service has already become pretty regular. I've included the exams for each subject here on the bottom. When you get ready, you can take the test – with no help from anyone – then mail them to me to correct. That way I can certify you and promote you to the next grade."

Jesse beamed, then a crease crossed his forehead. "But, Mr. Drake, what if I don't understand something and have trouble, say with an arithmetic problem?"

"Well, if Mrs. Haynes here can't help you, just write me a letter, and I'll answer as soon as I can."

They left the school house a few minutes later. Claire smiled at her little brother as he walked beside her, his arms laden with books. "How about we take those things home, and we'll have a cup of tea together? Our last little time alone in our Encampment house."

He nodded his agreement, and they continued in silence.

In only a short time, Claire sat opposite the small table from her brother. Two cups of steaming tea and a plate of ginger snaps between them. "Jesse, I've been thinking 'bout something since we left the school. When you first got here, you hated school and never wanted to go, but you never would tell me why. You haven't complained for the last year, but I thought it was because you knew it wouldn't get you anywhere. Today, it seemed to me that you have grown to really love school and learning. What changed?"

Jesse's eyes dropped to the ground. He sat still for so long, Claire wasn't sure he was going to answer her. When he did, his words stunned her.

"After you left to go live with the Behls, Papa sent me to school for a while. Each day, since I was so little and all we had were draft horses, Uncle Horace would put me on the back of his horse and ride me to the school. At first, I was excited about it all, but then I started to hate those rides. Uncle Horace would make fun of me going to school. He'd tell me that I was the runt of the litter and I'd never be able to learn anything. He'd say that book learning wasn't what real cowboys were interested in, and that Papa and Mama only sent me to school to get me out of their way. After a while, he started talking about the girls in my school. He'd ask me about one of them then ask me if I kissed her. He began telling me that to prove I was really a man, I needed to do stuff to them, ugly things, Claire, things I never want to do."

Claire tried not to react. She concentrated on breathing normally, willing herself to stay calm. Finally, Jesse continued, his voice quieter. "By the time I'd get into the school, my stomach would hurt so much that I couldn't think about what the teacher was saying, so then I'd get into trouble. After a few weeks, the teacher sent a note home telling Papa that I wasn't learning and that maybe I should stay home until I was a little older." Jesse took a shuddering breath and finished, "Mama told me it was okay if I wasn't good at reading, but Papa backhanded me and told me I'd shamed him. Later, I guess it was the next day, they were out in the barn I heard them talking about it. Papa and Uncle Horace both laughed that I was dumb, then they joked about how breeding a top bull with a bad cow always turned out a bum calf."

Claire never suspected that their father's wrath and meanness was ever turned towards her brothers. She physically felt sick with the knowledge that not only had her father abused his young son, but that Horace had as well.

Seeing the tears in Claire's eyes, Jesse apologized. "I should never have told you this. You didn't need to know it."

"I thought when you lived at Haddie's, that you were looking forward to going to live with Papa when you were older. She told me that you asked her all the time when he was coming back for you."

Jesse hung his head again. "I was so afraid that he was coming back for me that sometimes I couldn't sleep at night. I asked Haddie because I was dreading it. Papa told me he'd come back and get me, but I made a plan to run away before I'd ever go with him."

Jesse searched his sister's face, then added, even more quietly, "I'll bet Haddie also told you that I was mean sometimes to her girls."

She nodded, afraid to hear what he was going to say next.

"Uncle Horace told me that all men wanted to touch girls and do things to them. He said that when I got older, I'd like doing those things and that it didn't matter what a girl said or if she cried, she really liked it. I was afraid that someday I'd get the urge to do something to Marney or Milly. They both are so pretty and they were real nice to me. I liked them. So, I was mean to them so they'd stay away from me and be safe."

Claire was horrified. She tried to keep her voice even.

"Do you ever think about doing things to the girls at your school? Do you think Horace was right about what he said?"

"I never want to hurt anyone. Those things he said were terrible, and I never did think he was telling the truth. I've watched how Daniel treats you – how you treat each other. You are so different than Mama and Papa. I've heard what the preacher says at church. I think if you make someone cry for any reason, they don't like it."

They talked until their tea was gone and Claire was satisfied that Jesse understood that Horace's view of women was evil and selfish and that he didn't have to make those choices. She also told her brother that she would never let Hiram or Horace take him.

"You promise?"

"I promise." Claire smiled.

***

Later in the afternoon, Claire found herself at Ella Parkison's door. Ella's mother answered. "How nice to see you again," she smiled. "Ella is resting out on the back porch."

Claire stopped at the doorway, taking in the scene. Ella sat in a rocking chair, the baby tucked into the crook of her arm. She still looked a little tired, but smiled when she saw Claire.

"There you are. Come in and sit down. Tell me about something other than babies!" she laughed.

"What else is there to talk about other than how beautiful he is?" Claire responded.

"I know. My perfect Hoyt Shields Parkison. What a big name for such a little guy."

Claire settled into a chair beside Ella just as Ella's mother returned carrying a tray containing a teapot and two cups.

"Mother, please, come sit and join us," Ella asked.

"Thank you, dear, but since you have someone here with you, I'm going to get some fresh air. I saw a few weeds in the front flower bed that I thought I might pull for you."

After she'd left, Ella shook her head. "Mother has been a godsend. She is so patient with me and doesn't ever seem to get tired or irritated. Would you like to hold Hoyt? I'll pour the tea."

Claire smelled Hoyt's sweet baby smell as she kissed the top of his head. He fluttered his eyes at being moved around, then settled back to sleep.

"I'm serious, Claire, I am happy to be a mom, and I wouldn't trade Hoyt for anything, but I get a little tired of the subject. Talk to me about something else."

They laughed together as Claire related the outcome of their visit to the schoolhouse then began telling Ella the progress of their moving preparations.

"Two miners that work with Daniel agreed to help. They should be here tomorrow morning, along with Daniel. They are going to load all our things into a wagon, and the miners are going to haul them up to the mountains. Daniel, Jesse and I are going to go up separately. We will stay at the hotel here tomorrow night, then leave in a rented carriage."

"Can you make it all the way to Dillon in one day?"

"No, it's just too far. Since we aren't hauling anything, it will only take us two days. Mary Nell invited us to stay at their home in Battle."

"That's really nice of her. I'm sure you'll have a good visit.

"I've missed her. But did you hear, they've decided to move up to Dillon, too? Paul bought a tract of land very near to ours, so Mary Nell and I'll be neighbors."

"That leaves me down here on the plains pretty much alone." Ella complained. "I've told Ed that I want to go back to Denver."

Claire wasn't surprised. She knew that Ella was unhappy in Encampment, far from her family.

"This house is so drafty, and it certainly isn't large enough for anyone else to join our family. Hoyt's cradle is in our room, there's not a room for him here at all."

"Do you think Ed will agree to move back to Denver?"

"I think he is warming to the idea. The manager here at the store is very trustworthy. Ed is thinking that it might be better for us to be in Denver, at least for a while. He's talking about opening a fourth store there."

"He really likes it here, though, doesn't he?"

"Yes, he does, and he is convinced that this area is going to continue to boom. He told me last night that if we do move back to Denver, it won't be forever, and we'll come back."

"How do you feel about that?"

"I just told him his stunt last time of carrying me and the bed out of the house wouldn't work a second time. I promised him I'd never come back here unless he built me a decent house, one with two stories, a large kitchen and room for my piano. I'm not going to raise a brood of savages, I want the children to grow up civilized."

Claire laughed, knowing that while Ella sounded like she was making a joke, she was also serious. Claire pitied Ed if he thought he could change Ella's resolve.

247

"Now that the North American Copper Company has bought out Julia Ferris and taken ownership of the mine, there are going to be a lot of changes here in Encampment."

"There's no doubt of that." Ella nodded. "Did you know they paid a million dollars for the mine and holdings? Can you imagine?"

"I wonder what Ed and Edith Haggarty will think when they get back and find that out. Daniel always said that Rumsey, Deal and Haggarty should have held on for a while and they'd have made more money."

"What I'm excited about is that they have the power plant nearly completed. I told Ed that our new house here has to be wired for electricity. I'd love to have electric lights instead of smelly old kerosene lamps."

"What an idea!" Claire agreed.

They chatted for a while longer, until baby Hoyt started to fuss. "He's probably hungry," Ella smiled at the child in Claire's arms with a tenderness that Claire hadn't ever seen before from her friend.

"I need to go. Thank you so much for the tea and the visit. I will miss you so much!" Claire returned Hoyt to Ella's arms, then the two friends shared an awkward embrace with a squirming baby between them.

On her way out, Claire said goodbye to Ella's mother, who was kneeling by a garden rich with peonies in full bloom, then headed home.

32
June, 1902
Dillon, Wyoming

Claire felt the deep rumble in her chest before she heard the muffled roar. She put her hand against the door frame of her little cabin and looked up into the draw towards Rudefeha. "God, please protect him," she prayed. Then, she continued drying the bowl she held in her hand. Was that the third or fourth blast today? She couldn't remember. She only knew that every time the earth shook, her heart danced a wobbly pirouette.

Shaking off her disquiet, she focused on tidying up the house. She nestled the bowl with its mismatched mate in the small cupboard to the left of the stove, and folded and hung the towel on the bar under the window. Absently, she reached for the straw broom and began sweeping the smooth wood floor in the small room that served as kitchen, dining room and parlor. The cabin was cramped, smaller than the house they'd rented in Encampment, but Claire loved it. *Strange*, she thought. *This is a tiny home, but I've never felt more comfortable or happier anywhere else.*

She looked around, making sure everything was in place. Most mountain cabins were finished inside by simply adding thick chinking to the insides of the log walls to provide insulation. That meant the inside walls were log, rough and rustic. Ceilings in the cabins were often left with the beams exposed, creating a larger feel to the space. Daniel was fearful that Claire would get cold in the winter without thicker, more insulated walls. A material that he called plywood had just become available in America, and they had sheets of it at Jameson's Hardware, so he insisted that the builders add smooth, plywood walls and a ceiling to the inside of their cabin. Packed in the wagon of their belongings, Daniel brought a

249

can of white paint to cover the plywood. It hadn't taken long for him to paint the inside of their new home and get their furniture arranged. The open common room was cozy with Addie's chair and sofa plus their tables. Daniel had the builders add a small window, complete with glass, looking out to the front of the house, making the room light and cheery.

In the back left corner of the common room sat the small dining table and three chairs. The right wall hosted the stove and a kitchen work area, plus the dish cupboard and some shelves for food. There was a back door that provided access to the privy outside. Claire, certainly, would have preferred a new, modern indoor privy like those she'd seen in *Ladies Home Journal*, but that advance wasn't available here.

With her sweeping finished, she emptied the dustpan in the trash bucket beside the stove. She left the main rooms through a door in the right wall to enter a small hallway. She turned to the right and entered the bedroom she and Daniel shared. Their mahogany sleigh bed and matching tables, a wedding gift from Daniel's parents, filled the small room. Claire checked the glass chimneys on each bedside lamp to make sure they didn't have soot on them, then turned to look at herself in her grandmother's mirror.

She pulled the pins that had been holding a messy bun and began brushing her hair. *Happy twenty-fourth birthday*, she told herself in the mirror. The unwelcome memory of standing in her attic room in South Dakota in this same way, fixing her hair and congratulating herself on her sixteenth birthday crowded into her thoughts. For a brief moment she recalled that morning and the way her mother had greeted her with a slap and hard word. *My mother was weak and didn't protect me from my father's backhand or my uncle's groping,* she thought. *Other parents love and cherish their children, mine were the source of hurt and danger or at the very kindest a silent witness.* Claire put down her brush and quickly twisted her hair back into a bun. She clamped down on the memory and pushed it away. Turning from the mirror, she picked up her tatting and left the room, sending her mind somewhere – anywhere - else.

Claire sat down and pulled her tatting shuttle and a ball of thread onto her lap. Since today was Thursday, she had spent the morning ironing and doing a little patching. Thursdays were light work days for her. Daniel planned to take her and Jesse out to dinner tonight, so she didn't have any cooking to do either, so she found herself with the afternoon free.

Claire thought about Ella Parkison, and how it was her leading that got Claire on a schedule. Since the Parkison house was just around the corner from Claire and Daniel in Encampment, the back doors of both houses opened onto a common area complete with clotheslines for each house. Claire remembered waking up, still bleary-eyed and noticing that Ella already had sheets and towels snapping in the breeze every Monday morning.

It took Claire several weeks before she mentioned it to the quiet Ella. "Do you get up in the dark on Monday morning to get your laundry done so early?" she asked.

Ella smiled patiently. "My mother always quoted Abraham Lincoln when he said, 'Whatever you are, be a good one.' She said that we women have to make a name for ourselves by being the very best we could be at our house keeping job. Right after Ed and I got married, I began a routine I rarely stray from. On Mondays I do the wash. Tuesdays are for baking. Wednesdays I do the cleaning. That leaves Thursdays for ironing and patching and Fridays for shopping. Of course, I sweep and tidy up every day."

Claire missed Ella - whose calm, quiet confidence contrasted with Claire's own feelings of inadequacy. In her last letter, a short note really, Ella confirmed that they were moving back to Denver and that news made Claire sad, thinking that they would lose touch.

She'd completed only a few stitches when there was a knock at the already open door. "Come on in," Claire called.

Mary Nell stepped into the room and happily plopped down onto the sofa opposite Claire. "How's your day going?" she smiled.

"Good, how about you?"

"I'm great. I can't tell you how happy I am that Daniel talked Paul into moving up here to Dillon. I liked living in Battle, but I was lonely. Now we're here, and you're here, I'm sure there will be more soon. It's so great!"

Claire put down her shuttle and smiled. "It amazes me how just a few months ago this was 'man's country' and none of us had ever been up here and now there's a booming, bustling town full of people.

"You're right. For over two years Rudefeha was some sort of holy shrine open only to men, and then Mr. Dillon came along and here we are. He is such a charming man, have you met him, Claire?"

Claire stood up as they talked, moving to put the teakettle on the stove. She stoked up the firebox, returned to her chair and continued. "No, I haven't yet, though we are going to the restaurant tonight for supper and maybe I will then."

"That's right! It's your birthday! Happy day to you!"

"Thanks, it has been a good day."

Mary Nell continued, "I met Mr. Dillon once a few weeks ago, but only briefly. Now that the hotel and restaurant are open, I imagine we will meet again. He's quite a man. He's a bit dodgy about where he came from, and Paul suspects he could have some secrets in his past, but he was very polite and gentlemanly."

Claire wanted to change the subject quickly. "Did you hear all the blasts this morning?"

"Yes, Paul warned me that they were working on a new, deeper shaft so there'd be lots of rumbling this week."

"It makes me nervous. I worry about Daniel getting trapped down there."

"I just try not to think about it," Mary Nell tossed her head, making Claire think of a wild pony she'd once seen in a corral.

"Daniel has told me over and over that hard rock mines like this one just don't cave in the way coal mines do, but I still get worried."

"I do too, really. Paul said that same thing, and I said to him that if the mine was so safe, why are they building a huge, two-story hospital down in Encampment? He just shook his head and grinned."

"Have you heard who is moving into the two new cabins being built on the other side of Main Street? The ones in the trees closer to Haggarty Creek? It looks like they are almost done."

"That's what I came to tell you, actually," replied Mary Nell with a smile. "Paul was talking about it last night. One of them belongs to Harv Whitley. You might remember him from church down in Encampment. He's a tall, heavy set guy with reddish hair."

"I do remember him. He's very quiet and polite."

"Apparently he has a wife that no one has met. She stayed in Illinois somewhere when he came out to work at Rudefeha. Now he's sent for her and they should be here any day. I think Paul said they have a couple of children. I don't know about the other cabin."

The tea pot began its shrill whistle on the stove. Claire made tea and then returned to her conversation. "I can't imagine a single miner building a house in Dillon and living here alone when the bunkhouse and mess hall at Rudefeha would be so much easier, so it will be fun to see who arrives to fill that one."

"There are going to be a lot of single miners living here in Dillon by the end of this month," Mary Nell sipped her tea.

"Why is that?"

"I can't believe you haven't heard. Now that Mr. Dillon's saloon and boarding house are finished along with the hotel and restaurant, he's made an offer that any miner can live at the boarding house rent free for an entire year, just as long as they promise to do all their drinking at the saloon!"

"Not really?" Claire laughed. "Daniel is going to be horrified. He is worried about drunk miners at work, this will give him fits."

"The managers at the mine are fuming, but there's nothing they can do." Mary Nell finished her tea and stood up. "I'd better go. I don't have anything planned for supper."

Claire smiled as her friend left. For every way Ella was intentional and organized, Mary Nell was haphazard and spontaneous. One of Ella's strengths was her perfectionism, yet sometimes that made her too serious. Mary Nell was much quicker with a smile and often spoke before she thought about her words. Claire treasured both women. She tatted for a while longer, thinking about how she would like to be a combination of both her friends.

Daniel's footfalls on the front steps pulled Claire out of her thoughts.

"Where's my birthday girl?" he said as we walked in. "Have you had a good day?"

She lingered in his embrace and answered, "Yes, it was pretty quiet. I had a terrible time patching that pair of your work trousers, it doesn't look very great. You'll have to decide if you want me to tear it all out and start again."

"Humpf," Daniel responded. "I'm going to wear them down in a big, black hole where the only light is strapped to my head and the heads of the other miners. No one takes even a second to look at the seat of my pants! I'm sure they are perfect."

She laughed with him then started to step away.

"Where are you going? I like this touching stuff, stay here." He held her closer.

"I love that you can bathe and get cleaned up at the mine. When you get home you smell so good."

"I like that, too. It's handy to leave my work clothes in my locker there and use the bunk house baths to wash off the day. Walt even suggested I just add my work clothes to the laundry up there. It would be so much easier than you trying to get all that dirt and mud off."

"That would be wonderful," Claire agreed. She hated the chore of washing Daniel's work clothes. She always did them last, but felt that she ended up sloshing them around in muddy water instead of actually getting them clean. Even adding more Borax and using the washboard didn't seem to help much. "Doing the laundry is so much easier now that we have my new washtubs and the stand and wringer. I never could get much water out wringing by hand, and the wringer makes all the difference, but having someone else do your really dirty work clothes would be a godsend."

"Good, I knew you'd appreciate it."

They stood for a little longer; Claire listened to Daniel's heart beating and felt so thankful. "Hey, are you hungry? I'm starved." Daniel declared, finally releasing her. "Where's Jesse?"

"He's just out back, working on those old skis he got from Cody. He's been out there all afternoon sanding them and then putting tung oil on them so he can use them when it snows."

Daniel kissed her again, then headed outside. In just a few minutes he and Jesse filled up the little kitchen. "Let's go down to the restaurant. I stopped on my way up and asked Malachi to hold a nice table for us."

"That's sweet of you. I just need to tidy my hair and put on a hat."

Soon the couple was walking hand in hand the short two blocks to Dillon's main street as Jesse followed close behind. When they stepped onto the boardwalk of Main Street, Claire stopped for a moment to take in the surroundings.

"I don't think I'll ever get tired of looking at how pretty these mountains are."

Dillon sat at the bottom of a wide bowl. Mountain peaks and saddles soared high around them. Those to the north and east were the highest and formed the Continental Divide for North America. Most of the tall lodge pole pines had been cut down for use in the mine and buildings, so the hillsides were covered in stumps and slag piles along with high mountain grass ablaze with orange, purple and yellow wildflowers. Cabins dotted the hills.

Claire marveled at the growth of the town in such a short time. At only a few months old, downtown Dillon, Wyoming was quite a sight. Main Street was a wide, unfinished avenue filled with jagged rocks and plenty of dust. When afternoon rains came, the road became a shallow creek which quickly changed to a muddy mire. A large boulder curiously sat directly in the middle of the street in front of the Dillon Hotel. One of six buildings on Claire's left as they turned toward the main business district, the three-story hotel was regal among the others. Its tall, rectangular front facade was plain, red brick with three windows over the main floor's ample doors and windows. One small window on the third floor hinted at the sleeping area there. From where Claire stood at the south end of the street, she could see that the hotel's narrow front belied its size. The building reached far back from the street, its roofline filled with dormer windows. The hotel's back wall dug into the slope of the hillside and ended with a wooden storehouse.

Buildings on each side of the Dillon Hotel were two- and three-story structures. Daniel explained to Claire on their first day in town that Malachi Dillon had insisted that buildings near the saloon and hotel be built with ample room between to keep the whole town from burning in the event of a fire. Because of the steep slope of the valley floor, downtown Dillon didn't have a continuous boardwalk like most towns. To accommodate the hillside, the front doors on the businesses on the upper side of the street each had wooden stairs leading to porches for their entrances, necessitating a broken walkway instead of a continuous boardwalk like in Encampment. There were streetlamps along both sides of the avenue, and the little family stopped by the corner of the hotel to watch as the lamplighter used a short pole to lift the glass and set the wick to burning.

In comparison to their neighbors, businesses on the right side of the street appeared much shorter even though they were also mostly two story wooden buildings. These buildings were also more tightly grouped. Claire couldn't help thinking that the wide avenue and taller buildings coupled with the hillside worked together to give the appearance of two rival armies facing each other before battle instead of a harmonious little town.

Dillon was, in fact, anything but a sleepy little town. Blasting at the mine rattled windows with regularity. Shift work meant that at any time of the day or night miners were coming and going from Dillon to Rudefeha, happily stopping at the saloons for cards and drinks. The sharp calls or whistles of hostlers driving freight wagons pulled by fifteen horse or mule teams rumbled by at a constant rate.

While a few families with women and children lived in Dillon, most of the population was men, hard-working and tough. Miners, drivers, mechanics – men who lived rough with their hands and muscles were the mainstay of the town. These citizens were used to working long days with sore backs and dirty faces without expecting any of life's courtesies. Herders, their sheep grazing nearby, came into town nearly daily for supplies or a beer, smelling of sheep and sweat.

Claire, who had become accustomed to hard-living men in Rapid City, was able to see past the dirt, swagger and crude manners of the men in town easier than Mary Nell or some of the others. She walked the business district with caution but not fear while her friends rarely ventured even to the mercantile alone.

Daniel held the door for a miner coming out of the restaurant then ushered Claire and her brother inside. She was immediately impressed by how nicely it was furnished. The large room was light and cheery, partly because of the windows that looked out onto the main thoroughfare but also due to the ornate lamp sconces lining the other three wallpapered walls. Instead of the cheap pine tables that filled the saloon in Rapid City, here were thick, oak pedestal tables with matching, carved chairs.

"I'm Daniel Haynes, I think you have a table waiting for me."

"Of course," the host greeted them. Claire smiled as the man, dressed in a sharp black evening coat and white tie, led them to a small table on the side.

"This table is beautiful," Claire remarked as the man held her chair. "I didn't expect china plates or crystal glasses."

"It is an embarrassment to me that we are not using tablecloths, but as you well know, the water situation up here demands that we conserve."

Claire looked up to see the speaker was a barrel-chested man with a handlebar mustache dressed in formal evening wear. Daniel rose and shook the man's hand, then introduced Claire. "Darling, this is Malachi Dillon, the proprietor of this establishment. Malachi, my wife Claire and my brother-in-law Jesse."

Dillon shook Jesse's hand then reached for Claire's, kissing it sweetly. "It is my pleasure to meet you, Madam. Your beauty lights up this entire room. Welcome to Dillon, and welcome to my little restaurant."

"Thank you. This is a lovely place." Claire's cheeks were hot from the man's praise.

"I'm glad you like it. I've always wanted to own a fine restaurant and hotel. This one isn't quite like the Brown Palace in Denver, but I hope it will be someday."

"It is wonderful," Claire repeated smiling at the graciousness of her host.

"I will leave you in peace for now – I have to go check on the chef. I'll stop back by in a while to check on you. Happy Birthday, Dear Lady. Enjoy your evening out."

As he walked away, Daniel smiled at Claire. "He's quite the gentleman."

"He doesn't have Ed Haggarty's English accent, but he acts like a British gentleman. Where is he from?" Claire asked.

"I'm not sure. I think someone said California. When he started working at the mine, I thought he was just a prospector even though I knew he'd been involved with getting Encampment going. When he took over managing the kitchen, we were all impressed."

The restaurant was quiet and not crowded since it was a weeknight. They enjoyed the waiter's attention. They ordered their meals and sat back to enjoy the evening.

"Dan, do you think there'd be any work I could do at the mine?" Jesse asked.

Claire instantly shook her head. "Jess, I don't want you at the mine, it's too dangerous. What about your studies?"

"But, Claire," he began but Daniel interrupted.

"Jesse, I think Claire's right to keep you focused on your education. I wouldn't be where I am without it. I am not opposed, though, to you getting a part-time job."

"At the mine?"

Claire's withering glare stopped them both. Daniel cleared his throat and answered. "I wasn't thinking at the mine, no. I was thinking more here in Dillon. You enjoyed working at the livery in Encampment. Have you talked to anyone at the livery here?"

"No, not yet," Jesse answered him. "I wanted to wait and see what you said."

"I'd check there first."

The meals arrived, interrupting the conversation.

The family was quiet as they began eating. Finally, Claire addressed her husband, "Daniel, you seem a bit worried about something tonight. Is everything alright at the mine? I heard so many blasts today."

"I'm sorry, I don't mean to be distracted. Everything is fine at the mine. The blasts went perfectly. The narrow gauge rail system we put in the mine is working perfectly, which makes it so much easier and faster to clean out the debris. Things are going well."

"But...?" pushed Claire.

"It's really nothing, and certainly nothing to spoil your birthday. We've gotten word that 150,000 miners went on strike in Pennsylvania because the management refused to let the union in. I'd hate to see trouble like that start here."

"Is there any indication that the miners are unhappy or thinking of trying to start a union?"

"No, and I'm sure I'm just worrying for nothing. Between the push all over America to unionize, and hearing how many stocks George Emerson is offering for North American Copper, I just feel skittish. Maybe I'm just over tired."

"You've been working long hours. You are off on Saturday this week, aren't you?" Claire began. When Daniel nodded she continued. "We haven't been outside of Dillon since we arrived. How about if I put together a picnic and you show us some of these beautiful mountains?"

Daniel smiled. "That's a great idea. I could see about renting a horse and buggy for the day."

"Could we just go by horseback instead? " asked Jesse.

"Would you mind?" Daniel asked Claire. "It would really be more comfortable, I think."

"I don't mind at all. I've never been very skilled on a horse, though I rode a little when I lived on the farm. I hate to think

258

about bumping along in a wagon, though. Coming up here was a rough trip!"

The meal was tasty. The threesome enjoyed their relaxed time together. The plates were then taken away, and Claire savored a cup of coffee when they were interrupted by the waiter holding a platter containing three servings of chocolate cake. The plate he put in front of Claire was adorned with a lit candle. Other diners noticed and turned to watch, then join as Daniel and Jesse began singing.

> *For she's a jolly good fellow, for she's a jolly good fellow*
> *For she's a jolly good fellow, and so say all of us*
> *And so say all of us, and so say all of us*
> *For she's a jolly good fellow, for she's a jolly good fellow*
> *For she's a jolly good fellow, and so say all of us!*

Claire was touched and thought she might cry. Jesse saved her by handing her a small package. "Claire, this isn't much, I bought them with my own money, and they come with a promise that I'll help you plant them." Clearly he had wrapped the present himself. The brown paper, a bit askew, was adorned with a drawing of mountains with red flowers in front of a line of trees. The gift was three packets of flower seeds.

"Poppies, and hollyhocks, and marigolds. Jesse, this is a great present. We'll plant them out in front of the cabin to make it look beautiful. Thank you!"

Next, it was Daniel's turn. Tears did spill over when he handed her a small box from his breast pocket. She untied the red ribbon and lifted the lid, then froze.

"I've regretted that your wedding ring is so plain. From the start I wanted something beautiful that could remind you how deep my love is for you, but I couldn't afford it then. I looked at rings the last time we were in Denver and found this at the Denver Dry. Do you like it?"

Claire stared at the ring. Its gold band matched her own, but mounted on the top were a trio of diamonds. The middle diamond was largest, and sparkled in the lamplight as if it harbored a flame within. She lifted it from the box and slid it onto her finger. "This is so beautiful. How did you know about the size? It's perfect."

Daniel's smile was mischievous. "Remember that day in Denver when you and Addie were baking bread? You'd taken off your ring to do the kneading."

"Do I remember! I was frantic when I couldn't find it later. I thought I'd baked it into a loaf of bread for the church bazaar."

"I grabbed it and drew a circle around it on a piece of paper so I could know your size."

"I'll never trust you again," Claire laughed. "Daniel," she became serious. "This was so expensive, I'm sure. You shouldn't have."

"Yes, I should have and much sooner. God has blessed us with a good income and a limited amount of places to spend. Our bank account is healthy, so that's not a worry. My worry is that you know that you are treasured and loved."

"That's a beautiful ring, Mrs. Haynes." Claire looked up into the smiling face of Malachi Dillon.

"Thank you," she answered. "Won't you join us for our coffee and dessert?"

"I'd love to," he replied. He pulled up a chair and motioned to the waiter for another cup.

"Has everything been to your liking?"

"Absolutely," Daniel responded. "This was a very fine meal. The trout was perfect. Did it come from Haggarty Creek?"

"Either the creek or over at Battle Lake. I have several mountain men who supply me with fish and game on a weekly basis. Beef is a little harder to come by but mutton is plentiful. It keeps the cook happy to have a variety."

"It didn't take you long to develop a supply chain."

"No, it's gone well. Now that there are two roads into here, it helps. The road along Haggarty Creek provides the quickest access to Rawlins. Wagons come into the mountains at that stand of aspen trees they call Aspen Alley then up to Copperton. That's where they meet the Haggarty and come up. Folks and supplies from Encampment usually come in over the top, by Bridger Peak, but that's a long, hard trek."

"That's the way we came," responded Claire. "It is beautiful up there, but I was weary by the time we arrived."

"It's better now that they're establishing towns along the way."

Dillon nodded and then replied. "This little mine at the top of the Sierras is causing a fuss, to be sure. I've heard that there are now about a hundred people living in Elwood, just at the tree line above Encampment. Battle townsite is booming, last I heard there are close to two hundred living up there. They just put in another hotel. Then there's Rambler and Copperton. I don't expect either to ever get too big, but they sure do help the freight wagons coming up. When Jack Fulkerson or other hostlers are driving up big equipment and using a twenty mule team to do it, it takes a long time to get up here."

"I can't even imagine that. Do you have a house here in Dillon?"

"No, I live on the third floor of the boarding house in a set of rooms. No sense in rattling around in a house by myself."

"So there isn't a Mrs. Dillon?"

"There was once." Dillon's smile faded and his eyes looked sad. "I married my Nellie in 1886, I was thirty years old. Those were the happiest six years of my life, but they came to an end when she caught scarlet fever and died."

"I'm so sorry," Claire immediately regretted asking.

Dillon patted her hand. "Don't be. In my forty six years on this earth, I have seen good times and bad. After Nellie died I went a little crazy and spent some time at the bottom of a whiskey bottle. Did some things I'm not at all proud of. Then the good Lord got ahold of me and taught me His forgiveness. It took some healing, but I pulled on my britches and tied up my boots and started over."

"Forgiveness is a powerful thing," Claire said quietly, glancing at Daniel.

"Yes, Ma'am, it is. It's a mystery that I don't understand but I'm thankful for every day."

Claire was relieved when Daniel changed the subject then, and the men began discussing the smelter in Encampment and plans for an aerial tram system.

"It makes all the sense in the world," Daniel was saying. "The mountains are so rugged it takes more manpower to get the copper to the smelter than out of the ground. A tram system to transport it will lessen the manpower and make the trip so much quicker."

"I agree, in theory, but a sixteen mile long tram has never been built before in the world. I just hope we can get it operational and it doesn't end up making us the laughing stock of the west."

"What will power the tramway, Daniel?" Jesse asked.

"Mostly gravity. Since Encampment is so much lower than the mine, they can use that. There will be a couple of steam stations, though, to add to the reliability of it and help the speed."

"It sounds very complicated."

"I agree, Mrs. Haynes, and that's my point. I'm afraid there's just too much to go wrong."

Claire sipped the last of her coffee and breathed deeply.

"I need to take your leave. Thank you for your company and your patronage here at my little establishment. I need to go check on the kitchen staff."

"This has been a wonderful birthday," Claire smiled as Mr. Dillon again kissed her hand and departed.

"I hate to end this evening," Daniel said. "You are beautiful tonight, and I love being out with you. But, I have to work in the morning."

Claire reached around for her shawl as Daniel signaled for the check. The waiter came right away. "Mr. Dillon has taken care of everything, Sir. He asked me to wish the lady a happy birthday again for him."

As they exited the hotel, Jesse asked, "Claire and Daniel, would it be alright if I went over to Joey Logan's for a few minutes? I'll only stay a few minutes."

"Sure," answered Claire. "Tell Mrs. Logan hello for us."

"Thanks." Jesse was off at a lope in the the opposite direction.

"I'm so thankful for the Logan family. Joey is a good boy and he and Jesse have such fun together."

On the short walk back up to their cabin, Claire and Daniel's conversation turned to Malachi Dillon. "I'd like to talk to him more, he's very interesting."

"He is," agreed Daniel. "I like what he said about forgiveness."

"Me, too. I know God forgives us, it's just not as easy to forgive ourselves."

Daniel kissed her hand then paused to look at her new ring. "This looks so pretty on you. You deserve only the best, most beautiful things."

But that's just it, Claire thought, *I don't deserve it at all. Not at all.*

33
August, 1902
Dillon, Wyoming

Friday morning dawned slowly. The sky was overcast. Claire pulled on a sweater and sighed. The mine was keeping Daniel busy and preoccupied, though he rarely talked about it. Dillon was growing every day it seemed. Cabins sprang up quickly, dotting the hillside. Five streets lay parallel to Haggarty Creek. The middle one was named Main. Seven short roads intersected those five, creating nineteen city blocks. Claire and Daniel lived on the corner of Third and Copper Street, two blocks above Main. Mary Nell and Paul were just three cabins away on Copper closer to Fourth. Main Street held all the businesses. Besides Dillon's boarding house, saloon, hotel and restaurant, Main Street boasted Embry's Café and the Dillon Mercantile Company. Two more buildings were under construction, one of which was for the bank and additional office space for an attorney and an assay office. The Miner's Exchange sat at the end of the business district. Claire and Mary Nell giggled like school girls the day they went to the Miner's Exchange. They assumed it would be a store similar to Lamb and Schmitz in Battle, filled with boots, lamps, ropes and mining supplies. Mary Nell hoped to buy some nails and cord to hang curtains with. Both ladies were shocked to realize that the shelves were filled with liquor and that there were tables in the back. They left quickly, giggling all the way.

Claire put down her tea cup when she heard the rumble of the water wagon. Haggarty Creek, while a good, steady source of water, was a quarter of a mile from town, much too far to carry enough water for a household. Sahara Sam solved the problem by delivering it.

"Good morning, Mrs. Haynes," Sam called as he jumped off the wagon seat. "Looks like we could be in for an early winter by the looks of this sky."

"It sure is chilly this morning," Claire answered. "Good morning to you."

Sam lifted the lids from the two barrels on the side of the cabin. "I like how your husband rigged up this rain trough to fill these barrels when it rains."

"Thank, you. They work well, if only it would rain. It's been pretty dry this week."

"One barrel is empty and the other half full. Shall I top them both off for you?"

"Yes, please."

Claire watched as the man ran a hose from one of the many barrels on his wagon to hers, then put his mouth to the end of the hose to begin the siphon. He leaned against the side of the cabin as the barrels filled. Sam was short, shorter than Claire, and stocky. Both his full, bushy beard and the wild curls that showed under his dusty hat were amply peppered with grey. His face was leathery, the deep lines seemed to be a roadmap for the hard life he'd lived, yet his eyes twinkled merrily.

"Did you hear about the newspaper?" he asked.

"Newspaper?"

"Yeah, old Dillon's new plan to make this town great is to start up a newspaper. He's ordered a printing press, should be here within a month, and he hired some high fallutin' writer from Denver to come run it."

"That's very interesting." Claire thought about the handsome Mr. Jones she'd sat next to at dinner in Denver and wondered if he was the 'high fallutin' writer.

Replacing the lids carefully on both barrels, Sam said, "That will be fifty cents, Ma'am."

He tipped his hat and pocketed the coins, then bounced up into the wagon seat. "See you next week," he called as chirruped the horses and moved off down Third.

Claire looked in on Jesse, whose head was bent over a book. "How are you doing?"

"Alright, I guess. These calculations are still hard, but the last letter from Mr. Drake helped a lot."

"You've been at it quite a while this morning."

"Yeah, but I just have a little more to finish for today. If I keep to the schedule you and I made, I will be done with this book in just three more weeks."

"Then you can study and I can give you the exam for it."

"Yeah, I hope I can remember everything. Hey Claire, Daniel said that Jack Fulkerson is due in to the mine this afternoon with a load of supplies. He says that he's probably pulling it with a fifteen horse team. Do you think Joey and I could ride up and watch?"

"Is it alright with Mrs. Logan?"

"Yes, Joey and I talked to her about it yesterday."

"I think that would be alright, just be real sure not to get into anyone's' way. Be sure to walk the horses up that first grade out of Dillon, those rocks are so loose, the horses slip easily."

"I promise. Thanks, Claire."

A few minutes later, Mary Nell knocked at the door, basket in hand. Claire pointed at the loaf of bread wrapped in waxed paper on the counter. "Can you add that to your basket of goodies?"

"I certainly can," she answered. "I'm really looking forward to this. Getting a Ladies' Club started here will be so nice. I'm a little nervous about this winter, but knowing we have friends to talk to between snow storms will help it pass easier."

"That is so true. It was nice of Catherine to agree to host us this morning."

The friends walked four blocks, chatting as they went. Soon, they found themselves sipping tea from dainty cups around a large pedestal table covered with a white lace cloth.

"Are you going to let us try these secret treats you brought, Mary Nell?" Catherine Whitley teased.

"Yes, and you are going to be over the moon about them when you've had a taste. They are called Palmer House Brownies. My mother and father went to the World's Fair in Chicago in 1893. My mother tasted these while they were staying at a posh hotel called the Palmer House. How she talked the chef out of the recipe, I'll never know. Apparently, he created these because Mrs. Palmer wanted to take some ladies out to the fair and wanted boxed lunches with a dessert for them. Just wait until you try these."

She served each of the four women at the table a small square. The room was silent for a moment, then Veronica sighed. "Hmmm, these are indescribable! I love how they are chewy inside and crunchy on the edges."

"Is that apricot glaze on the top?" asked Catherine.

"Yes," answered Nell, "Do you agree that these are the best?"

"All in favor of Nell bringing these to every meeting say aye."

A chorus of "Ayes" followed by laughter rang through the cabin.

The ladies' discussion eventually turned to planning. They decided that they would meet on Friday mornings, rotating homes every week. Each woman was encouraged to bring sewing or handwork to do while they talked. The hostess would be responsible for light treats and tea or coffee.

"What do you think about having a devotion each week?" suggested Claire.

"I like that idea," responded Catherine. "Though it doesn't seem fair that the hostess should have to provide treats and a planned devotion. Let's set up a different rotation for that."

"How about the person who hosted one week is the discussion leader the next week?"

"I'm not very comfortable with leading a Bible study, does the discussion always have to be a devotion? Maybe we could sometimes discuss a poem or story, or something happening in the news?" Mary Nell looked around for support.

The ladies all nodded. "I think that is a good idea. As the 'Grand Dame' of this group – meaning of course the oldest – I think a little poetry or literature would be wonderful," laughed Catherine.

They talked further about inviting others to join. "As far as I know," began Veronica, "There are only a few other women in town so far, and we should invite them I talked with Elizabeth Janing at the mercantile. She'd like to come, but can't since she minds the store each day."

"Isn't there a woman living in the cabin way up in the trees behind you, Claire?"

"I think there is, but I never see her out or in town. Maybe Elizabeth would know more about her."

"There are the women who work at the saloon, and I certainly don't want to invite them," Mary Nell's voice became a little sharp. "I hate that they are here at all."

The other women nodded in agreement, Claire sat silently.

Catherine added, "We'll have to keep an eye out. When one of us notices someone new in Dillon, it is up to her to stop over and invite her to join us."

"What if we get too big to meet in our homes?" Veronica wondered.

"I suppose then we'll have to either split into smaller groups or find a common place to meet."

"How about at the Miner's Exchange," Mary Nell began to giggle and looked at Claire. Laughing, Claire explained their experience.

Claire finished her tea and smoothed her skirt. "Catherine, this has been so nice. Thank you for being our first hostess. You have a lovely home."

"Thank you. I think, then, that next week it's my turn to plan a discussion. In whose home are we meeting?"

"How about mine?" offered Mary Nell. "Our cabin is much smaller, but we can make enough room at the table."

"Do you mind if Rachel and Beth come with me?" asked Catherine. "At three and four I can't really leave them alone."

"They are welcome. They can play in our bedroom."

"Thank you. I'll bring them some paper dolls to work on."

"I have shopping still to do, so I better be going," said Claire finally. "Nell, how about you, are you shopping today?"

"Yes, I have quite a list."

The ladies thanked their hostess again and made their goodbyes. As they went toward the mercantile, the ground rumbled. "That was a good blast," Nell remarked. "I hope everyone is safe."

"I'm glad that Dr. Wilson has arrived to man the hospital at Rudefeha. It makes me easier to know that if something does happen, help is close by."

When they entered the mercantile, Elizabeth Janing was helping an elderly man. They looked around until she was free.

"Good morning Elizabeth. I have a list for you today," Mary Nell handed her a paper.

"If you don't mind, Nell, I'll gather this order this afternoon and have Richie deliver it," Elizabeth replied. Nell nodded ascent.

"I only need a few things," Claire added. "I can pick up most of them myself."

A small, dark haired woman with large green eyes came around the table.

"Oh, Ladies, I want you to meet Andriette Jameson. She's Nathan Jameson's new wife."

Mary Nell interrupted with a short squeal, "Nathan's wife! How clever of him to get married and not tell anyone!" they all chuckled and Elizabeth finished the introductions. They stood and chatted for a few minutes, exchanging information about themselves. Both friends, of course, knew Nathan and his mother from Encampment. They were happy to congratulate his new wife and tell her how much they liked him. "When I lived in Encampment, Lillian Jameson was one of my most favorite people. I was in a Bible study with her. She's such a lovely woman," confided Claire.

"Yes," answered Andriette shyly. "She was very kind to me when I arrived. She made me feel welcome and at home."

"Isn't her house beautiful?" Mary Nell asked. "I love the white stone walls."

Elizabeth left them to wait on a new customer as they continued to talk. Andriette asked about the coming winter.

"I'm not too worried. My husband, Daniel, has cut piles and piles of wood for the stove. He was up here last winter, and says that the snow can pile up ten or fifteen feet in places, but that here on the side of the hill, it shouldn't be that deep."

"Mr. Dillon is ready for it, though," laughed Nell. "He's built a two story privy for the hotel guests."

"How on earth can you have a two story privy?" asked Andriette.

They explained the trap doors and chutes that would enable the bottom level to be closed off for use of the top floor, resulting in laughter all around.

Claire told Andriette about the Ladies' Club and asked her to join.

"I'm not sure how that would work, since we live about three miles down Haggarty Creek, but I certainly would like to."

They walked with Andriette outside and pointed up the hill, describing their cabins and how to find them.

"The next time you are here, please stop by. I'd love to offer you a cup of tea and some good conversation," offered Claire.

Andriette agreed, and they left her in front of the Mercantile to head home.

Supper was noisy that night. Jesse recounted, minute by minute, his adventure of watching a fifteen-horse team make its way to the mine. "It was just like when we saw him that time in Saratoga, only then he had a much smaller team. He still sits on the back horse and only holds one set of reins in his hands. Golly, I just can't imagine being that good at training horses. I wish he'd agree to take me on as an apprentice and teach me how to do that myself."

Daniel looked up with a gleam in his eye. "Have you tried to talk with him, Jess?"

Jesse's eyes grew round. "No Sir! He's got such a gruff way about him, he actually scares me nearly to death if he just looks at me!"

They laughed at his admission, then Daniel added, "Don't feel bad, he scares me too. He's an ornery man, and you'd be wise to stay out of his way."

After supper that evening, Claire and Daniel sat contentedly on the front steps of the cabin, enjoying the night air and the peace and quiet. The street was deserted but they could hear an occasional clink of a dish or muffled voice from a neighboring cabin.

"I like how our cabins are spaced far enough apart for some privacy," Claire said, thinking about how busy and cramped it was in Rapid City.

"I agree. Maybe someday we could buy a place a little further out."

"I'm not sure I want to be as far removed as Nathan Jameson and his new wife. I met her today at the mercantile."

"I'd heard he married himself a mail order bride."

"Daniel! I can't believe that. She's very sweet and pretty. But, really, a mail order bride?"

"That's what I heard. They hadn't actually met until the day before they got married."

"I can't imagine that. She'd have to be very brave to marry a man she didn't know. Happily, we know that Nathan is a nice man. She seemed nice, however they came to be married. You and I met in an interesting way, and that doesn't diminish how precious our marriage is," Claire reached for Daniel's hand. "Does it?"

"Not at all, my love," Daniel kissed her hand and held it tightly. "Not at all."

"Anyway, it sounds like they are living very remotely."

"I talked to Nathan a few weeks ago about that. He's set up a saw mill not far from Copperton near Haggarty Creek. It gives him good access to timber. They are improving the road up here. He was pretty excited about it."

"I just am not sure I could stand living so far away from other people. I like our privacy, but that's pretty extreme. She must get very lonely."

"Hey, I have an idea," Daniel said, kissing her hand again. "Remember last month when we took the horses and went on a picnic?"

"Yes, it was such a lovely day."

"Well, how about we do that again and go visit the Jamesons? You can have a chat with her and I'll get to see his set up."

"Daniel, that's a great idea. Tomorrow is Saturday, but we already accepted a dinner invitation to Catherine and Wally's house. Can we go next Saturday?"

"We'll plan on it."

***

Claire looked forward to their outing all week. Daniel came home on Wednesday reporting that he'd seen Nathan at the mine and let him know of their plans, so Claire was no longer worried about intruding. Jesse decided not to go with them because he was invited to Joey's instead. She baked a loaf of raisin bread to take and on Saturday morning she tucked a jar of apricot jam into the basket alongside the bread.

The day was crisp and clear. The sky was a thick, deep blue with only an occasional high cloud. They left Dillon on horseback at a walk, keeping Haggarty Creek to their left. Soon, they were in the trees that lined the rushing creek. The sun there was muted, dappled. Bright spots of sunshine danced on the ground as the leaves above shifted with the wind.

"The sounds here are so different," Claire whispered after a few minutes. "Human noise is gone, replaced by squirrels and birds."

It was as though they didn't want to interrupt the serenity, and they continued on in silence, each relishing the beauty unfolding around them. Claire searched the trees to find the woodpecker she heard knocking and smiled when a hummingbird zoomed past her.

"We have to cross the creek a few times on our way down," Daniel explained when they came to the first crossing. "The water isn't deep this time of year, and it isn't running very fast, but the rocks might be slick. Hold on tight in case the horse stumbles, okay?"

Claire smiled and reassured him that she'd be fine. She waited as he forded the creek and then stopped to watch her come across. When she joined him, he smiled and fell in beside her. "This is a beautiful little canyon," she said.

The road stayed close to the creek most of the way as it curved its way down the narrow, tree lined arroyo. Claire marveled at several pools formed by fallen logs and debris and at small waterfalls chortling happily. They stopped once as they rounded a curve to watch a cow elk and her calf calmly drinking from a small pool. When the mama saw them she nudged her baby with her shoulder, and they silently moved off into the trees. Twice they spooked up deer. Claire delighted in watching them bounce away.

They'd been riding for a bit over an hour when Daniel led the way onto a smaller, less travelled two-track road on the left. They crossed the creek one more time and headed up a short but steep incline into thicker timber. Only a minute later, they came into a small clearing which held a large piece of machinery on one end and a small, cozy house at the other.

Nathan Jameson stepped out from behind the cast iron belly of the machine and greeted them. Daniel got down from his horse and shook his hand, then helped Claire dismount. Nathan explained to Daniel that his sawmill was steam powered, and showed him how it worked. Claire stood by, not understanding all the details, but getting the main idea of how the boiler created steam that drove the saw. She took the few minutes that the men talked to stretch and then look around the clearing. Sheepishly, Nathan and Daniel rejoined Claire, who was holding the horses.

"I'm sorry for my rudeness, Mrs. Haynes," Nathan said. "I get a little prideful about my set up."

"No need to apologize," Claire chuckled. "I listen to Daniel about the mine all the time, and he gets the same look in his eyes."

As they laughed, Daniel took the reins from Claire and they walked toward the cabin.

"Hello the house!" Nathan called as they neared it. Andriette opened the front door.

There were greetings and introductions, ending with an agreement that they'd dispense with formalities and use first names. "I'm so looking forward to becoming good friends," Claire said as they went inside.

The cabin was smaller than Claire and Daniel's, and instead of having separate bedrooms, this one had just one large room and a dirt floor. Claire admired the furnishings and remarked at how cozy and inviting the cabin was.

Andriette served coffee and thick slices of bread with butter. The four sat down to enjoy their snack and talk. Eventually, the men made their excuses and headed to the sawmill, leaving Andriette and Claire alone. They tidied up the table, leaving the cups and saucers in the sink. "Can I show you my garden?" Andriette asked.

The back of the house held an unexpected surprise. In the space surrounded by the back of the house, the barn and the privy, was a small protected courtyard which held a thriving garden. Claire marveled at bright green carrot tops and strong green bean vines beside three tall tomato plants full of ripening tomatoes. "This is wonderful, you are so clever!"

"Oh it wasn't me," explained Andriette. "Lillian and Abby, Nathan's sister, came up before I arrived and planted the garden. All I had to do was take care of it once I got here."

Andriette motioned to a small bench and they sat down. "Nathan built this bench just last week. He said he needed somewhere to sit and watch me work out here, though it isn't much work, really, and he's always too busy to actually watch me."

The ladies sat and talked as the afternoon passed. Claire learned that her new friend was raised by two aunts who barely invested themselves in their niece and a father who was cold and strict. Without revealing the whole story, and without mention of her uncles, Claire shared that her father also saw no value in female children and that he had at times been tough on her physically.

"When was the last time you heard from him?" Andriette asked.

"Not since the day I found out he'd been stealing the money I was making." Claire answered bitterly. "I hope I never see him again."

Andriette shook her head regretfully. "I've written to both my father and my aunts several times. I want them to know that I pray for them and that I care for them."

"How can you say that when they treated you so poorly?"

"It just takes so much energy to stay angry at them. My aunts became responsible for me, but they didn't ask for that responsibility. I can't blame them. My father is a busy and successful man. He didn't intend for his wife to die. What happened wasn't his fault, either, so I can't really blame him."

"But you said yourself that they treated you unfairly and didn't show you warmth and kindness."

"Yes, that's true, but maybe they didn't have any to give."

"The Bible says we have to ask for forgiveness. My father has never acknowledged even remotely that the way he treated my mother and me was wrong. Why should I forgive him when he feels no remorse?"

Andriette sat quietly for a few moments. A squirrel scolded from a tree above and the wind whooshed through the trees. When she spoke finally, her voice was a soft whisper. "I learned that forgiving my father wasn't about him. Forgiving is about me and my relationship with God. I felt that I couldn't stand blameless before God if I was holding on to anger and resentment."

Claire heard the words, but just couldn't agree. Neither lady was willing to let their conversation hamper the day, and soon the subject changed to lighter topics. They were talking about the Ladies' Club when Nathan and Daniel returned. Nathan was thoughtful as Claire invited his wife to their weekly meetings.

"I appreciate the invitation," Andriette answered. "I'd love to come. Maybe Nathan and I can work something out so that when he goes to Dillon on Friday I can come with him."

"I'd love that," answered Claire.

The afternoon was waning when the two couples said goodbye and Daniel and Claire started towards home. They rode in silence for quite a while, then Daniel spoke. "Did you enjoy your visit?"

"Oh yes, very much. And just for the record, Andriette is not a mail order bride."

"I never said she was, just said that was the rumor." Daniel grinned.

"They met through a mutual friend and wrote to each other for many months before they started planning to get married."

"It was meant to be," Daniel quipped.

"Oh, stop mocking me!" Claire returned, then she kicked her horse to a faster pace, laughing as she went.

34
December, 1902
Dillon, Wyoming

"Oh my," was all Claire could say when she and Daniel entered the Dillon Hotel's restaurant. "It's almost magical how different it looks in here."

The tables were festooned with red tablecloths topped with a pine garland. There were red bows and greenery hanging from each of the wall lamps. The room was warm in comparison to the snowy night air outside and brimming with the fragrance of pine and spice.

"There sure are a lot of people here already," Daniel responded. They had barely entered the room when they met Keith and Elizabeth Janing. Daniel and Keith began discussing the mine. Elizabeth turned to Claire. "Last winter this valley was void of everything but snow. Tonight, here we are in the middle of a booming town, in this pretty room. And look at all the people!"

"It's quite amazing," Claire agreed.

"Did you hear that we are going to get a new restaurant and boarding house soon?"

"No, when did that come up?"

"Two women were here this week, both from Slater. One, her name is Maggie Humphrey, bought two lots on Main Street and signed a contract to have it built. She's planning to move up as soon as the building is ready to open."

"I wonder how Mr. Dillon feels about that."

"He's got more business than he can handle, he may welcome her with open arms."

"What about the other woman? Is she moving here, too?"

"No, she and her husband are farmers, and she was here to

sign a contract with the Transportation Company to supply hay and oats for the stock. The two of them stopped into the store while they were looking around town and we had a nice visit. Both Mrs. Humphrey and Mrs. Morgan seemed really impressed with the town."

"What's not to be impressed with?" The ladies looked up from their conversation to find Grant Jones standing beside them.

"Good evening, Mr. Jones." Claire smiled. "It's nice to see you again."

"Lovely to see you, as well," he answered.

"I want to complement you on the latest edition of the *Dillon DoubleJack*." Elizabeth told him. "I very much enjoy reading the news, but my favorite part is *Grant Jones' Anvil*. You are a talented and creative writer." Claire added her assent.

"Thank you so much, Ladies. I appreciate that. She's a humble little paper at this time, but she's growing. Now that I've made everyone in the area an honorary reporter for the '*Jack*', I have been getting some good information to pass along."

"It's an interesting idea." Claire responded.

"It certainly helps me to know what is going on. I didn't know how the idea would be accepted, but I have gotten a steady stream of information from here in town and all the mines, logging camps, and even some of the sheepherders. It makes covering such a large area much easier for me."

Elizabeth chuckled, "It's actually fun to be a reporter. The information about the new restaurant will be in the next *Doublejack* because of me!"

Jones patted Elizabeth's arm, "Yes, I expect you are going to be a wealth of news for me."

They spoke a bit longer, then Jones excused himself to refill his drink. Claire watched as he walked away. "He's already a bit unsteady on his feet and the evening is still young," Elizabeth remarked.

Claire waved when she spotted Mary Nell and Paul. Nell greeted them as Paul joined the men's discussion. "You look so pretty," Nell complimented Claire. "You have such fine dresses. I love that the hat matches so perfectly. I've not seen that one before."

"Thank you," Claire said as she smoothed the green brocade of her dress self-consciously. She remembered the night that Estelle and Lela had given her the hat, marveling at how far she'd come. "I brought this with me from Rapid City. The hat was a gift from two friends."

"Well, I love it. I'd like to have friends like that!" Mary Nell laughed.

Claire thought to herself, *No, Nell, you'd be horrified.*

Elizabeth unwittingly rescued Claire and changed the subject. "Look, there's Chris Christenson."

"Where?" Nell asked, looking around.

"He's by the bar, see there?"

Claire looked around. She didn't know the man, but spotted a fellow making his way to a table with the help of crutches under each arm.

"Poor man, he could have been killed. Paul told me that he's lucky that the cave-in was small and he was the only one hurt."

Claire remembered what Daniel told her. "It wasn't a cave-in like you are picturing, Claire, so don't worry. The shaft is stable, it was just a large rock on the ceiling that cracked and gave way. No one else was really in danger, and old Christenson just happened to be under it when it fell."

"Will he go back to work when he's healed?" wondered Elizabeth aloud.

Mary Nell shivered. "I sure wouldn't."

Someone rang a bell and began to ask the guests to find their seats. Daniel reached for Claire's hand as they found seats at a table towards the back.

Claire found herself sitting with Daniel at a table for six beside Harriet DeWitt and her husband Clarence and two men she didn't know. The men, Claire guessed, were both in their late twenties. Both were robust, with wind-tanned faces and rough, weathered skin. Daniel reached across the table to shake hands, introduced the DeWitts , then Claire and himself.

"My name is Charlie Comer," began the shorter of the two. "I go by C.G. This here's my partner, Peter LeMieux."

The men shook hands, and nodded politely at Claire and Harriet.

"I don't think I've seen you at the mine," Daniel began. "What brings you to Dillon?"

"We're up here to scout for the telephone lines," LeMieux answered. Claire was taken with his thick French accent and his shy smile.

"We start work in January to bring the telephone to you."

Claire enjoyed the ensuing conversation. LeMieux, a French Canadian, and Comer arrived in Encampment two weeks ago. They had just completed mapping out the route they planned to use to bring a telephone line up just shy of Bridger Peak, then along a high ridge, finally dropping down to the mine.

"Isn't that about the same route they are planning for the tramway?" DeWitt asked.

"Yes," Daniel answered. "The tram, when completed, will be about a quarter mile shy of sixteen miles long. It will carry the ore we take out of Rudefeha in large buckets all the way down to the smelter in Encampment."

"It is the same for the telephone line," agreed LeMieux. "We are working with the Southern Wyoming Tramway Company and the engineer they hired. He's a fella named B.C. Riblet. Riblet's got a crew working with us to stake out the line. They want to begin building the tramway in February.

"The snow is so deep this time of year," remarked Harriett. "How ever do you manage to get around out there?"

Comer laughed. "Well, Ma'am, I'd venture to guess that Peter here could snowshoe before he could walk. It's like those webs are part of his legs. I've spent a lot of time in snowy mountains myself, so we just strap on the snowshoes and go."

"That's hard work, for sure," DeWitt said.

Claire turned to him. "Mr. DeWitt, I'm so happy that you've agreed to be the postmaster for Dillon. I'm sure it will take a lot of your time away from running the Mercantile, but I love that we now have mail service right here."

"Thank you. I don't expect it will be that much of a burden. We've added a counter and the proper shelving to satisfy the postal service to the back corner of the store. The first bag of mail arrived last week."

"I hated not having mail here." Harriett added. "The postmaster at Osceola, that's the actual name of the office at Rudefeha, seemed to take forever with sorting out the mail. Then someone had to go up there to retrieve it."

"It certainly is wonderful."

Claire's comment was interrupted by the bell. Nearly everyone was seated, and the guests turned to face a tall, portly gentleman in an ill-fitting suit. Claire smiled to herself. Clearly this man wasn't used to the suit or the attention he was getting, his discomfort lingered about him like a cloud.

"Well, folks, as most of you know, I'm Walter Bunce, the superintendent for the Rudefeha mine." There was a smattering of applause. "I want to welcome everyone to our holiday party. We're thankful to have work at the mine slowed down a bit in this week between Christmas and New Year's, and we're happy you've joined us for our little party.

"I want to acknowledge a few people here that have worked their fingers to the bone to get the mine going. There's the mine's bookkeeper, J.K. Jeffrey and Dennis Reedy, the foreman." He paused while the men stood and the crowd applauded, then continued. "We also have Mr. A.E Loizeau joining us tonight. Mr. Loizeau is from the North American Copper Company main office in Denver here to keep an eye on us and audit our books." The applause was subdued.

Bunce also introduced Daniel and several other men to acknowledge their work, then added, "Now I'm not going to talk very long. We've got a nice meal to eat and we don't want to cause Mr. Dillon heart failure trying to have his staff keep it all warm while I talk too much. I just want to thank everyone for your hard work at the mine. We've uncovered a deep, rich vein of copper that's beautiful to behold. We've got the water seepage under control, even down in the deep shafts, and we're hauling ore out around the clock. The most exciting news to me is that the tramway is being constructed and scheduled to be ready to haul ore sometime this summer. The smelter in Encampment has shut down for a time in order for workers to be sent up to build the stanchions that will hold the cables. Even in the snow, in the next few weeks, the mountains will be crawling with hearty men building the longest aerial tramway in the world." The applause was loud and long, real and heartfelt this time. The men in the room along with the women who supported them felt a collective pride in their own efforts.

"Now I want to leave you in peace to enjoy our meal. Again, thank you for being here and thank you for all you do to support the mine." Bunce sat down to another round of applause as waiters began serving plates to the tables.

***

Claire held Daniel's hand as they slowly sauntered back up the ridge when the party had ended. The night was cold and by the time they reached their cabin her nose and gloved fingers were cold and Daniel's cheeks were red. Soon Claire had the kerosene lantern blazing and Daniel stood by the newly stoked stove warming his hands.

"What a fun night," Claire said as she leaned into an embrace.

"Yes, it was, and you were the most beautiful woman there."

Claire nuzzled in closer, absorbing her husband's warmth.

"I know the snow is deep, but it surprised me that George Emerson and Barney McCaffrey weren't there tonight."

Daniel growled. "They don't usually miss a chance for attention, that's for sure. Emerson is probably out somewhere selling more shares to the mine."

"That's a good thing, isn't it?"

"At this point, I'm not so sure. He and his North American Copper Company bought the mine and all its rights for a million dollars. They've already sold more than three million dollars' worth of shares, though."

"I don't understand, why does that bother you? Surely there is that much copper there."

"Oh yes, there's that much copper there, but remember, selling shares is like borrowing money from investors. Those investors expect a return on their funds. In this case, they are being told they'll get a big return."

"You don't think they'll get it?"

"I think that Emerson is a great salesman when he thinks there's something in it for him. They are spending money left and right. The tramway is costing them a pretty penny, and so are the upgrades on the mine, the smelter and the town of Encampment. Emerson and McCaffrey both are living very high on the hog. I just don't trust him."

Daniel kissed a line on the back of Claire's neck, then turned her in his arms and continued kissing until he reached her mouth, where he lingered.

"Mmm," he sighed. "We aren't alone in this cabin very often. How about we continue this over there?" he said before he blew out the lantern light.

35
June, 1903
Dillon, Wyoming

Claire thought of Ella Parkison as she pinned the laundry on the line. *Ella would be shaking her head in dismay at me, getting the wash out so late in the day*, thought Claire. She pinned up another towel then stopped to rest. Her arms felt like lead. Though she'd slept well, she was tired already. Resting, she looked around. The hills were aglow with wildflowers in a rainbow of colors. The sky was clear and blue. Somewhere nearby lambs bleated. A rumble of wagon wheels echoed from below. *It's a beautiful day, but here I am feeling anxious and droopy.*

She finished pinning up the wash and returned to the house. The water in the teapot was still hot, so she made herself a cup of tea and took it out to the front porch. She sat down heavily on one of the two wooden chairs and sighed.

Claire's thoughts wound around for a few minutes but finally came to rest on the letter she'd received last week. Haddie always supplied the latest news and thoughts, and never failed to make Claire smile. This letter was no exception until the end. *I want you to know that your father and his brother are back in Mitchell. William ran into them last week. William says he's looking old and ill kept. He asked about Jesse, and talked about 'wanting to retrieve his son'. William didn't know what to say, so he told the truth, that Jesse was with you. Will did not tell them where you are, though.*

Since she got the letter Claire's nights were haunted with dreams of her father's fists and her uncle's roaming hands. Every quiet moment during the day was consumed with memories of her life as a near prisoner on the farm. She thought about what Jesse had shared with her about how Hiram and Horace had teased and mocked him, and the evil suggestions Horace made to little Jesse about the girls at school. She brushed off Daniel's concern for her, not ready to share with him or anyone else the worry Haddie's letter had brought her.

The Ladies' Society was meeting at Veronica's house. Claire looked around the table. Nell had just arrived. She sat between Veronica and Catherine and said, "Andriette, we're so very happy that you are here. It's always fun when you can join us."

"I'm excited to tell you that you'll probably be seeing me much more often from now on. Nathan bought me a horse, so I can come to town now without him."

Claire was especially happy to hear the news. Since the day last summer when she and Daniel had visited the Jamesons, the couples had met several times, enjoying evenings at one another's homes. Claire and Andriette had gotten together several times as well. Claire appreciated Andriette's faith and gentleness, and cherished their growing friendship.

As Andriette described her new chestnut mare named Daisy, her eyes sparkled and her smile permeated the room. Claire commanded herself to let go of worrying about her father and Horace. She laughed as Catherine described the latest antics of her two girls.

The afternoon grew more serious when Mary Nell began the formal discussion. "As we all know, Mr. Grant Jones passed away at the beginning of this month. It is a terrible loss. The news he provided in the *Doublejack* has brought our town together, and his beautiful writing has enriched us all." Everyone knew that Grant Jones died while he was at Battle. He had come down with a bad cold, some say bronchitis, and another traveler at the boardinghouse offered him some morphine to help him sleep. The combination of the morphine and drink allowed him to sleep well that night, but kept him from ever awakening again.

Catherine cleared her throat. "When Mr. Comer and Mr. LeMieux died in that terrible avalanche in February, Grant Jones' eulogy in the paper was one of the most beautiful things I've ever read."

"I agree," continued Nell. "He's made us laugh with his stories of the screaming emu and the coggly-woo, and made us cry when something bad happened like the avalanche. His passing creates a big hole here in Dillon. I for one will miss seeing Mr. Jones on the streets and having a courteous word with him. He was always a gentleman."

"Yes," agreed Veronica. "Even though he was always a bit drunk, he was quite a handsome and suave man."

"That's exactly what I want to talk about." Nell adjusted her skirt and leaned forward. "Dillon is a wonderful town full of good people, but we have three saloons, if you count the Miner's Exchange, and there is just too much alcohol and debauchery here. I've been reading about the Women's Christian Temperance League back east and the push to prohibit alcohol in America. I think we should start a chapter here to rid our town of alcohol and those horrible harlots who lure the town's men in with their low necklines and even lower morals."

The discussion was spirited.

"I don't think we have much chance of running the saloons out of town or getting the miners to stop drinking," declared Catherine. "It's just part of our town whether we like it or not."

"Maybe that is true," Nell agreed, "but I think we could succeed in getting rid of those women who work there. They are devils. They smile and flirt in broad daylight, and corrupt our innocent men."

"Nell, I hate to break it to you, but our men aren't innocent."

"Don't be flippant, Catherine. Do you like it when our husbands are subjected to even seeing those floozies on the street? Paul came home the other night and asked me why I never flirt with him. That's the devil's influence without a doubt."

Claire listened to the ladies without comment. She grew increasingly uncomfortable as Nell grew increasingly passionate.

"All I'm saying is that there is no place in a town with ladies and children for women who are so low. They snatch up good men and teach them their evil."

Claire had heard enough. She took a breath and quietly but firmly replied, "Men choose to enter a saloon. They choose to pay for their drinks and they choose to pay for a saloon girl's company and attention. The women don't go out and grab the men."

"I can't believe that you would stand up for this evil right here in our town!" Nell's voice grew louder.

"I am not defending anything about the situation, I am just saying that a man goes into a tavern for a reason. Sometimes they just want a drink, other times they want more. It's not the alcohol that is the problem, it's the man's choice to drink too much. The women who work there are victims themselves. Since women can't vote and have such diminished rights, there's no remedy for them. Mr. Jones was a very nice man, but he had an addiction with alcohol that began with a choice. Closing the bars or running the saloon girls out of town would not have solved it."

"But those women are in this town intent on ruining our men," retorted Nell. "We need to get rid of them."

"I bet there are many reasons a woman ends up as a bar girl that would break your heart. I can't imagine that any of them grew up aspiring to do what they do." Claire's voice was low and quiet, she wasn't quite sure where her courage was coming from.

Mary Nell's face grew red. "I can't believe you or any self-respecting lady would argue against this. Claire, what is the matter with you?"

Catherine cleared her throat and smiled. "Well, this has been a thought-provoking discussion today. Thank you for leading us, Mary Nell. Who is going to lead our discussion next week?" With that, the subject was firmly changed and the group seemed to release a collective sigh of relief at the respite.

Not much later the ladies made their goodbyes and began to leave Veronica's. Nell left alone, barely nodding at Claire. Claire watched her for a moment, recognizing the possibility that she'd just lost a friend. Andriette stood beside her.

"I still have a few minutes before I need to start for home," she said.

Thankful for the support, Claire responded, "I'd love it if you'd come up to the cabin for a few minutes, will you?"

They walked up the hill together in silence. Andriette led Daisy behind them. She tied the gentle horse loosely to the clothes line pole near a patch of weeds then joined Claire on the porch.

"Not everyone has had the kind of upbringing Nell has talked about. She's mentioned before how kind and loving her parents are and how close she is to her siblings. I think it may be harder for her to understand hard choices than it is for others."

Claire stayed silent, afraid of what she might admit if she started talking.

Andriette smiled a sad, joyless smile and added, "My mother died birthing me so I never knew her. From that moment on I was simply a sad reminder to my father of what he'd lost and a burden to the aunts who had to care for me. I thank God every day for Nathan. I can't imagine what I'd have done if we hadn't begun writing to one another and if I hadn't chosen to come here to marry him."

"My father only saw my mother and me as possessions, there to do what he wanted," Claire finally said, carefully.

They sat quietly for a time. Sparrows chirped in a nearby pine while the breeze rifled the tufts of grass in front of the cabin.

"How can you not still hate him?" Claire finally asked.

"My father? I used to. I seethed at the thought of him for a long time. I hadn't done anything wrong, but he couldn't forgive me for taking my mother. He actually said that to me once, that I had taken his wife away from him by being born."

"So how is it that you don't hate him still?"

Andriette laughed. "I've spent a lot of time praying. Once Nathan and I were married and I understood what being loved felt like, I began to understand that losing my mother's love must have been a hard thing for my strict and rigid father. I stopped being angry at him and started feeling a bit sorry for him. Then, as that settled in, along with a lot of prayer, I decided that I had to let it go. I didn't want to have any part of me become cold and hard and indifferent like he had, so I made a choice."

"I admire that," Claire said honestly. *My father wasn't indifferent like Andriette's, and I have the scars to prove it. I think letting go what he did to me might be a harder task.*

"You look a little pale, are you feeling alright?" Andriette said after a few moments.

"Yes, I think so. I've been feeling tired lately. I bought some Dr. Kilmer's Swamp Root Remedy at the mercantile last week, but it doesn't seem to have helped."

"I tried that once, it didn't do anything for me either. Do you think you might be, well, could you be in a family way?"

Andriette's words hit Claire like cold water. "Well," she stammered, "I'd not even thought of that.' She thought back then said, "Oh my, I could be!"

The women giggled together like school chums, excited at the idea.

Later that evening, Claire looked at the calendar, concluding that she was, in all likelihood, going to have a baby. She rubbed her tummy, trying out the idea and deciding to wait before mentioning anything to Daniel.

36
July, 1903
Dillon, Wyoming

July fourth arrived in Dillon with clear warm skies and a hubbub of excitement. Business owners in town banded together with the mine to offer a daylong festival of food and fun for everyone in the area. Claire finished putting the last of their lunch remains in the picnic basket. She and Daniel sat on one of the quilts dotting the clearing just north of town. Jesse and his friend Joey sat across from them, licking their fingers and searching the basket for any crumbs left.

"Hey everyone!" a loud voice called, "We'll be starting the relays and three legged races right after the baseball game between the prospectors and the miners. The game will start in about half an hour. In the meantime, you might want to come down to Main Street to watch the double jacking demonstration."

Daniel stood up and then held out his hand for Claire. The boys ran ahead, as they walked with the crowd chatting with neighbors to a space on the boardwalk in front of the Dillon Hotel.

"It looks like someone is finally going to put that rock to good use," Daniel commented. Claire had always wondered why someone didn't move that rock from the center of the street, and smiled at Daniel's comment. Three men stood in a triad around it. Other men were blocking off the street on each side, and slowly the crowd began to venture closer.

As they got nearer Claire could see one man held a large sledge hammer. "What is that man holding?" Claire asked Daniel.

"That's an eight pound sledge hammer."

"No, I know what a sledge hammer looks like." Claire laughed. "I just can't see what the other man has."

Daniel put his arm around his wife, pulling her in to him. "Oh, he's got a drill bit." The man turned so that Claire could see clearly that he held a long bar, perhaps four feet long, that came to a sharp, chiseled point

The third man in the circle addressed the crowd, "Ladies and Gentlemen, Charlie and Lucky here are going to give us a double jacking demonstration. Some of the time down deep in the belly of mother earth, a man uses a four-pound hammer and holds his own chisel bit to create a hole in the rock. That's called single jacking. Other times, especially when excavating in hard rock, like in the Rudefeha, the job takes two men working together. Now I'm going to time these two. We're going to give them two minutes. At the end of those two minutes we'll see how far they've managed to bore down into this solid boulder."

The announcer moved back while the men stepped up on opposite sides of the rock. "Charlie is the guy with the hammer." Daniel told Claire, "and the other guy is Lucky."

Claire watched as Charlie leaned the hammer against his leg, then spat on his hands and rubbed them together. He picked the hammer back up and nodded. The other man, Lucky, held the long bar against the rock then nodded to the announcer.

"On your mark, get set, go!"

The crowd cheered as the men began. Between each strike of Charlie's hammer Lucky, using both hands, first lifted then twisted the bit about a quarter of a turn. The men fell into a quick rhythm, each concentrating all their efforts on the bit and stone. Claire watched in amazement as the bar seemed to grow shorter with each blow. The crowd cheered and hollered. Charlie's face grew red and his shirt was sweat soaked when the announcer called one minute. With almost no break in the rhythm, Charlie handed the hammer to Lucky and kneeled down to hold the bit. Lucky began swinging the hammer, increasing the pace even when it didn't seem possible to go faster.

The crowd got louder as the seconds ticked by. The long drill bit disappeared stroke by stroke until finally time was called. Lucky put down the hammer. His arm shot out to shake his partner's hand as the announcer stepped up. He grasped the bit at the rock line and lifted it up so everyone could see. Another man came with a measuring tape. After a few seconds to measure and confer, the announcer called out, "Let's hear it for Charlie and Lucky. They just drilled a total of three feet two inches in just two minutes."

The crowd applauded, stomped and yelled their approval. "Do we have any takers? Anyone think they can beat that performance? Just let me know, and we'll get another team set up to try!"

Claire could hear comments of "No way" and "Those two are the best" as she and Daniel walked away. On their trek back to the clearing Claire questioned Daniel about the hole the men made. "The result of their double jacking was a clean hole through that rock. What happens next?"

Daniel smiled and replied quietly, "This is one of the many reasons why I love you so much. You always ask such interesting and good questions. Miners drill holes that deep so that we can fill them with dynamite or blasting powder. When you have several of those charges set in strategic spots, a fuse is run that will ignite the powder in all the holes at once. Then, the charge boss makes sure all the other men are out and somewhere safe, lights the fuse and runs for cover."

"Then those are the blasts I feel and hear."

"Exactly. Other times, though, whether the hole is made by a double jack team or individual miners who are single jacking, once they get a hole about eight inches deep they switch to a wider chisel bit to crack the rock off. A team of miners are doing that while others are cleaning up the waste rock and carrying it out of the way."

Daniel and Claire found themselves back at the edge of town. They sat on their blanket with friends all around and spent the next two hours watching the miners versus the prospectors in a game of baseball. "Those poor saps just can't hit the ball as far as the miners can," Keith Janing complained as the game concluded. The victorious miners were celebrating.

The sun was nearly touching the mountains to the west when Veronica's husband Harv Whitley called out, "Hey Haynes, the last event of the day is about to start and I need a partner for the three legged race. Come on!" Daniel hesitated, but Claire pushed him forward.

"I'll be cheering for you," she called as Daniel was whisked away towards the starting line. She folded the blanket and laid it on top of her picnic basket. She left it there and moved to find a spot about halfway down the field with a good view of both the starting and finish lines. Spectators filled in quickly, and soon Claire was standing with Mary Nell not far away on one side and Elizabeth Janing and her husband on the other. Claire smiled and greeted her friends. The Janings returned her hello warmly. Nell smiled and asked how she was. Ever since the Ladies' Society last month Nell had been standoffish and distant, and Claire was happy at Nell's greeting. *Maybe she'll come around and we'll be friends again like we were,* Claire thought.

While she waited for the race to begin, Claire thought about how perfect her life was at the moment. She couldn't imagine a better day, or a better summer. The look on Daniel's face the evening she told him about the baby was etched on her heart. While their life was modest, and living on the Continental Divide presented new challenges for them often, she cherished the safety and love that surrounded her.

Everyone cheered as the race began. Claire chortled at the antics on the field. Watching grown men, serious miners, try to run while tied to a partner was a funny sight. Daniel and Walt fell twice, and were so tangled the second time they had trouble getting up again. Claire's side hurt from laughing as she watched the race end with her competitive husband nearly last. The spectators began breaking up when strong hands grabbed Claire by the shoulders and spun her around. She found herself face to face with a rough looking man with a two-day beard and dusty hat.

"I thought that was you, Purty Girl! I thought that was you!"

It took Claire several moments to recognize the man. He'd been a frequent customer at Jack's Saloon in Rapid City.

"I'm sorry, Sir, you must have be mistaken for someone else," Claire stammered as she tried to free herself from his grip.

"Now Darlin', don't play hard to git. You must remember old Curly here. I was one of your best customers."

"Please," Claire said, trying to keep her voice down and not attract attention. "Please let go of me." She could smell the whiskey on his breath as he continued to hold her. "I'm not who you think I am."

Confusion clouded the man's eyes. He held her a few seconds more, then released her. "I can't believe you don't remember me," he whined. "We had some good times together."

"No, we didn't," Claire argued. She was shaking all over, gripped in fear. Her only instinct was to get away and find Daniel.

She turned and fled through the crowd.

By the time she found Daniel, her head was pounding. He and Walt each had a mug of beer in hand. Walt proposed a toast to their worthy partnership and they clinked glasses. Daniel was caught in the moment of fun and revelry, and didn't notice anything amiss with Claire. Soon, Veronica appeared by Walt's side, then Clarence and Harriet DeWitt joined them. The couples joked and talked. Eventually, insulated within the nest of her friends and the safety of Daniel's presence, Claire regained her composure and began breathing normally again.

The group's conversation was interrupted by the sound of a large cowbell. When Walter Bunce, the mine superintendent, had everyone's attention he called out, "Folks, we've built a dance floor in the vacant lot next to the Miner's Exchange. Some of the guys put together a band and they've been practicing after their shifts for the past two weeks. I'd like to invite you to come join us and do some dancing under the stars."

Daniel led Claire over to where they'd left the picnic basket. He carried it in one hand and held hers in the other. Jesse, still with Joey, ran up to tell her that they were going to head back to the cabin.

"What are you going to do at the cabin?" Claire asked.

"I thought I'd grab a clean shirt and then we'd go to Joey's" was Jesse's answer. "Would that be alright?"

"To spend the night?"

"Yes,"

"Have you asked Joey's mom about this?"

"Aw, Claire. If it isn't okay with her I'll come home."

"Okay, then. Be good." She pecked him on the cheek.

"Will you take the basket with you, please, and carry it to the cabin?" asked Daniel.

"Sure," was all Jesse said as he snatched it up and turned uphill.

Claire was tired and her head was pounding, but Daniel was in such good spirits that she didn't want to ruin the mood. She walked along with him, joined by the other revelers. By the time they reached the boardwalk, harmonica music lilted through the streets drawing them in. The band consisted of a guitar player, a violin and the harmonica. They easily got the crowd going and soon the dance floor was filled with couples enjoying the end of the Independence Day celebration.

Claire and Daniel danced their second waltz, "Are you thirsty?"

"Yes," Claire answered. "I'm parched."

"I'll step into the Miner's Exchange and get us each a root beer."

"Hmmm, that sounds wonderful," Claire turned to watch the dancers as Daniel stepped away.

As Daniel entered the tavern, a drunk man he'd never seen before brushed his shoulder. The man weaved unsteadily past without a word.

Claire took a deep breath and looked up at the bright array of stars overhead. Elizabeth and Keith Janing twirled by her as the band played a rousing polka. Claire clapped along with the music as she waited for Daniel. When she felt someone brush against her she turned, expecting her husband. Instead, someone grabbed her hand and pulled her onto the dance floor. Before she could react, Curly wrapped his arm tightly around her waist and pulled her into the swirl of dancers. Claire didn't know what to do. This man had held her and danced with her just like this before. From his point of view he was just dancing with a bar girl from Jack's Saloon.

"Let go of me!" When she tried to push away from him, he pulled her closer, her feet barely skimmed the floor as they swirled around. She could smell whiskey and sweat and felt dizzy and sick. Afraid to make a scene or call attention to herself, but wanting to be free of this man, she continued to push against him and repeat that she wanted him to stop. In his drunken state, he plowed into Elizabeth and Keith, knocking them apart. They bounced against first one couple on the dance floor, then another, causing partners to separate and stop. In only a few moments, the floor was a mass of chaos. As more and more couples stopped dancing and stepped back, more room was created for Curly and his unwilling partner. He continued to drag Claire around, stumbling and laughing all the time.

One by one the band members noticed the disturbance and stopped playing. The harmonica player was the last to quit just as Claire once more implored her partner to stop.

Daniel stepped out of the Miner's Exchange holding two mugs of root beer to see his wife, looking pale and frightened, in the arms of a tall man on the dance floor. He dropped the drinks and raced to the floor, reaching Claire just as the harmonica player stopped playing.

The man's back was to Daniel, so he grabbed the back of his collar and pulled. Curly stumbled backwards, still holding tightly to Claire and the pair began to fall. Daniel let go of the man and reached for his wife, catching her just as the drunk let her go. Daniel and Claire stumbled a few steps before they were able to regain their feet, and stood staring at each other, stunned for a few seconds. In the meantime, Curly hit the ground on his right side, rolled to his hands and knees then came up fighting mad. Daniel saw him out of the corner of his eye and moved so that Claire was safe behind him and he could face the onslaught. Curly took an off-balance swing with his right fist that Daniel easily side stepped.

By the time Curly was steady enough to attempt another punch, two miners ran up and grabbed him. As they escorted him off the floor and away from the crowd, everyone could hear him hollering, "Hey, I was going to pay her just like always, I didn't expect to get it for free."

Sure that the man was subdued, Daniel turned to Claire.

"Did he hurt you?"

"No, I'm just dizzy."

The couple was quickly surrounded by friends and acquaintances, all asking Claire if she was alright and offering help. Daniel took Claire's arm and they moved off the dance floor. Someone pulled up a chair so that Claire could sit down.

Daniel read Claire's look and knew he needed to divert attention away from her before she was even more overwhelmed. "It's a good thing the band quit playing. That fella was so drunk he'd have probably tried to dance with me next!" The crowd laughed and began to break up. Soon the band was playing a quiet waltz.

"Are you sure you are alright?" Elizabeth and Keith remained at Claire's side. "He was holding you so tight, I hope you don't have bruises."

"I'm sure I'm fine, just tired. Thank you for your help."

Daniel reached for Claire's hand. "Are you steady enough to walk home?"

"Yes, of course," she smiled and stood. "Thank you again, Elizabeth and Keith."

The couple walked slowly up to their cabin. Music followed them, as they climbed the hill.

When they were safe inside the cabin, Claire sat down at the kitchen table, put her head down on her arm and began to cry. Daniel pulled his chair close to her and stroked her hair. After a few minutes, she raised her head. Daniel handed her his handkerchief and gently used his thumb to capture a tear from her cheek.

"I've embarrassed you, how can you ever forgive me?"

"What?"

"Now the whole town knows that I have a soiled past. You must be so ashamed of me."

"Claire, look at me. I don't know what you are thinking, but this wasn't your fault."

"But Daniel, I knew him. I've been with him. I was foolish to think that we could just move away and pretend I wasn't a, a …"

She stopped talking when she saw Daniel's face. He was angry.

"Claire, the God of the universe has promised you that your sins are washed clean because of Jesus' love for you. You've been promised that your sins are gone in His eyes. Who do you think you are? Are you more important or wiser than God that you can choose to hold onto those sins when He doesn't?"

"But what about the town? Your bosses, the other miners, our friends? It will be all over town tomorrow about me. Now everyone knows."

Daniel took a breath and ran his hand through his hair, then knelt down in front of Claire's chair. "All anyone knows is that a drifter got drunk and grabbed you for a dance. It could have been anyone."

"It wasn't just the dance. I saw him earlier. He talked to me earlier. He told me he missed me and that Jack's wasn't the same without me. I'm sure others heard that, too."

Daniel was tired. He was weary of the fight. "Claire, we've been through this over and over. We agreed when we got married that the past was in the past. I've told you many times that I have nothing to hold against you, I love you and that is all. You are forgiven by God. The only one who continues to hold a grudge against you is you. Until you decide to let it go and forgive yourself, you are always going to be a prisoner of your past. I'm going to bed."

Daniel shrugged and turned away. Claire listened as he moved around the bedroom, heard the bed squeak as he got in and rustled around for a few minutes. She didn't move. She sat, hearing the stillness settle into the cabin. For a while she could hear fragments of songs or a peal of laughter drift up from Main Street, then the stillness got a foothold there as well and the night became silent.

From somewhere inside her, or more probably from Somewhere outside her, Second Corinthians 5:17 announced itself. Claire reached for her Bible and opened it to read, "Therefore if any man be in Christ, he is a new creature: old things are passed away; behold, all things are become new."

Claire read the verse through several times, then sat and let the beauty and simplicity of it sink in. "I am a new creature," she whispered to herself. "I am become new."

Eventually, after time in prayer and a few more tears, Claire slipped quietly into bed beside Daniel. He didn't wake, but turned towards her and drew her close. Claire snuggled deep into his arms and fell asleep.

37

July, 1903
Dillon, Wyoming

The morning after the celebration Claire awakened late, still tired and very queasy. She made a quick trip to the privy. Returning to the house feeling a bit better, she settled heavily into a chair by the table.

"What's that on your arm?"

Claire examined her forearm. There was a hand-sized bruise above her elbow. Daniel was instantly beside her. He tenderly kissed her arm and then her mouth. "You need some rest. You look tired and I don't like that bruise."

Daniel took Claire's hand and led her back into the bedroom. "Your job is to stay in this bed and relax. I'm in charge of the house today."

Claire tried to argue, but in the end, she agreed. She snuggled back into bed to the sounds of Daniel clanging pots. Soon, he perched at the end of her bed to watch her eat a bowl of oatmeal. Despite a few lumps, her breakfast tasted good and warmed her stomach and her heart.

Daniel stroked the side of her face and kissed the tip of her nose when Jesse came home. She slept and read through the day, feeling lazy and spoiled. It wasn't until he brought her a bowl of Campbell's tomato soup and some crackers for dinner that Daniel finally sat down beside the bed to talk. She told him about the Bible verse, in fact she recited it to him, and explained what happened after he went to bed.

"You were right. I was the only one holding on to the past. I spent a lot of time thinking about it and praying last night. I'm going to remind myself every time I start to feel guilty about my past that I am a new person, forgiven and loved."

She finished her soup and suggested a game of checkers.

Claire stayed home, not in bed but taking it easy for the next few days. She didn't walk the few blocks into town, but instead busied herself with writing letters to Haddie and Marcus to share the news about the baby. She made a list of items they needed to purchase before the baby arrived and even sketched an idea she had for adding another room onto their cabin.

***

Five days later, Claire found herself at Catherine's house for the Ladies' Society meeting. Andriette sat beside her on the sofa, Veronica perched on a wing backed chair across the small parlor. Catherine answered the door and welcomed Nell. When she stepped inside, Nell looked across the room at Claire and said, "Oh, you did come today. I thought maybe you wouldn't."

"Mornings are a bit rough still, but they are getting better."

"That's not what I meant. I just am surprised that you could face us after that shameful show you put on at the picnic." Nell turned to Catherine, "I brought a loaf of bread for you for later. Can we put it in the kitchen?"

The two women headed towards the kitchen as Andriette turned to Claire. "What did she mean?"

Veronica answered before Claire could say anything. "Poor Claire! After you left the dance, Andri, some drunk grabbed her and took her out on the dance floor. He was so drunk, he knocked Harv and me clean off the floor, along with several others. It was a miracle you weren't hurt, Claire. It was like he was using you as a battering ram."

Catherine and Nell came in and settled themselves as Veronica described the melee. "I'd never seen the man before, I don't think he is a miner. Daniel was a real champ in how he handled the situation. Harv said that he would have cold-cocked the guy!"

Nell's voice was cold. "My husband Paul, along with John Fischer escorted the man away. He kept claiming that he was old friends with Claire and that he used to pay her for lots more than just dancing with him. He said that Claire here worked in a saloon in Rapid City, and that she had shown him a good time quite often.

The man knew her name and all about her, so it is clear he didn't mistake her for someone else."

Stunned silence descended. The ladies stared at Nell, not quite comprehending. Claire felt as if all the oxygen had been sucked from the room. She couldn't breathe. She felt hot and clammy-cold at the same time. Wishing she could simply disappear, Claire sat, mute and still.

When Claire didn't answer, Nell continued. "Maybe that explains why you stood up for those harlots at the saloon a while back. You are one of them."

Catherine gasped. "Nell, how could you say such a mean thing?"

Nell met Claire's eyes. "Well, go ahead and deny it if it isn't true."

Claire took her time. She inhaled a steadying breath and let it out slowly. *I am a new person, forgiven and loved,* she reminded herself.

After a short wait, Nell continued, "I just don't understand how you can call yourself a Christian and sit here with us and study the Bible with the past you have."

With these words, a sort of warm calm flooded her, and after taking one more breath, Claire said to the group, "It is because of all that has gone before me in this life, that I claim Jesus as my own and choose to follow Him and study the Bible. The most perfect day was the day that I realized that I was forgiven and loved by the Creator of the Universe.

"Mary Nell, you and I are friends. We've known each other since we lived in Encampment. We've done Bible study together and shared jokes and recipes. You know that I am a believer and you also know who I am now. If you choose to hold something against me that happened before we were friends, before I knew Jesus, I can't stop you." Claire held Nell's gaze until she looked down.

Claire looked around at the rest of the group. "I'll leave now, I don't want to disrupt the study anymore."

Andriette put her hand on Claire's arm at the same time that Catherine spoke up, "We are all sinners here, we've all been forgiven. Please stay, Claire."

With that, Nell rose. Without a word, she put down her teacup, picked up her Bible and left the room. The ladies sat in silence for a few seconds after the front door slammed.

Catherine coughed and stood up. She offered everyone a refill of their tea cups then said, "Andri, isn't it your turn to be discussion leader?"

Claire was thankful that the group let the subject pass. Andriette forged ahead with a discussion about the miracle of the loaves and fishes.

"I'm going to spend some time in prayer for Nell," Andriette said as the two walked away from Catherine's. "She seems pretty unhappy."

"Does what she accused me of bother you?" Claire asked quietly. "Now you know the truth."

Andriette considered the question. "I completely agree with what you said to Nell. There are many seasons in a person's life. The important time is now. I think that's all that matters." She looked up to see tears of gratitude in Claire's eyes.

***

Sitting so close to the Continental Divide at nearly ten thousand feet above sea level, summer in Dillon is a fleeting prospect. By late August, the town had already seen one brief snow shower, and temperatures dipped to nearly freezing most nights. Everyone worked to stockpile enough wood to heat homes and enough food and supplies for the winter. Claire and Daniel were looking through the Sears and Roebuck catalog one evening when Daniel saw Claire's sketch for an addition to the cabin. He furrowed his brow.

"This will never do."

"It was just an idea. I don't like the idea of asking Jesse to share his room with the baby, and there's barely space in either room for a cradle."

Daniel's eyes twinkled. "I wasn't saying we couldn't add on, I was pointing out that while there's an added room for the baby, that doesn't help with all we need." He took the pencil from her hand. "How about we also add an enclosed porch room and pantry right here? We could put a door here. By keeping it closed in the winter, the cold air from outside won't cool down the cabin as much. We won't heat that room, so it will be a good place to store supplies, but it won't get cold enough to freeze. We can make it big enough to hold a couple of water barrels so that we don't have the problem like last winter of the water barrels freezing."

They'd discussed a couple options and settled on a plan. Daniel arranged for a small crew to build their addition. Now, it was the end of September and the rooms were complete. The small nursery was right next to the larger bedroom, with an adjoining door to allow Claire to hear the baby easily. Since the nursery faced the north, they'd chosen to add a small window high up on the wall. The window didn't open, so it wouldn't allow a draft into the room, but it did provide light.

Claire idly rubbed her protruding belly as she sat on the built-in bench in her new porch. Daniel found an old dynamite box that fit perfectly beneath it to hold hats and mittens and scarves, leaving plenty of room for their boots. The cross country skis they used to get around in deep snow leaned against the wall behind the back door and three pairs of snowshoes hung beside.

From her vantage point, she peered into the open pantry, mentally taking stock of the provisions she'd amassed so far. The shelves were colorful and pretty as they held jars of green beans, tomatoes and carrots, pickled cucumbers and beets, and preserved meat. Claire was proud that she'd learned, with Catherine's help, to use her pressure cooker and do much of her own canning. Beside her own jars, the cheery red and gold labels announcing her stock of Campbell's condensed soups and vegetables sat alongside plain cans of sardines and kippered herring. Bins of straw on the floor held potatoes, onions, and more carrots. She had bags of flour, sugar, coffee and tea enough to last.

Claire smiled as she looked at one row of small cans. While she fully intended to nurse the baby, she wanted to be sure he or she had plenty to eat. In one of his letters, Marcus told her about Pet Milk, a kind of canned milk that he enjoyed in Cuba while with the Rough Riders. The mercantile happily ordered some for her. Hidden behind the milk Claire had three boxes of Cracker Jacks. The molasses covered popcorn was one of Daniel's favorite treats, so Claire tucked the boxes away so she could surprise him during a blizzard.

Rested and satisfied that she was quite ready for winter, Claire closed the pantry door and went to tidy the kitchen.

Daniel arrived home later than usual that evening. As Claire watched him trudge up the street, she started to worry. His head was down, his shoulders slumped. She slipped quickly into the cabin and poured a glass of tea. When he finally made it to the porch, kissed her cheek and sat down heavily in the chair next to her, she handed it to him.

"You are so thoughtful," he said after drinking half the glass.

"How was your day? You look dead tired."

"I am. Keeping all one hundred and twenty five miners working and safe is more than I can handle some days."

"Is that why you look so discouraged?"

"I didn't know I did, but no. I have something else on my mind."

"I'm listening."

Daniel smiled at her and finished his tea. He rubbed the back of his neck. "I've been hearing some talk and rumors for quite some time, both in Encampment and around here." He reached into his pocket and withdrew a folded paper. He unfolded the envelope and retrieved a short sheaf of papers.

"Just mostly out of curiosity, I wrote to Peter in Denver with what I'd heard and asked him to look into it if he could. I checked the mail this morning before I caught the wagon to the mine, and here's Peter's reply."

"What's this about?"

"You know that I'm not fond of George Emerson and his partner Barney McCaffrey?" Claire nodded and Daniel continued. "Emerson's just too slick for my liking. He's always the hero of his own story. He's a windbag. McCaffrey is Emerson's shadow, his henchman. Anything Emerson says or does, McCaffrey is right there nodding his head." Claire smiled as she nodded hers. She'd heard Daniel's opinion of the two men before.

"It galls me how Emerson is always claiming credit for being the founder of Encampment when it was Charlie McConnell, Jim Rankin and Malachi Dillon who hired Tom Sun to do the initial surveying. You've heard him claim to have named Idaho Falls, Idaho when he started a company called Eagle Rock Land and Townsite Company. It made me start to thinking about what else Emerson has been involved in and what he's exaggerating."

"So what does Peter have to say about it?"

"It's actually worse than I suspected it might be. Peter contacted the new owners of the mine in Cripple Creek, Colorado. That's where I first met Emerson, when he was one of the owners of the *Jack Pot*. Turns out that the claims Emerson made about how much the mine was making were highly exaggerated. The owners are suing, claiming that Emerson and his partners salted the mine."

"I've heard that term before, but I'm not sure what it means."

"It means that they are suspected of planting ore in the mine so that it looked rich when it really isn't.

"But then there's even more. Peter also contacted some folks in Idaho Falls. It seems that Emerson also was a partner in a business called the Great Western Canal and Improvement Company, which promised a canal and irrigation to prospective farmers. You've never been to Idaho. That area is high desert, yet they sold land for farming. Then, Emerson and McCaffrey moved to Chicago, without building a canal in Idaho. In Chicago they started another canal company that never happened."

"It sounds like Emerson has lots of good ideas that he has trouble getting going."

"If that was all it was, there wouldn't be much of a problem, but everywhere he goes, it looks like he ends up making a lot of money and then leaves others holding the bag. One more thing Peter uncovered was something that a newspaper in Kansas called "the Kansas Sugar Swindle." Emerson built a sugar mill and demonstrated it to the local farmers, who were excited to have sugar mills built close to them instead of having to transport their crops so far. According to reports from the newspaper reporter who covered it, Emerson and his partners – including McCaffrey - got over two million dollars by selling bonds to construct the mills then never built them and disappeared."

"That's horrible!"

"It makes me really nervous, Claire. I know now that Emerson has a habit of bilking people out of grand sums of money, and I also know he is selling millions of dollars in shares of the Rudefeha Mine."

"So you suspect he's got some sort of scheme going here."

Daniel ran his hand through his hair. "Yes, I do. Right now the mine is sending out tons of ore a day. Ever since that first bucket of ore arrived at the smelter in Encampment on the tramway on June ninth, the operation has been keeping a steady supply of copper arriving. Everyone is hopeful and happy, but I just can't shake a feeling that the bottom could drop out at any minute."

"Is there anything you can do, anyone you can talk to?"

"I have talked to Walter Bunce about it. He doesn't trust Emerson, either, but his opinion is that there are enough other people involved in decision making for the mine and smelter that Emerson can't hurt the operation." Daniel sighed. Claire walked around behind him and began rubbing his neck and shoulders.

"You've been putting in many long hours between the mine and getting this house ready for winter. I think we need a day of fun and rest. Could we take one last picnic on Sunday afternoon?"

Daniel caught her hands and held them. "I can't imagine you'd be very comfortable riding in your condition," he pulled her around him and she sat down on his lap.

"You're right about that. I would be up for a nice walk to that little clearing at Haggarty Creek, though."

"Then it's settled. A day alone in the woods with my wife. What could be better?"

38
December, 1903
Dillon, Wyoming

"Happy sixth anniversary, my beautiful wife." Daniel came into the kitchen, pulling up his suspenders. He crossed the small room and hugged Claire from behind as she stirred the biscuit dough.

"Happy anniversary to you. It's hard to work when you are hugging me," she teased.

"Well, with the babe taking up the front of you, the only way I can get close is from this direction." He reached around and rubbed her belly. The baby kicked at that moment, and he chuckled and nuzzled closer. "Hmmm, you smell good."

"I smell like bacon and you are hungry." Claire laughed and slid from his hold. "Pour yourself some coffee while I get the biscuits in the oven."

Daniel did as he was told, then picked up a newspaper. "The *Dillon Doublejack* just isn't as pleasurable to read as it used to be. Thank you for getting me a subscription to the *Cheyenne Daily Leader*. Between that and the *Grand Encampment Herald*, I figure I know most of what is going on in the world."

"With the snow as deep as it has been we haven't gotten much mail at all this winter." Claire said as she used a drinking glass to cut biscuits from her rolled-out dough. "Elizabeth Janing told me that over at Battle the snow is so deep that they've had to shovel off the roofs, but don't even need a ladder to get up to do it."

"That's one of the good things about the wind in this valley," Daniel replied. "The snow seems to get blown off our roof better than in Battle, though I think it also helps that we put on a metal roof. The snow slides off easier."

Claire put the biscuits in the oven and turned to the stove to start the gravy. "What are you reading about?"

Daniel was quiet for a minute, then finally answered. "Earlier I was reading about the first ever World Series baseball game. The Boston Americans beat the Pittsburg Pirates with a score of five games to three. That Cy Young, who pitches for Boston, must be a sight to watch. The article said that Honus Wagner did a poor job of hitting, not at all like he usually does.

"Just now, though, I was just reading about Tom Horn. They finally hanged him on the twentieth of November."

"That's an interesting case, isn't it? He confessed while he was drunk, but then had other people testify that he didn't do it. I'll be interested in reading that article."

"I think you shouldn't. The article is a very detailed account of the hanging."

Claire shivered. "Thanks for the warning. You're right, I don't want to know the details.

"It's such a treat for you to be home today, on a Thursday. It was nice that Mr. Bunce declared a holiday for most of the miners for New Year's. It feels like a vacation that you are off for four whole days."

"Yup, I don't go back until Monday. I'm glad, too. It's made me nervous leaving you here all day with the baby due any day."

"I'm not alone, though. Jesse is here to help if I need anything."

"I do have a few small jobs I'd like to get done around here, so I'll try to stay out of your way."

By mid-afternoon, Daniel and Jesse had refilled the water barrels, split wood and restocked the wood pile inside and helped shake the rugs. Claire looked around her tidy kitchen and rubbed her back. It had been getting more and more sore as the afternoon progressed. She sat down, but got up again in just a few minutes, unable to get comfortable. She felt out of sorts. She was standing in the parlor, deciding if she wanted to cry or eat a leftover biscuit, when she heard her men stomping the snow off their boots on the porch. Soon Daniel folded her into a sideways hug, his face red from the chilly wind outside.

"You look a little pale. Are you feeling alright?" he asked as she snuggled into his shoulder.

"No, I really don't feel very well. My back is killing me and I feel anxious and unsettled."

"Can I do anything to help?" His eyes said everything she ever needed to hear. When she shook her head he smiled. "Let's get your mind off how you feel. Would you like to play Parcheesi or checkers? I always make you laugh when we play Slapjack."

"Parcheesi would be fun. I don't think I'm up for all the yelling and excitement of Slapjack."

"I'll get the cloth board and the dice. Why don't you fold up a towel to sit on and see if that gives you a bit of padding for your back?"

Jesse agreed to play with them, and they'd been playing for about half an hour when Claire felt a tightening in her belly that turned into a dull, aching pain. She took a deep breath and closed her eyes as it passed. When she opened her eyes, Daniel was studying her. "Was that...?"

"Yes, I think so." She smiled at him wanly and reached for his hand.

It was a long night. Since Catherine had already birthed two healthy children, she had offered to come help when the time came. Daniel sent Jesse to summon Catherine, then sent him to stay at Joey's until after the baby's birth. When Catherine arrived, Daniel's job became pacing and praying. Just as the sky was tinting itself with the muted blue of sunrise, Daniel heard Claire groan followed by the new, urgent cry of a baby. Soon, a wrinkled and red faced child lay in his arms. He walked back and forth, cradling his son.

39
August, 1907
Dillon, Wyoming

Dear Haddie,

I can't believe how quickly time passes when there are children in the house. Did you feel this way, too? It seems as if yesterday Michael Paul was just a baby, and now he is the big brother to baby Gregory Daniel and I'm a mother of two! How can that be? I love being a mother, but I'll admit that I'm tired more than not. At six months old, Greg is already crawling about and getting into things. Michael, at three and a half, is my little policeman. He likes to holler "Baby!" when Greg is into something he shouldn't. It is really very comical.

Life in the high mountains is the same as always. Jesse is doing fine. For his seventeenth birthday, Daniel and I bought him his own horse. You should have seen how excited he was! He's not at all interested in mining – he still hates tight places. I imagine it is due to the time he spent trapped in the grain binder. Daniel has been encouraging Jesse to do something that keeps him close to animals. Now that he's graduated from high school, with the years of help and support he received from the headmaster in Encampment, Jesse is working full time at the Transportation Company. He takes care of the livestock mostly, but he is also driving a freight wagon some of the time. He always admired a local driver here, and now he is learning to handle teams for himself.

It still makes me nervous to hear, like in your last letter, that Hiram and Horace are back in Mitchell again, but I worry less and less. Jesse is too old now for them to cause him many problems or take him away from me.

The mine is doing well, Daniel says we will never see the end of the copper in this mountain in our lifetimes. He never stops worrying, though. Ever since the Penn-Wyoming Company bought out North American Copper, it seems that there has been no end of bad luck for the whole operation. Last year a fire destroyed the concentrating mill down at Riverside. Then, just a month ago there was a fire at the smelter in Encampment. Copper is selling at twenty eight cents per pound, though, which is the highest it has ever been, so they should be able to rebuild. Daniel trusts the Penn-Wyo bosses and board much more than he ever did George Emerson, who sold out and left about two years ago. We weren't sad to see him go.

Claire heard the unmistakable sounds of her youngest son beginning to wake up from his nap, so she put a quick end to her letter. By the time it was safely sealed in an envelope, both boys were awake and hungry. "How about a walk to the post office?" she said to Michael as he ate a piece of bread and butter and she nursed Greg. "When we finish here, we'll put your shoes on and take a walk."

She tucked a blanket around Greg as she belted him into her Allwin Folding Go-cart. The stroller had been a gift from Addie and Peter, and Claire was so thankful for it. The large wheels allowed her to push the baby easily up and down the hills plus there was a little room for a few purchases and a diaper bag for the boys. She wasn't sure how she would have managed to walk to the store without it.

When they got to Main Street, Michael stepped up on the back of the cart and held on. He giggled as they bounced along, as he did each trip. It was a beautiful day, warm and clear. The sun was warm on Claire's back, and she felt light and happy. She greeted neighbors and friends as she walked the boardwalk towards the bank, it seemed like she knew nearly everyone in her small mountain home. Bending down so that she was eye to eye with her oldest son, she said quietly, "When we go into the bank and then the store, what is your job?"

Michael's face was serious, "M-my hands are behind my back and I need to be bery quiet."

"Yes, Sir. That's right. Very quiet. It will only take a minute."

Claire struggled with the door for a few seconds until a gentleman leaving the bank held it for her and the baby buggy. She thanked him then got in line at the teller behind Mrs. Drury, a minor's wife Claire had met once or twice. While they waited, Claire looked around. The bank was small, but elegantly furnished. The oak paneled walls matched the thick oak desks and the counter for the teller. The wood floor was polished to a fine sheen.

Just as Claire thanked the teller and turned to leave, a door in the back opened and three men emerged. Claire was surprised to see that Daniel was among them.

"Daddy!"

Michael instantly put his hand over his mouth and looked at his Mama, knowing that he'd broken the 'quiet rule'. Claire hushed him, but smiled and nodded. Michael ducked under the handle of the buggy and hurried to Daniel.

Daniel picked up the boy, shook the banker's hand and then joined Claire at the teller window. Claire finished making the deposit then turned to greet him.

"I didn't expect to see you in town today."

"Harold asked me to come with him, he had some business with the bank and wanted my input."

"Are you heading back up to the mine now?"

Daniel hugged Michael and then put him down. "Yeah, I wish I could take you three out for a cup of coffee, but Harold said he needed to make a quick stop for some supplies at the hardware then we'd head on up."

Daniel helped Claire maneuver the buggy outside then said, "I hope you three have a good day. I shouldn't be late tonight." He leaned closer to Claire and kissed her softly on the cheek. "I don't want to be inappropriate in public, but I can't help myself."

Claire smiled and watched him walk away. "Are you ready to go shopping?" she said to Michael.

"Yes, Mama. And I will be real good."

"I know you will," she said with a smile.

Claire was tucked into one of the long aisles at the mercantile, looking at fabric for shirts for the boys while she waited for Elizabeth to fill her order. When the front door opened, she smiled to see that Catherine was stopping in to shop as well. The two women greeted each other with a hug, and Catherine rubbed Michael's head. They talked for barely a minute when the door opened again and Jesse came in. He looked around urgently and then hurried over to Claire.

"Claire, I'm glad you told me you were coming to shop. Papa and Horace are here. They must've come in yesterday because their horses were in the stable when I got in there this morning. When I questioned Barney about the new mounts, he said that two men rode in asking about you."

He hesitated then finished, "and me. They spent most of the night last night at the saloon. They are eating breakfast at the Dillon Hotel right now and asking around for us."

Claire felt sick. "Have you talked to them?"

"No, I'm not sure I want to at all. I came right away to find you, so you'd be forewarned."

Catherine put her hand on Claire's arm, offering friendship when she didn't understand the need. "You went pale all of a sudden, and you are shaking. Can I help somehow?"

Claire took a breath and steadied herself. "No, I'm fine," she began then stopped. "Catherine, would you be willing to take the boys with you? I'm not sure whether my father and his brother even know about my boys, but I want my babies as far away from those two as possible."

"Of course. I'll take them home with me as soon as I drop this list off for Elizabeth."

The relief Claire felt was evident. She'd never spoken about her father or Horace to anyone here beside Andriette. Catherine, though not understanding the details, understood the urgency Claire was radiating. "I'll fill you in about the situation later, if that's alright?"

"Only if you want to."

"Oh, would you ask Elizabeth to just hold my order? Jesse and I will stop back for it later."

"I'm sure she'll be fine with that."

Claire knelt down to talk to Michael. "Little guy, Miz Catherine is going to take you and Baby Greg home with her for a bit. I'll see you in a while."

"OK, Mama," Michael answered as she kissed his cheek. He turned to Catherine. Taking her hand he asked, "Can we play with the blocks?"

Claire stepped away from her sons, giving Catherine a wane smile.

"Claire, what are we going to do?"

"If they are asking around, eventually, someone is going to tell them where the cabin is. I'd rather meet them in a public place instead, so I am going to the hotel. If you don't want to see them, I thoroughly understand. I can tell them you aren't here if they ask."

"I don't want to hide. I'll go with you."

Buoyed by having him by her side, Claire and Jesse headed for the hotel. As they walked, Claire summoned her courage and reminded herself that she wasn't the same timid and naïve little girl her father had known. She whispered a prayer, then said, "Jesse, we will just sit down and have a short visit with them. We don't have to give them details about our lives here or invite them to supper, we'll just have a cup of coffee and send them on their wandering way."

Jesse's voice was steady and deep when he answered her, but he slipped his hand into hers as they neared the hotel. It was as cold as ice.

Claire's brave resolve came close to shattering to a shimmering pile when they entered the dining room. Her father, grey and gaunt, leaned on the table with an empty plate pushed to the side and tumbler of brown liquid in front of him. Even though he looked half asleep, that one look was enough to ignite Claire's fear of him. Across the table, Horace was leaned back in his chair. He stretched one arm over his head and then rubbed the back of his neck. Claire and Jesse stood in the doorway. She wanted to turn and run, but knew she had to face them. Horace was the first to see her. She watched as he scanned the room, his eyes stopping as they met hers. A sly grin spread across his unshaven face and he kicked his brother under the table. Hiram jumped then looked around.

On legs that felt wobbly and unreliable, Claire led Jesse around the other tables. Neither man stood and neither smiled.

Claire's voice surprised her, it was steady and confident, and not angry or accusing. "You've been asking about us?"

"Well, look at you all grown into a round, full woman, no more skin and bone for you." It was Horace. Claire grimaced at the touch of his voice.

Her father looked past Claire and settled on Jesse. It took a few heartbeats before recognition dawned. "Why Jesse, my lost son." He stood up then, and stepped toward the boy. Jesse reacted by taking a step backward.

"Is that any way to treat your old Dad? I've missed you, Cowboy, and I'm glad to see you so tall and manly."

Jesse's cold resolve melted a bit at the sound of his old nickname. When his father put out his hand, Jesse responded. The two shook hands, and Hiram pulled his son into a clumsy embrace. "It's good to see you, we've been searching for you for quite a time. Sit down, now, and have some breakfast."

Jesse pulled a chair for Claire, then moved around the table and sat opposite her. "You've been looking for me?"

"I've been back to Dakota twice to see if there was news of where she'd taken you away to. That Foster woman was supposed to keep you safe and sound until you were old enough to come with me, but then your sister took you away and no one seemed willing to say where."

The reference opened an old wound in Claire. In her memory, her father had never called her by name. *Even after all these years, I still don't have a name, just a role. 'Your sister'*, thought Claire.

He motioned to the waitress, then asked for a cup of coffee for Jesse when she arrived.

Claire sat at the table, inches away from her father yet completely invisible and alone. Once Hiram had seen his son, her existence no longer mattered. The dynamics felt familiar and somehow normal, and the old hurt and confusion rose in her. The conversation was lost to her. Jesse was warily answering his father's questions and hearing stories of gold panning in Nevada, but the words were a blur to Claire. She took in the scene, removed and unheeded, and felt a whole lifetime of yearning pour down on her. All she'd ever wanted was to be acknowledged, to have him look at her the way he was studying Jesse. The anger and bitterness built up as she faced once again how truly unimportant she was and always had been to her father. Her fists clinched and she felt as if at any moment she might lose control and begin screaming. For a brief instant, she watched herself hitting this man, whose fists had been his only touch to her, and imagined the satisfaction she'd feel if she could just rake his cheeks with her fingernails or leave bruises to rival the ones he'd given her.

She sat quietly, though, and didn't move. Her fantasy passed quickly and left in its wake a clearer picture of the man sitting next to her. His hair was thin and grey, his eyes rheumy and sad. While he talked on about staking a claim in the Yukon, Claire's eyes focused on his hands. Once, she'd feared them and the blows they delivered, now they were gnarled and twisted with oversized knuckles filled with arthritis, and no doubt, pain. The skin was mottled with age spots and scars.

A quiet voice spoke from deep inside her. It had taken years for her to finally forgive herself and let go of her own past. Now, she knew, it was time to let this go as well. She remembered, then,

Andriette saying that as she had begun forgiving her own father, she'd started to feel a bit sorry for him. Claire's hands unclenched and the tension in her shoulders eased. In a moment of stark clarity, Claire released herself from his hold. She felt years of resentment and longing, bitterness and hurt tumble away from her. She sighed a wordless prayer and rejoined the present.

"We woulda made a fortune in Dawson if the land office hadn't been crooked. Now we're on our way to California, your Uncle Horace won a deed to some property near Modesto in a card game last month. The fella who lost it said it had almond trees there just ready to pick. We're going to move there and do us a little farming. We need your young, strong back to make a go of it. How long will it take you to pull your stuff together? Do you have a horse of your own?"

Claire watched as Jesse sat back. She could read in his eyes that he didn't know how to say no.

"Jesse, do you want to leave with these two?" Her voice was quiet and strong.

Their father looked surprised. "You aren't part of this, Girl," he sneered. Claire accepted his tone and his menacing look with new courage and confidence. She smiled as she realized that her fear of this man had evaporated with her hatred for him.

Hiram swiveled around to look at his youngest son. Fortified by Claire's support, Jesse cleared his throat and answered. "It's been nice to talk with you and good to see you both, but I have a good job here and a home where I belong. I'm not interested in California or farming."

Claire recognized the growing rage in her father's eyes. "What do you mean? You want to stay here, attached to this woman's apron instead of being a man? We've been searching for you, we've worked hard to come retrieve you."

Claire saw Jesse's fear rising, understanding what it was like to be in his shoes and the focus of that anger.

"Jesse is not a lost possession that you misplaced. He's the son you abandoned because he was young and a liability. Now that you need him to come help do your work and be useful, you want him."

Hiram's temper was near boiling over and his voice grew louder. "This is hogwash. You are my son and you are coming with me." He banged his fist on the table. Claire glanced around the half-filled dining room, worried about the scene they were making. People at the other tables were glancing their way, looking uncomfortable. Malachi Dillon and a burly bouncer from the bar were standing in the doorway, watching and ready.

Jesse's voice came out quiet but strong, "I truly appreciate the offer, Sir, and that you came for me. That means a lot. But, I am staying here."

Hiram turned back to Claire his voice loud and mean. "This is all your doing, you've poisoned his mind about me. You never were worth a damn."

"I'll bet that's not what you thought when you used me as a punching bag in your drunken rages, or allowed your perverted brother to fondle me. You certainly reaped benefits from me when you sent me out to work. I worked for nearly two years before I caught on that you were stealing my earnings. Papa, I forgive you, but forgiving doesn't mean forgetting or allowing you to hurt me or anyone I love again."

She stood up then. Slowly and deliberately. Jesse stood as well.

Hiram's face turned red, his eyes narrowed into slits. He pushed out of his chair menacingly, and it toppled over, thudding loudly on the hard wood floor. "Jesse, you will be ready to ride out with us in one hour." He moved closer to Claire, staring into her eyes.

"And you, you will stay out of this or else."

Sitting in the chair, he'd looked old and weak. Now he towered over her, close enough for her to smell the dirt from his clothes and the hardness of his breath. There were loud, familiar boot steps at the door but her focus was on the man in front of her.

She never blinked. "I am no longer afraid of you." She held his gaze with calm determination. When he raised his hand in a movement she'd seen a hundred times, she didn't flinch or try to duck. Instead her own hand shot out and caught his arm just before he attacked. They stood there – merely a second perhaps, but a moment locked into forever. "Never again." She said it quietly as she pushed his arm away from her.

Hiram growled a low, savage sound, but he stepped backwards and turned back to Jesse. "I said, go get your belongings, we are leaving within the hour."

Jesse moved to stand at Claire's side. At the same time, Claire heard those familiar footsteps again and without taking her eyes from her father, she felt Daniel's presence beside her. "No, Sir," answered Jesse. "I am not interested in going with you now or ever."

Daniel spoke, then. "I think my family has made it clear that we are finished here. It's time for you both to leave. Now."

Horace, forgotten until now, spoke to Daniel. "Well now," he started, standing up leisurely and sporting the same sneer that had haunted Claire's night terrors. "Who do we have here? Must be, you're the fella that finally got this little one. You could take a minute to thank me for the things I taught her."

Daniel was on him in a second, his muscles leaping to the task. He reached out and grabbed Horace's collar at the neck with his left hand. Before anyone could react, Daniel's fist, hard as the rock he mined, slammed into Horace's face three times in quick succession leaving his nose misshapen and bloody and a small gash over his right eye. Daniel pushed the stunned man back into his chair and turned to face Claire's father, anticipating what might come.

Hiram, though stunned at the quickness of the onslaught, had just raised his fist to come to his brother's aid when Daniel met his eyes. Hiram froze at the threat in Daniel's stare. Quietly, Daniel growled at the old man, "Go ahead, take that swing, but it will be the last one you ever do."

Claire's father unclenched his fist and stepped back. His fear was apparent as was his shame. Along with everyone in the room Hiram knew that this wasn't an idle threat. Daniel held his eyes on the man until Hiram lowered his head, then turned to Claire with a cocky smile. "I told you if I ever met him…"

Claire's knees felt weak again, but she managed a smile.

Daniel reached for Claire's hand and turned his back on Horace and Hiram in a final gesture of complete defeat. With a voice now relaxed and friendly he said, "Mr. Dillon, since you and Pete often act as the law in this town, may I ask you to see that these two thugs get themselves well out of town?"

"Absolutely, Dan, it would be our pleasure."

Protectively, Daniel took Claire's arm then motioned Jesse to move ahead of them. They walked out of the hotel together into the sunshine. The fresh air steadied Claire, and after a few steps, she said, "How did you know? How did you know they were here and Jesse and I were at the hotel?"

"As Harold and I were leaving the Miner's Supply we met Catherine with the boys. She told me what she knew, and I came right away. You really didn't need me, it looked like you had the situation well in hand."

They walked a few steps when Jesse spoke for the first time. "Thank you, Claire. Thank you for standing up for me and with me." He slipped his hand into hers, this time it was warm and strong.

A few more steps and then he added, "Daniel, can you teach me to hit like that? That was fiercely impressive."

Daniel's answer was a chuckle that turned into a belly laugh. Claire caught his mirth and for a few moments their laughter drifted down Main Street on the breeze.

EPILOGUE
1908
Dillon, Wyoming

"Don't look so sad, Claire," Daniel folded his wife into his arms amid the crates and boxes holding their belongings.

Wiping her eyes, Claire sniffed once then answered, "This has been our home for so long, I just don't want to leave it. It just doesn't make any sense."

"I agree. There's more copper left in that mine than we've taken out, so it's a complete shame that Rudefeha is closed down, but that's the way it is."

"It's prophetic that you worried from the beginning about how the number of shares George Emerson was selling was over capitalizing the mine and would end it up in trouble."

Daniel pulled her closer. "Maybe the company could have survived that debacle if so many other things hadn't gone wrong as well. There are a lot of ifs."

"I understand. If the Saratoga and Encampment railroad line would have been completed sooner so that transporting the copper would have been easier and cheaper."

"Right. And if fire hadn't destroyed the concentrating mill last year or burned down the smelter this year. Certainly the biggest 'if' is if copper prices hadn't fallen so drastically in the past six months."

Claire pulled away enough to look into her husband's gentle face. "I understand all that, and it will be nice to be back in Encampment where it's warmer and the snow doesn't get so deep. The boys will have a real school to go to, but at the same time I love this little cabin. This was where they were born, and I hate to just leave it here, sitting alone and empty in a ghost town.

"People aren't even boarding up their windows before they leave."

"Some will be back to dismantle some of the buildings and haul them off, but others are just walking away."

Claire sniffed again, her eyes filling as she thought of leaving. Daniel released her as they heard Jesse's voice out front as he pulled up the freight wagon. Soon, Jesse's frame filled the doorway. He looked tired.

Claire asked if he was alright.

"Yeah, just weary. I've taken four families down the mountain this week, we've been working sixteen hour days. I got a good night's sleep last night, though, so let's get us moved." He smiled at his sister's concern.

"I brought Joey with me to help fill the wagon, I think if we are smart, we'll get everything in one trip."

By noon, they were ready to go. Jesse and Daniel finished loading the freight wagon first, and Jesse had already gone, driving a rig with six steady draft horses that he'd bought to go into business for himself. Claire sat beside Daniel on the buckboard as they pulled away from the cabin. She kept her face straight ahead so that her boys, sitting behind her in a nest of trunks and blankets, couldn't see her tears. Daniel patted her leg and smiled, allowing her to feel the loss of their home.

She reminded herself that Daniel's new position as an engineer for the city of Encampment would be less dangerous with more benefits, and she was happy that her old friend Ella Parkison was back in town and only two blocks from the new house. She knew she'd be happy in Encampment, but the leaving was hard.

Daniel turned the buckboard onto Main Street and they rode in silence past the Dillon Hotel and the bank, already empty, with their blank windows reflecting the rugged mountains all around. The town was nearly deserted and desolately quiet. A hawk wheeled above them, its haunting scream echoing through the valley.

HISTORY GEEK INFORMATION, PICTURES, ACKNOWLEDGEMENTS AND GENERALLY INTERESTING ITEMS

Miners inside the Ferris Haggarty-Mine

Compressed air powered locomotive in front of the
Ferris-Haggarty mine

From the J.E. Stimson collection, Wyoming State Archives, Department of State
Parks and Cultural Resources

Tramway with the encampment smelter in the distance.

Rudefeha

From the J.E. Stimson collection, Wyoming State Archives, Department of State Parks and Cultural Resources

Ed and Ella Parkison   Circa 1920

Photos courtesy of the Parkison Family

First Parkison store in Encampment, Wyoming, 1899.

From Left: Belle Shields, Ella Shields Parkison, Ed Parkison, unidentified individual, John Parkison

Photo courtesy of the Parkison Family

Ed Haggarty

Photos courtesy of The Grand Encampment Museum

Downtown Dillon, Wyoming
(Note the large rock in the center of the street.)

The Dillon Hotel

Photos courtesy of The Grand Encampment Museum

325

The People of Peaks and Valleys

In both *Mountain Time* and here in *Peaks and Valleys*, I have
tried to combine the factual and real with my imagination in a way
that tells a good story with an historically accurate backdrop. To do
this, it was necessary to portray actual people and to create
characters of my own. This gets a little tricky sometimes, especially
when the lives of the historical humans are not thoroughly
documented. The result, of course, is that the actions and words of
the historical characters are invented for the most part, and I allow
myself freedom within the facts that I do know to make all the
characters, both historical and imaginative, be as real and alive as I
can. To the best of my ability, I have kept major facts about
historical characters as accurate as possible. What follows here is a
listing of the characters who appear in *Peaks and Valleys* so that you
might know who came from my own imagination and who were
historical.

Person	Description	Fictional (F) Historical (H) Mentioned only (M)
Claire Atley Haynes	Main character	F
Hiram and Dorinda Atley	Claire's parents	F
Marcus and Jesse Atley	Claire's brothers	F
Horace and Clancey Atley	Claire's uncles	F
Haddie and William Foster	Claire's neighbors	F
Matthew, Marney, Milly, and Marshall Foster	Haddies' children	F
George and Felicia Behl Lucas, Jolene, Abigail, Darcy	Claire's second employer and his family	F

Thomas Sweeney	Claire's third employer – owned Rapid City hardware store	H
Lucy	Co-worker at Sweeney's hardware	F
Robert Murphy	Lucy's beau	F
Jack Clower	Saloon owner	H
Mrs. Payne	Boarding house owner	F (M)
Estelle and Lela	Bar girls/ Claire's friends	F
Daniel Haynes	Claire's husband	F
Mr. Smithfield	Postmaster in Rapid City	H
Mark and Catherine Crosby	Pastor in Rapid City and his wife	F
Addie , Peter Jeremiah and Richard	Daniel's sister and brother in law and nephews	F
Jack Fulkerson	Teamster	H (m)
Ed Haggarty	Prospector	H
Edith Crow	Ed's wife	H
Ed and Ella Parkison	Mercantile owner	H
Hoyt Shields Parkison	Parkison's son	H
Mary Nell and Paul Baker	Friends/miner	F
J.M. Rumsey, Robert Deal, George Ferris, and Ed Haggarty	Original owners of Rudefeha mine	H
Mr. Whiteson	Rented them the house in Encampment	F
Tom Sun	Surveyor of Encampment	H (m)
Bernard "Barney" McCaffrey	Partner in the mine	H
Willis George Emerson	Partner in the mine	H
Abigail Gillingworth	Guest at New Year's Eve party	F
Miss Mary Bohn	Hotel owner in Encampment	H

G.W Henry	Insurance agent in Encampment	H
Alkali Ike	Wanderer	H (m)
James Graham	Attorney	H (m)
Grant Jones	Journalist	H
Malachi Dillon	Entrepreneur	H
Julia Ferris	Wife of George Ferris – owned the mine	H (m)
*Lillian Jameson	Hardware store owner in Encampment	F
*Nathan Jameson	Lillian's son	F
*Andriette Jameson	Claire's friend	F
Mr. Macfarlane	First post master in Encampment	H
Harv and Veronica Whitley	Neighbors in Dillon	F
Catherine and Wally Holden Rachel and Beth	Neighbors in Dillon	F
Sahara Sam	Water hauler	F
Dr. T.W. Wilson	Doctor at Rudefeha mine	H
Elizabeth and Keith Janing	Store clerk in Dillon	F
Charlie Comer and Peter LeMieux	Telephone line men	H
B.C Riblet	Tramway Company Engineer	H (m)
Clarence DeWitt	Owner of Dillon Mercantile and post master of Dillon	H
Harriet DeWitt	Clarence's wife	F
Mrs. William Morgan	Farmer from Slater	H (M)
Mrs. William (Maggie) Humphrey	Owner of restaurant and hotel/boarding house in Dillon	H (M)

Chris Christensen	Miner hurt in a cave in	F
Walter Bunce	Rudefeha mine superintendent	H
J.K. Jeffrey	Rudefeha mine bookkeeper	H
Dennis Reedy	Rudefeha mine foreman	H
A.E Loizeau	NACC Denver office auditor	H
Curly	Drunk	F
Charlie McConnell	Founding father of Encampment	H
Jim Rankin	Founding Father of Encampment	H (m)
Robert Simons	builder in Dillon	F
Joey Logan	Jesse's friend in Dillon	F

*Andriette Jameson is the main character in *Mountain Time* by donna coulson. Lillian and Nathan are also main characters in that novel.

Peaks and Valleys Timeline

One of the great aspects of historical fiction is that it allows history to feel real and alive as opposed to just being cold lists of dates and names. In order to help myself while I was writing *Peaks and Valleys*, I created this timeline of historical events, then placed my story alongside. Hopefully, this will be an interesting addition for you, my reader, as well.

Year	Historical Event
1856	May 28 -Willis George Emerson born in Blakesburg, Iowa Franklin Pierce is president (1856-1857) Malachi W. Dillon born in California
1857	James Buchanan is president (1857 – 1861)
1861	Abraham Lincoln is president (1861 – 1865)
1865	Andrew Johnson is president (1865-1869)
1866	December 6 - Ed Haggarty born in England
1869	Ulysses S Grant is president (1869-1877)
1871	Grant Jones is born
1874	Man named Harper discovers copper float near Rambler
1876	June 25-26 - Battle of the Little Big Horn Gold is discovered in the Black Hills
1877	Rutherford B. Hayes is president R (1877-1881)
1881	September 19 – James A. Garfield becomes president Chester Arthur becomes president (1881-1885)
1884	December 6 - Washington Monument completed
1885	Grover Cleveland becomes president (1885-1889) Ed Haggarty arrives in the US from England
1886	Ed Haggarty arrives in Cheyenne February 25 - Malachi W. Dillon marries Nellie Fagan in Carbon County
1887	Willis George Emerson comes to Wyoming
1889	Benjamin Harrison becomes president (1889-1893) November 2 – North and South Dakota become states November 8 – Montana becomes a state

1890	July 3 - Idaho becomes a state October 1 - Yosemite National Park created
1891	June 10 - Wyoming becomes a state
1892	April – Johnson County Cattle War Malachi Dillon found guilty of voluntary manslaughter in Utah
1893	Grover Cleveland becomes president again (1893-1897) Panic of 1893 – worst depression to date in the US – high unemployment until 1898 The Corn Palace is built in Mitchell, South Dakota
1894	Ed Haggarty works for seven months in Cripple Creek, CO Labor Day becomes a national holiday on the first Monday of September
1895	Ed Haggarty finds copper in the Seminoe Mountains
1896	Jan 4 - Utah becomes a state May 18 - Supreme Court – separate but equal – Plessy V Ferguson August 16 - Gold discovered in the Yukon Ed Haggarty makes three claims in Sandstone country Karl Elsener attaches several tools to a pocket knife using a spring and creates the Swiss Army Knife.
1897	William McKinley becomes president (1897-1901) June 20 – Ed Haggarty spots promising area for copper in the Sierra Madre mountains, Wyoming- snow is too deep to investigate further July 25 – Haggarty stakes 21 acres as Rudefeha mine Ferris sends supplies and nine men to work through the winter Encampment is surveyed and laid out by Tom Sun
1898	April 25 through August 12, Spanish American War (10 week war) Hawaii annexed Shaft House built at Rudefeha

	August 25 – dynamite blast to 30 feet exposes copper vein
	September 17 – logs are cut for bunk house and mess hall at Rudefeha
	September 25 – whim is working and getting the spring water out of the shaft
	October- first load of ore goes to Ft. Steele by wagon – workforce is tripled to 27 men
	April 1 - Alkali Ike is in from the hills
	False report about lynching of Jas. H. Graham
	Ed and Ella Parkison arrive in Encampment and open a store
1899	March 9 – shaft is 85 feet deep and vein is 7 feet wide.
	August 20 – George Ferris is killed in a wagon accident at Snowslide Hill
	James Rumsey sells out for $1,000
	Ed Haggarty sells out for $30,000
	New investors: Emerson and McCaffrey
1901	Theodore Roosevelt becomes president (1901-1909)
	Rudefeha mine employs 55 men and produces 50 tons of ore a day
	Ed Haggarty and Edith Crow are married and honeymoon in England
1902	Dec 22 – post office in Dillon opens Clarence D. Dewitt postmaster
	Boston-Wyoming Company sells its holdings to North American Copper Company for $1 million.
	Hoyt Shields Parkison is born to Ed and Ella in Encampment
	Elizabeth Cady Stanton dies
	In 1902, residents build the Grand Encampment Opera House to use as a meeting place
1903	June - Grant Jones dies
	June 9 – first bucket of ore arrives in Encampment on the tram- 350 tons of ore can now be taken out each day
	October 1 – 13th First World Series

	November 20 – Tom Horn is hanged in Cheyenne Rudefeha mine employs 125 men 4th of July celebration in Dillon
1904	Teabag invented by Thomas Sullivan Emerson sells out and moves to California
1905	January - Penn-Wyoming buys North American Copper Company
1906	Fire destroys the concentrating mill at Riverside Parkison family moves to Denver (still own the store) Mildred Parkison is born to Ed and Ella in Denver.
1907	November 16 - Oklahoma becomes a state Fire destroys part of the smelter Copper sells at peak of 27 cents per pound Parkisons return to Encampment
1908	Lydia Willis begins building a stone house in Encampment to be a bordello August – Saratoga and Encampment Railway reaches Encampment October 1 - Ford makes and markets Model T Rudefeha Mine and smelter are shut down for good Russel Parkison is born in February in Denver but lived only a short time

Acknowledgements and Bibliography

My deep thanks to Hillary Wilkerson, editor extraordinaire. Her insights, ideas, and attention to details have been a Godsend. (She's a really terrific daughter also!)

Thanks to my son, Sam Coulson – a talented author himself - for all his help with the technical aspects of getting this ready to publish.

I've been in love with the history of Dillon and Rudefeha and have absorbed stories and facts about them since I was very young. To make sure that my understanding of the history of the times and place were as accurate as possible, I relied on many sources for great and factual information.

 I am indebted to all those at The Grand Encampment Museum in Encampment, Wyoming. The staff there is amazing, and the museum holds a vast wealth of information, from unpublished letters, pictures and journals to actual buildings and historical items from this era. I've spent very enjoyable days there, reading through files, taking notes and talking to the staff. Check out their website at http://www.gemuseum.com/

My deepest thanks go to John D. Farr, former board member at the Grand Encampment Museum and fellow history geek. He has been my #1 fan and supporter, always encouraging me and either answering my questions or putting me in touch with someone else who could.

A special thanks go to Mary Jane Cozzens and her siblings Ed H. Parkison and Martha Morris. They are the grandchildren of Ella and Ed Parkison. They have been so generous in sharing pictures, letters and information about their grandparents that not only helped me understand Ed and Ella and the mercantile they owned and operated in Encampment, but also the whole town. I loved my email exchanges with Mary Jane regarding her grandmother's life and personality.

A really wonderful website full of great information is *Wyoming Tales and Trails*. This site has lots of information about not only the Grand Encampment and its nearby mines and history, but about all of Wyoming. I used this site as a 'go to' for many facts in this novel. Their website is http://www.wyomingtalesandtrails.com/.

The *Dillon Doublejack* was published in Dillon by Grant Jones from December 1902 until he died in June of 1903. It continued under the editorship of several other men until 1908. Only six editions of the *Doublejack* are known to still exist, and I have had microfiche copies of those editions since I was in high school. There are few things that can make a history geek smile more than reading old newspapers. My understanding of many of the businesses, people and events of Dillon as well as the products and fashions popular at the time came, at least in part, from reading the *Doublejack*.

If you ever want to read old newspapers for fun or to research a specific topic or event, a terrific resource the Wyoming Newspaper Project at http://newspapers.wyo.gov/

For general research about small details (Who *was* president in 1898? When did the World Series begin?) I will admit that I really appreciate Wikipedia. I am well aware that this is not a scholarly admission, but it's fast and easy. ☺

Below is a partial list of other resources, either for background knowledge or for facts, I used in writing *Peaks and Valleys*.

Books:

The Treasure of Hidden Valley by Willis George Emerson. Published by Forbes Company, 1915.

Lora Webb Nichols: Homesteader's Daughter, Miner's Bride by Nancy F. Anderson. Published by The Caxton Printers, 1995.

Articles and newspaper stories:

"Discovery of the Ferris-Haggarty Mine" by Agnes Wright Spring. 1939. From the Grand Encampment Museum Collection.

"How a Woman May Retain Beauty" Good Housekeeping Magazine. June, 1897 Volume 24 Number 6 as archived at the Albert R. Mann Library, Cornell University. http://hearth.library.cornell.edu/

"Thick Cream From the Sierra Madres" by Beryl M. Williams. In *Wyoming* magazine April/May 1972.

Tom Horn: "Hung By The Neck Till Dead". *The Cheyenne Daily Leader.* Friday Morning November 20, 1908 Vol. XXXVII Number 88

Websites on the following topics:

American History Timeline: www.history-timeslines.org.uk/events-timelines/14-american-history-timeline.htm

Billy Sunday: http://billysunday.org/timeline.php3

Books that Claire read: "Books that Shaped America" Library of Congress. www.loc.org/exhibits/books-that-chaped-america/1850-to-1900.html

Campbell's Soup: https://www.campbellsoup.co.uk/history

Churn dash quilt pattern: http://www.quilting-in-america.com/churn-dash.html

Claire's baby stroller, the Allwin folding go-cart: http://www.ebay.com/itm/1908-Ad-Allwin-Folding-Go-Cart-Baby-Stroller-Carriage-Edwardian-Woman-YDL5-/371491643769?hash=item567ea0a179:g:3pwAAOSwgyxWUL~2

Colorado School of Mines: www.mines.edu/History

Corn Palace History: www.cornpalace.org/Information/corn-palace-history.php

Cripple Creek: http://visitcripplecreek.com/heritage

Dime novels: http://www.ulib.niu.edu/badndp/dn-b.html

Doublejacking: https://www.youtube.com/watch?v=ZaZ5cuhipHk

Encampment smelter: http://www.wyohistory.org/encyclopedia/encampment-wyoming#sthash.Sn7Kv6h0.dpuf

Fashions: http://vintagefashionguild.org/fashion-timeline/1890-to-1900/

First Aid and medicines in the 1800s:
www.kilmerhouse.com/2013/06/from-1888-to-2-13-celebrating-the-125th-birthday-of-the-first-aid-kit/ and also
"The Great Dr. Kilmer – Swamproot King"
www.bottlebooks.com/drkilmer.htm

Galena, South Dakota:
www.ghosttowns.com/states/sd/galena.html

Gold in Iowa:
http://iavanburen.org/FactsAndFolklore/GoldInIowa.htm
and also
https://sites.google.com/site/nationaltreasuresonline/national/iowa

Gold mining in the Black Hills:
www.blackhillsvisitor.com/featured-articles.html

Grain Binders: "History of the Grain Binder" by J.F. Percival
www.farmcollector.com/steam-traction/history-of-th-grain-binder.aspx

Gypsies: "Gypsies in the United States"
www.smithsonianeducation.org/migrations/gyp/nichel/html
and http://james-a-watkins.hubpages.com/hub/The-Gypsie
(Note: Claire's encounter with the gypsies is from my memory of my mom telling me about her own experience as a child encountering a gypsy caravan.)

Hairstyles:
http://bartocollection.com/vehairstylesyera/hairstylesthegay90s.html

History of Coffee: www.gocoffeego.com/professor-peabody/history -of-coffee/1800

History of tennis:
http://www.historyorb.com/events/date/1896/august

History of the brownie:
http://www.palmerhousehiltonhotel.com/recipes/#sthash.C5r3VdZA.dpuf

Jamesway chicken feeders:
www.comercialappeal.com/photos/2011/jan/27/207419/

McGuffey Reader Collection: Library of Congress.
www.loc.gov/rr/rarebook/coll/152.html

Mowers and Reapers: "Walter A. Wood Mowing and Reaping Machine Company (1865-1924)" from the Hoosick Township Historical Society.
www.hoosickhistory.com/shortstories/WalterWoodPlant.htm

Percolator Coffee pot inventor Hanson Goodrich: "Inventor Goodrich Was In Our Town" by Veronica Voss. The Times-Leader Thursday, March 21, 1968.
www.carolyar.com/Illinois/Newspaper/Goodrich.htm

Pet Milk: www.petmilk.com/history/

Prostitution: www.soileddoves-doves.com

Rail lines in South Dakota, Nebraska and Wyoming: *South Dakota Railroads* published online by South Dakota State Historic Preservation Office and from www.usgwarchives.org/maps/southdakota/statemap/dakterr/1882.jpg

Rapid City, South Dakota facts: *The Rapid City Walking Tour: An informative Guide to the Downtown Historic District* http://www.rcgov.org/Growth-Management/hpc-walking-tour.html

Rough Riders and the Spanish American War:
www.cov.gov.rr/hispanic/1898/roughriders.html and also 'The Battle of San Juan Hill" www.history.com/this-day-in-history/the-battle-of-san-juan-hill and also "The Sinking of the Maine" www.historytoday.com/richard-cavendish/sinking-maine

Saratoga and Encampment Railroad:
http://www.wyohistory.org/encyclopedia/encampment-wyoming#sthash.Sn7Kv6h0.dpuf

Steven Foster:
http://www.pitt.edu/~amerimus/Fosterbiography.html and http://www.spinner.com/2010/07/02/stephen-foster-music/

Tapeworm eggs for weight loss: (Eew! Yes, this is factual!)
http://www.health.com/health/gallery/0,,20653382,00.html and http://www.diet-blog.com/07/vintage_weight_loss_sanitized_tapeworms.php

Typical wages in 1860 to 1890:
http://outrunchange.com/2012/06/14/typical-wages-in-1860-through-1890/

Willis George Emerson and Barney McCaffrey
http://www.wyomingtalesandtrails.com/encampemerson.html

36272373R00193

Made in the USA
San Bernardino, CA
18 July 2016